"It's Mr. Cowb racing to the door.

Then to Sophie's utt[...] Tanner, "Houston, [...]

Tall, lanky and lean, with wide [...] that looked perfect for leaning on, Tanner Johns was every woman's fantasy cowboy.

Not *her* fantasy cowboy, of course, but—

"What's the problem, er, Houston?" His gaze rested on Sophie.

Sophie couldn't explain because there was something wrong with her breathing. As in, she couldn't. Then Davy came racing down the stairs, tripped on the perpetually loose runner at the bottom tread and tumbled headlong into the cowboy's arms. Tanner caught her son and held on just long enough to make sure Davy could stand on his own.

"Something I said?" he joked, winking at her.

The man *winked* at her! The control Sophie had almost recovered vanished. She figured she probably looked like a beached fish, gulping for air. Stupidly, she wished she'd had time to fix her hair.

Where's your independence now?

Lois Richer loves traveling, swimming and quilting, but mostly she loves writing stories that show God's boundless love for His precious children. As she says, "His love never changes or gives up. It's always waiting for me. My stories feature imperfect characters learning that love doesn't mean attaining perfection. Love is about keeping on keeping on." You can contact Lois via email, loisricher@gmail.com, or on Facebook (loisricherauthor).

Leann Harris has always had stories in her head. Once her youngest child went to school, she began putting those stories on a page. She is active in her local RWA chapter and ACFW chapters. She's a teacher of the deaf (high school), a master composter and avid gardener, and teaches writing at her local community college. Her website is leannharris.com.

The Rancher's Family Wish

Lois Richer

&

The Cowboy Meets His Match

Leann Harris

HARLEQUIN® LOVE INSPIRED®

 LOVE INSPIRED BOOKS

PLEASE RECYCLE • THIS PRODUCT IS RECYCLABLE

Recycling programs for this product may not exist in your area.

ISBN-13: 978-1-335-14609-0

The Rancher's Family Wish & The Cowboy Meets His Match

Copyright © 2019 by Harlequin Books S.A.

The Rancher's Family Wish
First published in 2016. This edition published in 2019.
Copyright © 2016 by Lois M. Richer

The Cowboy Meets His Match
First published in 2016. This edition published in 2019.
Copyright © 2016 by Barbara M. Harrison

www.Harlequin.com

Printed in U.S.A.

CONTENTS

THE RANCHER'S FAMILY WISH   7
Lois Richer

THE COWBOY MEETS HIS MATCH   213
Leann Harris

THE RANCHER'S FAMILY WISH

Lois Richer

For James, who teaches me about love and trust.

Fan into flame the gift of God that is within you.
—*2 Timothy* 1:6

Chapter One

"**M**r. Cowboy!"

Lost in thoughts of his upcoming meeting, Tanner Johns barely registered the call of the child standing outside the door of the Tucson grocery store he'd just left.

"Hey, Mr. Cowboy!"

When the call came a third time, Tanner realized the girl had to be addressing him since there was no one else in the parking lot wearing cowboy boots and a Stetson, no one else who could even remotely be called a cowboy. He walked toward the child, taken aback by her extraordinary beauty. The piercing scrutiny of intense blue eyes enhanced her ivory skin and flaxen hair. He was a few feet away when he noticed the obvious signs of Down syndrome.

"Were you calling me?" Tanner glanced around to be certain.

"Uh-huh." Her smile made her skin glow.

"Why?" Tanner automatically smiled back. This little cutie was a looker with a grin that would melt the most weather-beaten hide.

"'Cause you're a cowboy and cowboys have ranches." Her bell-like voice carried on January's breeze as it whispered across blacktop shimmering in the Arizona heat.

Several people turned to study them. After a glimpse at Tanner their focus veered to the child, benevolent smiles widening when they spied the big cage at her feet. Wait a minute—rabbits? How had he missed that?

"A ranch is a good place to keep bunnies," she said.

"Uh, how many are there?" Tanner couldn't decipher one ball of fur from another.

"Only eight." She was probably five or six, he guessed. Sadness filled her voice as she explained, "We can't keep them anymore."

"I see." In spite of Tanner's reluctance to get involved, her innocence evoked a memory long buried inside him. Had he ever been that guileless?

"What happened to your face, Mr. Cowboy?" The question was open and honest. Tanner liked her steady stare better than others' quick gawks. Empathy beamed out from her blue eyes. "Does it hurt?"

"A little," he admitted. "I scratched myself on a wire fence."

"People stare at you." She nodded. "They stare at me, too. It's 'cause we're different."

"They stare at you because you're beautiful." Affection for this spunky child flared inside him. "And because you're special." He meant her Down syndrome.

"I'm not special." She shook her blond head firmly. "I'm just me. Mama says I'm exactly the way God made me." The happiness wreathing her round face made Tanner wish he'd had a mother like hers. His brain skittered away from that sensitive subject.

"Where is your mom?" Tanner glanced around curiously.

"Getting my brother." She pointed to a young woman with glossy, shoulder-length hair. It was clear the mom was trying to reason with a reluctant boy whom she held by one arm as she drew him forward. Her brightly flowered sundress billowed around her slim figure. She looked too young to have a daughter and a son. "That's Davy. He gets mad. A lot."

"What's your name?" Tanner forced his gaze from the brunette's lovely face to the girl in front of him. Mother and daughter shared translucent skin that seemed to bloom from within, but that's where the resemblance between the cute mom and this blonde sweetheart ended.

"I'm Beth. I'm almost six." When she grinned, dimples appeared in her apple cheeks.

"Pleased to meet you, Beth." Tanner held out a hand. He suppressed a laugh when she shook it heartily, her face completely serious. Beth's trusting gaze made him feel ten feet tall.

"Cowboys have horses, don't they?" Beth scanned the parking lot with a frown.

"Yes." Tanner choked down his mirth. "But today I left Samson at the ranch."

Beth's mother arrived breathless, studying him with a protective look flickering in her cocoa-toned eyes. Beauty certainly ran in this family.

"Hello. I'm Tanner Johns. Beth was just asking if I'd take her rabbits to my ranch."

"Will you?" A desperation the harried mother couldn't mask leached through her words before she huffed a laugh. "Sorry, that was rude. I'm Sophie Armstrong. This is my son, Davy—David."

"Nice to meet you both." Tanner took one look at the surly-faced boy and returned his attention to the easy-on-the-eyes mother.

"So can you take the rabbits?" The pleading in Sophie's voice was hard enough to resist, but that sound— half hope, half desperation—that's what got to Tanner. "I'd be very grateful."

"I—uh—" *You should have walked away, Tanner.*

"Do we have to give them all away, Mama?" Beth's gaze implored her mother to rethink her decision.

"I'm sorry but we do, honey. Mrs. Jones is very upset that the bunnies got out of their pen again and ate her flowers." The gentleness of Sophie's "mom" voice and the tender brush of her fingers against her daughter's flaxen head didn't need translation. She loved this child.

"Who cares about stupid old rabbits?" Davy scoffed. "Good riddance."

The words were a bluff to hide his anger. Tanner knew that because as a kid he'd used that same tone when life had jabbed him with reality once too often. But when Beth's blue eyes watered and her bottom lip wobbled, Tanner's chest tightened.

"Davy, that's mean," his mother reproved. "Beth loves the rabbits."

"She shouldn't. We always have to let go of stuff we love." The boy turned away to scuff his toe against a hump in the pavement, head bent, shoulders stiff.

Sophie's face fell and her amazing smile dimmed. Though Tanner understood the pain behind the words, he wanted to ream out the kid for hurting his lovely mother and sister.

Whoa! You don't do getting involved, Tanner, his brain scoffed. *Never have, though Burt tried his best to teach you. Walk away.*

But two pairs of eyes, one a rich Arizona sky blue and one dark as the dust trails on Mount Lemmon's highest slopes, wouldn't let him leave.

"I can't—that is, uh, I don't know anything about keeping rabbits." Tanner gazed longingly at his truck, his way of escape. Why had he answered Beth's call in the first place?

"Okay, thanks anyway." Sophie smiled politely as her fingers squeezed Beth's shoulder. "Come on, kids. Let's get these guys loaded up. We'll have to take them to the pet shelter. I don't dare take them home again or Mrs. Jones will call the landlord."

"Old bag," Davy muttered almost under his breath.

"Manners, David," his mother reproved. "Now let's get moving. I'm working tonight, remember?"

"Again," Davy complained in a grumpy tone.

"Yes, again. Because that's how I pay for those new sneakers you're wearing. So carry the cage, Davy, and let's go." Sophie Armstrong offered Tanner a distracted smile before urging the children forward.

As they walked away Tanner heard Beth protest.

"This morning you said the pet shelter can't keep them," she said. "What will happen to our bunnies, Mama?"

"God will take care of them." Sophie paused long enough to glance Tanner's way. He thought he glimpsed a hint of guilt in her brown eyes before she resumed her speed-walk to a red van. "After all, He cares for the sparrows and the lilies of the field, remember?"

Nice sentiment but her tone held no assurance.

It's not your problem. That did nothing to lift the blanket of guilt weighing down Tanner's shoulders. As he turned from watching Davy wrangle the cage into the van, his gaze slid past then returned to the logo printed on the side.

Sophie's Kitchen—Home-Cooked Food Without the Hassle.

Home-cooked. Tanner studied the bag in his hand.

Doughnuts again? In his head he heard the other church ushers' laughter. *Is that all you ever eat, Tanner?*

An idea sprang to life. He whirled around and saw Sophie, er, Mrs. Armstrong getting into her van. "Wait."

She frowned at him but waited for his approach. "Is something wrong?"

"No, yes—" He pointed at the writing on her vehicle. "You make food? For people to eat?"

"That's usually what they do with it." Amusement laced her voice.

"Do you ever make desserts? Or treats for coffee time?" Tanner felt ridiculous. But the thought of serving the same old store-bought doughnuts he always provided, the thought of overhearing the same snarky comments made him wait, albeit impatiently, for her response.

"Cakes, tarts, that kind of thing? Sure." She noticed Beth licking her lips and winked. Eyes dancing, Sophie looked young and carefree, not at all motherly.

What would it be like to be loved by a mom like her?

She frowned. "Look, I'm in a hurry—"

Tanner took a leap of faith. "I'll take the rabbits and make a home for them on the ranch in exchange for something."

"What?" Suspicion darkened her brown eyes.

"You making me some kind of dessert for tonight." Sophie's face said she wasn't sold on the trade. Hoping to sweeten the deal, Tanner glanced at Beth. "You could bring your kids to see the rabbits in their new home if you want, to make sure they're okay."

Sophie's eyebrows drew together. "What kind of dessert?"

"I don't care." He glanced down at the bag he still clutched. "As long as it's not doughnuts." He knew from the furrow on her forehead that she was considering his offer.

"You haven't given me much notice," she complained.

"Can't help it. That's the deal." Tanner tipped back on the heels of his boots, Stetson in hand, and waited while she deliberated. "There will be twelve of us."

"All men?" Sophie asked.

"Yes. Does that matter?" She nodded. "Why?" he asked curiously.

"Well, for one thing, women often appreciate different desserts from men, say something like cheesecake over pie," Sophie explained.

"Pie?" Tanner's stomach tap-danced in anticipation. "You could make pies for twelve people for tonight?"

"You'd only need three, maybe four." She tapped her chin. "That's not the problem."

"What is?" Could she see he was almost salivating at the mere thought of cinnamon-scented apple pie with a scoop of vanilla ice cream dripping down its sides?

"I have a catering job tonight, which means I couldn't possibly bake *and* deliver your pies today." When she shook her head, strands of shiny chocolate-toned hair flew through the air in an arc then fell back perfectly into place.

Tanner loved chocolate. Even more so now.

"I'm sorry, I can't do it."

"But you don't even know where I live." He wasn't giving up so easily.

"Doesn't matter. I don't have time to bake and deliver," she said. "If it could be tomorrow—?"

"It has to be today. Maybe I could pick them up. Where do you live?" He noted her hesitation. Why not? She had a couple of kids to think of. "Or perhaps your husband could meet me somewhere with them?"

"I'm a widow." The note of defiance buried in her comment intrigued Tanner.

"Well, I could pick them up," he offered. She wrinkled her nose. "Would it make a difference to you if my pastor vouched for me?" Even as Tanner said it, he wondered what his life had come to that he was willing to ask someone to vouch for him in order to get pie.

"I don't know." She hesitated.

"The meeting tonight is for our church ushers' group.

I'm head usher so it's at my place and I'm supplying the food," he explained before she could say no. "We get together every three months or so to organize the schedule of who's covering which services when at Tanque Verde First Community Church."

"Hey, that's where we go," Davy said from the backseat.

"I thought you seemed familiar." The furrow of worry disappeared from Sophie's forehead. "You're Burt Green's successor at Wranglers Ranch."

She knew Burt? Well, of course she did. Tanner figured pretty well everyone at First Community Church must know about the burly rancher and the transient kids he'd often brought to church.

"I was sorry to hear of Burt's passing." Sophie glanced at the van's clock, hesitated a moment then nodded. "Okay. It's a deal. You can pick up your dessert at my place in exchange for taking the rabbits. But I'm not promising pie."

"Oh." His balloon of hope burst.

"I'll make you something delicious, though, don't worry." Sophie tilted her head toward the rabbits. "I really appreciate this. It's a great relief to find a home for those guys but—I have to go. My roast is due to come out of the oven."

"Wait here." Tanner drove his truck next to her van, loaded the rabbits and promised Beth she could come see them anytime. With Sophie's address tucked into his shirt pocket, he handed her one of Burt's cards with the phone number at Wranglers Ranch.

"So you can let me know when I should come and pick up the desserts," he said. Sophie nodded, fluttered a hand, then quickly drove away.

Chuckling at the goofy sunflower stuck on the van's rear bumper, Tanner started his engine. Thanks to Sophie, his usher friends were going to get a surprise when they arrived at Wranglers Ranch tonight.

That's when it occurred to Tanner that he didn't even know if she was a good cook. For some reason that worry immediately dissipated. Strangely he felt utterly confident that whatever Sophie Armstrong made would be delicious. Tonight was going to be a good meeting.

Tanner gave the doughnut bag on his seat a glare, but he couldn't bring himself to throw it out. Living on the street in his teens, he'd felt that painful gnawing ache of hunger once too often to ever waste food. Spying a solution, he pulled a twenty-dollar bill from his wallet and handed it, the doughnuts and a business card to a disheveled man sitting in the parking lot by a light standard, exactly what Tanner would probably be doing if not for Burt Green.

"Hello. Buy yourself a meal to go with these doughnuts. If you need a job come see me at Wranglers Ranch," he said.

Tanner drove to the exit and left the city limits, marveling at the simplicity of the interaction. Maybe Burt's teaching wasn't totally wasted on him.

But that optimism faltered the closer Tanner got to Wranglers Ranch. Whom was he kidding? He didn't have the first clue how to carry out Burt's ideas for Wranglers even though the ranch had been his home for the past ten of his almost twenty-six years. Tanner had been thrilled to work alongside Burt, to share in helping the street kids he mentored, kids who wouldn't or couldn't fit into the institutions of Tucson. Foster parent Burt, with Social Services' permission, gladly nurtured each one, feeding, clothing and teaching life skills on his working ranch.

Ten years ago Tanner had been one of those kids. Other kids eventually found their families who'd missed them, wanted them back. Tanner was the only one who'd stayed. Nobody had ever come for him.

"Tanner, God's given me a new goal," Burt had announced last June. "I believe He wants us to make Wranglers Ranch into a kind of camp retreat for kids." The surprise of his words hadn't diminished even six months later.

Tanner might have been stunned by Burt's new goal but he'd never doubted his mentor would do it. He'd only been curious about how. Unfortunately a fatal heart attack had kept Burt from turning his goal into reality. Tanner had mourned his mentor, assuming Wranglers Ranch, which had been his home for so long, would be sold. He'd been stunned to learn that Burt had entrusted Tanner with his ranch and the fortune that went with it. Burt's will had just one condition: Tanner had two years to turn the ranch into a kids' camp. If he failed, then the ranch would be sold.

Tanner desperately wanted to live up to Burt's trust in him but he couldn't figure out how to make the dream happen. He had no difficulty running the ranch. That was easy. But the scope of creating a refuge for kids like the ones Burt had described overwhelmed and intimidated him. In six months he hadn't made even a tiny dent because he had no idea how to start. Shame over his failure left him feeling unworthy of Burt's trust. Failure meant he could never repay the enormous debt he owed the man who'd coaxed him off the streets and into a life in which faith in God now filled his world.

Fan into flame the gift of God that is within you, Tanner. In his mind he could hear Burt's voice repeating the verse from Timothy. Yet even now, after living at Wranglers so long, the meaning of that biblical quote still wasn't clear to Tanner.

What is the gift that's within me, Burt? Same old question. Still no answer.

Tanner knew he lacked Burt's easy ability to reach into a street kid's heart and help him gain a new perspective. He'd taken a foster parenting course and tons of psychology classes but they hadn't helped. He had the head knowledge. The problem was, Tanner Johns was a loner, plagued by his past mistakes.

The old insecurities returned as they always did when Tanner thought about his past. Once more he became a painfully shy seven-year-old foster kid, utterly devastated when he'd overheard a social worker say Tanner's mom abandoned him before he was a day old. In the years that followed he'd learned exactly what it meant when nobody wanted you, not even your own mother. From then on, a family was all Tanner had ever wanted. He'd finally found that family in Burt. But now he was gone and Tanner was alone.

Ignoring the rush of loss that bulged inside, Tanner pushed away the past and refocused. Even if he could somehow coax kids to come to the ranch, Burt's vision had been to turn Wranglers into a place where kids would find God was the answer to their problems. But how? Tanner had repeatedly asked God to send someone to show him. Then, as Burt had taught, he waited for God's leading. So far Tanner's prayers remained unanswered.

Show me how to do this, God, his heart cried once more.

With a sigh, Tanner turned his truck into the winding road that led to Wranglers, his spirit lifting at the beauty of the place. Burt had claimed the ranch showed its best in March and April when the desert bloomed with life. But January was Tanner's favorite month because it was a time of new birth, beginnings and hope.

The swaying leaves of the massive eucalyptus trees brought powerful memories of Burt and his unending life lessons. The only thing that wily man hadn't been able to teach Tanner was how to let go of his shameful past. Of course Burt hadn't known that by accepting his invitation to come to Wranglers, Tanner had abandoned the girl-friend who was going to have his child. In fact, it was only much later that Tanner himself understood that though he'd gained Burt and a home, he'd done exactly as his mother had—he'd thrown away his chance to be a father, to have the family he'd always craved. How could he possibly be forgiven for that?

With a sigh of regret Tanner pushed away the past and decided he'd focus on recruiting kids tomorrow. Right now he needed to relocate these rabbits so if a cute little girl, her grumpy brother and her pretty mom came to visit, he could allay their fears about their pets.

Moses Featherbed sat on the porch swing at Wranglers, watching as Tanner hefted the cage out of the truck. The elderly Native American had called Wranglers his home long before Tanner's arrival and thanks to a stipend from Burt's estate, Moses remained, refusing to retire, let alone stop rehabilitating the abused horses Burt had always welcomed on his spread.

"You raising rabbits now?" Moses, never short for a comment, lifted one bushy eyebrow.

"Not intentionally." Conscious of the old man following, Tanner carried the cage to a fenced area he'd built last November to house a pair of injured Canadian geese that had since flown away. "I made an exchange." He set the cage inside and opened the wire door.

"Rabbits for...?" Moses eased his arthritic hip onto a nearby bale and watched the animals hop out of the cage to explore their new home.

"Rabbits for pie or something like it for my ushers' meeting tonight." Tanner couldn't hide his smile of anticipation.

"Good deal, especially if a pretty lady comes with it," Moses approved with a chuckle.

"She's pretty all right," Tanner assured him. Then he frowned. "But that has nothing to do with the pie. I mean—uh—"

"Right." Moses's amused chuckle echoed through the

feathery mesquites, over the spiky barrel cactus and tumbled down to the bubbling brook three hundred feet away. "The Lord's ways surely are mysterious."

Mysterious or not, the Lord wasn't in the matchmaking business for Tanner Johns, because pretty as Sophie Armstrong was, God knew perfectly well that Tanner didn't get involved with women. Never again.

"I sure hope your cowboy likes these kinds of pie." Sophie studied the fluted golden crusts with a critical eye.

"He will." Beth smiled dreamily, her mind obviously elsewhere. "Do you think the rabbits are happy, Mama?"

"On a ranch? I think they're ecstatic. That means very happy," she clarified when Beth frowned.

"Mr. Cowboy will be really nice to them." Beth went back to coloring her oversize rabbit-picture-thank-you card for the rancher.

"How do you know that?" Curious to hear the response, Sophie listened before completing a last-minute mental check on her catered meal.

"'Cause he was really nice to me. Only he's got sad eyes. I think he hurts inside. I don't think he has anybody to love him." Beth added a few blue lines to her drawing before she murmured, "*I* love him."

I could almost love him for taking those rabbits. Immediately Sophie quashed the errant thought. *Never falling into that trap again*, she reminded herself. *Independence is too precious.*

"I love Mr. Cowboy lots." Beth sounded the way Sophie had felt when she was fifteen and Marty Armstrong, the coolest guy in school, had first shown an interest in her.

"That's nice to say, sweetie, but Mr. Johns is a stranger. You can't love a stranger." It was the wrong thing to say to her very literal daughter, and Sophie knew it the moment Beth's blue eyes darkened to storm clouds.

"The Bible says to love everybody." She glared at her mother, her voice accusing.

"That's right. Thank you for reminding me, Bethy." Sophie pressed a placating kiss against her daughter's head, then checked the kitchen clock. Where was the man? She had to leave for her gig in less than five minutes. "Maybe that's him," she said when the phone rang a second later.

It wasn't Tanner Johns calling.

"I can't babysit, Sophie. I'm so sorry." Edna Parker's breathy voice sounded horribly weak.

"What's wrong, Edna? Where are you?" Sophie asked worriedly.

"At the hospital. My son brought me. I fell and broke my hip while you were out trying to get rid of the rabbits. They're going to do surgery soon." That weepy tone told Sophie her elderly neighbor was very frightened.

"You stop fussing now," she said gently. "The doctors will make everything better."

"But I can't babysit for you tonight," the woman wailed in a feeble voice.

"I'll get someone else to watch the kids. Don't worry about us. And I'll run over later and look after your cats. I have your key, remember? Everything's going to be fine." She heard a sigh of relief. "The kids and I will come see you as soon as we can. Don't worry, Edna."

"Thank you, dear." Somewhat calmer, Edna chatted for a moment before saying, "I'm so glad God sent you into my life." Then she hung up.

"I wish God would send me someone into *my* life. Where am I going to get a sitter at this time on a Friday night?" Sophie couldn't mess up this catering job. She needed it to pay next month's rent. "I need help, God."

A loud rap on the front door startled her out of her silent prayer.

"It's Mr. Cowboy," Beth yelled, having raced to answer

the door. Then to Sophie's utter dismay, her daughter said to Tanner, "Houston, we have a problem."

Tanner's startled gaze moved from Beth to Sophie. One corner of his mouth kicked up. Dark green eyes, which earlier had been hidden behind sunglasses, were startling in his tanned face. Sophie gulped. Tall, lanky and lean, with wide denim-clad shoulders that looked perfect for leaning on, Tanner Johns was every woman's fantasy cowboy.

Not *her* fantasy cowboy, of course, but—

"What's the problem, er, Houston?" His gaze rested on Sophie while his fingers gripped the black Stetson he'd removed when he stepped over their threshold.

Sophie couldn't explain because there was something wrong with her breathing. As in, she couldn't. Then Davy came racing down the stairs, tripped on the perpetually loose runner at the bottom tread and tumbled headlong into the cowboy's arms. Tanner grunted as he caught her son and held on just long enough to make sure Davy could stand on his own.

"Something I said?" he joked, winking at her.

The man *winked* at her! The control Sophie had almost recovered vanished. She figured she probably looked like a beached fish, gulping for air. Stupidly, she wished she'd had time to fix her hair.

Where's your independence now?

"Our babysitter can't come," Beth explained. "Mama's gonna lose this job and we need it to pay our bills." The words were an exact repeat of her mother's earlier meant-to-be-silent mutterings.

Sophie almost groaned out loud. Tanner so needed to hear that sad story, he of the billion-acre ranch with money coming out of his ears, thanks, according to church gossip, to Burt's generosity. Now he'd feel sorry for her. Sophie thrust back her shoulders, independence reasserting itself.

"That's enough, Beth. You and Davy get your sweaters.

You'll have to come with me and sit quietly in a corner of the kitchen while I work. Go now. Monica and Tiffany will meet us there." She said hello to Tanner and beckoned him to follow her to the kitchen.

"Monica and Tiffany?" he said in a dazed voice. "You have more children?"

"They're my catering helpers." Sophie pointed. "Your pies."

When there was no response, she paused in lifting the pan holding her perfectly sliced roast from the oven to look at him. Her heart gave a bump of pure sympathy. The poor man was gazing at her pies as if he hadn't eaten for months. So maybe his massive inheritance couldn't buy everything, but she had no time to think about that now.

"Tanner?" She said it more crisply than she intended. He lost the hungry look and snapped to attention. "Sorry to rush you. You'll have to wrap them yourself. The foil's over there. I've got to load up and get going."

"I'll help you." He took the heavy metal server from her and insisted she lead him to the garage where the van was open, waiting. He stored the container where she indicated, then carried out the other dishes, refusing to let her lift even one though she assured him she'd done it many times before.

"Thank you for your help," Sophie said when everything was placed so it couldn't move during the trip. "Now I must leave. Beth. Davy," she called.

"Aw, Mom. Do I have to go?" Her son glared at her. "I'm not a baby, you know."

"I know you're growing up fast, but you're still too young to stay alone. Now please come on. I don't have time to waste arguing." Too aware of Tanner standing next to her, Sophie reached out to grab her son's arm to draw him forward.

"I could take your children back to the ranch with me while you work."

The cowboy's offer stunned her. It must have stunned him, too, because Tanner gawked at her, green eyes stretched wide as if he was in shock.

"It's very kind of you to offer but you're a stranger," she said as nicely as she could. If only she could accept. It would save— What was she thinking? It was impossible.

"There will be eleven other men at the meeting. One will be Pastor Jeff and at least two others are church board members. You can call any of them for references if you want." Tanner waited. Could he know how desperately she wanted to accept his offer? "Please let me help," he murmured when she'd wasted several more moments. "These pies—you've no idea what they mean to me. I'd like to return the favor, if you'll let me."

"You already did by taking the rabbits," Sophie reminded. He only smiled and waited, watching her with that intense contemplation that had turned more hazel now that flecks of copper glinted in the depths.

"Can we go to his ranch, Mom?" Davy's hopeful voice broke the silence.

"What about your meeting?" Sophie knew Davy wouldn't settle while she was working, and that would disturb Beth, which would distract her. She desperately needed tonight's job to go right. Dare she risk leaving her kids with this man?

"I draw up the usher schedules ahead of time. It's just a matter of everyone confirming dates and then sampling your pie." Tanner's grin made her stomach swoop so she felt off balance. "It's an excuse for guy time. Your kids won't be an issue, Sophie. Moses will make sure of that."

As Tanner explained to the kids about a Native American man who lived at the ranch, Sophie could no longer resist his offer. She lifted her cell phone from her pocket and dialed the pastor's number. Once she'd laid out the situation, Pastor Jeff gave his wholehearted reassurance.

"Tanner's a great guy, Sophie. He's going to turn Burt's ranch into a kind of outreach camp. I'm hoping our church can partner with him." His effusive praise for the rancher went on and on. When she didn't immediately respond, Jeff said, "If you're still worried, know that I'll be there to make sure nothing happens to Beth and Davy."

"I appreciate that, Jeff." She ended the call, closed the phone, then looked at Tanner. "Thank you, I'd like to accept your offer."

He nodded and turned away, probably to hide the embarrassed flush rising up his neck. Sophie regretted causing that but she had to be sure the kids would be safe. She drew Davy aside and stared him straight in the eye.

"Same rules as at home, buddy. You don't go anywhere on the ranch if Tanner isn't there. You obey him and Moses without question. If I hear one word—"

"You won't." Davy eagerly grabbed his jacket and held out his sister's. "Come on, Bethy. We're going to a real ranch."

Davy's use of the old pet name for his sister made Sophie smile. His good mood probably wouldn't last, but while it did she'd enjoy it.

It took only minutes to store the now-covered pies in the side boxes of Tanner's truck, minutes more to kiss her babies and promise to pick them up as soon as she was finished working. Sophie searched her brain, worried she'd missed something, forgotten something important.

"Go do your job, Sophie." Tanner's quiet reassurance brought back the reality of time. "I promise I'll keep Beth and Davy safe for you."

"Thank you," she said sincerely. A moment later, with her kids safely belted into their seats, Tanner drove away and Sophie left home with her meal, clinging to her wobbly faith that this time God would be there for her.

She'd almost forgotten the Sunday she'd been on cleanup duty after a potluck at the church and overheard Burt speaking to someone about Tanner.

"He had a rough childhood and his teen years weren't much better. His past dogs him. But there isn't a man I trust more than Tanner Johns. His integrity, honesty and uprightness are part of what makes him tick."

The old man must have truly trusted Tanner to bequeath his beloved Wranglers Ranch to him. Burt's latest dream for the place was something the whole congregation had learned about from a presentation he'd made a few weeks before his death. The reason Sophie remembered that specific conversation, though, was because of Burt's last words.

"As I keep telling Tanner, we must fan into flame the gift of God inside us."

So, Sophie wondered, what was Tanner's gift? Knight in shining armor?

The mental image of him riding a white steed, or in this case his white truck, to her rescue made Sophie blush. She got back to work forcing away that image and the memory of the way her senses had reacted to the big cowboy, especially to that slow, easy smile of his. She'd been this route before with Marty, and life had been a painful teacher.

Her husband Marty's greatest attraction had been his charm. He'd been as big a kid as his own children, fun-loving, living for the moment, never giving a thought to tomorrow, often to the detriment of his family. In the two years since his death Sophie had finally put her life back together and regained control. Sure, every day was a struggle to make ends meet, but it was *her* struggle, *her* bank account to hide away for real emergencies. *She* was the person she depended on. No way was she giving up her independence or security now.

Sophie wasn't ever going to be dependent on any man again, even if he was a big strong cowboy with a smile that made a zillion butterflies skip in her stomach.

Chapter Two

"**I**'m afraid I wore out your kids." Tanner liked the way Sophie's upswept hair left her graceful neck free for his inspection.

"I hope they behaved." Three and a half hours later the cook's black fitted blouse and slacks still looked pristine. In fact, Sophie appeared relaxed and calm, exactly the type of competent professional you'd want catering your occasion. "Davy..."

"Loves horses. I could barely keep him from saddling up. His enthusiasm is great." Tanner chuckled at her surprise. "No kidding. He's a natural cowboy. They're sleeping in the other room. Want to check?" She nodded so he led the way.

Sophie's lovely face softened when she saw Beth curled in Burt's chair in front of the fire next to Davy, who'd thrown his arm across her shoulder in a protective manner. Tanner pointed to the kitchen and after a long moment she nodded and followed.

"Thank you," Sophie said quietly.

"They're good kids. After my meeting ended I took them out to feed the rabbits. They approve of the bunnies' new home." He smiled at her eye roll. "How did the job go?"

"Perfectly. I have just enough beef left over to make us a stew tomorrow and not a spoonful remains of my chocolate cherry trifle." Despite the lines of weariness around her eyes, Sophie looked happy. "And I have two new jobs."

"Great." He motioned to the stove. "Do you have time for tea? I just made a pot."

"I'd love a cup. Thank you." Sophie sank into the chair he offered. "Somehow I didn't see you as a tea drinker."

"Burt only drank coffee in the morning. He refused to make it after that. Since my coffee is worse than mud it was easier to drink whatever he made. It's pretty hard even for me to mess up tea bags." He poured tea into two mugs before realizing he should have used the good cups. "I have some pie left. Would you like a slice?"

"No, thanks. I like making pie but eating it is bad for my waist." Sophie frowned at him. "Which kinds were left?"

"One apple and one strawberry rhubarb." He sat down across from her thinking that there was nothing wrong with her waist. "Don't make that face. It wasn't because they didn't like them," he reassured her. "They did. I knew most of them would take seconds or thirds so I hid two pieces before they got here."

She frowned. "Why?"

"Because I wanted some for tomorrow." He shrugged when she grinned. "Self-preservation. You make very good pies."

"Thank you but I'm sure your housekeeper keeps you well fed." Sophie's gaze moved around the kitchen.

"I don't have a housekeeper. The hands are all married and eat at home. Moses prefers his own cooking. It's just me." She looked dubious. "It's true. When he was alive, Burt did the cooking or we ate out."

"What a shame with a kitchen like this. It's a cook's dream." A soft yearning look filled Sophie's face as she studied the stainless steel appliances. "You have every piece of equipment any cook could dream of."

"Probably." He shrugged carelessly. "Burt had this room redone several months ago and then asked the Public Health Department to certify it as commercial. He hoped to use it for meal preparation when he got the camps going."

"When will that be?" Sophie leaned back in her chair, mug in hand, and let the steam bathe her face.

"Good question." Tanner forced himself to stop staring at her and admitted, "I'm struggling to get things started because I don't have Burt's gift for striking up conversations with kids. I'm not even sure how to start a camp or whatever for them. Actually I'm scared witless at the thought of hosting a group of troubled kids for a whole week, but that was Burt's goal."

"Why must you start with a full-week camp?" Sophie tilted her head, her face thoughtful. "Couldn't you try a one-day riding camp first, maybe get some practice at running that before you branch out?"

Tanner blinked. He'd been overwhelmed by the scope of Burt's impossible dream, but this smaller step seemed feasible.

"How do you see that working?" He waited with a wiggle of excitement flaring inside, for Sophie to expand on her idea.

"Hmm. Maybe the kids would arrive Saturday morning between seven and eight? You could have a buffet breakfast while they assemble. Kids are always hungry." She smiled, her full lips tipping up in a way that set his heart thudding. "After that they could mingle among the horses."

"That way we could assess their skills without being too obvious." Logical and organized. Tanner liked that about Sophie. "Also they could get to know their ride. But we'd need some time to prepare the horses," he mused with a frown.

"So maybe a little explanation about the horses while you prepare. After that you tell them the rules for the trail ride and what to expect." Sophie glanced at him, eyebrows lifted in a question. "Then you mount up."

"And just ride?" He thought that sounded boring.

"You could break up the ride." Sophie didn't laugh or mock him for his lack of ideas. Instead she chewed on her bottom lip, a frown marring her smooth forehead as she thought it through. "Maybe you'd stop along the way to explain about the desert, the animals that live here, talk about Wranglers Ranch and how it came to be—stuff like that."

"That'd be Moses's job," Tanner said, thinking how easily her plan came together. "He knows everything there is to know about this spread and the desert adjoining us."

"Perfect." Her smile made him feel as if he could handle this.

Suddenly Tanner didn't find Burt's dream quite so daunting.

"At the end of the ride you might have a campfire picnic or maybe a chuck wagon dinner." Sophie studied him, assessing his response. "Doable?"

"Sure. We could follow that with stories, maybe bring up God's creation," Tanner added thoughtfully. "It's a good plan. A small group would give us a chance to do a trial run, iron out problems."

"It wouldn't be hard to turn that into a two-day camp, either, if you had somewhere on the ranch for people to camp out overnight. Breakfast in the desert, ride back to the ranch for lunch, then head home. It sounds—" Sophie's smile faltered. "You're frowning."

"Because I don't see how this plan attracts street kids." Tanner avoided her gaze. "They were Burt's primary focus."

"Maybe to get there you have to start with other kids," Sophie said in a thoughtful voice. "Maybe if you got a buzz going about this place, street kids would come out of curiosity. There are lots of needy kids who could benefit from coming here. Building a rapport with a horse and the people who care for them could be a bridge to reaching many kids."

"You think?" Tanner hadn't considered that.

"Sure. I'd enroll Davy in a program like that if it was available and I could afford it." Sophie set her cup down and placed her hands in her lap. Her voice dropped. "Actually I'm willing to try almost anything to engage him. He's not yet nine but he's already gotten in with a bad bunch of kids. His behavior and attitude are suffering at school, too. I'm his mother but I feel like I'm failing him."

"I sincerely doubt that." Tanner didn't think a caring mom like her would ever disappoint her child or abandon him as his own mother had.

"I homeschool Beth and that takes a lot of prep time, but I have to do it. She just wasn't progressing at her school." Sophie sighed. "By necessity she gets a lot of attention from me. So does my job and when I've finished that—"

"You're wiped out," he completed, seeing the weariness in her posture.

"Yes." Sophie's head drooped. "And Davy suffers. His 'friends' have already persuaded him to steal a candy bar. I reprimanded and punished him but I'm worried about what comes next. I don't know what to do. I'm doing the best I can but..."

Tanner had to say something to erase the misery on her face.

"Davy was great tonight. He even offered to help Moses muck out stalls." He grinned as astonishment filled Sophie's face. "Don't worry, I didn't let him. I said we'd need your permission first, but Davy is definitely intrigued by the animals. He went from tough bravado to quiet gentleness in about three seconds flat when he met an abused horse someone dropped off today."

"My son—gentle?" Sophie's big brown eyes stretched wide. "Davy?"

"Davy," Tanner affirmed. He liked her honesty about her son. "Maybe that's an interest you can build on, which is also why this idea of yours could be worthwhile." His brain whirled with ideas. "If Wranglers helped only Davy it would at least be a step toward making Burt's dream come true."

"Doing that means a lot to you?" she said softly.

"It's the only reason I accepted his legacy of Wranglers. I have less than two years left to turn Burt's dream into reality. Maybe a day camp is the way to finally start down that path." Tanner grabbed a pen and pad of paper from near the phone. "For me the biggest issue will be the food. Hey!" He grinned at her. "Could we hire you to cook?"

"I'd need to check dates but I'm sure we could work out something." Sophie didn't look at him as she asked, "Maybe I could cook in lieu of Davy's fee to attend?"

"We could talk about that." Tanner saw hurt flicker through her eyes when he didn't immediately accept and mentally kicked himself for causing it. But his strong re-actions to this woman scared him. He didn't want to en-courage anything that could be construed as personal with her. Or anyone else. "I need to keep everything business-like," he excused quickly.

"Of course. So do I." The hurt look disappeared as she nodded. "Profit and loss to make it official. Then when you've done several camps you'll have built a résumé that you can use for schools or public agencies so they'll see you're not just playing at this. Good idea."

It hadn't been his idea at all. It was hers. And a good one at that.

"Thank you for understanding, Sophie. But I would like

to have Davy attend the first camp." He saw her surprise. *Don't say anything about what he did. Don't get involved*, his brain ordered. Too late.

"Why?" Sophie's gaze narrowed. "Because you feel sorry for him?"

"Sorry?" How could he phrase this without offending her? "No. I see Davy as sort of a guinea pig. Maybe I should say 'test subject.'" Sophie's dark eyes narrowed so Tanner hurried to clarify. "If Davy was part of the first ride, I could question him afterward and see from his perspective where we missed a need or should do something differently. I wouldn't want to ask a guest those kinds of questions. But if Davy was part of my team—" He saw skepticism in her intelligent gaze. "You don't want that."

"I think it's wonderful of you and he'd love it, I'm sure." The frown furrowing her forehead returned. What a concerned mother she was. "But what if he does something he shouldn't? What if he messes up?"

He already has.

"Then we'll learn from that, too." Tanner smiled at her. Somehow it seemed important to reach this boy. At least he could do that, couldn't he? "Davy's a little kid. What could happen?"

"You'd be surprised." A wry tilt of her lips told Tanner Sophie's equanimity was returning. "Okay, but I hope you don't regret this idea. You do realize Davy doesn't know how to ride."

"So we'll teach him." Tanner shrugged to show her it was no big deal. Suddenly he wanted to know more about Sophie. "Your husband must have been glad of your quick thinking." Immediately shutters dropped over her eyes, telling him it was the wrong thing to say. "That's private. I'm sorry."

"No, it's fine." She huffed out a sigh and then sipped her tea. Just when he thought she would get up and leave,

Sophie lifted her head and looked him in the eye. "I guess Marty did depend on me. He certainly didn't have a head for business."

"Is Davy like him?" Tanner asked, curious about the man this lovely woman had married.

"I hope not." Sophie smiled at his startled look. "I loved my husband but he wasn't what you'd call responsible. Marty was like a big kid, carefree, enjoying himself without worrying about the future."

"Tough on you," he murmured.

"Yes. I was the heavy, the one who said no to his wilder ideas, and Davy was old enough to see that." Sophie's pretty face tightened at the memory. "I'm trying to teach my son that responsibility is part of growing up, that nobody gets out of it."

"Is that what Marty tried to do, get out of his responsibility?" It was none of Tanner's business but he had to ask. His stomach knotted when Sophie slowly nodded. What would she think if she knew of his past irresponsibility? "How did Marty die?"

Normally Tanner would have steered far away from such personal questions. But here, in the intimacy of his kitchen, he had a strange feeling that Sophie wanted to share her past and that she needed to talk to someone. He'd guess she didn't do that often but maybe with her kids asleep and her job finished, she could finally relax. She'd helped him. He wanted to help her.

"I'm a good listener, Sophie," he assured her quietly. Silence yawned.

"Marty died riding bulls at the rodeo."

It wasn't so much those seven words as the way Sophie said them that told Tanner how much her husband's decision to take that risk had affected her. He made no comment, simply waited for her to continue.

"Beth was three months old and our medical bills were

huge. Marty was looking for an easy way to pay them off." She bowed her head as if ashamed about her debt. "The rodeo purse was a large amount. Marty being Marty never considered it was so large because no one could ride the animal, or that he might get hurt trying. After three seconds, the bull threw him, then trampled him. Marty was unconscious for four days before he died."

Leaving Sophie with even larger medical bills and no one to help her. Irritation toward the careless husband built with a rush of—what? Not pity. Sympathy? Compassion— that was it. And a wish that he'd been there to help her. But why was that? Tanner was a loner. He barely knew Sophie Armstrong. So why should he feel she needed his help?

"That must have been very hard for you, alone with a newborn and another child." A thousand questions bubbled inside him. "What did you do?"

"I cried for a while but that was useless so I grabbed control of my life." Sophie's voice hardened. "I felt like I'd lost it in high school when I learned I was pregnant with Davy. My parents were furious their daughter had strayed from the Christian path." Her voice showed the strain of that time. "They insisted Marty and I get married. I obeyed them even though I had a lot of doubts about marriage and motherhood at sixteen."

"Sixteen? Wow. That is young." Tanner gulped down the memory of his own life at sixteen and the mistake he was still running from, the thing that made him utterly unworthy of Burt's trust or anyone's love. "When Marty died, did you contact your parents?"

"His and mine both, to tell them of his death. I could have used my parents' support then but I couldn't take their recriminations." Sophie's usually laughing lips tightened. "My parents are big into rules and judgment. I didn't need the guilt of hearing about how my sins were coming back to roost."

"His parents couldn't help, either?" Sophie shook her head. "So you were alone. How did you survive?" Tanner was aghast that this young woman had faced life as the sole support for two very young children.

"Marty had an insurance policy. I got it the day he bought a house that was beyond our means. The policy paid off our mortgage but we couldn't afford to live there so I sold the place and everything else we didn't absolutely need." Sophie's chin thrust out as if she expected some argument from Tanner, as if she'd had to justify her decision before.

Tanner remained silent, amazed at her pluck and grit.

"That money, a cleaning job with a neighbor babysitting for free and the food bank gave us a cushion while I figured out my next step." She shrugged. "People liked my cooking so I started selling it at farmers' markets to make a few dollars extra. That grew into catering and eventually allowed me to stay home with Beth. We manage now."

"So you have your own business." Tanner felt enormously proud of Sophie and he barely knew her!

"It hasn't been easy, but yes, I love being my own boss." She grimaced. "Along the way I've struggled to figure out God's plan but—hey, that's enough of my life story."

"Thank you for sharing it with me," Tanner said and meant it. "You're a remarkable woman, Sophie Armstrong."

"I'm just a mom trying to do the very best for my kids. They come first." She said it with a fierce purpose, her eyes dark with determination. "Davy and Beth are why I keep pushing through the problems. My kids are my life. I will never knowingly endanger them. I will also never again allow my life to be controlled by someone else."

Sophie's darkened eyes and stern voice brooked no argument. Her harsh life had obviously strengthened her but Tanner hated to see the tiny fan lines of stress at the sides of her eyes.

"So now you believe Davy needs to learn responsibility?" He waited for her nod, feeling slightly guilty for thinking he had something he could teach this boy, he who had abdicated fatherhood of his own child. "How will you teach him that?" he asked curiously.

"By finding something he loves and then indulging it as much as I can afford. Maybe he'll begin to understand that some things are worth working for." Her firm clear voice and focused gaze told him Sophie needed no greater motivation for her life than her kids.

How Tanner admired that motherly devotion. "And Beth? What does she need?"

"Beth—" Sophie paused, her face momentarily reflective. "Beth will be fine." Her dark eyes softened and the hard thrust of her jaw relaxed. "She takes whatever life hands her and turns it into a rainbow. She's adaptable. Davy's different." Her lips pinched tight. "He needs something...more."

"God certainly knew what He was doing when He made you their mother." Tanner was positive he'd never known anyone more determined than Sophie Armstrong. He noted her quick glance at the wall clock, saw it swerve to rest on Beth's card sitting on a shelf. Her smile returned. "It's a pretty card," he said. "More tea?"

"No, thanks. I must get home." She rose, set her cup in the sink then faced him. "I can't thank you enough for helping me out tonight, Tanner."

"I think four pies more than covered that bill. This ranch will have a new reputation at church thanks to you. The best eats ever at Wranglers Ranch." He grinned and when she smiled back he decided Sophie's pies weren't the best thing about her. Her smile was.

Silence yawned between them. Tanner's gaze locked

with hers and he couldn't look away from those intense brown eyes until Sophie's cough snapped the electrical current running between them.

"I need to go," she said again. "But if I can somehow help with your project here at Wranglers, I hope you'll tell me."

"Thanks." How generous to make such a gracious offer with all she had on her plate. "I will."

She nodded once before she stepped around him and walked into the living room. "Come on, guys. Time to get home."

Tanner watched in silent admiration as Sophie gently shook Davy's shoulder, then Beth's, wakening them in a tender loving tone. The children roused easily, yawning as they straightened.

"We had the bestest time, Mama. Thank you, Cowboy Tanner." Beth insisted on calling him *Cowboy.* Tanner liked it. It made him feel as if he was somehow more noteworthy than the men she usually encountered. He basked in her sweet smile.

"You're welcome, Beth. I hope you come again." Tanner surprised himself with the invitation. Sophie's presence here made his pulse speed up, and that made him nervous. He was all about not getting involved, yet there was something about Sophie and her little family that drew him, made him want to interact with them again.

"Hey, Mom." Davy was fully awake now and full of information. "Bethy was telling Tanner how you homeschool her and how you're the leader."

"I'm just chairman of the homeschool association," Sophie corrected gently.

"Whatever. Anyway I remembered you said you have to arrange an outing for the homeschool kids." He grinned at his sister. "Beth and me think coming to Wranglers Ranch would be fun. I could come, too. To help," he added, his chest puffed out.

Tanner hadn't encouraged Davy when he'd posed the thought earlier, and he was glad he hadn't because a doubtful look washed over Sophie's face as she glanced from her son to him.

"You'd be a big help, son. But I don't know about visiting a ranch. Not all the homeschool kids can ride horses. What would they do out here?" she asked.

"There's tons of stuff to do." Davy grinned at Tanner. "This old guy, Moses, knows all about the original settlers and the Indians that lived here first. He tells lots of cool stories."

"And the horses need people to feed and brush them," Beth added. "I got to pet a white one. It's called Jeremiah, right?" she asked Tanner, who nodded.

"I'd rather ride Gideon. He looks like he's fast." Davy's eyes glowed with excitement.

"Moses, Jeremiah and Gideon. Sounds like you've got an Old Testament theme going at Wranglers Ranch." Sophie smiled at Tanner.

My, how he liked that smile.

"Burt's idea. Every time he read a passage about a Bible character's struggles, he'd figure out how he could apply that lesson to his own life. Then he'd use the hero's name on a rescued horse to remind himself." Tanner nodded. "We have Melchizedek, Ehud, Balaam—want me to continue?"

"I get the idea. Old Testament heroes." She rolled her eyes.

"And heroines. Burt was an equal opportunity *namer*." Tanner couldn't smother his laughter when Sophie's face twisted in a droll look. "No kidding. We have Rhoda, Abishag and Bathsheba to name a few."

"Abishag?" Sophie's chortles lifted the gloom that had

settled over the house since Burt's passing. Tanner felt as if the joyful sound swept the house free of grief and loss and replaced it with—hope?

"Maybe you haven't read about her. Abishag was a beautiful young woman who was chosen to marry David in his old age and cherish him." Tanner shrugged. "I'm not sure what Burt's lesson about her was but there must have been one because he chose that name for a mare."

"Abishag is a really pretty horse. She has black and white spots." Davy turned to Tanner. "What kind did you say?"

"A pinto," he said, then fell silent as the children regaled their mother with all the things they'd done with Tanner.

"Okay, odd names aside," Sophie said when they finally ran out of stories, "since my kids are so impressed with Wranglers Ranch, maybe you and I *should* have a discussion about arranging for the homeschool kids to come here. This sounds like a great place to visit."

Davy cheered so loudly the dog started to yowl.

"Sheba, quiet." Tanner tried to shush the excited animal.

"Sheba." Sophie slid her arm around each child's shoulder. "As in queen of—?" She arched one dark eyebrow in a question.

"Everything." Tanner laughed at her groan. It was such fun teasing with Sophie. He walked with her as she shepherded her family out to her van, waited till they were all buckled in, then leaned toward the driver's open window. "I really appreciate those pies, Sophie. And I hope you'll come again soon. Your homeschool kids are also welcome if they want to visit."

"I'll see what the rest of the board thinks. They might want to visit your ranch first." She frowned. "Would that be a problem?"

"Not at all, but you should give me a heads-up before you come," he said quickly. He liked to be prepared, get his barriers up, Burt would have said. "We're working on replacement fencing up in the hills and I'm not always here."

"Okay." Was Sophie's hesitation because she was as loath to leave as he was to have her go? "See you."

I hope so.

He nodded and waved. When the van's red taillights disappeared around the bend, Tanner let his hand fall to his side, marveling at how alone it suddenly felt in this place that had been his home for so long, the place he enjoyed particularly *because of* the solitude. Tonight he'd welcome company to stop him from thinking about Sophie, but Moses had disappeared to his little cottage after the kids had fallen asleep.

Tanner walked back inside Burt's home, then jerked to a stop, suddenly seeing the rooms through new eyes. The updated modernity of the stainless steel kitchen and pristinely tiled bathroom didn't match the worn and shabby masculinity of the living room. Whenever possible Tanner avoided sitting in Burt's leather chair, the place where the kids had slept, because it had a spring that hit him in exactly the wrong spot. And it was becoming increasingly difficult to get comfortable on the stained and sagging plaid sofa, which was far too tattered to be restored by simple cleaning.

Tanner kept the place as tidy as he could, but tonight, through Sophie's eyes, he wondered who in their right mind had chosen the dreary red-and-black wallpaper, which in no way went with the horrible mud-brown carpet that was alternately matted in places and threadbare in others. There was no warm, cozy feeling here, not like at Sophie's home.

He thought about her suggestions for a day camp, which in his opinion had real merit. But if he pursued it there could be occasions when groups would have to come inside, say if it was raining or too windy outside. Burt had worked hard on the exterior appearance of Wranglers Ranch because he wanted those who visited to see his ranch in top-notch condition. Shouldn't that include the inside of the house, as well?

This room definitely didn't say "welcome." Tanner didn't have a clue how to achieve a hospitable feel, but he figured there were people in Tucson who did. He'd told Sophie he'd be working on fences, but his ranch hands were more than capable of doing that. He went along only in hopes the open spaces would help him figure out how to make Burt's dream live. Instead Sophie had showed him how to start.

Tanner went back to the kitchen, grabbed his Bible from a shelf and sat down, prepared to ask God about his next move. Immediately his nose caught Sophie's citrusy fragrance and his brain framed her laughing face.

Would she come back to Wranglers? Soon?

And why did it matter so much?

Chapter Three

Two weeks later Sophie ended her morning visit at the hospital after praying for added strength for Edna.

She thought God would answer that prayer because of Edna's strong faith in Him. But as she drove to Wranglers Ranch, Sophie couldn't bring herself to ask Him to affirm her decision to return to the ranch and the man she couldn't stop thinking about. She just couldn't trust that God would help her get over this silly attraction to a real-life cowboy.

"Do you think Cowboy Tanner missed us?" Beth asked from the backseat, completely ignoring Sophie's advice to stick with plain Tanner. "Bertie's mom told Cora Lee's mom that it was about time you got us a new daddy. Are we getting a new daddy, Mama?"

"No, honey, we're not." Sophie forced herself to unclench her jaw. Why did Beth's best friend have to be the son of the block's biggest gossip?

I am not interested in Tanner Johns.

Her brain laughed. Okay so she hadn't been very successful at banishing a host of mental images of the rancher and his lazy smile. But nobody needed to know that, especially Bertie's mom.

"I want to ask you something, honey," she said, changing the subject quickly.

"Okay." Beth nodded. Her blue eyes sparkled with excitement. "Is it a secret, like what Bertie's mom said?" She frowned. "Maybe I wasn't supposed to tell what she said."

"Oh, that wasn't a secret," Sophie reassured her with a mental grimace. The whole block probably knew about Tanner now. "Listen, Bethy. I need to have an important talk with Tanner and I don't want you to interrupt. I brought your crayons so you can color while we talk."

"Okay." Her daughter smoothed out the skirt of the dress Sophie had made her. There'd been no talking Beth out of wearing what was meant to be her Sunday best to the ranch today. Beth had a big crush on her Cowboy Tanner. Like mother, like daughter? "Can I see the rabbits, Mama?"

"If you don't interrupt, maybe you can see them when we're finished." Sophie frowned. "Do you understand?"

"Only interrupt if it's important," Beth promised.

Of course, Beth's *important* never meant what it did to others, but Sophie knew it was the best she could hope for. Talking about it more now that they were arriving would only confuse her daughter. She turned the corner, frowning as she noticed a group of people scattered all over the front yard. Some sat on the patchy grass, sipping from cans of soda, while others carried stuff from a big delivery truck. What was going on?

She parked her van in what she hoped was an out-of-the-way place, then she and Beth walked toward the door. Tanner met them, his grin wide and welcoming.

"This is a bad time for you," Sophie said, dismayed because she knew Beth wouldn't settle with so many people around. Even now she was chattering a mile a minute to a man she'd never met. "You should have put me off. I need to talk to you but it isn't urgent."

"There's no problem," he said easily. "Hey, Beth." He smiled at her daughter, admired her dress, then turned back to Sophie. "They're almost finished with the deliveries. Just taking a break while the designer rearranges a few things."

Designer? For a place for street kids?

Stop judging, Sophie.

"We can come back another time if it works better," she offered.

"Actually I was hoping you'd take a look while you're here and tell me what you think of my changes," he said with obvious eagerness. "Come on in. You, too, Beth." He took the little girl's hand and led her inside.

This was not the entry Sophie had used last time, but it led directly into the same room where her kids had fallen asleep. Only it wasn't the same. The dowdy old room had been transformed with the addition of a bank of windows facing north.

"It's so pretty, Mr. Cowboy." Beth's eyes were huge.

"Brilliant idea to make the windows floor to ceiling." Sophie was astounded by the light flooding the room.

"They're actually doors." Tanner showed her how one door folded against the other until the entire wall was open. "The workmen out there are creating a stone patio with lots of seating, including around a fireplace."

So Tanner was using Bert's fortune for himself. A flicker of disappointment wiggled through her but Sophie shrugged it off. Why did it matter to her that he was making his living quarters more comfortable? This room had been ugly and desperately in need of a face-lift. Tanner had the funds and there was nothing wrong with modernizing.

"I'm sure it will be lovely," she murmured.

"Actually you gave me the idea," he said, shocking her.

"Me?" Sophie blinked. "I said nothing about redecorating."

"No, but after all you said about day camps I got thinking how this room would be a great place to bring guests if it was raining or something. That grew into 'why not have a patio area, partly covered, where people could relax after their ride?' Or it could be for entertaining. I might have to do that if we get groups—" He paused. "I don't think you approve, Sophie," he said with a frown. "Is it the furniture? Maybe leather sofas are too much, but the designer said they're the easiest to clean if someone spills. I've heard kids usually spill."

"Yes, they do." She couldn't get over the difference he'd made. The room was warm and welcoming, inviting conversations in any of the casual groupings scattered around the big open space. Pale cream walls left no indication that redbird wallpaper—they had been birds, hadn't they?— had once nested there.

"You think I wasted Burt's money." He sank onto the arm of a sofa, his face defeated. "Maybe I did. I hemmed and hawed over this decision a lot." His tone grew somber. "It kept me awake thinking how many meals all this could buy for someone on the street."

Sophie tried to mask her feelings. "But you went ahead anyway."

"Yes, because of something Moses said." A funny look flickered across Tanner's ruggedly handsome face. "He asked me if I'd rather eat in a dump or a palace."

"That makes sense." But Sophie wasn't swayed. She'd heard the same kind of rationalization from Marty too many times.

"Moses helped me realize that people who've known toughness and hurt appreciate comfort just as much as the rest of us. I want everyone who comes to Burt's ranch to be comfortable." He rose slowly. "I'm sorry you don't approve."

"Oh, Tanner." Sophie hated that she'd spoiled his happiness. She touched his arm, wishing she hadn't immediately thought the worst of him. Independence was a fine thing but it was time to realize that not every man was like Marty. "I didn't say I didn't approve."

"You didn't have to." He seemed disappointed, his earlier joy gone. "It's in your face and your voice."

"I was just surprised. Anyone would love to come here. You've created a very comfortable, beautiful place." Sophie smiled at him. "I'm overwhelmed by the change. It's so different."

"Thanks." He looked relieved. "I particularly wanted this room perfect because further down the line, when things are more established, I hope to invite Social Services or some organization like that to come see what Wranglers can offer kids." He made a face. "I doubt they'd be impressed by the former decor. If they one day agree to partner in a program for needy children, I want this place to be ready."

"You've changed, also." Sophie studied the bright glint in his green eyes. "When we talked before you seemed as if you were struggling to begin Burt's dream but now you're charging ahead full speed." It wasn't a criticism. More that she couldn't quite define the change she saw in him.

"Because of you. You planted ideas that wouldn't go away." Tanner's steady stare made Sophie blush. "God's been working on me. I couldn't see how Burt's idea would work with me in charge. I still can't. But I'll start with your day camp idea and wait for God to lead me from there."

"I hope He comes through for you." How could she have imagined Tanner would be sidetracked by Burt's money? Everything he'd done here was with a view to fulfill Burt's dream.

"God always comes through, Sophie. It's just that sometimes it's in a different way than we expect." He smiled, his straight, even teeth flashing. "At the very least I owe you dinner for helping me get started."

"You don't owe me anything." No way did she want

this man to think there would be more than business to their relationship.

"Yeah, I do." His lazy smile was so attractive. "I want to repay you for helping me realize that I don't have to have the whole plan up and running right away. Burt once said it took years for God to get him used to the idea of using Wranglers Ranch for kids. I'll trust God to keep pushing me forward."

"I wish I had your strength," Sophie muttered, not intending him to hear it.

"Lady, you're a lot stronger than I'll ever be." Tanner leaned against the door frame, his hand stuffed into his front pockets. "I could never handle a job, two kids, one of whom I homeschool—"

"Where's Beth?" How could she have gotten so caught up in Tanner that she'd forgotten her daughter? Sophie glanced frantically at the work site where stone masons chiseled a patio.

"I'm here, Mama. I'm coloring." Her daughter sat on the floor in one corner, a book in front of her, crayons neatly organized. "I didn't bother you, Mama. So can we see the bunnies?"

"Sweetheart, you never bother me. And you've been very patient." Sophie hunched down beside her child and pressed a tender kiss against her head. "Just a few minutes more," she promised.

"Okay." Beth happily returned to her crayons.

"She's such a sweet kid," Tanner murmured, his dark green gaze resting on Beth. "It must be great to have a daughter like her. She brims with joy no matter what."

"Yes, she does." Sophie wanted to hug him for saying that. So many people saw only Beth's handicap, yet Tanner— She quashed her admiration for the rancher and returned to the reason she'd come here. "The homeschool group wants to plan an outing to your ranch, if you'll allow them to come."

"Sure." His forehead creased. "When? And what kinds of things will you want to do? I remember you said that not all the kids would be able to ride."

"For this first trip there'll be no riding. Instead we're looking for educational as well as fun." Sophie laid out the board's ideas: a nature walk, a discussion and perhaps a demonstration about a day on the ranch followed by refreshments. "Is that doable?" A leap of pleasure sprang inside at his nod.

"Provided you handle the refreshment part," he said with a grin.

"No problem." A wash of relief filled her at the ease of working with him. "When is a good time for you?"

Tanner consulted the calendar on his phone before giving her a choice of dates. She noted those, promised to get back to him, then glanced around.

"Is something wrong?" he said.

"Just wondering when the patio will be finished." A dozen scenarios for using the area played through her head.

"By the end of tomorrow, I hope. That's what they promised." He smiled at Sophie's surprise. "They'd better finish then because the youth pastor, Mike, is bringing some kids out on Friday evening and he wants them to have a sing-along around a fire."

"So you're already getting kids out here." She grinned at him. "That was fast."

"That was your daughter's doing." He glanced at Beth and chuckled.

"Beth?" Sophie liked Tanner's smile, an open, sharing kind of expression, not the kind of cagey grin that made you worry about what would come next. "What did she do?"

"She spoke to Mike last Sunday. I don't know exactly

what she said, but apparently Beth is a great salesgirl. He called me up that night to ask if we could arrange something especially challenging for some tough kids in his group who haven't been engaged by whatever he's been arranging. He's planning a mini rodeo for Friday."

"Can you handle that?" she asked curiously.

"Oh sure." Tanner winked at her. Sophie's stomach dipped. "We'll take out Jezebel, Obadiah and a few other old-timers for the kids to ride. They're gentle and don't spook. We won't be setting any rodeo records but it's all for fun anyway."

"Jezebel and Obadiah, huh?" Sophie couldn't smother her laughter.

"Yep." He grinned at her. "Actually I intended to phone you to see if I could order some snacks," Tanner added. His cheeks turned slightly pink when Sophie checked her watch and then raised her eyebrows.

"Tanner, today is Wednesday. Your event is Friday. I pride myself on freshly made delicious food, but I need time to make it," she scolded. "I have an event on Friday night and another on Saturday."

"I'm sorry. I got caught up in other stuff. Never mind. I'll go to the bakery." He looked so sad about it that Sophie's irritation melted.

"And ruin Wranglers' reputation for the best eats ever?" she teased. "How many kids and what kind of snacks?"

"You'll do it?" Could a grown man's eyes twinkle? "The church is supplying hot dogs and fixings. I thought I'd buy some chips so you'd only need to make treats. For around twenty, Mike said. I figured a couple pieces for each kid."

"You don't know kids' appetites." Sophie inclined her head. "I'll make lots. If you have leftovers you can freeze them for another time or take them to church potluck."

"Good idea." His attention strayed to the patio under construction. "Will the homeschool kids eat here or would you rather have some kind of picnic elsewhere on the ranch?"

"The patio would be perfect. A smooth surface makes it a lot easier for kids in wheelchairs." Sophie knew it was time to leave yet she lingered, savoring the lazy drape of the mesquite trees where they shaded the corner of the new patio. Neither the murmur of voices behind her as deliverymen finished filling the room nor the construction noise in front detracted from the peace of this place. "You're so lucky to live here."

"Blessed," Tanner agreed, his voice coming over her left shoulder. "I thank God every day that Burt found me and brought me here."

"I never heard the whole story. Will you tell me?" Sophie asked quietly, intrigued by the glimpse into Tanner's past.

"Not much to tell. I was almost sixteen, living on the streets. I'd run away from my foster home." He grimaced. "I was auditioning for membership in a gang when I met Burt." His cheeks stained red. "Actually I was trying to steal his truck. He invited me out to lunch and I was starving so I went."

"And that's it? You came here?" she asked in disbelief.

"Not quite." Tanner chuckled. "I ate the meal, even had seconds, but when he started talking about God I walked out on him. That didn't stop Burt. He came back, again and again. I must have cost him a fortune in food but the man was relentless."

"So eventually he talked you into coming to Wranglers." Sophie nodded, then stopped at the look on Tanner's face. "Not quite?"

"Not hardly. Burt had done some foster parenting years before so he had connections. He went to a social worker who was a friend of his and reported me." Tanner grinned at her surprise. "She appeared with some cops to take me to a juvenile detention center unless I agreed to have Burt as my guardian. He'd talked a lot about his ranch and since I was keen on horses I agreed to go with him. I figured I'd spend some time at Wranglers, enjoy the food and let my bruises from a street fight heal. Then I'd run away again."

"But you didn't." Sophie's interest grew.

"I didn't have the energy." Tanner shook his head, his face wry. "That man about wore me out with chores around this place. When he wasn't watching me, Moses was. I almost left the night before I was supposed to go to school, but I couldn't get away from them. Then I realized some of the kids admired me because I lived on a ranch. Me! So I decided to stay for a while."

"And you've never left." Sophie had heard Burt speak about Wranglers Ranch but she'd never realized how much effort he'd put into his work with Tanner.

"God and Burt wouldn't let me." Tanner's face grew pensive. "That man had a faith that astounded me. He prayed about everything and God answered. I couldn't leave because I was desperate to figure out why that was. Because of Burt I finally accepted God in my life. I've never regretted that. God's love changed my world."

Tanner sounded so confident in his faith. Sophie wished she was. But somehow lately she felt out of touch with God, as if He ignored her pleas for a way to build her catering business, to help Davy, to enrich Beth's life. And she still battled to be free of the condemnation her parents had heaped on her head when they'd first learned she was pregnant all those years ago.

Everybody pays, Sophie. For every action there is an equal and opposite reaction. If you break God's laws, you have to pay the price.

So now she was a widow, broke and alone with two kids, one mentally challenged and one well on the path to trouble. When would she have paid enough?

"Mama? Can we see the rabbits?"

Sophie shook off the gloomy thoughts to smile at her sweet daughter. Beth wasn't a penalty. She was a blessing. So was Davy.

"Why don't you ask Tanner?" She tossed a glance at the man who was becoming her best customer.

But he couldn't be more than that because Sophie wasn't about to trust Tanner or any other man with more than simple friendship.

When Tanner caught himself straightening a cushion for the fifth time on Friday night, he knew he was fussing too much. Moses knew it, too.

"What's bugging you?" the old man demanded from his seat on the patio. "You're like a cat on a hot roof. Is it that lady?"

"Sophie?" He saw the gleam in the old man's eyes and chided himself for taking Moses's bait. "She said five. She should have been here by now."

"That young pastor is waiting by the front gate for the second bus from the church. Guess I'd better go take the hooligans to the north pasture." Moses swallowed the last of his water, then rose. "They're playing a game about a flag."

"Capture the flag," Tanner said.

"That's what he called it." Moses nodded and pointed to the dust trail. "That could be your lady."

His *lady*? Tanner didn't have time to sort through the rush of excitement that skittered inside his midsection because Sophie pulled in front of the house and braked hard. She jumped out of her van and hurried to the back.

"Is anything wrong?" He strode toward her, noticing Beth's tear-streaked face in passing. Davy didn't look at him.

"Very wrong," she muttered, handing him two large

trays of assorted goodies. Her face was white, her eyes troubled. "But I don't have time to go into it now. I've got to serve crudités at a black-tie event in half an hour."

"The kids?" he asked, balancing the trays in each hand.

"Are staying with me," she said, her voice tight. "They can sit in the corner while I work." Clearly Sophie was steamed.

"Why not leave them with me? They can—" Tanner swallowed the rest of his offer when her dark brown eyes flashed a warning.

Sophie slammed the van's rear door closed, nodded toward the house and, after ordering the kids to stay put, followed him into the kitchen.

"He stole from you." Her fury showed in her stance, in the flicker at the corner of her mouth and in her lovely pain-filled eyes. "My son stole from you."

"Ah." Tanner clamped his lips closed and said nothing more.

"You knew?" If anything her anger burned hotter. "You knew and didn't say anything?"

"Sophie, he made a mistake. He took the arrowhead without thinking and then he didn't know how to put it back," he said in a soft voice. "But he would have. Davy's not a cheat."

"You could have fooled me." Her shoulders sagged. A rush of compassion filled Tanner. She hadn't even started her job and she was worn out.

"You can't do your best work worrying about them. Leave Beth and Davy here," he insisted softly. "Moses will talk to Davy, and trust me, Moses knows exactly what to say to get your son to consider his actions."

"Reward him by letting him stay?" Her brows drew together.

"Sophie." He watched her watch him. "Davy knows right from wrong. You don't have to bat him over the head with it. What he needs is to see how his actions affect others." He touched her shoulder. "Besides, Beth shouldn't suffer for his mistake. Leave them here. We'll talk later."

She studied him for several minutes, caught sight of the clock and heaved a sigh.

"Are you sure?"

He nodded.

"I don't feel good about this," she said. "I feel like Davy's getting paid for stealing."

"He won't feel like that when he leaves here tonight, I assure you." Tanner squeezed her shoulder. "Go do your job. You can deal with the rest afterward."

"You're always bailing me out," she murmured.

"Seriously?" He waved his hand at the trays of baking. "Who's bailing whom? But let's not argue it. You've got a job waiting and I need to check if Moses needs help. I'll get the kids so you can get on the road."

"You are a very nice man, Tanner Johns." Sophie spared a long moment to study him before she led the way back to her van. "No wonder Burt trusted you." She opened the van door. "Okay, you two, out. You're staying with Tanner till I'm finished with work. And no, this is not a vacation, Davy."

Tanner watched her pin the boy with a severe look that sent him scuttling out of the van. Sophie looked as if she'd say more but Tanner had a feeling Davy needed time to process what he'd done, time away from his mom.

"See you later," he said with a wave, then shepherded the kids toward the house.

Sophie drove away.

"Did Mom tell you?" Davy muttered as they walked.

"That you took something that didn't belong to you?" Tanner shook his head. "She didn't have to. Neither did Moses."

"How come?" Davy frowned as he peeked at Tanner through his lashes.

"I saw you take it when Moses showed you the collection."

"But you never said anything," Davy sputtered.

"Why would I want to hurt your mom by telling her you stole from us?" Tanner looked the boy square in the eye and watched him squirm. "Your mom loves you. It must have hurt her a lot to find out what you did."

"Yeah. I didn't think about that." Davy tried to smile when Beth slid her hand into his and hugged him.

"I love you, Davy," she said.

Tanner's heart pinched. What a special child. They both were. He wanted to reassure them they'd be okay but they weren't his to reassure. All he could do was support Sophie.

"Come on. We need to help Moses with a group that's visiting." He saw Davy lagging back and urged him forward. "What's the matter?"

"I have to apologize to Moses," the boy said, head down. "What I did was wrong. I knew it and I did it anyway. I wish I hadn't."

"That's the first step to learning," Tanner assured him. Sophie might think she had a problem with this kid but from his perspective, Davy seemed a good kid who'd simply given in to an impulse. Her parenting skills were not at fault and he was going to tell her that the next time they got some time alone together.

Tanner had a hunch Sophie might not like the rest of what he was going to tell her, but he'd just had an idea about how he could help her teach Davy about responsibility, an idea that if carried out, was going to mean he'd have a lot more contact with the single mom.

Now, why did that make him smile?

Chapter Four

"I can't believe it." A week later Sophie stared at the son she'd struggled to control. "A few hours of after-school work at Wranglers Ranch and Davy seems a different child."

"It's the horses," Tanner said. "Animals who've been abused or mishandled always seem to have a life-changing effect on people who work with them."

"I think it's your effect, too, Tanner." Embarrassed that a stranger could manage her child better than his own mother, Sophie quickly averted her gaze from his intense one.

They stood side by side, silently watching as Davy half carried, half dragged hay to the freshly cleaned stall. The boy glanced once at Tanner, waited for his nod of satisfaction, grinned at Sophie and then continued working, his forehead shiny with perspiration.

"Look at him. I can barely get that same boy to clean his room." She managed a huff of laughter to mask the feeling of failure that bubbled inside.

"Davy's beginning to realize the satisfaction that comes from giving to others." Tanner turned to face her. "Where's Beth today?"

"A friend's birthday party. Believe me, it wasn't an easy

choice for her, allotting her favorite cowboy second place to attend a birthday party," she teased.

Tanner shrugged. "Love is fickle."

"You can say that again." Sophie knew he didn't understand how much she meant those words, but since she didn't want to explain and spoil this moment of sharing, she leaned against a fence rail and allowed the dappling sun to warm her. The heat felt good after three hours spent catering in frigid air-conditioning.

"You're tired," Tanner said after studying her. "Do you have time for some tea while Davy finishes his job?"

"That's kind of you." It sounded strange to hear that her son had a job. Sophie debated a moment before she said, "I'd rather have coffee than tea, though."

"You don't want my coffee." Tanner gave a slight shudder.

"I'll make it," she offered, unable to quash her longing for a jolt of caffeine. "It would go well with the leftover cake from my event, if you're interested?"

"Silly question. I'm always interested in cake." Tanner licked his lips before telling Davy to come to the house when he was finished. Then in a much quieter aside he asked his foreman, Lefty, to watch Sophie's son.

"Thank you," she said after she'd retrieved the leftover dessert from her van. "I appreciate your thoughtfulness."

"More like common sense." He held the kitchen door open for her. "We don't leave guests alone with the horses, ever."

"So how is the guest thing coming?" After scooping grounds from the tin he handed her, she added ice water from the fridge and turned the coffee machine on. "Anything new?"

The freshly brewing aroma wafting through the kitchen teased Sophie's nostrils. Apparently it had the same effect on Tanner because he closed his eyes, inhaled and smiled, his mouth stretching wide. Her insides quivered at the attractive picture he made.

"How come I use the same machine, the same coffee, and I never get this aroma?" he demanded when he finally opened his eyes.

"Don't know," she said with a shrug. He grimaced.

"Okay, keep your secrets. Guests?" He nodded, green eyes intense. "We're getting some calls. Not the street kids I was aiming for, but kids. We have four groups booked for next week."

"Our homeschoolers come on Monday so—three groups besides them? That's good. Isn't it?" Sophie didn't understand why he wasn't smiling. As soon as the coffee finished brewing she poured out two large mugs, opened the cake box in front of him and sat down.

Once he'd fetched cream for his coffee, Tanner sat opposite her. With delicate precision he selected the largest piece of cake, laid it on a plate, then slowly sampled it.

"Is it okay?" she asked, worried by his silence.

"I guess it'll do." He winked as he took a second helping. "Can you make this again next week?"

"I could." She smiled. That wink got to her. Made her feel skittish. Nervous. *Young.* "Things must be improving if you're feeding a group."

"Not for a group. I want to take it to church for potluck Sunday." Tanner licked the icing off his fingers.

"Better not. Everyone at church knows this recipe is mine. I've taken it several times." She chuckled at his glower. "I could make you something else, though."

"Hard to beat this chocolate." He eyed the two remaining pieces but left them.

"Had enough?" Sophie couldn't hide her surprise.

"No way. But Davy will want some." He savored his coffee. "About the groups—I'm getting interest from several different organizations, but I'm hesitant to accept many bookings until we've had your group through and figured out what to expect. I've considered many scenarios but reality is far different from imagining."

"You've checked into insurance and all that?" Funny, Sophie mused to herself. She didn't feel the usual anxiety she experienced when her children weren't under her direct control.

Because she trusted Tanner? No! She couldn't afford to trust anyone.

"What if someone falls or a horse bolts or—"

"Our lawyer says we're covered, Sophie. Not that our horses bolt." Tanner tossed her an abstracted smile, but his forehead furrowed.

"But you're still worried. Why?" Sophie felt his intense scrutiny before he spoke.

"What if that's all we become, Sophie, a kind of entertainment for locals?" His hesitant voice dropped. "Burt's goal was so much bigger than that. The day he found me—" He stopped.

"Doing some initiation for a gang, wasn't it?" She was eager to hear the story behind the story so she asked, "How did you get involved in a gang?"

"I'd been living on the street." He shrugged. "I was a lifer." When she frowned he explained. "Lifelong foster child."

"You never knew your mother?" Sophie saw sadness fill his face.

"As I understand it, she gave me away right after I was born." A twinge of hurt edged Tanner's husky tone. His chin jutted out defensively. This insecure man was far different from the competent-cowboy image she usually saw.

"Oh, Tanner." She couldn't help reaching out to touch his arm and press her fingers against his warm skin. "I'm so sorry."

"I found out when I was seven. I didn't really understand it then but it didn't take long to figure out that no-body really wanted me, not the way other kids' mothers wanted them." He tried to smile but there was no humor in his next words. "I never stayed in a house more than six months before I was moved. The last one was abusive but the social worker didn't believe me so I ran away."

"And lived on the streets in Tucson," she added.

"Yeah." He nodded. "It was a lot safer than that home." He drained his cup and rose to fetch the coffeepot. When Sophie declined his offer he refilled his own cup. "But I wouldn't do drugs and that put me up against a guy who did."

"You got into a fight and Burt rescued you," Sophie finished.

"Burt sure blabbed." Tanner smiled. "Street life was tough but it wasn't all bad. I made some good friends. It was just that when they got high they turned into differ-ent people." He shrugged. "Anyway I came to Wranglers and stayed."

Sophie knew there was a lot more to the story, things he hadn't said. She wondered what they were but before she could question him further, he turned the tables.

"What about you?" Tanner said. "Why haven't you mar-ried again?"

"I don't think I'm the type to be married." Sophie strove to make her response sound carefree, airy. "Anyway I have to focus on my kids."

"And when they're grown?" Tanner arched one brow in a question.

"That'll be ages. Beth will probably be with me for a long while." Sophie couldn't think of anything else to add without going into detail, which she did not want to do.

Fortunately Davy appeared. He gobbled down the cake and a tall glass of water and filled the gaps between with nonstop enthusiasm about his work.

"I want to hear all about it, son," Sophie said half an hour later, delighted by the excitement she heard in his voice. "But you'll have to tell me the rest on the way home. We need to pick up Beth in twenty minutes."

"Aw, Mom—" The words died midsentence when Tanner cleared his throat. Davy wiped his face on his napkin, rose and stored his dishes in the dishwasher. "I'm ready when you are," he said moments later.

"Great." Blinking her surprise, Sophie glanced at Tanner, who was nodding approvingly at her son. "Could you bring that empty cake box, please?"

Davy instantly obeyed, then stopped in front of Tanner. "Tomorrow's Saturday. Will I be needed for work then?" he asked, his tone quiet and respectful.

"Yes. If your mom can bring you out." Tanner glanced at her, waited for her agreement.

"Bringing him here isn't a problem," she agreed as they walked to her van. "But I'm not sure about picking him up. I'm catering an anniversary tea tomorrow afternoon and I don't know how long I'll be."

"Why don't you come when you're finished?" Tanner invited. "We can share a pizza."

Something about the way he said that sent a frisson of worry tiptoeing up Sophie's spine, sending her independence surging. A pizza might be the first step toward getting involved in a date-type of situation, and she did not want that. She rapidly postulated excuses to refuse, discarding all of them.

"You don't like pizza?" Tanner asked with a frown.

"Yes, I do, but I'm not sure that will work," she said finally.

"Aw, Mom." This time Davy didn't even glance at Tanner, his disappointment in her obvious. "We never do anything special after you finish work."

"It so happens I'd planned pizza and games for tomorrow night," she said quickly. Too quickly.

"Great! Can Tanner come, too?" Davy's brown eyes glowed with excitement.

What could she do but graciously agree? After all, the man had singlehandedly managed to get her son started down a different path. Pizza was the least she owed him.

"Of course you are welcome to join us, Tanner." She hoped her genial tone masked her uncertainty.

"I don't think so." He smiled at Davy to soften his refusal before his gaze returned to Sophie. "Thanks anyway, but you'll be tired after working. Anyway I get the feeling Saturday nights when you're not working are family nights. I don't want to intrude."

"You won't be," Davy insisted. "We need four people to play the games. Otherwise Mom has to play two spots and that takes too long. We need Tanner, don't we, Mom?"

Need him? No, she didn't *need* him. And even if she did she couldn't afford to need anyone. Still, Davy's plea and the obvious pleasure he found in the cowboy's company was her undoing. Besides, if Tanner came, her son wouldn't nag to go out with his "gang."

"Please join us, Tanner." Sophie swallowed all her inhibitions and smiled. "I'm not Italian but I make a decent pizza."

"With onions?" Tanner kept a straight face when Davy choked off a complaint. "And anchovies?" A burst of laughter exploded from his chest when Davy couldn't control his horrified expression.

"I'm afraid the best I can do is cheese, ham and pineapple, maybe some pepperoni." Sophie mentally checked her store of groceries. She had paid for the ingredients for today's job and tomorrow's tea, which meant her cash was low. There was always her credit card but Sophie hated using that. After Marty died she'd been mired in debt once, and now that she was free she was never going the credit route again.

"A Hawaiian pizza sounds fantastic." Tanner smiled at her. "Thanks. I'd like to come if you're sure I won't be in the way."

"You won't." Davy was all smiles as he climbed into the van. "And you can bring me home so Mom won't have to come get me," he added, his eyes shining with excitement.

"Would that work?" Sophie felt self-conscious as she climbed into her van with Tanner watching.

"Sure. What can I bring? Doughnuts?" He winked at her startled look. "Kidding. Maybe some soda. Or ice cream?"

"You don't have to bring anything," Sophie said. "Just yourself. I've really got to go now. Beth will be waiting. See you."

"Yes, you will, Sophie." Tanner's low words sounded like a promise and that produced a warm glow inside that grew when he smiled at her. "See you tomorrow morning, Davy."

Sophie drove away while ordering herself not to glance in the rearview mirror. But she couldn't help it. She gulped at the sight of Tanner standing there, watching them leave, hat tipped back on his head, hands thrust in his pockets, calm, in control.

What she wouldn't give to feel like she was in control of her world.

"It's great that Tanner can come tomorrow night, isn't it, Mom?" Davy said. "You better make a lot of pizza and something nice for dessert."

"Why?" she asked curiously.

"'Cause Tanner always seems hungry. When I got some water out of the fridge today all I saw was an apple and some juice." Davy went silent for a moment, forehead furrowed as he thought. "Maybe when I go tomorrow I should take some extra sandwiches so I can share my lunch with Tanner."

Sophie sighed. Another mouth to feed. And yet she couldn't smother the smile that lifted her lips. Tanner was so appreciative of whatever she made. It was a pleasure to cook for him.

Watch it! It's just a plain little family dinner, for the kids' sake. You don't want more than that, remember?

No, she didn't. But it *was* nice to have her cooking appreciated.

Did that explain the kind of fuzzy afterglow that lingered for hours after Sophie had left Wranglers Ranch?

Tanner walked into the grocery store with purpose. Only he wasn't exactly sure what that purpose was. What did one take for pizza dinner with a gorgeous woman and two kids?

He should have brought Davy with him instead of dropping him at home to clean up. Now he pushed his cart up and down the aisles, puzzling over choices.

Garlic bread? Nah, Sophie probably made her own. Soda? She probably didn't like to give her kids so much sugar. Milk. That was an okay choice, surely? He chose two gallon jugs, then added a couple of pounds of butter. Everyone used butter, didn't they?

Tanner made several trips around the produce section before he came to a decision. Fruit was good for kids. He grabbed a big watermelon, two bags of grapes and three packs of strawberries. He thought only a moment before adding a pail of ice cream. Maybe Sophie would use it for one of her yummy desserts.

Stuff for a salad seemed a healthy idea, so Tanner added fresh vegetables. Sliced salami beckoned and he paired it with a package of sliced ham, just in case she didn't have enough meat to put on the pizza. He selected the largest onion he could find just to tease Davy, then added his crowning achievement—three pounds of freshly ground coffee.

Please, Lord, let her make that fantastic coffee again, Tanner prayed silently. He had to go back to get some cream, stomach growling at the thought of homemade pizza and Sophie's delicious coffee laced with cream. It was going to be a good evening.

Unable to think of anything else, he walked to the checkout.

"Stocking up, huh?" The clerk raised her eyebrows as she checked him out. "No doughnuts today?"

"Nope." Tanner almost burst out laughing at her surprise. "But I will take this." *This* was a pack of candy bars, Davy's favorites. The boy had enthused over them for twenty minutes yesterday. "These mints." For Beth. "And this."

There wasn't anything wrong with taking some flowers to his hostess, was there?

Tanner loaded the bags in his truck while noting the presence of the homeless man in the same place he'd seen him last time. He thought for a moment, returned to the store and purchased a container of soup from the snack bar, a thick ham sandwich and a bottle of icy lemonade. He tucked another ten-dollar bill into the sandwich bag before carrying them outside.

"Hi. I just bought my dinner but it seems I've been invited out and won't need it. Interested?" He held out the items and waited until the man stood. "I'm Tanner Johns."

"The doughnut guy." The man nodded. "I'm Tom. Tom Parker." He peeked in the bag. "I'm not a street person."

"Doesn't matter to me, man. It's just—I used to live on the streets and old habits die hard."

"Yes, but—"

"Wasting a fresh meal seems silly if someone else can

enjoy it." Tanner somehow felt it was best not to push for answers just yet. "Still got my card?" When Tom nodded, he said, "Call me if you want. The job offer still stands."

"I can't work—" Tom paused. The pain in his eyes made Tanner want to offer a way for him to avoid explaining. "Not yet anyway."

"I'm sorry, Tom. Listen, I want to talk to you but I can't stick around now or I'll be late, and trust me, there's no way I want to make this lady wait." How could he keep this connection going? "Maybe next time you and I meet we could go for coffee at that ice-cream place? I need an excuse to visit there."

After some hesitation Tom nodded. "Sure. Okay. *If* we meet again."

"We will." The two words slipped out.

"How do you know that?" Tom asked curiously.

"Because I believe in God and He works all things together." Tanner grinned. "Be seeing you, Tom." He swung into his truck and headed for Sophie's. "What do You want me to do about him?" he prayed aloud, but for the moment God wasn't explaining. That was okay. Tanner was learning to wait for God's direction, just like Burt had tried to teach him.

It was only as Tanner pulled into the Armstrong driveway that he started wondering if he'd bought too many things. Sophie certainly seemed to think so when he handed her the flowers, then asked Davy and Beth to help him carry the rest inside.

"Thank you but—what is all of this?" Sophie's dark eyes stretched wide as they plunked bag after bag on the counter. She looked really pretty in a fitted red shirt, cheeks flushed from the warmth of the kitchen, long legs covered in shabby jeans and bare feet.

"I wanted to bring a couple of things, you know, my

share of the meal." Tanner inhaled the mouthwatering scent of a robust tomato sauce, spices and freshly baking dough.

"Uh—" Sophie cleared her throat. "A couple of things?" She waved a hand at the stockpile. "You must be planning to eat a lot."

Heat singed his cheeks as he muttered sheepishly, "Maybe I got carried away."

"You think?" She arched one perfectly shaped eyebrow. Tanner had a hunch Sophie would have liked to send some of the bags home with him, but she couldn't because the kids were enthusing over the grapes as if they were some kind of delicacy.

"Thank you for the mints, Mr. Cowboy," Beth said, her sweet smile lighting up her face. "And for everything. Mama said we wouldn't have milk for a while. I love milk."

"Oh. Good. Drink all you like." Tanner smiled to hide his concern. Wouldn't have milk? What did that mean?

"You can have milk with your pizza, Beth." Sophie's voice came out choked. She coughed, regrouped and thanked him again. "You certainly didn't have to go to all this trouble, though. It's only pizza."

"Homemade pizza," he clarified and winked. "I wanted to make sure I get seconds."

"Seconds and probably thirds." Sophie seemed tense, off-kilter, as if she wasn't sure she wanted him here, in her home. "I have a couple of things to do before it's ready. Would you like to talk to the kids in the other room?"

"I'd like to help, if I can." He waited for instructions but it was clear Sophie preferred to have her kitchen space to herself because she shooed him away. "I'll call when I'm ready," she promised when he hesitated.

"Okay." He followed the kids into the living room and agreed to play a game of checkers.

The coffee table wobbled when he pressed too hard on it and Sophie's couch had some of the same issues Burt's chair had suffered from, so after a few minutes on it Tanner moved to the floor. He saw a number of other problems in the little house that needed addressing—drooping wallpaper, a screen on a window that had come loose and, of course, the stair with the loosened carpet that Davy had tripped over the first time Tanner had visited.

He made a mental note of all of them, though he figured it would be pretty hard to fix them. Sophie seemed like one of those folks who had a lot of pride and wouldn't welcome his notice of the problems in her home. Still, maybe with Davy's help—

"The pizza's ready if you'd like to come to the table." Sophie glanced at him, something dark and worried lingering at the back of her gaze. Then her smile reappeared as her children hurried to the table. When everyone was seated she glanced at Davy. "Would you please say grace?"

Davy began to protest, then stopped, glanced at Tanner and bowed his head. "Thanks, God, for this good food and for Tanner bringing chocolate bars. In Jesus's name, amen."

"Amen." Tanner stifled his chuckle and watched as Sophie lifted a huge pizza from the oven and set it on the table. His mouth watered just looking at it. He'd never known you could make a pizza look pretty. This one had happy faces all over it.

"Would you like some juice?" Sophie asked, the container of orange juice he'd bought in her hand.

"Just water for me, please. Unless you've made coffee?" She blinked in surprise, then shook her head. "Water is fine. Thank you."

She served him the first piece, the kids next and then herself. Tanner waited until she was seated, amused to notice Davy hurriedly put down his pizza and waited, too.

"Please, go ahead," Sophie said.

Tanner bit into his pizza, unable to speak for the flavors bursting on his tongue. When he asked about them and Sophie explained, Tanner simply listened to her musical voice, knowing he'd never remember what spices she listed. He was too busy enjoying her pretty face. Finally aware that she was watching him with a frown, he savored his pizza and the salad she'd made to go with it.

"I never thought of putting oranges or almonds in a salad but it's delicious," he said. "You have an amazing gift with food, Sophie Armstrong."

"I don't think it's a gift," she demurred, cheeks hot pink. "I just know how to cook."

"That's a gift. A great one." He leaned back in his chair, replete for now. "If you hadn't already done it, I would have suggested you choose cooking as a vocation. Your return rate for customer satisfaction must be amazing."

"I could take on more jobs if I had more time, more equipment and a bigger kitchen," she admitted. She glanced at her children. "Maybe someday I will." When she couldn't coax anyone to eat the last three slices, she lifted the pan off the table. "Ready for dessert?"

"What is it?" Davy asked as Tanner's stomach groaned.

"Banana splits." She set round dishes in front of each of them—not a traditional split but better, much better, Tanner decided as he sampled his portion.

"This is good, Mama." Beth's cheeks were smeared with chocolate sauce but her face glowed with happiness.

"It certainly is, Beth." Tanner frowned. "But you hardly have any, Sophie. Here, take some of mine." He was about to scoop some into her dish when she blocked him.

"This is plenty, thank you." She flushed. "Chocolate heads directly for my hips."

"Does it do that to mine?" Beth twisted to get a better look at her backside.

"Not yet," Sophie assured her, eyes dancing.

Tanner thought her laughter filling the kitchen was the loveliest sound he'd ever heard.

The children finished their dessert, then cleared the table while Sophie made a pot of her delicious coffee.

"I wish I knew how to make this," he said after swallowing his third cup. "There has to be some secret you're not telling me about because the stuff I made this morning, according to your directions, didn't bear the slightest resemblance to this."

"I don't know what to tell you." She studied him for a moment. Tanner felt as if a current ran between them. It gave him an odd feeling, one he'd never had before. He was relieved when she jumped up to wash the dishes. He helped with cleanup, startled by the electricity that sparked when their gazes met or their hands touched. Those sparks were enjoyable.

"Aren't you ever going to be finished?" Davy asked plaintively. "When I do them—"

"Don't go there, son," Tanner warned him with a wink.

"No, because next time it's your turn, Davy." Sophie laughed at his glower. "We're finished." She rinsed out her dishcloth and hung it on the sink, took the last dish from Tanner and set it in the cupboard. "Let the games begin."

Tanner had never played many board games so he lost most of the time, even though Beth tried to help him. Midway through Sophie made popcorn and cocoa and Tanner crunched on the warm buttery corn in between answering questions about the ranch. When he lost all his play money he knew it was time to go.

"I don't know how you won," he said to Beth, chucking her cheek with one finger.

"She always wins," Davy complained.

"It's because Beth is patient. You are too much like me. We want what we want now. Our way." Sophie's rueful words were accompanied by a wry grimace. "Bethy makes the best of what comes."

"I'll share my money with you, Mr. Cowboy." The little girl shoved a pile of paper money toward him. Tanner's heart melted.

"That's very kind of you, Beth. You keep it safe for us, okay? It's time for me go home." He rose, hating to leave this family for the loneliness of the ranch house. His gaze rested on Sophie. "Thank you for a wonderful dinner, a delicious dessert and a fun time. I enjoyed myself very much."

"I'm glad." She rose and walked with him to the door, handing him the hat he'd hung on her coat rack. "Come again."

Tanner thought the words were rote, said out of politeness, but he grabbed at them anyway.

"Thank you. I'd like that." He studied her, one arm wrapped around each child. "You're a blessed woman, Sophie. And so are your kids. You have each other and that's a lot." Before he revealed his envy of her, Tanner dragged open the sticky door. Another project. "Good night."

"Good night," they called.

He climbed in his truck, started the engine, but sat there for a moment, watching as the front door closed, the downstairs lights snapped off and the bedroom lights winked on.

What would it be like to have someone like Sophie in your life with a family who was always there for you?

Tanner drove home imagining someone with Sophie's laugh waited for him at Wranglers Ranch.

Chapter Five

The homeschoolers' visit to Wranglers Ranch was like nothing Sophie expected, mostly because Tanner's efforts outdid her highest hopes for the afternoon.

After a general welcome, he escorted the students on a ramble around the ranch that the children in wheelchairs could easily handle. He paused periodically at stations he'd specifically set up to illustrate different aspects of ranch life.

"Wranglers Ranch is home to a small flock of Navajo-Churro sheep," he explained. The curious children gathered around him, eager to touch the lamb he held before they moved on to examine multicolored balls of wool spilling out of a handwoven basket. "We sell the wool to artists who use it for their work. On a ranch it's important to have different sources of income."

Sophie's appreciation for the cowboy grew when, after they arrived at the horse station, he hunkered down to answer the smallest child's query.

"That's a good question," he praised the disabled boy. "We put those hoods on our horses' heads to keep out flies. If we don't, the flies will lay their eggs in the animals' eyes. That would make them really sick and sometimes cause blindness. We want our horses to be healthy."

Tanner's explanation about the brook's importance drew giggles when he said its most important function was to cool off cowboys on hot summer days. He introduced Moses, who delighted the children by escorting them to the remains of an old covered wagon that had once rumbled through Wranglers Ranch. Sophie found herself listening to the man's history lesson as carefully as the children did. Their rapt expressions made their formerly dubious parents smile with approval. Sophie was glad she'd suggested the ranch to the homeschool association. Positive word of mouth from these moms and dads could help Tanner gain new clients.

"Can we come back and ride your horses sometime?" Beth's friend Bertie asked in a loud voice. "I want to ride the white horse and go really fast."

"You'll have to ask your parents about coming back, Bertie." Tanner winked at Sophie. "But maybe you should choose a different horse. Methuselah doesn't go very fast because he's quite old. Actually he's a grandfather so mostly we let him eat and rest."

"Oh." Quieted for the moment, talkative Bertie fell into step with Beth as Tanner continued the tour. At the completion of it, when the cowboy had finally answered all the kids' questions, their host invited the group to enjoy lemonade and a snack on his new patio.

After ensuring everyone had been served, Sophie turned to find Tanner next to her, offering a glass of lemonade. "Thank you."

"No problem. Thank you for making all these snacks. This should cover it." He held out a check.

"Tanner, I don't expect you to pay for food I made for our homeschool group." Relieved that the parents weren't near enough to overhear, Sophie shook her head in refusal.

"I insist. It's important for Wranglers to track all its expenses. If we know how much our programs cost it will allow us to plan more effectively. Today's visit is a great opportunity to see how our plans worked out."

"But—"

"Also, if future visitors bring food to Wranglers, it will cause a whole mess of issues with the health department." His megawatt grin made Sophie's heart rate soar. "But you're a licensed caterer. Your home-cooked treats make our experience more authentic. Believe me, that's worth paying for."

"Tanner, you've done more than enough by letting us visit," she protested but his smile only grew as he pressed her fingers around the check. He pulled his hand away, then he turned his focus to the trays of treats she'd laid out on a nearby table. After several moments' deliberation he chose a brownie.

"This is amazing," he said after he'd tasted it.

"Personally I like the lemon bars better." Sophie shrugged. "But then I'm not a chocolate addict."

"Like me, you mean?" He chuckled when she wrinkled her nose in dismay at blurting that out. "That's the only kind of addict I don't mind being." Something in the tone of his words made Sophie realize that Tanner's past still troubled him, but she lost that thought when he asked hesitantly, "Do you really think the visit went well?"

"Far better than I ever imagined," she assured him. "Moses was a hit and those stations with your explanations really helped the kids appreciate the past and present at Wranglers."

"The stations were your son's idea." Tanner took another brownie, smiling at her surprise.

"Davy?" She blinked at his nod. "How could he…?" Confused, Sophie waited for an explanation.

"He talked to some of the kids who came here with the church youth group the other night and realized that many of them had no idea about life on a modern-day ranch." Tanner chuckled at the memory. "Davy confessed he didn't, either, and pointed out that it would be a lot easier for him to help at Wranglers if he understood what we were trying to achieve. So he and I came up with those information stations. He's got a good head on his shoulders, your boy."

"Good to know." Though he'd never said so, Sophie suspected her son longed to earn Tanner's respect. "Davy has changed, thanks to you. I know he has a long way to go to prove himself, but even in the short time he's been coming here, he's grown less self-focused."

"Because he feels needed," Tanner suggested. "Everybody wants to feel like their presence is important to someone, that they have a place. I guess Wranglers is becoming Davy's place."

"I don't think Davy's the only one," Sophie murmured as she glanced around the patio. Parents and children were happily sharing the beautiful space. "This was a good idea."

"You didn't think so at first, though, did you?" His grin dared her to refute it. "When you saw the men putting down the flagstones that day you weren't impressed. But this—" He waved a hand. "This is what I wanted. A space for people to relax, enjoy God's beauty and each other."

"You have a lot of ideas about Wranglers' future, don't you, Tanner?" She knew that she'd underestimated him, hadn't truly considered how he'd use the ranch to minister to kids. "What else would you like to accomplish?"

A strange curiosity welled inside Sophie, a need to share his hopes and dreams. Maybe because it seemed her own dreams would never happen, that she would never escape her desperate scramble to keep a roof over their heads and food on the table.

Tanner didn't have to worry about those mundane things. His dreams could soar. Unlike her he had the means to achieve his goals. And strangely Sophie wanted to be part of that, though she didn't want to get too close to him. Relationships were not part of her life plan.

"I'd like to figure out a way to keep a vet on staff full-time. The county is asking for a medical assessment on each abused horse we take in. It's time-consuming, expensive and hard on the horse to transport, and that's not even mentioning the difficulty of getting in to see a vet in the city. Most don't want to come way out here."

"Great idea," she said. His gaze shifted to something distant, something she couldn't see. "What else?"

"I'd like to build some cabins," Tanner said. "So we could have overnighters."

"Won't that bring additional problems? I mean, sometimes street kids have issues." She frowned, dubious about the idea.

"The whole idea of Burt's camp is to help kids with issues. Everyone has issues, Sophie." He studied her for a moment, then spoke in a quiet, husky tone. "Or maybe I'm just trying to recapture my childhood."

"How so?" Curiosity about his past ballooned.

"When I was ten, I went to summer camp." His voice altered, his joy obvious in his sparkling smile. "It was the one and only time. I've never forgotten the experience because for a while, for one short week, it was okay just to be myself, a kid, and to have fun."

A lump filled Sophie's throat.

"Six of us stayed in a ramshackle leaky cabin with a counselor. It was a dump but I thought it was paradise. I could let myself sleep at night because the counselor was there protecting us." A quirky smile lifted Tanner's lips.

Sophie's heart gave a bump at the sudden rush of attraction that surged inside her. The cut on his cheek she'd seen the day they'd met had almost completely disappeared.

She thought perhaps making Burt's dream live was helping Tanner heal in many ways.

"The best part wasn't the sleeping, though," he continued. "The best part came just before sleep. Everyone was in bed. The cabin was dark and quiet. That's when the counselor would talk to us. Not preachy stuff, just telling us we were loved, encouraging us not to ever give up on our dreams. He'd urge us to resist the bad stuff we encountered, make us feel hopeful about our future. It was the first time I can ever remember feeling safe."

He hadn't felt safe until he was ten—almost Davy's age. Sophie's mother's heart ached for that young boy who'd been so alone.

"I've hung on to those moments through some pretty tough times in my life." Tanner smiled at her. "Those feelings—hope and safety—that's what I want Wranglers to give kids. I want this place to show God to kids so they'll yearn to know Him because He's the answer to every seeking heart."

"I think you'll do it, Tanner." How could she not support a dream like his? "There's a lot of space on this ranch and plenty of little groves where cabins wouldn't have to stick out."

"I'm praying for someone, an architect maybe, to show me how to do that, but I need a lot of things in place before building cabins can happen." He shrugged. "Like maybe—clients?"

"They'll come." Somehow Sophie was certain of that. Tanner was the kind of man who reached for his dream and got it. Not the kind of selfish dreams Marty had chased; not for an easy way to make his own world better. Tanner's dreams had a plan and a spiritual grounding. They were for others, not to benefit himself.

Sophie liked the rancher's selflessness. Liked it a lot. Too much for a woman who was never going to let her heart feel anything again.

* * *

"Sophie, I really appreciate you doing this on such last-minute notice." Tanner stood in the doorway of Wranglers' kitchen several days later stunned by the number of food trays covering every possible surface. "How did you manage to produce so much so fast?"

"I always keep frozen stock." She looked lovely even with a dab of flour on one cheek.

"Pastor Jeff didn't tell me much, only that something had happened to the couple's venue and they were forced to cancel their wedding," he explained. "Apparently they've waited a long time and desperately want to get married today. Pastor Jeff seemed to think the ranch would be the perfect place for that."

"Didn't they have a caterer lined up?" Sophie swung a tray from one of the ovens and quickly replaced it with another.

"They did. Unfortunately that was canceled with the venue and the chef took another job." Noticing the line of perspiration dotting Sophie's upper lip, he offered to help.

"That's kind of you but it only looks like chaos." She grinned. "Actually I'm fine and Monica and Tiffany will be here soon to help." She glanced around and nodded, apparently satisfied with her creations. "What about outside?"

"Outside?" Tanner glanced out the window. "What do you mean?"

"Decorations. Something to make it look like a wedding." When he stared at her stupidly, Sophie pointed. "Those bougainvilleas—why don't you drape them to make an arch? It would be the perfect place for the couple to say their vows. There are fairy dusters around the edge of the patio so their colors will really stand out, but maybe you and Davy could snip some brittlebush flowers."

"Moses will put up a fuss if I appropriate your son.

Davy's *helping* him with a new horse." Tanner chuckled when she rolled her eyes.

"If we had flowers we could put them in small glasses on each of the table for centerpieces. Beth's gathering petals off those bushes next to the sycamore trees. She loves scattering them." Sophie's brown eyes softened with love. "But something with stems would be nice."

"Centerpieces, huh?" Tanner studied her. "How do you know about this stuff?"

"I was a bride once." Sophie thrust out her chin. "Not that we had a fancy wedding. My parents weren't anxious for their friends and neighbors to know I had to get married." For a moment she looked grim. Then her irrepressible grin reappeared. "I'm a girl, Tanner. Weddings are in our genes."

"Ah." He felt awkward and ignorant on the subject so he went outside to work on the bougainvilleas as requested. When he stood back to get the full effect, he realized how right Sophie was. The arch made a perfect focal point for a bride and groom.

"Mama said you'd show me what to do with these petals." Beth stood at the edge of the patio, a basket hanging from one hand.

"She did?" Tanner gulped, totally out of his depth. "What do you think we should do with them?"

Beth considered for several moments, then smiled, her blue eyes glowing.

"We can make a little path to that," she said, indicating the arch. "And we could sprinkle some on the tables and benches. They smell nice."

"Can you show me how to do it?" he asked hopefully. Beth did, insisting he handle the petals gently. Ten minutes later his patio looked romantic and sort of dreamy.

"Good job," Sophie approved. She hugged Beth, then addressed him. "Maybe with your petals decorating things we don't need centerpieces." She turned to Tanner. "If I were you, I'd order some tablecloths, maybe black, to fit these tables. Then you'd have something fancy to dress up this area for other special occasions. Who knows, you might get other weddings."

"I hope not," Tanner told her, aghast at the thought.

"Wasn't it you who told the homeschool kids that a ranch needs many sources of income?" Sophie shot him an arch look. "Not only could weddings do that, but it would get you additional exposure."

Maybe she was right but surely there were other ways to do that without getting involved in something as personal as a wedding. Tanner stuffed down his inhibitions long enough to help her set up the two portable tables she'd brought. Then he stood back and watched as she and her staff, with Beth's help, organized a beverage station around a punch fountain.

"Would you be able to man this?" Sophie faced him with a speculative look.

Him? Serve punch in those itty-bitty plastic glasses? Tanner gulped and shook his head. "No."

"Why not?" She frowned. "Change into black pants and a black shirt, or white, and you'll look like one of us." When he didn't agree, Sophie glared at him. "I can't do the food *and* serve punch *and* watch the hors d'oeuvres. We need your help and there's not much time."

She was doing this to help *him*. Tanner sighed, raced upstairs and took a quick shower before changing into the requested clothes. He added the jacket he'd bought for Burt's funeral, gave his boots a swift shine, then hurried back downstairs. And stopped dead in his tracks. Sophie had wreaked bridal magic in less than ten minutes.

"I hope you don't mind," she said from behind him. "That lace tablecloth was in the drawer. I thought it made a nice background for the signing table. And the candles were just sitting in a cupboard. They were half-used but now that they're lit you don't notice that." The words spilled out, as if she expected him to object.

Did he look that dumb? Tanner wanted to hug her.

"Moses and Davy brought over the wagon wheel and the hay bales," she continued. "And your hands helped us set them up. It'll make a good backdrop for pictures."

She'd even found the old bell Burt had unearthed last year from a nearby abandoned mission. It hung above the arch, grit and grime removed, shining in the sunlight.

"You need to expand your business to wedding planner," he praised. "This is amazing."

"I hope they like it." Sophie's brown gaze gave him the once-over. "You clean up nice, Mr. Cowboy," she said with a giggle in her voice.

Tanner absorbed the sweet sound of her laughter. No matter how busy, Sophie made every occasion fun. He couldn't have asked for a better partner.

Partner? Wait a minute…

"Sounds like the guests are arriving. Can you welcome them and show the way, Tanner?" Sophie called her staff, gave Beth a keep-busy job and hurried to the kitchen. She paused at the door to frown at him. "Tanner?"

"Yeah?" *Partner?* He didn't need, didn't *want* a partner.

"As the host at Wranglers, getting the guests to the patio is your responsibility." Her tone asked why he was still standing there.

"I'm hosting a wedding. Right." Tanner took a deep breath as he absorbed this new role. He walked to the front of the house while ordering his brain off the subject of Sophie Armstrong. She was a friend, a very helpful friend. But that's all she was. All she could be. Because his goal was to make this ranch a haven for kids, not to get sidetracked by a lovely mom.

But why had God sent a wedding his way?

A couple stood beside their car, clearly wondering where to go, so Tanner squared his shoulders and stepped forward. He could do host as well as the next guy—he hoped.

"Hello. Welcome to Wranglers Ranch. Are you here for the wedding? Come this way, please."

Twenty minutes later when the patio was almost filled with guests, an old Chevy, fully restored, pulled up. A senior man in a black suit escorted an older woman in a pretty cream silk outfit from the car. Arm in arm, they walked slowly toward Tanner, the woman evidently needing the man's support.

"Hi. We're the bride and groom. I'm Herb Jenkins and this is my bride, Vanessa." Herb thrust out his hand and Tanner shook it.

"Congratulations," he said, suddenly aware that Sophie was beside him.

"I'm Sophie. We thought you might like a bouquet." She handed Vanessa a bunch of multicolored roses he recognized as coming from a shrub out back. "Our friend Moses picked them for you and wrapped them in his handkerchief. Something borrowed."

"Oh, thank you, dear." Vanessa clutched the little bouquet as if it were from a renowned florist. "It's lovely. Now all I need is something blue."

"I have a blue ribbon." Beth squeezed in beside her mother. "You can borrow it," she offered with her sweet smile as she slid a bow from her hair.

"Thank you, darling. You are all so kind." Vanessa sniffed as Beth tied the blue ribbon around her flowers. The groom chuckled as he dabbed at his bride's cheeks.

"Now, Van, don't start crying or we'll never get down the aisle." He looked at Tanner. "Where is the aisle?"

"The patio is this way. Please, follow me." Sophie and Beth slipped through a hedge near the kitchen as Tanner led the couple on a route that emerged at the rear of the patio behind their guests. "Pastor Jeff is waiting for you up there," he said to the groom, who smiled fondly at his wife-to-be, let go of her hand and strode eagerly forward.

"Thank you for doing this on such short notice," Vanessa said. "We've waited for this day since I was diagnosed with breast cancer a year ago. Herb stayed right by my side the whole time while the Lord came through for us. And He's done it again. This is a beautiful place."

"I wish you the very best in your marriage." Tanner glanced around. "Are we waiting for someone to walk you down the aisle?"

"No." Her face saddened. "Our children don't approve. Would you—no, never mind." Her hopeful look died. Tanner couldn't stand it.

"I'd be honored to walk you down the aisle, ma'am."

"You're so kind." She touched his cheek. "Would it be too much to ask the little blonde girl to be my flower girl?"

"I'm sure Beth would love that." Tanner hurried away to have a quick word with Sophie, then returned with Beth. "Here we are. Vanessa, this is Beth."

"Hi, Beth. Thank you for being part of our wedding." Vanessa touched her cheek, her eyes misty. "You remind me of my daughter when she was your age."

Afraid the bride would start crying, Tanner cleared his throat.

"You know what to do?" he asked Beth, who calmly nodded. As if this was a normal day in her life, she took her place in front of the bride, waiting. "Okay. So whenever you're ready, Vanessa." He held out his arm for her to slip her hand through.

"I've been ready to be married to Herb for such a long time." Eyes riveted to her smiling groom, Vanessa took his arm, then glided over the flagstones as if they were glass. "Hi, Herb," she breathed as if she hadn't seen him for days.

"Sweetheart, you are so beautiful."

Tanner's heart thudded at the love flowing between the couple. He'd never quite believed such love existed until today, but it was clear that these two belonged with each other. Though Tanner had never been in a wedding party before, he suddenly knew exactly what to do. He lifted Vanessa's hand from his arm and tucked it into Herb's.

"Be happy," he said, then, grasping Beth's hand, he stepped aside. They slipped out of the way between two shrubs so the guests' view of the couple wasn't blocked. He followed Beth, who headed for Sophie, who stood near the open doors of the house watching as Pastor Jeff greeted the guests and then addressed the couple.

"Herb and Vanessa, you have already loved each other through better and worse, through sickness and health. You know that love isn't about finding the right person, it's about being the right person, one who stands firm against life's storms but can also give way when needed. One who helps you be the person God created." The pastor's fondness for the couple laced his words. "I'm very proud today to lead you through your vows to each other."

They were the kind of old-fashioned vows that were heartfelt, filled with promise. The kind that said, "I'm sticking with you forever." The kind Tanner had once longed to hear.

What woman would say those vows to you if she knew you abandoned your own child?

"I now pronounce you husband and wife. You may kiss your bride."

Wondering if the ceremony brought back painful memories for Sophie, Tanner glanced at her and was startled to find her dark eyes fixed on him, something he couldn't understand swirling in their depths.

"Vanessa and Herb invite you to sample the punch and

hors d'oeuvres while they sign the papers," Pastor Jeff said, breaking the spell that held them.

"Okay, we're on," Sophie whispered. "You're pouring the punch, Tanner." She nudged his arm to jolt him out of his fugue.

"Right." He straightened and thrust away his dreams of getting married, having a family. Hadn't he learned that wasn't for him? Instead God had given him Wranglers and a camp to run.

"If you need anything, motion to the girls or me but stay at your station. Okay?" Once he nodded, Sophie hurried away to check the trays her helpers were holding, ready to mingle among the group.

Tanner should have been nervous. Hosting a wedding was something he knew less than nothing about. But he had only to glance at Sophie to know that everything was going perfectly. Classical music played in the background—who'd thought of that?—and a low hum of conversation carried on the gentle breeze as Sophie's staff circulated among guests. Tanner kept pouring until he was sure everyone had a glass of punch to join in the pastor's toast to the happy couple. Gentle laughter filled the air as everyone cheered.

The guests mingled, sometimes sitting at the tables, moving, eager to sample the changing variety of food that Sophie offered as they laughed and shared stories about the couple. Tanner snitched several samples and found it delicious. How had Sophie managed to create a feast in such a short time?

"Tanner, can you help me, please?"

He hadn't seen Sophie come up behind him. Swallowing the last bite of food, he dabbed his mouth on a napkin. "What do you need?"

"Help to move the wedding cake," she whispered. "I

thought we could use the signing table and set the cake on that."

He was game to help until he saw the cake. Trepidation made him freeze.

"What's wrong?" Sophie hissed.

"What if I drop it?" He flinched at the glare she threw his way.

"Don't" was her gritted response.

Heart in his mouth, Tanner held the board on one side of the two-tiered cake and gingerly moved it with her out the door and across the patio under Beth's soft directions.

"Good girl, Beth," Sophie said, her voice tender. "Just stay there, okay?"

"Okay, Mama." Beth smiled her unconcerned smile, trust in her mother complete. Tanner wished he'd known that kind of trust for his own mother. He wished he could instill that kind of trust in his own family. That wasn't going to happen.

"Can I set it down now? Please?" he begged, heaving a sigh of relief when she nodded, glad the cake finally rested on the table. "When did you get a wedding cake, Sophie?"

"I baked it after you phoned me about the wedding last night. I hope it's okay." She arranged some sugar roses in soft pastel hues on the top, added some pale colored sprinkles and a gathered-fabric thing around the base.

"But I phoned after eleven o'clock last night," he gasped. How did she manage to look so rested creating so much? "It looks amazing," Tanner complimented when she stood back to survey her work.

"Thank you." She motioned to one of her helpers to bring plates and pulled a cake server out of her pocket. Once everything was arranged, she stood back for one more look and nodded her satisfaction. "I sent Davy to tell Moses to get some pictures of this. Tanner, you can tell our couple they can cut the cake whenever they're ready."

"Me?" he protested but Sophie had disappeared inside the house. He sent a quick prayer that she was making coffee, then did as he was told.

"A wedding cake? We never expected that." Vanessa's glow brightened to an even higher wattage. "You've made this a wonderful day. A perfect day."

"I'm glad." And he was, Tanner realized. Not that he'd done much. It was all Sophie. She was an amazing woman.

"Cake cutting," Pastor Jeff announced.

Tanner moved away as the group crowded around the couple to watch with Moses snapping madly. When the cake was cut, Tanner felt vaguely disappointed to see Sophie had made them a lemon wedding cake. He'd hoped for chocolate. Which was silly. This would be as delicious as everything else she made.

When he saw her struggling to carry a big urn across the patio, Tanner hurried to help. Her assistants set out cups and spoons along with cream and sugar and two massive teapots. When all was ready for the guests, Tanner followed Sophie to the kitchen, carrying two cups of steaming coffee.

"Sit down and relax," he ordered as he placed one in front of her. "Celebrate another of your successes."

"I hope everything was okay." She sipped her coffee. After a huge sigh she leaned back in her chair. "That was a rush."

"Do you think there will be any cake left?" Tanner asked, noticing that Beth had a piece and was eating it.

Sophie burst out laughing after she stopped Beth from offering hers.

"What's so funny?" he asked with a frown.

"I made Beth her own cake. I made you one, too." She laughed when he licked his lips. "Well, you'll have to share with Davy and Moses, but mostly your own."

"Where is Davy?" He eagerly accepted the plate of cake

she handed him. Lemon cake was light-years better than no cake. "I haven't seen him for ages."

"He and Moses are up to something, a surprise, Moses said. Should I be worried?" Sophie didn't look worried. She looked happy, relaxed, satisfied.

"With Moses? Probably. This cake is amazing." Tanner debated hiding the rest for later, then decided Moses would find it anyway. He'd have to share. "So is the coffee. Your mama is an excellent cook," he said to Beth. "She's giving Wranglers quite a reputation."

"Is that good?" Beth paused, her forkful of cake hanging in midair as she studied him.

"It's very good," he assured her.

"I think so, too." She calmly resumed eating her cake.

"You're a very smart girl, Beth." Tanner smiled at her, loving the way her blue eyes glowed at the compliment.

"I am? Why?"

"Because you don't worry about things. You trust." Tanner figured there was a lesson there for him.

"Don't you?" The little girl frowned. "In the Bible God says to cast your cares on Him. Right, Mama?"

"Right." Sophie leaned over to nudge Tanner's shoulder with her own. "It's her favorite verse so don't argue."

"Wouldn't dream of it." Her tone spoke of her pride in her child. What a great mom she was, Tanner thought.

"But that's not all of the verse, Mr. Cowboy." Beth studied him with an intensity that made him sit up straight. "Do you know why we cast our cares on Him?" Her blue gaze demanded an answer.

"Uh, no." A six-year-old girl was teaching him the Bible. "Tell me why, Beth."

"Because He cares for us." Her smile spread from cheek to cheek.

He'd never heard the truth of God's love given so succinctly with such passion.

"As I said, you're a very smart girl." Tanner brushed her cheek with his knuckles in a fond caress while his heart yearned for a child like Beth to love.

You turned your back on that opportunity.

All Tanner could do now was enjoy Sophie and her kids and pour his heart's desire to be part of something bigger than himself into Wranglers Ranch.

And pray that would be enough to satisfy the ache to be loved that had been throbbing inside him for years.

Chapter Six

"My mom wasn't too impressed with me and Moses tying those cans on the bride and groom's car," Davy told Tanner a few days after the wedding.

Because neither of them could see her sitting behind her house, Sophie grinned. Truthfully she'd been amused by the action, but that had been tempered by worries about the bridal couple's reaction when they saw the crude cardboard sign proclaiming Just Married. Thankfully Vanessa and Herb had hooted with laughter, so Sophie had tempered her scolding of Davy for touching other people's property, especially after Moses insisted the idea was his.

"I like doing things with you, Tanner. You make everything fun." There was Davy's hero worship showing again. In fact both her kids adored the big rancher, and Sophie had to admit she wasn't immune to his charms, either. The thing was, though catering at Wranglers Ranch was fun, she couldn't depend on it. She could depend only on herself.

"I like doing things with you, too, Davy." Tanner paused, a hesitancy in his voice that tweaked Sophie's attention so that she focused on his next words. "I never knew my parents. Sometimes when I'm with you, I think about them and all the things we could have done together."

"I heard about people finding their real parents. Couldn't you do that?" Davy asked.

"My mom gave me away when I was born. I don't think she'd want me to find her." Tanner sounded definite.

"That must make you sad." Sophie wanted to cheer for Davy's sensitivity.

"Sometimes." Tanner cleared his throat. "I'm glad you're out of school today. I'm hoping your mom won't mind if you and Beth come out to Wranglers. I need some help with an idea I have, kid kind of help."

Sophie could almost see the grin on Tanner's face. She knew his eyes would be dancing with fun. And for some odd reason that made her stomach skip.

Get a grip, Sophie.

"Your mom is welcome to come, too, if she wants," Tanner added.

Like she was an afterthought. Sophie's smile faded.

"I'll ask her. Mo-o-o-m!" Davy's bellow echoed through the house.

"She's cutting the rosebushes," Beth called back.

Sophie jumped from her lawn chair, grabbed her pruning shears and barely made it to the bush before Davy and Tanner appeared in the backyard. "Hi," she said to Tanner. "Davy, don't yell, please."

"Tanner wants me and Beth to go to Wranglers," Davy said.

Sophie looked at Tanner curiously. "To do what?"

"If you want to come along, I'd rather show you." He glanced at her rosebush. One eyebrow lifted. "You don't seem to be making much progress. You could do this later."

"I don't know if I can do it at all," she admitted self-consciously. "I'm not good with roses. Apparently I cut off too much last year but the book says they need to be pruned so..." A funny expression washed over his face so she stopped talking.

"I don't think what you're doing is *technically* called pruning," he said, a muscle flicking at the corner of his lips as if he was trying not to smile. "Butchering, maybe. May I?" He held out his hand for her shears.

"Go for it." When she handed them over, he gripped them, studied the shrub for a few moments, then began deftly clipping away branches. A second later droplets of blood dotted his hands where the thorns had pierced.

"You should have gloves on, Tanner." Sophie peeled off her own and held them out. "Those barbs can cause a lot of damage."

"To you maybe. I have tough skin." He ignored her gloves, swiped away the blood and continued working. A few minutes later he leaned back to admire his work. "There. If you leave it alone it should soon start to bloom."

"That'd be the first time since my dad bought it," Davy mumbled after a sideways peek at Sophie.

"Thanks for that, Davy." She gave him a pseudofierce look, took the shears from Tanner's outstretched hand and stored both in her tiny work shed. When she turned around, Tanner had carried the thorny stems to the trash container at the back of her yard. "Thank you."

"You're welcome. So can you come to Wranglers?" He sounded eager for her acceptance. Sophie's heart gave a little skip, which she ruthlessly suppressed. "You don't have to cater today, do you? Not on Martin Luther King Day."

"I don't have *catering* scheduled, no." She wanted to go with him, wanted desperately to escape the thousand repair jobs that never seemed to get done and have fun. But being the one in charge meant facing responsibility. "However, I do have a long list of things that need doing. I want to finish them today."

"Okay. We'll help." Tanner's eyes, dark emerald with swirls of turquoise, danced with fun. "With Davy and Beth and me pitching in, your list will soon be done and then we can all go. What's first?"

"But—" Sophie hadn't expected this. "I—er, that is, I don't know if you can help." She so did not want him to examine the inadequacies of where she lived. Maybe he'd think she wasn't a good mother for raising her kids in such a tumbledown place.

"Try me." When Sophie didn't respond Tanner turned to Davy. "What's first on the list?"

"Fixing that stupid carpet on the stairs." Davy's sour look said it all. "Every time I come down those stairs I trip."

"Carpet repair it is. Do you have a hammer and some small nails?" Tanner asked Sophie.

She hesitated but there was no point. She knew from his face that he wouldn't give in. He'd made up his mind and he was going to help her, whether she liked it or not. And actually, Sophie liked it.

"Thank you. That's very kind of you." She smiled at him, secretly hoping Tanner would also notice the loose board on the downstairs landing. She'd caught her toe on it last night and it still throbbed. "Davy can show you where the stuff is in the shed. I'll get Beth started on cleaning the cupboards."

Once she'd demonstrated to Beth how to clean one cabinet, Sophie got to work washing windows. Inside was simple, but the outside glass required a ladder. She was struggling to move it out of the shed when it was lifted from her hands.

"What's this for?" Tanner asked. "And where do you want it?"

"I'm cleaning windows. I'll start at the back." She thanked him when he'd placed the ladder and was about to climb up with her bucket and cloths when Beth called for her help. "I'll be right back," she promised.

Once Beth was settled, Sophie returned outside. To her surprise Tanner and the ladder were missing. She walked around the side of the house and found him polishing the big picture window at the front.

"Two more on the side and this job can be crossed off." Tanner's wide grin stretched across his face. "Many hands make light work," he said, inclining his head toward Davy, who was washing a basement window.

Funny how the more she got to know Tanner, the less she noticed his faults—if he had any. Sophie had often wondered if she found fault in men because it gave her a good reason to avoid connections with them. But with Tanner...

"What should I do when I'm finished here?" he asked, scrubbing vigorously.

Sophie had dearly hoped to clean up the pile of debris outside her back gate. But she certainly wasn't going to ask Tanner to pick through her garbage. Without answering she hurried inside to answer Beth's call. By the time she returned outside Tanner was storing the ladder in the shed.

"Was painting the fence on your list?" Tanner inclined his head toward the paint cans sitting on a shelf.

"I asked the man I rent from to have the fence painted but he refused. So I told him I'd do it if he'd buy the paint." Sophie felt foolish when Tanner's lips tightened. "I thought if I did some home improvement that he didn't have to pay for, he wouldn't raise my rent."

"Painting is something I could show Davy how to do," Tanner said quietly, his gaze tracking Davy as he picked up debris around the yard. "He wants to feel like the man of the house."

"I know," she murmured, glad when Davy disappeared to discard his trash and couldn't overhear. "I am trying to teach him responsibility but I don't want to put too much on him yet. He's still just a little kid."

"Sophie, Davy is very bright. I think a task like painting would make him feel like he has an important part in the good of his family," Tanner insisted in a quiet tone. "Besides, a newly painted fence is something he could show off to his friends."

"True." How did a single rancher know so much about kids? "But it's a lot of work for you. And he'll make a mess."

"So? What's a mess when you're building character? Burt taught me that." He waited, watching her. "Should we do it?"

"Are you sure you want to?" Sophie asked, dubious about letting Tanner help so much.

Tanner grinned but didn't answer. A moment later he carried the paint cans outside and Davy brought the paintbrushes. He and Davy stashed the debris by the gate in trash bags, then Tanner began showing her excited son how to load his brush and reach the nooks and crannies.

"We'll do this right, Mom," Davy promised in a proud voice. "You don't have to watch us." Tanner winked and made a shooing motion, eyes glinting with fun.

"Thank you, gentlemen." Sophie hurried inside, where she could give her laughter free rein. Might as well admit she liked the owner of Wranglers, liked him a lot. It was good to have a friend who so generously lent a hand.

As long as she didn't let it become more than friendship.

"Mama? I'm finished. Can I paint with Davy?"

Uh-oh. Beth's expectant blue eyes begged her. But Sophie wasn't going to saddle Tanner with another child. Not yet anyway.

"You can," she agreed. "Only we're not going to paint the fence. We're going to paint that cupboard I bought at the garage sale. What color do you think it should be?"

"Blue," Beth said predictably. "I like blue."

"I know you do." Sophie risked a quick glance out the

window and did a double take. Tanner was making swift progress. "How about if we paint the cupboard white and then add some blue flowers?"

"I like blue flowers." Beth nodded with a sweet biddable smile.

"I love you, Beth." Swallowing a rush of emotion, Sophie wrapped her sweet daughter in a hug. "You're my blessing."

"Count your blessings," Beth sang in an off-key tone as she nestled against her mother for a moment, then drew back. "Can we paint now?"

Chuckling, Sophie went to find a drop cloth, paint and brushes. Maybe Tanner's appearance outside the grocery store that day had been an answer to prayer for her little family. It certainly had been for those rabbits! But Sophie wasn't ready to entirely trust God with her future because relying on someone other than yourself always led to hurt when the person disappointed you.

In her adult faith journey, Sophie had endured a bellyful of disillusionment. All through her marriage she'd known she wasn't a good wife. She'd repeatedly begged God to show her how to love Marty as a wife should in spite of the financial predicaments he kept putting them in.

She'd pleaded for His help every time her husband blew their tiny savings and waited interminably for God to respond. His lack of response had left her scrambling to survive after Marty's death. Those desperate days had made Sophie determined she would never be that vulnerable again, never again be totally dependent on anyone but herself.

Like God, Tanner was great to have around. But also like God, he had his own goals, his own desires and his own plans—plans that didn't mesh with hers. One day Tanner wouldn't be part of her world anymore. Sophie needed to keep repeating it to herself. She couldn't let herself rely on him.

That way lay pain and Sophie never wanted to hurt like that again.

"So my idea is to make a climbing wall here."

After Sophie had checked off all her jobs and couldn't think of another thing, she'd provided a delicious picnic in her backyard. It was such fun that Tanner was loath to break it up, but when they'd eaten and cleaned up, he'd insisted on driving them to Wranglers Ranch.

Now he gave voice to the tumble of ideas that had begun swirling in his head before midnight last night and were still going strong. He felt a surge of relief that Davy and Beth were busy playing with the rabbits because he wanted to hear Sophie's honest perspective.

What he hadn't figured out was why her concerns seemed so important to him.

"A climbing wall? Here?"

The time Tanner had spent with Davy at Sophie's house today had made him aware that not only had he missed special moments like those with his own parents, but also with his own child, the one he'd never known. Suggesting ways Davy could reason with the school bully, empathizing over his fatherless state and explaining why the stars moved in the sky were the kind of things a kid needed a parent for.

Throughout the day Tanner's self-doubts about his decision to never contact his child grew. Davy and Beth's nonstop questions were the very things his own child might ask. Who'd been there to answer them? Who was there now, teaching his son or daughter about God's love? Bad enough Tanner had cheated his child of a father, but was he also cheating his child out of a spiritual relationship with God?

"Tanner?" Sophie's hand on his arm stirred him from his troubling thoughts. "What's wrong?"

"Uh, just thinking," he mumbled, hesitant to share his dark secret past with her.

"About what?" She glanced to check on her children. Then her dark brown stare returned to him, a question in its depths.

Dare he ask her opinion? It took but a moment for Tanner to decide. Sophie was level-headed, totally focused on her kids' welfare. She'd know what he should do.

"A friend broached me with a problem. I'm not sure how to help him. Care to offer an opinion?" he said, deciding he'd frame the situation as hypothetical.

"I don't know that my opinion would count for much," she demurred.

"Oh." Tanner couldn't help it. His face fell, his shoulders sagged. He exhaled.

"But if you want to tell me the issue, I'll tell you what I think, even if it's not what you want to hear," she said with a quick grin.

"Great." How to begin? "This guy…he walked away from his pregnant girlfriend when he was just a kid—a teenager." Tanner saw her face tighten into a scowl and hurried on. "It was a bad decision. He soon realized that, but when he went back to find her she was gone. He lost all contact. Now he's thinking that he should find his child."

"So why doesn't he?" she demanded, her voice spirited.

"He's worried that doing so might complicate his former girlfriend's life, or the child's. He doesn't want to mess things up for them simply to salve his own guilt, but he does want to know his child. He's always wanted that." As a scowl furrowed her forehead, Tanner began to wish he hadn't said a word. But he could hardly stop now. "You're the kid expert, Sophie. What would you advise him to do?"

"Seriously?" She looked furious. "You're telling me this

guy abandoned his pregnant teenage girlfriend—what? Eight or ten years ago?" He nodded. "And you think he should waltz back into their lives now because he has this sudden yen to know his child?" The sarcasm in her voice chewed him out.

Guilt fell like a shroud. But guilt wouldn't help.

"It's not sudden. He's wanted—I think he's wanted," Tanner substituted, trying to remember that he was talking about his friend, "—to know his child from the beginning. But he was only sixteen and he was scared and—"

"He was scared. Oh, well, that changes everything," Sophie snapped. "Because she wasn't scared, I guess. She was alone, pregnant, struggling as her body went through changes, giving birth alone, a kid trying to care for her baby on her own, and he was scared. Really?"

Desperate to end her scathing opinion of *his* actions, Tanner went for levity. "So I'll take that as a 'No, you don't think he should find his child'?"

"I think it's too late for his regrets. If he wants to salve his conscience he should write a check." The way she glared at him made him wonder if she'd guessed it was his child they were talking about.

"What if the child needs help?" Tanner sighed. "He made a mistake, Sophie. We all make them, but now he's trying to make amends. You can't just write him off. He's looking for practical advice to do what's best for his child. Shouldn't I suggest he find the mom and the kid and make sure they're okay?"

She frowned at him, her eyes scanning his face. Tanner wondered if he'd pressed her too hard.

"It sounds like this guy must be a really close friend of yours," she said finally. "I'm sorry if I dissed him. It's just—I have no patience with people who opt out when the going gets tough. Especially when there are kids involved."

"I know and admire that trait in you." He smiled, savoring the fiercely protective glance she directed toward her giggling children and suddenly wishing she was the mother of the child he didn't know, the one he'd abandoned.

With a mother like Sophie his child would be deeply loved because that's what Sophie did. Of course, if she was his child's mother, Tanner was pretty sure she wouldn't allow him within fifty feet of their child. Sophie would be as protective as a mother bear of her cub.

"I suppose the responsible thing to do would be to investigate, make sure mom and child aren't starving in some hole, or living on the streets," she finally agreed, brown eyes dark and brooding.

He nodded. "Agreed."

"Maybe the woman's married now, with a family. If the kid is fine, the least selfish thing this guy could do is to not disrupt their lives and get on with his own, preferably doing something that will make a difference in the world and maybe help make up for his past mistake."

Tanner gulped at the distaste lacing her voice. What would she say if she knew he was trying to do that by turning Burt's idea into reality? And yet, he didn't think this was only about Sophie's repugnance toward some nameless man who'd abandoned his child. Something in her tone said there was more to the antagonism behind her stiff words.

"You sound really angry toward my friend," he said in a quiet tone.

"If I do it's because I know what it's like to be on your own, the only one your kids can depend on," she said, still bristling. "Can you imagine what it feels like to know you haven't got a cent and no way to make one but know that in half an hour your child will be hungry and you have no way to feed him?" Her face tightened. Her voice broke slightly and she paused to regroup. "That even if you can find something for that meal, there's tomorrow and tomorrow after that to worry about? I hope you never know that helpless feeling, Tanner." Her hands fisted.

"That's how Marty left you." In that moment he understood the scared lurch of her voice and the passion behind her words. Sophie was still afraid. "You were left alone with two kids to feed, clothe and house. That must have been terrifying."

"Yes." She bowed her head, as if ashamed to admit it.

"I'm so sorry," he said as he touched her shoulder. "I wish I'd been there to help you through that. But at least you could count on God."

"Could I?" She studied him for a moment before her gaze veered away to study something in the distance.

"Of course you could." He was suddenly uncertain, given the flash of anger through her dark eyes. "You're here. You made it. You and the kids."

"Thanks mostly to the food bank." She lifted her head. Defiance blazed from her face. "If it hadn't been for that, we'd have starved."

"And the church." He saw something blaze across her face. "Oh, Sophie," he groaned. "You did tell someone at church, didn't you?"

"Of course not." Sophie glared at him. "Do you think I wanted the congregation talking about us, choosing the silly, clueless mom and her kids as their newest charity case?"

"Sweet, sweet Sophie." Tanner brushed his fingertips against her cheek, touched by her independence but frustrated by her attitude. "Is that what *you* think when you take your trays of leftovers to folks who need them?"

She frowned. "How do you know about— Davy," she breathed in an exasperated tone.

"Would you think of Edna, whom you help, as stupid or silly because she's fallen on hard times?" he asked. "Is that why you're over at her house taking care of things while she's in the hospital?"

"Davy talks too much," she mumbled.

"Or do you help," he continued, ignoring her comment, "because you see someone who just needs a hand, which you're glad to offer because it makes you feel as if you matter, as if someone needs *you*?"

"It's not the same." She winced at his bark of laughter. "Okay, it's quite a bit the same but back then I had to stand alone, to solve my own problems."

"Why? That's completely against the whole point of faith." Tanner frowned.

"Huh?" She stared at him as if he had two heads.

"By definition faith is trusting in something you can't explicitly prove. Or if you prefer a biblical definition, Hebrews eleven, verse one says 'faith is the assurance of things hoped for, the conviction of things not seen.'" He grinned at her, wishing he could hug her and watch those brown eyes lose their shadows. "In other words, believing God has it taken care of so you don't have to fuss about it."

"Tanner, that sounds good but practically it makes no sense." She glanced at her kids. "That's like saying I should let Davy and Beth climb this wall without any advice or protection because God will watch out for them."

"I'm not saying that. I'm saying the *worry* is unnecessary." Tanner sought to explain himself. "Faith is saying 'I can't be here all the time for my kids but I've entrusted them to God and I trust Him to do His best for them when I can't.' It's leaving the results up to God."

"Is that what you do?" she asked, her forehead marred by a frown, her voice hesitant.

"Not all the time," he admitted shamefacedly. "Sometimes I try to work things around to ensure the result I want and then something I didn't foresee happens and I wish I'd left it up to God." He winced at her nod. "It's a journey, Sophie. I'm learning to walk by faith. I still make mistakes."

"I tried that," she admitted in a whisper-soft voice, her head bent. "After I got married, I promised God I'd do the best I could if He'd be with me." She lifted her head and looked directly at him, her brown eyes welling with tears. "He wasn't."

"Of course He was." Tanner's heart ached for the doubt that plagued her. "In Second Timothy it says, 'Even when we are too weak to have any faith left, he remains faithful to us and will help us.' That proves how much God loves us."

"But I never *feel* like He's near, Tanner." Sophie's big brown eyes shone with tears. "I always feel like I'm alone."

Her raw whisper got to him. With a groan for her pain, Tanner gave up restraining himself and pulled Sophie into his arms, stunned by how right it felt. "He's always right beside you, sweetheart. Always leading you, always guiding you."

"Even when He let Beth...be the way she is?" Sophie's hesitant whisper came as she lifted her head to search his gaze for reassurance.

The satin strands of her hair brushed against Tanner's cheek, carrying the faintest scent of lilac and bringing feelings of affection and comfort and belonging. Of Sophie.

"Honey, Beth is a living testament to faith. She's vulnerable and yet there's this trusting spirit inside her that allows her to trust God in a way that makes me envious." Tanner pressed his forefinger under Sophie's chin so she had to look at him. "God knew exactly what He was doing when he created Beth. She's His gift to us."

"That's what I think, too," Sophie murmured. "But sometimes—"

"Sometimes you let fear take over," he said softly, brushing a hand against her smooth cheek. "And that opens the door to doubt. That's when you have to cling hardest to your faith. God is here. He will do his best for us. Count on that, Sophie."

As her intense brown eyes locked with his, Tanner couldn't tamp down a rush of affection for this woman. She was so strong, forcing her way through her misgivings to be the mom her kids needed. What was this need inside him, to be here for her, to protect and support her—why did he feel compelled to protect Sophie Armstrong?

She was so beautiful, so utterly lovely inside and out. His arms tightened around her. He needed to get closer. He dipped his head—

"Are you going to kiss Mama?"

Pulling away from Sophie, Tanner called himself an idiot. Was he so desperate to be part of a family, to share his life and his work with someone who could understand and support him, that he would kiss Sophie in front of her kids?

Yes! his spirit groaned.

"I'm glad you finally left those rabbits to come over." Tanner dropped his hands to release Sophie and fought to control his voice. He winked at Beth. "You can tell me what you think of my climbing wall." That reminded Tanner that his goal was to fulfill Burt's dream by reaching kids—which superseded any personal wants.

Trouble was, the more Tanner worked with Sophie, the more his yearning grew to be part of a family, preferably a family with a mom like her! His skin reacted to her hand when it rested fleetingly against his arm with a burst of electricity.

"Thank you, Tanner," she murmured too quietly for the kids to hear. "I'll look up the verse tonight. Maybe some Bible study will help rebuild my faith in God."

Tanner was surprised by just how much he wanted that for Sophie. But caring meant he was getting too close to her. He had to stop trying to get his own desires. The thought made him grin.

Faith was sure easier to preach to Sophie than it was to live by.

Chapter Seven

"I can't believe I let you talk me into this." Tanner's visible gulp as he surveyed the twenty-odd kids who were mounted up and impatiently waiting for their trail ride to begin made Sophie smile. "There are way more of them than I expected."

"They're just kids wanting to learn to ride," she encouraged. "You've done that before. And Moses will be there as well as two of your hired men." Sophie hid her smile at Davy's proud stance on his horse, confident of his skill when his classmates were not. "And Davy will help, too."

"Nice to hear you have faith in your son." Tanner studied her for several moments before lifting his reins. "Does your trust extend to me?"

Sophie wasn't going to answer that because she didn't have an answer. She was comfortable with leaving her kids in Tanner's care. She knew he'd protect and care for them. But trust him? That was asking a lot more than she could give.

She swerved her gaze away, stepped back and watched Tanner lead the way over the trail. Davy's school class followed in pairs, their teacher in the middle with Moses, and two of Wranglers' hands in the rear. It was the first large trail ride Tanner had attempted and he was doing it mostly because Davy's teacher, after noting a huge change in him, hoped Tanner could make her science project on animals come alive for the rest of her class.

Please, please let everything go okay, Sophie prayed. It was the first time in ages that she'd actually asked God for something. *Now have some faith*, she reminded herself. Faith. That was the hardest part.

"Why couldn't I go on the horses with Davy, Mama?" Beth's usually happy face drooped with disappointment.

"You can go another time, sweetie. This time is for Davy's class to have a riding lesson." She tried to soothe her daughter but Beth wasn't in a soothing mood.

"I wish I had school friends to ride horses with," her daughter muttered before turning toward the house.

"You don't like being homeschooled?" Sophie asked, surprised by Beth's discontent. She struggled to quell the rush of hurt she felt. She'd tried so hard…

"I love you, Mama." Beth hugged her tightly and pressed a kiss against her arm. "I like being with you, too. But I want lots of friends like Davy has."

"What about Bertie and Cora Lee?" Sophie sat down on Tanner's patio and patted the seat next to her for Beth to also sit, probing this uncertain territory with a worried heart.

"They're nice but I want more friends. Lots of them. And I want to sing in the kids' choir." Beth's lips pressed in a firm line that warned Sophie she wasn't about to be swayed.

"Still?" Sophie's heart sank a little at Beth's swift nod. Her daughter was so not musically gifted.

"I want to sing songs to God like that lady and her girl did on Sunday." Beth leaned her head against Sophie and sighed. "I know I don't sing very good, but I could learn, Mama. I could try really hard to learn."

"Oh, honey, I know you'd try." Sophie drew her sweet

child into her arms and held her, trying to soothe what could not be soothed. Beth couldn't sing.

After a moment Beth drew away so she could look at Sophie, blue eyes sad. "Remember that book we read about the lonely puppy. I think I'm like him, Mama. I'm lonely."

The words cut a swath straight to Sophie's heart. She'd tried so hard to do everything right for this precious child, to protect her from the scathing hurt of other kids who didn't understand her disability. Instead she'd made Beth feel isolated.

"Do you mean you want to go back to school?" she asked in a careful voice as fear bubbled up inside. How could she protect...

"No." The answer burst out of Beth, accompanied by a swift shake of her head.

"But you just said— Why not?" Beth's sudden retreat puzzled her.

"I shouldn't have said anything." Her blond head drooped.

"Why not?" Something was going on.

"Davy said I'd hurt you if I asked." Beth's bottom lip quivered and a tear rolled down her cheek. "I did, didn't I? I don't ever want to hurt you. I love you, Mama." She wrapped her arms around Sophie's waist and squeezed.

"Well, I love you, too, sweetie. That won't ever change. But I want you to tell me why you don't want to go back to school." She saw several emotions vying for supremacy on Beth's expressive face. Finally her daughter spoke.

"I don't want to go 'cause I'm too dumb just like Bertie said." Beth hung her head.

"Honey!" Appalled, Sophie lifted her chin to peer into her eyes. "You are not dumb."

"Bertie said the other kids say that's why I can't go to school anymore. They said you have to teach me 'cause I'm too dumb to learn at school." Beth began to weep as if her heart was broken. "I don't want to be dumb. I want to go to school like Davy."

"Oh, Bethy, I don't think you're dumb." Sophie tamped down her anger at the slur, comforted her child and searched for a way to handle her daughter's unhappiness. "But actually I'm glad you told me because I've been thinking it's time for you to get back in the school. I homeschooled you because I didn't think you were happy at school. But you're older now and you need to be among your friends. I was just waiting for you to be ready."

"But I don't want you to be sad," Beth protested.

"Why would I be sad?" Sophie couldn't figure it out but she had a hunch Davy had something to do with this. Beth's next words rendered her speechless.

"Because if I go to school you'll be all alone with nobody. Davy said that I shouldn't say anything because when I'm at home you don't worry so much." Beth sniffed. "Davy and me don't like it when you worry, Mama."

So she was causing problems for both her kids. Sophie cringed inside. Davy must have guessed she hadn't removed Beth from school only because she was struggling but mostly because she'd heard the horrible taunts of other kids and wanted to save Beth from unhappiness.

"I can do it, Mama. I can learn at school." Beth's blue eyes implored her to understand while confirming Sophie's realization that her children understood far more than she'd given them credit for. "Anyway I don't care what other kids say about me."

"You don't?" she asked, stemming her tears.

"Nope. You love me and Davy loves me and God loves me." Her daughter's sweet smile lifted Sophie's hurting heart. "God will help me. That's what He does. He helps people who need him." Beth's trusting words added to the lump inside Sophie's stomach.

A child shall lead them.

"If we trust God to help us, He does, Mama. That's what Pastor Jeff said."

Each word was a prick against Sophie's heart. *Trust.* Beth trusted God but her mother couldn't? Humbled and ashamed, she realized that not only hadn't she trusted her sweet child, she hadn't trusted God to protect her daughter, either. She wasn't the example her daughter needed.

"I'm sorry I hurt you, Mama." Beth's hand touched her face, trying to soothe pain she hadn't caused.

"You didn't, darling. You make me very proud. I love you, Bethy." Sophie hugged her daughter tightly. "I'm sorry I didn't trust you," she whispered against Beth's flaxen head. "I'm so sorry."

And Beth, being Beth, immediately forgave her.

This is what your refusal to trust brings, a voice inside her head chided. *When are you going to trust God? He loves Beth even more than you do.*

"Mama?" Beth wiggled to get free. "When are Mr. Cowboy and Davy coming back?"

"Soon," Sophie said after checking her watch. "Want to help me get things ready?"

"Sure." Beth trailed beside her into the house. "Then we can talk more about me singing." She tilted her head to peer into Sophie's face, her concern visible. "Are you worrying, Mama?"

"No, sweetie," she said past the lump in her throat. "I just want you to be happy."

"I am." Beth did a pirouette, eyes shining with joy. "I'm always happy."

"I know." *Why aren't I?*

And then Tanner's image slid through her mind and an effervescent giddiness began bubbling inside. He was such a great guy. Thinking about him made her happy. And it shouldn't.

As Sophie worked to assemble lunch, she had to remind

herself that these soft feelings for Tanner had to be routed. He was committed, caring and determined to fulfill Burt's dream. That was great. But there could be nothing romantic between them.

Because you won't trust him? her brain demanded.

"I can't," she whispered. "I just can't take that risk again."

Trusting in others had ended badly before. No matter how much she admired Tanner Johns, Sophie could not get past those memories.

"It seems I keep repeating this, but thanks again for serving a great lunch, Sophie. Those pizza bun things were delicious." Tanner waved as the school bus filled with happy kids pulled out of the yard. "I think Davy's classmates had a good time *and* learned something."

"I'm sure they did." She edged away from him and entered the kitchen, distracted by the way her pulse leaped whenever he was near. "Davy said you made it very interesting. And of course he loved Moses's spiel. History seems to be growing on my son."

"What's wrong?" Tanner gripped her arm so she had to face him. "I know something happened because Beth kept peeking at you with a worried look. So tell me."

"It's nothing important. Just—I'm sending her back to school." There. She'd said it. And now she felt like a part of her lay exposed and raw. "I've done the best I could these past months. I think she's learned a lot. But it's time for her to return to school."

"And that bothers you." He poured himself a cup of coffee and sat down. "Why?"

Sophie glanced toward the patio to check Beth's location, not wanting her daughter to overhear her fears.

"She's gone with Moses to see a new calf." Tanner patted the chair next to him. "Talk, Mama."

"I think I messed up by taking her out of school," Sophie admitted after she'd sat down. She sipped her coffee thoughtfully.

"Why did you do that?" he asked.

"I overheard some kids teasing her one day when I picked her up."

"Beth was upset?" Tanner's lips tightened. She loved him for caring so much.

"That's the odd thing. As I think back on it now, I don't believe it bothered her unduly. But it sure got to me. I was furious. I wanted to protect her," she admitted sheepishly.

"You wanted to punish the nasty kids," Tanner corrected and chuckled when she glared at him. "I think that's a mother's instinct. There's nothing wrong with that."

"Yes, there is." It hurt to admit it. Sophie set down her cup, picked up one of the cookies she'd made earlier and nibbled on its corner. A moment later she put it down. "I thought I'd decided to homeschool Beth to protect her, but actually I did it to make me feel better."

"Huh?" Tanner poured himself another cup of coffee, topped up hers, then returned to his seat across from her. He chose another cookie as he waited for her to continue.

"You might not realize it but I'm a bit of a control freak, Tanner." She frowned when he choked on his coffee, then coughed to clear his throat.

"*You* might not realize it, Sophie, but that's a bit of an understatement." His teasing amusement stretched a grin across his face.

"Okay. Make fun of me." Her face burned with embarrassment. "But my decision to homeschool has hurt Beth. I feel better when she's with me, but she doesn't. She's lonely and she wants more friends. I cheated her of that because I was too afraid to let her handle the teasing, the snubs and whatever else those kids dished out."

"Sophie, you did your best for her." Tanner's hand slid

over hers, warm and comforting. "That's what a mom is supposed to do."

"A mother isn't supposed to make her kid afraid to say what she wants for fear she'll make me worry." She pulled her hand from his, hating the knowledge that she'd failed her children. First Davy and now Beth.

What kind of mother was she?

"What are you really worried about, Sophie?" Tanner's quiet question surprised her. "Let me guess. You're afraid something will happen and you won't be there to protect Beth."

"Yes." She lifted her chin. "She's an innocent, Tanner. I don't want her hurt. Or Davy."

"But they will be hurt, Sophie," he said quietly. "One way or another life hurts all of us. It's part of living." He leaned forward to stare earnestly into her eyes. "You can't protect them from everything, and even if you could it wouldn't be healthy. Beth and Davy have to learn to deal with life's problems on their own. That's how they grow."

"It's just so hard to stand back and let it happen when I could prevent it," she murmured.

"Has preventing it made Beth happy?" He smiled when she shook her head, then reached up to brush the hair from her cheek so he could stare into her eyes. "Beth isn't alone, you know."

She frowned at him, enjoying the touch of his fingertips against her skin. "Meaning?"

"Beth and Davy are God's children and He loves them far more than you ever could." Tanner's soft voice oozed faith. "Whenever your kids encounter a problem, God's right there beside them, helping them through."

"Why doesn't He stop it?" she demanded, edging away from his touch because that familiar yearning to lean on him had started up again. "Why must they go through it?"

"Sophie, think back on your life. Would you prefer to be alone, without Davy and Beth?"

"No." She glared at him. "Of course not. They are my everything."

"But having two kids is hard on you. You went through a lot of suffering because you had two kids to care for, right?" He waited for her nod. "So wouldn't it have been better to have avoided all that by simply not having them or giving them away for adoption?"

She stared at him, unable to believe he'd said that. Then the light dawned. "You're saying sometimes the pain is worth it."

"Yes. Davy is quickly reaching the stage where you soon won't be in control of who he meets or where he goes." His voice rebuked her in a tender tone. "Isn't it smarter to give him to God and trust He'll keep Davy safe instead of fighting to control everything yourself?"

"You're single, with no family—at least not that I know of. How do you know so much about kids and parenting, Tanner Johns?" Sophie suddenly saw the big cowboy in a fresh light. "I think you're one of those men who are born fathers."

She smiled at his surprised look, then rose to clean up the kitchen. Tanner simply sat there staring at her as if she'd told him his cattle were dinosaurs.

"No, that's not it," he said in a choked voice, breaking a long silence. "That's not it at all. I'd be a lousy dad. I'll go check on Beth." He left, striding across the yard as if chased by a bull.

Surprised by his rapid departure, Sophie studied his disappearing figure and realized how alone the cowboy was. Despite a full slate of staff and his friendly interaction with anyone who came to Wranglers, Tanner somehow remained aloof. Because it just happened that way, or was that his choice?

Get your mind off Tanner, Sophie, and clean up this mess. You have that anniversary party to cater tonight, remember?

But her brain wouldn't leave the subject alone. When Tanner later waved her and Beth off, Sophie's last view of him was a solitary figure standing tall and strong, but alone.

She wondered what it would be like to live on Wranglers Ranch.

With Tanner? an inner voice asked.

She refused to answer it.

"Sophie's supposed to arrive soon with food for that Big Brothers group the church is bringing," Tanner said the following Friday, striving to mask the anger he felt. "Keep her and the kids away from here, okay, Moses?"

"Her boy won't like it," Moses reminded. "He likes to walk Goliath around this way."

"Not today. Tell Davy we need him to accompany the group on their ride. I'll clear it with Sophie." Tanner pressed his lips together. "Whatever you do, don't let anyone near this mess."

"You know who you ticked off that would do this?" Moses asked, surveying the charred remains of the old log cabin he'd been restoring.

"No," Tanner muttered but in the back of his mind he saw the face of Tige, a former street gang leader who'd been an addict back when Tanner had lived on the streets. Was their meeting in the grocery store yesterday coincidental?

A prickly warning he hadn't felt in ten years feathered up his spine. Was this fire Tige's doing?

"Ask Lefty to use the loader to clean this up, will you? He can scrape it right down so it looks like we're clearing a spot."

"Sure. The police?" Moses's arch look said the question was perfunctory.

"They're certain it was arson but found no clues so they're not hopeful about finding the culprit. Can you ask the boys to keep it quiet that we had some vandalism last night? We don't want to alarm anyone."

He waited for Moses's nod before walking toward the house, but he couldn't silence his brain from repeating the question uppermost in his mind. *What did I do wrong, God? Don't You want me to go for Burt's dream?*

It wasn't that he didn't trust God anymore, but they'd come so close to losing everything. Wranglers Ranch land was tinder dry. If he hadn't happened to wake up around two and smell the smoke…

Tanner checked that the wood was stacked and ready on the patio, the only safe place to have a campfire after the ride. Then he made sure the tack the group would use was in perfect condition. As he did his mind replayed the previous day's events.

He'd never expected to see Tige again, let alone in a grocery store. Nothing much had changed. Lulu still hugged his side like a leech, eyes glazed, blond hair stringy and thinner than Tanner had ever seen her. She was using. Tige was, too, though he was better at hiding the effect of his last fix.

"How are you, buddy?" Tige had slapped him on the back. Years ago that slap would have felled Tanner but he'd toughened up a lot since he'd been that helpless kid living on the street under Tige's auspices. "You still a cowboy?" he'd said, studying the boots and hat Tanner wore. "Musta stayed with that guy who kept hounding you, huh?"

"Yeah." Tanner hadn't wanted to give too much away. "And you?" Two kids hung on the sidelines. "These your babies?" He'd been astonished to see them so grown.

"Yeah. Teenagers are pests." Lulu had brusquely

brushed off the two teens' request for money for a soda and Tige's language to them was no less rough. The boys had cowered away with shamed faces and scared looks.

Tanner's heart went out to them. How well he remembered feeling shrunken, worthless and afraid when he was with Tige.

"Good-looking boys," Tanner said with a smile in their direction.

"Think they'd make good cowboys, like you?" Tige's smile held no warmth.

"Maybe." The ice cream in Tanner's hands dripped with condensation. He held up the container to show them. "This is melting. I've got to go. Good seeing you."

"Yeah. Likewise. Hey, maybe we can get together, reminisce about old times, huh?" Tige's cagey smile had bothered Tanner but he'd pretended to be enthusiastic.

"Sure. Where you at now?" he asked.

"Oh, here and there. No fixed address, you know." Tige's face turned cunning. "You?"

Since Tanner couldn't lie he gave the best answer he could. "Same place."

"Still with Amy?" Tige's sly tone said he knew the truth.

"I haven't seen her since the day I left," Tanner said, keeping his face impassive. He held up the ice cream. "I'm getting soaked. See you around."

"Say, Tanner." Tige's fingers on his arm were not gentle. "Can you lend me a couple of bucks?" His eager look bounced from Lulu to the kids and back. "My check got held up."

"I haven't got much but I'll give you what I can." Tanner had been glad he'd left his wallet in his truck. "Let's see," he said, pulling his money from his pocket. "I've got maybe a hundred and twenty five after I pay for the ice cream. Will that—"

"You can have your ice cream another time, okay?" Tige

had snatched all the money. "Thanks, buddy. Good seeing you." Clutching his cash, Tige had hurried away with Lulu in tow. The boys looked uncertain as to whether or not they should follow until their mother bellowed. They gave Tanner a look that begged for help.

So he'd done something he probably shouldn't have.

"If you two ever need a break, come see me at Wranglers Ranch," he'd said in a very quiet voice, too quiet for their parents to hear.

Now, a day later, this fire told Tanner he should have kept his mouth shut. He felt certain Tige had something to do with it because he'd tried to interfere in Tige's business by talking to his kids. If his old street mate visited again it would be because he'd figured out that Tanner owned Wranglers. When that happened Tige wouldn't be satisfied with a measly hundred bucks.

Worried about visitors, but especially worried that Sophie and her kids could be in danger, Tanner had told the police investigators about his past association with Tige. They'd brushed off his concerns. They knew Tige, insisted he wasn't into arson. He was into drugs, lots and lots of drugs that hurt innocent kids and dragged them down to a life of misery. But arson? They'd shaken their heads.

"Tanner?" Sophie's voice drew him out of his reverie and back to the present. "Are you okay?" she asked, staring at his bunched forearms.

"Yeah. Sure." He forced his muscles to relax and smiled. "Can't a guy daydream?"

"Looked more like a nightmare from your scowl," she said with a frown. "What was your daydream about?"

"My birthday's tomorrow," he said, blurting out the first thing he could think of to evade that curious brown gaze. "March first."

"Really?" Sophie stared at him for several minutes as if she had trouble believing him. "You looked upset."

"You'd be upset, too, if you had only three more years in your twenties. I'm getting old." She didn't look convinced by his joking so Tanner didn't push it. He just wanted the conversation off himself. "Everything okay for the ride?"

"Sure. Except I didn't see any ice cream in your freezer." She kept looking at him as if she knew he was hiding something. "I thought you said you were going to buy a gallon yesterday."

"I forgot. I can go get it now," he said, eager to escape her too-knowing gaze. "What flavor do you need?"

"No, don't make a special trip." She grinned. "Actually I don't *need* it. I made different desserts than I'd planned, chocolate ones. We'll be fine without ice cream." She paused, then asked quietly, "Tanner, what's wrong?"

Thankfully he heard the chug of the church bus just then.

"There are our guests," he said, forcing enthusiasm into his voice. "Let's go greet them. Where are Beth and Davy?"

"Talking to Moses." Sophie eyed him uncertainly but offered no objection when he threaded his fingers with hers and led her toward the group.

Tanner liked the feel of Sophie's hand in his. At least she trusted him that much. For now—until she learned that associating with him might be a problem. That thought made him release her hand. He couldn't endanger sweet Sophie or her kids. Maybe it was time to think about hiring some kind of security to prevent another issue like last night's fire.

Help me protect her and her children, he prayed silently as the group assembled with their horses. *Please, God, don't let anything happen to Sophie*. His heart hurt at the thought.

When had Sophie begun to matter so much?

Chapter Eight

"I can't believe you wrangled a birthday party at Wranglers Ranch without me guessing." Tanner's delight at church folks gathered on his patio warmed Sophie's heart. He thanked them, then asked her, "How did you manage this?"

"I had a little help while you were goofing off up in the hills today." She smiled at her ranch hand accomplices who led the guests to the pizza buffet line. "I hope I didn't miss inviting anyone who is important to you."

"Cowboys do not goof off," he said sternly, then smiled. "And everyone who's important to me is already here."

Tanner's soft, reflective voice and the way he looked at her made Sophie's stomach lurch and her heart race. Apparently only just realizing what he'd admitted, Tanner gulped, his Adam's apple bobbing as he did.

"I mean, it's very kind of you. Thank you, Sophie. I've never had anyone throw me a birthday party before."

Those words squeezed her motherly heart so hard her arms ached to comfort him. What kind of a life had young Tanner led not to have had even one birthday party?

"But Burt…?" she murmured, then dropped it when he shook his head.

"He'd take me out for supper and give me a gift." He

grinned. "But I doubt Burt would have known how to throw a party. Guess that's why I never had one before."

"Then you must enjoy this one," she said firmly. But instead of dissipating, the crackling awareness she always felt around him thickened. Desperate to break it before she said something she shouldn't, Sophie resorted to teasing. "By next year you might be too old to enjoy another."

"And here I thought you were so nice." He shook his head sadly, gave a mock sigh, then headed off to get his own pizza.

"When can we give Tanner his gift, Mom?" Davy asked, Beth by his side.

"After we have cake," she promised, smiling at Davy's excited face.

What a change the big cowboy had made in her son's life. So much so that Davy had insisted on using most of the small salary Tanner now paid him for helping at Wranglers. Amazing to think that the money Davy hoarded to buy a skateboard had been willingly depleted to purchase a special pocketknife for the cowboy. Her son was at last learning about giving and caring, and Tanner was the reason. How could Sophie ever repay him?

But not just for Davy. When Beth had confided her desperate yearning to sing in the kids' church choir to Tanner, he'd taken that as his mission. Amazingly he'd found a voice coach with a reputation for successful work with Down syndrome children. Though now retired, Mrs. Baggle agreed to meet Beth. The two had immediately bonded. Mrs. Baggle insisted she would teach Beth for no fee. Sophie refused until the teacher finally admitted she'd always wanted to host an Easter Sunday brunch for her elderly quilting friends. Sophie insisted on catering it as payment.

Mrs. Baggle understood Beth's vocal issues but Sophie doubted Tanner knew how difficult singing was for those with Down syndrome or that the genetic disorder made the voice lower, which required more energy and training to produce sound. Years ago the doctors had told Sophie that Beth might never sing on key at all, and she'd feared Tanner would get Beth's hopes up for something that was impossible. She hadn't trusted him, certainly hadn't believed he'd find someone who not only taught her daughter to sing on key but encouraged Beth by making her feel her singing goals were reachable.

The voice lessons and a return to school had revitalized Beth. Sophie had never seen either of her children so happy.

Thanks to Tanner. And God answering her prayers.

If only she could finally learn to let go of the controls and trust Him.

"Scrumptious pizza. Thank you," Tanner said. Sophie had been so deep in thought she hadn't noticed he'd returned to sit beside her or that he'd finished eating. "I guess I'd better make a little thank-you speech—" His jaw dropped and his eyes opened wide. "You didn't," he whispered.

"Oh yes I did." Sophie laughed at his surprise as Moses carried the three-layer chocolate cake toward him. Atop thick chocolate icing sparklers glittered and twenty-six candles fluttered in the soft breeze.

Beth immediately led the group in a rousing, if off-key, rendition of the birthday song. Then Tanner's friends from church teased about his age and made a big fuss about his inability to blow out all the candles.

"Does that mean you're an old bag of wind?" one of his usher buddies gibed.

"No, it means Tanner has a girlfriend," Beth explained in her most serious voice.

Suddenly Sophie felt the intense stares of everyone on her. Her cheeks burned at the knowing looks. Tongue-tied, she couldn't think what to say. Fortunately Pastor Jeff broke the embarrassing silence.

"Are you going to share that cake or hide it away like you did those pies?" he demanded with a wink at Sophie.

Laughter rippled across the patio. Monica and Tiffany brought plates and forks and a huge container of chocolate ice cream. At Tanner's urging they took over cutting the cake and added generous scoops of the frozen treat. Davy and Beth passed around the filled plates.

"Enough chocolate for you?" Sophie asked, tongue in cheek.

"Almost." He licked his lips then frowned. "You shouldn't have hired staff for this," Tanner scolded. "I'll pay Monica's and Tiffany's wages."

"You certainly will not." Indignant, she glared at him. "This party is the Armstrong family's gift to you. Are you rejecting it?"

"Nope." He blinked and shook his head as he licked a blob of ice cream that was tucked at the corner of his lips. "No way. Burt didn't raise a dummy. I am going to thank you for it." He grinned and cupped a hand against her thrust-out chin. "Thank you, Sophie."

And then Tanner kissed her.

That kiss was over and done before Sophie could react, but she was acutely aware that every eye in the place was on them. As if she needed that with every nerve in her body already tingling from Tanner's kiss. She wished she could melt into the patio stones, and yet she wanted to re-play that fraction of a second over and over, even knowing that now gossip about a relationship between them would run rampant at church. They didn't know a relationship with Tanner was impossible.

But you want a relationship. Don't you?

"Stop scowling, Sophie," Tanner whispered in her ear. "They're focused on the cake, not you."

Which was such a lie, but she loved him for it.

Wait a minute—loved him? No! She didn't love Tanner. She didn't even trust him.

And yet—was there anyone she'd ever relied on more than Tanner Johns?

"Mama, our presents *now*?" Beth's whisper nudged Sophie out of the fog she'd fallen into. She must have nodded because a moment later her daughter plunked the gift she'd helped wrap this morning in front of Tanner. "This is from Mama," she said with a big grin. "You open it first."

He opened the card, laughed at the joke, then carefully unwrapped the gift. For several long moments he studied the coffeemaker as if he couldn't quite understand it. Then Tanner lifted his gaze to hers and said, "Thank you," in a polite voice.

Sophie just smiled.

"There's more. Open my gift now." Beth handed him a wildly decorated bag she'd made. When Tanner didn't take out the contents fast enough she helped him, setting the six boxes of coffee pods in a row on the table in front of him. "These are to use with Mama's gift. Now you won't ever have bad coffee anymore, Mr. Cowboy."

It seemed to Sophie that everyone but Tanner understood how fitting the gift was because the entire crowd applauded.

"Now we won't have to make excuses not to drink his coffee when we come to Wranglers," Pastor Jeff called out. "Tanner can actually serve real coffee."

Seeing Tanner's confusion, Sophie leaned close and explained how the machine worked. "It makes a perfect cup of coffee every time," she assured him.

"Like you make?" he said, his breath brushing against her cheek, enhancing the intimacy of the moment.

"Probably better than mine." Realizing they were again the focus of everyone's attention, Sophie stood, desperate to put some distance between them so she could corral her wayward senses. "Later I'll show you how to use it," she promised and began collecting plates.

"Thank you, Sophie." The sincerity in his voice and the glow in his green eyes made her heart skip. Surely he wasn't going to kiss her again? She cleared her throat, desperate to get away and clear her head.

"I made the coffee tonight, not Tanner," she announced as Monica and Tiffany waited by the coffee cart. "I guarantee it's safe to drink."

As the group hooted with laughter, Sophie shifted away from Tanner. Some approached him to present their gag gifts while others headed for the beverage cart. All in all, she was fairly pleased with the way the evening had gone. She was about to go into the house when she saw Beth and Davy talking to two teenage boys whom she'd never seen before. Concerned, she approached them and heard Davy ask, "You mean you want to talk to Tanner? He's the one who owns Wranglers Ranch."

When the boys nodded, Davy hurried toward his hero.

"I'm Sophie. And you are?" She waited until the pair had exchanged a glance.

"Rod" came from one, followed by "Trent" from the other boy.

"We're having a birthday party for Tanner tonight. Would you like some cake?" She saw the direction of their eager gazes and added, "Or pizza?" At their nods she led them to an empty spot and motioned for Monica to bring two drinks while she retrieved a pizza.

Apparently starved, the boys gulped down several slices of the pie before Tanner appeared. Sophie saw surprise on his face.

"Trent and Rod would like to speak to you." Something in Tanner's manner made Sophie believe he wanted a few minutes alone with the boys. "Come Beth, Davy. We'll get some cake and ice cream for the boys. And maybe another drink." She shepherded her kids away to give Tanner privacy.

"Do you think those are some of the street kids Tanner talks to?" Davy asked with a backward glance.

"What do you mean?" Surprised, Sophie listened as she cut two large wedges of the remaining cake and handed Beth and Davy each a glass of iced tea to carry.

"Tanner finds kids who don't have a home or food. Sometimes he takes them for a hamburger," Davy said knowledgeably.

A flutter of worry about the big generous cowboy grew to a ripple. Tucson was mostly a safe city but still—a shiver tiptoed up her spine. "Does Moses go with him?"

"I don't think so." Davy frowned. "He told me not to say anything."

"I'm sure Tanner won't mind me knowing." Sophie led the kids to the table where the cowboy was holding an animated discussion with the boys, who vehemently shook their heads at whatever he was saying. Silence fell while she served the cake and drinks. "Eat up. If you want more, we have lots." Then with a smile at Tanner she gave her children jobs to help with the cleanup.

"Mama, are those boys friends of Mr. Cowboy?" Beth's face scrunched up in a frown.

"Why do you ask, honey?" Sophie paused to study her daughter.

"'Cause he's giving them money."

Sophie turned in time to see Tanner slip a bill into the palm of the oldest boy. Since Tanner didn't look upset or angry, she turned back to her work.

"They're leaving now. Mr. Cowboy is watching them. He looks sad." Beth dropped the paper she'd collected into the trash. "I'm going to give him a hug."

Sophie put her hand on Beth's shoulder. "Wait a minute, okay, sweetie? Give Tanner some time to himself."

"Can I pray for him?" her daughter asked, blue eyes glowing huge in her round face. "He's my friend. We pray for our friends, don't we, Mama?"

"That's a great idea," Sophie approved.

"'Kay." Beth sat down on a bench, bowed her head and began silently praying.

From the corner of her eye Sophie saw Tanner motion to Lefty and give him directions. The man hurried away and a moment later one of the ranch's four-wheel-drive vehicles left a cloud of dust as it took off down the driveway. Tanner turned and caught Sophie staring. He walked toward her.

Not wanting to intrude, she merely asked, "Everything okay?"

"They're two street kids whose parents are, I believe, abusing them. I met them in a store the other day when I saw an old—acquaintance." There was a pause before he said the word, as if he'd deliberately avoided saying "friend." "I told them to come here if they needed anything. They said they hadn't eaten today. Thanks for feeding them."

Sophie shrugged. "No biggie, as Davy would say. Feeding a kid is easy to do, not like trying to reach their souls, as you do on your street visits." She said it nonchalantly.

Tanner jerked as if she'd struck him. "How do you know—" Then he shook his head. "Davy."

"No secrets with kids around." Sophie sensed his reticence. "You don't have to tell me anything." She knew it was the right thing to say when he remained silent for a moment.

"I knew their father back in the days when I lived on the streets." He glanced around. "I need to mingle right now. But can I tell you about it when everyone's gone? You don't have to hurry home tonight, do you, Sophie?"

"It's Friday. No school and I don't have anything scheduled for tomorrow so I guess we could stay for a while," she agreed. "Go enjoy your party, Tanner."

"I am," he said, his eyes dancing. "Some parts more than others." His gaze rested on her lips.

"I need to check on Monica and Tiffany." Sophie said it quickly, feeling as if her face was on fire. "Excuse me." She hurried away, knowing he was watching her with that cute lopsided grin of his.

At the doorway she gave in to the urge to turn back and check. Sure enough, Tanner stood in place, watching her with those intense green eyes. But he wasn't smiling. He looked as if he were struggling with a decision. Then Beth tugged on his pant leg and he smiled at her.

Something was definitely bothering Tanner, and Sophie could hardly wait to learn what was going on.

"I dropped them off on Fourth Street, boss. That was as far as they'd let me take them."

"Thanks, Lefty, I appreciate it." Tanner watched his foreman leave the patio while his mind swirled with questions about Tige.

He put away the questions to entertain his guests, but when they'd all left and he was finally alone, he sat down on a bench to think about Trent and Rod. Had Tige sent his kids with that story? Tanner didn't think so but—

"Davy and Beth fell asleep." Sophie's glance around the empty patio told him she was waiting for that talk he'd promised. He didn't want to tell her anything about his ugly past, but his conscience demanded Sophie know the risk her kids might be taking if things escalated with Tige.

Are you going to tell her everything about your past? Including the child you abandoned? Because if you don't, you know that someday Tige will.

He ignored the voice in his head.

"Let's sit down."

"Okay." Sophie shivered slightly, prompting his realization that the night air had cooled.

Tanner added a couple of logs to the fire still burning in the fire pit to ensure she'd be warm enough. "First of all, thank you for making this birthday so special. I appreciate all the trouble you and the kids went to."

"It was our pleasure." Sophie sat with her beautiful face lit by the dancing flames.

"About those boys. Trent and Rod are the sons of a man I knew as Tige from my days of living on the streets." Tanner wanted to hurry through the past and avoid long-buried thoughts that still brought pain. "I happened to meet Tige the other day when I went to the grocery store."

"Happened to meet?" Her brown eyes narrowed. "That's odd, isn't it?"

"Yeah." He grimaced. "I don't believe in coincidences, either. Maybe word is getting out about Wranglers and he recognized my name. I don't know." He kept going, anxious to get it said. "He's not a nice man, Sophie. Neither is his wife, Lulu. For as long as I've known Tige he's been into drugs, selling and using, friendly when he's high, mean and nasty when he's not. Anyway in the store that day I noticed his kids seemed ill at ease and I felt sorry for them. I told them to look me up if they ever needed anything. I guess that's why they showed up today."

"Because they were hungry." Sophie sat silently watching him, her face impassive. Finally, her voice very soft, she asked, "Why are you telling me this, Tanner?"

"That day I met him—Tige hit me up for some money." He exhaled, hoping, praying she wouldn't grab her kids and run when he explained. "The morning after I saw him I found a fire blazing in one of the old buildings Moses has been restoring. Understand that there was no electricity, nothing in there that could have caused a fire. Yet it burned hot and fast." He could see she didn't understand his inference. "The police insist it is arson but they found no clues as to who lit it."

"You think Tige did it." Awareness dawned, then she frowned. "But why?"

"As a kind of message that he's watching me. At least that's how Tige used to operate." Tanner couldn't shake the black mantle of dread. "He used to pass out what he called 'warnings,' maybe a beating, maybe something else equally nasty, to let you know that he was always watching."

"And if you didn't do what he wanted?" Sophie whispered, her pupils wide.

"His usual modus operandi was violence to make sure you did." Now came the hard part. "His sons are scared." He condensed what the boys had told him. "Apparently Tige and Lulu got high after I saw them. Those boys hadn't eaten for ages. They know they'll get in trouble if Tige finds out they came here, but they had nowhere else to go."

Tanner noticed Sophie didn't ask him about Children's Services or any other agency. Was that because she trusted him to do the right thing? But Sophie didn't trust.

"So now you're worried about us," she guessed. He nodded, sobered by concern. "What will Tige do if he finds out you interfered with his kids?"

"Tige only goes after someone if there's a profit for him." Tanner saw her absorb that. Her eyes expanded in understanding.

"You mean—he'll ask you for money when he learns you own the ranch?"

"Yes." Tanner exhaled. He hated saying this, hated distancing himself from this woman he admired. But the thought of Sophie, Davy or Beth being hurt because of him was intolerable. "I don't know if you and the kids should come to Wranglers anymore."

"We have to!" She stared at him. "Unless you have someone else in mind to cater the camp next week? And the Easter morning sunrise ride?"

"No, but—"

"It's my job, Tanner, and I don't quit on a job. Ever." She leaned forward, covered his hand with hers and squeezed. "Isn't the whole purpose of Wranglers Ranch to minister to needy kids?"

"Yes." Fear churned in his gut, eating away his resolve. He had to protect her. "But what if—"

"You're always after me for not trusting." Sophie's beautiful smile curved her lips. "This time it's you who isn't trusting, Tanner. Think about those two boys. They know Tucson's streets because they grew up on them, right?"

Tanner nodded though he didn't get where she was headed.

"You're trying to help street kids. Maybe this is God's way of easing your foot in the door for this ministry." Sophie tilted her head to one side, thinking it through as she spoke. "Maybe Trent and Rod are the first steps in your outreach program for Tucson's street kids. Possible?"

What a woman! Not only did she chide him for his doubts, she saw past the immediate problems to the possibilities. How could he keep away from her? He couldn't.

Tanner leaned forward and brought his lips to hers. The kiss began lightly but quickly took on its own life, rapidly escalating into something more meaningful as Sophie wrapped her arms around his neck and tilted toward him. She kissed him back in a way that made Tanner certain she must have some kind of fond feeling for him.

A burst of yearning flared inside him. This woman felt so precious in his arms, like a wonderful gift he could never deserve. Tanner wished for more than a simple kiss but he didn't want to ruin the friendship she'd trusted him with. He was not going to repay this giving, caring woman by deepening the embrace, by asking for more than she could give. Sophie didn't want a personal relationship. She'd told him that. He'd respect her wishes no matter how much he hated letting her go. Besides, he didn't deserve Sophie.

Carefully Tanner eased away from her.

"What was that for?" Sophie whispered. She looked as shaken as he felt.

"Just—because." He pushed her soft brown hair off her face. "Because you're an amazing woman with amazing vision and amazing talents."

"Tanner, I cook. Hardly amazing," she scoffed.

"You don't just cook, Sophie. When you offer food, you meet a need by seeing into a person, past the barriers they put up to the hurting place inside them that aches to have someone care." He was saying too much and he knew it, but Tanner couldn't stop. "You can't pretend that you don't go over each menu for Wranglers very carefully, making sure it fits the ranch and whatever occasion you're serving. That detail and caring is evident in everything you do, from loving Davy and Beth to maintaining a house you don't own."

Afraid he'd said too much and given away how deeply he admired her, Tanner clamped his lips together and visually dared her to deny it.

"Thank you." To his surprise Sophie's eyes welled with tears. She squeezed his hand before letting go. "Thank you for saying that."

"It's the truth. You're a very special lady, Sophie Armstrong." Her gaze met his and somehow got tangled. For a brief moment, a yawning space in time, Tanner felt like he could see into the heart of the woman behind that brown-eyed gaze, who took on the world without complaint.

Then her lids dropped and hid her thoughts.

"I wish you'd tell me more about your past, Tanner." Her

eyes narrowed and her voice dropped to a wistful tone. "If I knew more about your time on the street, maybe I could better understand why you're so worried about this Tige and what he might do."

"I don't like to remember that time." Tanner ripped his gaze from hers, afraid she'd see how much he feared her knowing the whole truth about his past. He blinked when her fingertips brushed his cheek.

"I'm sorry. I don't want to bring back any bad memories for you," Sophie whispered. "I just want to help you."

"You've already helped me a lot." He felt like a traitor. Was it lying if you kept a secret like his? *Yes!* his brain yelled. "One day I will tell you all about Tige and my past," he promised. *And then she'll walk away from you.*

"I'll hold you to that," Sophie promised, though questions remained in her dark eyes.

How Tanner wished he could be totally honest with her. But he kept hoping that with time she'd come to know him better, trust that he wasn't the total jerk his decision back then seemed to make him; that if Sophie knew who he was in his heart she'd be willing to forgive him his youthful mistake. Maybe.

"But what are you going to do now? Because I'm not about to walk away from my commitment to help you and Wranglers Ranch," Sophie said in a firm voice. "I believe that through you, Tanner, this place is going to reach a lot of kids. There's no way we can let one messed-up drug addict stop God's work."

We. Tanner smiled. He liked knowing Sophie was on his side. Liked it a lot. But Tige—what was he supposed to do about Tige? *Lord?*

"I will hire a security firm tomorrow." He frowned as he studied her. "But I'm not sure that's enough. I can't guarantee your kids' safety when they're here, Sophie."

To his astonishment she smiled.

"What's so funny?"

"Not too long ago, I'd have insisted I was perfectly capable of caring for my kids," she told him with a chuckle. "Or I'd have hightailed it out of here and shuttered them up at home regardless of how they protested."

"You're not going to do that?" He knew before he asked that she wasn't. "Why not?"

"A certain man recently rebuked me about my faith, or rather my lack of it." Sophie chuckled at his sheepish look. "I'm glad you did. Your words made me think about my claim to be a Christian. I was really convicted when I read a verse in First John that says, 'If we are afraid, it is for fear of what He might do to us and shows that we are not fully convinced that He really loves us.' I've been living in fear, Tanner."

"And now you're not?" His brows drew together.

"Oh, I'm still afraid the sky will fall on me," Sophie joked, but the shadows in her brown eyes told him it was true. "I haven't gotten rid of that monkey on my back so easily. But lately I'm realizing how my lack of faith in God hurts me. And my kids. So I've been trying to work out my faith, or rather to let God work it out, by relinquishing my control."

"How's that going?" He didn't have to ask. Tanner could see by the look on beautiful Sophie's face that she would far rather cling to the reins of running her own life. His heart empathized at the difficult lesson of true faith in God that she was learning.

"It's not easy," she said in a low voice.

"Not supposed to be, honey. Trust is a process, one step at a time." He couldn't stop staring, appreciating the way she thrust out her chin, determined to trust no matter how much she hated it. "It gets easier, Sophie," he promised.

"I hope so." This time she didn't look away, didn't immediately end that sensitive current that zipped back and forth between them. Instead she studied him with an almost tender scrutiny. "Do you realize that you conducted your first real outreach tonight, Tanner? And you didn't even have to leave the ranch."

He blinked, stunned to realize that it was true. He'd invited Tige's kids to come without even thinking. Tonight he'd talked to them as a friend, not as the preacher he'd figured he was supposed to be. "It seemed to come naturally," he muttered, awed by the insight.

"That seems like the best way." Sophie grinned at him. "Congratulations."

"Thanks." He savored the moment, delighted to have her there to share it. But the reality of the situation returned like a wet blanket. "But what about Tige?"

"What about him?" Sophie straightened her shoulders and met his look with a stern one of her own. "He's nothing to me. We've never met. Why should he care about me or my family?"

"I don't know." Troubled, Tanner frowned. "Tige was never exactly rational…"

"Listen." Sophie wrapped her fingers around his arm and squeezed, catching and holding his attention. "In learning to trust I've begun to understand that I have to live in the now or I'll drive myself crazy with what-ifs. Let's just keep working toward Burt's goal and trust God to work things out. Let's 'fan into flame the gift that is within you.'"

"I still don't know what that is," he complained.

"You'll figure it out." She smiled a Mona Lisa smile. "I think I have."

"Oh." He hoped she'd tell him what his gift was but she remained silent, though her eyes glowed with some inner secret. "Thank you, Sophie," he murmured, returning the pressure of her fingers against his.

"For what?" She tilted her head to one side.

"Everything. The party. Making every guest feel welcome. Making me feel special. For helping me make Burt's dream come true. For being you." Without even thinking he leaned forward and kissed her again. It felt so right to have Sophie here at the ranch, by his side, being his partner.

She wouldn't be here if she knew why you're so afraid of Tige, especially of what he could tell her. Sophie wouldn't stay if she knew you walked away from your child and never looked back.

Brought back to reality by that warning voice, Tanner helped Sophie pack up the kids while resolve filled his head. Along with hiring security for the ranch he would hire a private detective to find his child. Wranglers Ranch and the message of God's love was too important to be sidetracked by a man from his past. If he told her, Tanner was certain Sophie would agree.

The voice in his head laughed at him for believing Sophie would ever condone his past actions. If she knew what he'd done, she'd probably hate Tanner for abandoning his child.

Please don't let Sophie hate me.

Chapter Nine

"I don't like the look on your face." Sophie tamped down the frisson of excitement that always fluttered across her skin whenever she was near Tanner. "Can you fix my oven or not?"

"Probably not," he muttered in disgust as he squeezed out from behind the appliance. "We'll find out when you turn on the breaker."

She did that, then returned to find him scowling. "Nothing?"

"Dead as a doornail. Sophie, the thing is older than time. You need a new one. Can't the person you rent from see that?" Obviously frustrated, Tanner gathered up his tools. "Why didn't you use the stove at the ranch?"

"I did use it for your Easter sunrise ride this morning," Sophie reminded him, wondering why she couldn't rid herself of this feeling that Tanner wasn't telling her something about his past. She'd felt it again earlier when she'd asked him if he'd heard from Tige and he'd brushed her off.

"You used our kitchen to great success." Tanner patted his stomach, smile back in place. "Your cooking was so delicious that I've decided we'll have a sunrise service at Wranglers every Easter." He frowned. "So why didn't you take these cinnamon rolls there?"

"Because they were still rising while I was at Wranglers. Besides, Mrs. Baggle's place is only a few blocks away from here. It seemed silly to haul everything out to Wranglers and then back to my place. Also, how was I to know this thing would cease working today?" She glared at the old stove. "I don't have time to take the rolls to the ranch now. Mrs. Baggle's Easter brunch is going to be ruined and that's all she asked in return for teaching Beth."

"Mom, Mrs. Parker's home." Davy burst through the door, basketball clutched under one arm. "She's got a walker."

"A man is trying to help her up the stairs," Beth added.

"Edna." Sophie grinned and exhaled her relief. "Of course. Thank You, Lord." She closed her eyes, whispered a prayer of thanks and picked up the phone. After speaking to her elderly neighbor for a few minutes she wished her a happy Easter, then hung up. "Tanner, will you help me carry these pans next door?"

"Uh, yeah. Sure." His confused look made her giggle. But the cowboy's face rapidly cleared as he followed her across the backyard to her neighbor's house. "You're going to use her oven," he deduced.

"Yes, I am. Edna's homecoming is an answer to prayer." Sophie was surprised by how frequently it seemed God had answered her prayers lately. This Easter held more promise than she'd ever experienced. Was that because she'd been spending more time studying her Bible? Or because of Tanner?

Though Edna had just been released from full-time care and was still slightly pale, she seemed very mobile and utterly delighted to see them. Actually she seemed most excited to meet Tanner and clung to the cowboy's hand as she introduced her son, Ronald.

"He's a good son but he's like his father. Not handy at

all," she complained. "I need a ramp to get in the door and Ronald doesn't know how to make one. Do you?"

"Uh, sure." Tanner handed the pan of rolls to Sophie and left to fetch his tools, Ronald following.

"Wow! Your Tanner's a hunk," Edna squealed when the door creaked closed behind them. "And so big and strong. It's good to have a man around, isn't it, dear? Didn't I tell you that?"

"Tanner's a good friend. I've been doing a lot of catering at his ranch," Sophie explained, embarrassed by her neighbor's garrulous appreciation of the cowboy. She hugged Edna. "You look good, Edna."

"I feel very well. It got much easier once I put my heart into doing the exercises. I was stubborn about obeying the physiotherapist." She twittered with laughter, then urged Davy and Beth to take a treat from the jar that seemed never to empty. "My, how you children have grown. Now, tell me about your mother's boyfriend."

"Boyfriend?" Davy frowned at Beth, then at Sophie.

"Tanner's not—" But she was drowned out by Beth, who was eager to share all she knew about the man who now seemed a permanent part of their lives.

But Tanner wasn't part of their lives. And Sophie couldn't let herself forget that, no matter how much she wished for more than friendship. She'd barely begun to trust God. Trusting a man was far more difficult, even if he was a man for whom she had increasingly strong feelings.

She'd tell Edna that later. For now she dashed between her neighbor's kitchen and her own, checking the food she'd prepared and sharing a smile with Tanner as he hammered and sawed under Ronald's gaze to form the ramp that would assist Edna.

Affection bubbled up inside Sophie. How many men would spend their Easter Sundays building a ramp for an old woman they didn't even know? Edna was right. Tanner *was* a hunk. And he was handy as well as very good-looking. He was also a good kisser.

She told herself to stop hoping that would happen again.

"It's time for me to deliver this food," she announced when the rolls were golden brown and oozing with sticky glaze.

"Leave the kids here with me," Tanner said. "They can help finish the ramp while you make your delivery." When she didn't answer he frowned. "Okay, Sophie?"

"Yes," she murmured, touched by his generosity. What would she do without Tanner's unstinting help?

It didn't take long to reach Mrs. Baggle's. There were eight older women waiting and they twittered and giggled like young girls as Sophie set out the brunch she'd prepared.

"Scalloped potatoes," Mrs. Baggle breathed. "I haven't had those for years. And baked ham with cherry glaze. How wonderful."

"I hope you enjoy everything," Sophie said as she arranged napkins. She set a covered square container in the fridge. "The dessert crepes are in here, ready whenever you are, Mrs. Baggle." She had to smile at the other women's eager expressions. "Now, shall I make tea?"

"Oh, no, dear. We'll do that after we've eaten. Will you join us?" Mrs. Baggle nodded when Sophie declined the offer. "Of course you want to spend your Easter with Beth and Davy. And your nice boyfriend. Go now, dear. You can pick up your containers tomorrow."

"Thank you. Happy Easter," Sophie called as she walked out the door, neglecting to correct Mrs. Baggle about Tanner. After all, he *was* nice.

The ladies' cheerful "Happy Easter to you, dear" made her smile.

For the first time in a long time, it truly *was* a *happy* Easter. Thanks in large part to Tanner.

I need to think of some way to thank him, she mused on the drive home. But how? Tanner was rich. He sure didn't need anything she could buy.

Sophie was surprised to find the big cowboy sitting on her front step with her children when she pulled up in front of her house. The kids jumped up and hurried toward her.

"Tanner says we're going to the zoo," Davy said, obviously excited.

"Are we?" Her heart skipped a couple of beats when Tanner winked at her.

"We are," he affirmed. "We're just waiting for you to change out of your work clothes."

"Okay, then." She eased past him, trying to erase the memory of being in his arms by focusing instead on the joy of spending an afternoon of free time with him—which did nothing for her heart rate. "I'll pack a little lunch—" Tanner's hand on her arm stopped her short. His touch sent a zing of warmth through her body. She couldn't tear her gaze from his.

"No more cooking for you today, Sophie," he said firmly. "We'll grab something there."

"But—" She stopped when he shook his head.

"It's Easter, a time to celebrate the risen Lord. Let's enjoy the day He's made for us." It wasn't so much Tanner's words as the wistful expression she saw in his green eyes that ended her argument. She had no intention of refusing. In fact, she could hardly wait to get started.

Funny how she always thought of Tanner as a loner. Was that an aura left over from his former street persona? How she wished he'd open up to her about his past. What was so terrible that he had to hide it? Drugs? Theft?

"Sophie?" His hand on her arm drew her from her introspection.

"Sorry. I'll change and be right out." She moved away from his touch while noting how much she liked it. Too much. "Beth, do you want to change out of your Easter dress?"

"Why?" Beth looked shocked by the suggestion. "It's an Easter dress and this is Easter," she said logically.

"Indeed it is. And a most lovely dress it is, too. The zoo animals will love it." Tanner grinned at Sophie. "We're waiting on you."

They didn't wait long. Sophie took mere seconds to change into her favorite sundress, loosen her hair from the topknot she favored for work and spritz on a few drops of her favorite scent.

For Tanner?

She ignored that mocking voice in her head and joined the others, inwardly glowing at his approving smile. She accepted his helping hand into his truck and made sure her kids were belted in before fastening her own. On the drive to Reid Park Zoo, Davy and Beth chatted with Tanner about Pastor Jeff's short sermon that they heard this morning at Wranglers' sunrise service. As Sophie listened to Tanner's answers to their questions, she was struck by the solid faith of the cowboy's answers.

"See, the thing is, Davy, that we are the center of God's plan." Tanner caught her scrutiny and smiled at her before he continued. "He dreamed up the idea of us and made us His children, part of His family, just because He wants to love us."

"Even if we do bad things?" her son wondered.

"Even if," Tanner affirmed.

"But God doesn't like us to do bad things," Beth corrected in a grave tone.

"Nope. You're right." Stopped at a stop sign, Tanner reached behind Sophie and tugged Beth's ponytail with a smile. "He doesn't like that. But it doesn't stop Him from loving us. No matter what we do He loves us because we're His kids."

"Sometimes I don't feel like God hears me when I pray to Him." Sophie saw Davy shoot her a quick glance as if he wasn't sure he should have admitted that. If he only knew how often his mother felt the same!

"We all have times like that." Tanner's tone grew pensive.

"Even you?" Davy asked in an awed voice.

"Especially me," Tanner said. "That's when I remind myself that nothing can separate us from God's love. Nothing."

"Does it say that in the Bible?" Beth asked. Sophie hid her smile at her daughter's fastidious insistence on knowing biblical references.

"It does. I'll show you later," Tanner promised. "It says something else, too. It says in Deuteronomy that the Lord our God is faithful and will keep His agreement of love for a thousand lifetimes for people who love Him and obey His commands."

"A thousand lifetimes is a long time," Davy murmured thoughtfully.

"Our God makes big promises. And He keeps them," Tanner said.

The kids seemed satisfied with that answer and so was Sophie, though when she got the chance she was going to ask Tanner some questions about her own Bible study. His faith seemed so much more developed than hers.

Rubbing shoulders with Tanner, she wandered through the zoo beside him as the kids dashed ahead. Then they'd run back to be sure the adults hadn't missed anything. It was a warm afternoon filled with fun and relaxation, and Sophie savored the closeness she felt with Tanner.

"Time for lemonade?" At her nod he bought them each a glass of the chilly beverage and they sat at a picnic table to enjoy it. Davy and Beth kept running off only to return full of information about the next exhibit.

"They're having so much fun. Thank you for bringing us here," Sophie said when they were alone for a few minutes.

"They're good kids. I enjoy being with them." Tanner smiled at her. She would have liked to read his eyes but they were concealed behind his sunglasses. For once he'd left his Stetson in the truck. "I enjoy being with you, too," he added in a quieter voice.

"It's mutual," she said, struggling not to grin at him and reveal just how much she was enjoying this afternoon. "I don't think Burt could have picked anyone better than you to run Wranglers Ranch."

"That's debatable." He shrugged, then grinned. "But I'm awfully glad he entrusted me with his dream. It's a challenge that's truly worthwhile."

"I agree." Sophie inclined her head to study him. "I noticed someone carved his verse about you into a piece of beech wood and hung it in the barn."

"I did," he admitted sheepishly. "I don't want to forget the things he told me."

"Fan into flame the gift that is within you," she quoted. "Do you know what that gift is yet?"

"Not a clue." His nose wrinkled. "I don't have any special gifts unless you count riding a horse. I can do that okay."

"A little better than okay, I'd say. Moses showed me all those rodeo trophies you won." Sophie liked the way he deflected compliments. In her opinion, Tanner Johns had a lot to be proud of and yet he didn't put on airs or try to impress. He just did what needed doing. "I think you have many gifts. But you don't think of them as gifts."

He leaned back with a frown. "Gifts like what?"

"The way you handle Tige's sons for one thing." Sophie wasn't sure he wanted her to discuss that. After all, he'd spoken about his former friend only one time and that was to warn her. She'd offered him several opportunities since but he hadn't confided anything more, so his past remained a mystery to her.

Tige's two boys kept reappearing at the ranch. Tanner acted as if that was perfectly natural. He never questioned them about their parents, simply treated them as if they were visitors—the same as other kids who'd recently begun to drop by. He made sure the two boys were fed, taught them how to sit on a horse and answered any questions they had. And he always invited them to come back.

"Being with Rod and Trent doesn't take any gift." He shrugged it off. "They're just kids."

"Kids in a bad situation. Lots of people would try to get them away from their parents or convince them to run away," she began but Tanner was vehemently shaking his head.

"I would never do that without a very good reason," he said in a harsh voice. "Families are precious."

"See?" Sophie grinned and nudged him with her elbow while wondering why he was so adamant on the subject of families. Her questions about him grew. "That's what I'm talking about. Everything you do is for the kids' sake. That's a gift."

Tanner made a rude noise.

"It's common sense. I'm a product of a foster home. Believe me I'm well aware that if Rod and Trent were put in foster care they could be better off. It could also be much worse."

"You've made sure they're okay with Tige and Lulu, haven't you?" she guessed and smiled when he shrugged.

"Judging parents isn't my mission. My mission is to help kids," he said, his voice unwavering. "That means gaining their trust and trusting them to know when to ask for help. And those two haven't. I think they're willing to come to Wranglers because I don't interfere."

"But it's not just those two. You have a gift with most kids, Davy included," she insisted. "I've seen the way you work with them after they fail at something they desperately want to do, like Davy trying to rope that calf the other day." She joined in his reminiscent chuckle, then sobered. "He was frustrated and ready to blow. You could have made fun of him or told him to practice. Instead you used that opportunity to teach him about patience. That's a gift."

Tanner let his sunglasses slide to the end of his nose so he could give her a rolling-eye look. "You're pushing the definition, Sophie."

"I don't think so. I think God is using you at Wranglers far beyond anything Burt could have imagined. God showed him those qualities in you—those gifts that you're fanning into flame." She stared into the distance thoughtfully. "I wish I had some kind of gift."

"You do!" Of course Tanner being Tanner, he raced to enumerate what he considered her gifts and compliment her. She cut him off.

"It's nice of you to say, but I don't have any real gifts," she murmured sadly. "I'm not the type of person God uses."

"Why do you think that, Sophie?" he asked quietly. "Why do you think God isn't using you?"

"Because I'm not fit. Because I can't quite trust Him." She hung her head, ashamed of the admission. "Not completely. I'm trying but—I'm just not there yet."

"Listen to me." He shoved his sunglasses to the top of his head, then took her hand in both of his. "Willingness to be used is what God looks for. Trust me, He is using you. And as He does you will learn to trust Him more and more. It's a process. Trust grows. The more we use it, the stronger it gets."

She stared at his hand holding hers and wondered for the hundredth time why Tanner Johns wasn't involved with someone. Were single women so foolish that they couldn't see beyond his humble cowboy demeanor and recognize his integrity and compassion?

Maybe he's hiding something that you can't or won't see.

Taken aback by that thought, Sophie immediately wondered if there was something about Tanner that when revealed would cost her. She liked, appreciated and respected him but...

Distrust moved in. Much as she hated breaking contact with him, she slid her hand from his while forcing a smile.

"Thank you for your encouragement." She watched her children dart from one animal enclosure to the next and admitted, "I know it's foolish but somehow depending on God seems like I'm abandoning my role as a mother. After all, I'm responsible for them. Leaving things up to Him seems like I'm letting go of the controls He's given me."

"You're not letting go, Sophie. You're being their mother in the best way you know how, by seeking His will," he said. "Then you act, trusting that He's directing you."

How did Tanner's explanations about God always make her feel better, as if she wasn't the failure at Christianity that she always felt?

"Recently I've been reading Isaiah. I've been struck by how much God yearned for His children to love Him." He shook his head as if he couldn't wrap his mind around why it should be so. "They were disobedient, they took other gods, they did exactly what God said not to and He had to discipline them. Yet there's such a longing in His words, begging them to restore their relationship with Him and to have their love again. Such love amazes me."

Sophie made a mental note to read Isaiah as Davy and Beth rushed back, finished their drinks and pleaded to move on.

As the afternoon waned, the children's restlessness gave way to quiet introspection as Tanner frequently commented about God's painstaking efforts to make His creation perfect. And always the big cowboy emphasized how much God loved His children. Tanner made God the father's love come alive.

Yet it wasn't so much Tanner's comments about family as the way he expressed them, combined with the lingering hugs he'd given Beth and Davy that bothered Sophie later that night when she sat alone in her living room.

She'd watched him as the kids raced away from him, into the house. She'd seen the loneliness wash over his face, felt his yearning to stay, to share her family.

Once more Sophie's questions about him ratcheted up. Why didn't he talk about his past? Surely he'd dated, fallen in love at least once?

Sophie's misgivings about Tanner came from concern that the rancher was hiding something she wouldn't like. She cared a lot about Tanner. But she couldn't get past the fear that trusting him would cost her dearly.

Chapter Ten

Tanner sat on his patio in the May sunshine, nursing a fragrant cup of perfectly brewed coffee, utterly stunned by the contents of the manila envelope in front of him. As he read everything in his private detective's update, hope shriveled inside him. Now he could only stare at the small picture that had been clipped to the report, desperately struggling to formulate a prayer for direction, for something to end this despair clawing at him. Nothing came.

All he could think of was that his child was gone. He'd never know that person, never see his potential or hear *Hi, Daddy*. His insides squeezed tight with pain and loss.

God?

Tanner didn't know how much time passed before he jerked to awareness at the sound of a vehicle arriving. He rose, stuffed the papers into the envelope and stored it under a plant pot, tucking the picture into his back pocket. Something else to hide.

His heart lifted as he caught a glimpse of a familiar van. Sophie and the kids. But she was catering a Memorial Day dinner today. She wasn't supposed to be here.

Something must be wrong.

Surprised by how glad he was to see her again, though only last night he'd enjoyed a barbecue dinner at her house,

Tanner suddenly realized that they now saw each other almost every day. Which was good and totally fine with him. It couldn't be too often for Tanner. Sophie and her kids felt like his family, the one he'd always wanted and now would never have. That secret was hardest of all to keep.

"Hey," he greeted, opening her door. She looked beautiful, as usual, though her lips were pursed in a thin line. "What's happening?"

"Not that stupid stove of mine." She frowned. "I hate to keep running to you—"

"Why?" he demanded, surprised by how much he disliked her saying that. He wanted her to need him. He'd have to think about that later. "Aren't we friends? Don't friends help each other?"

"Well, you certainly help me an awful lot." She sighed and slid out of the van.

Oh, Sophie. If only you knew how much I love helping you, being around you, touching you. Kissing you? A kiss wasn't nearly enough to satisfy his longing to hold her.

"I'm not sure you get as much as you give," she said, her tone wistful.

"Do you hear me complaining?" Tanner asked.

"Not yet. Guess the treats I've been leaving in your fridge must be working." Sophie laughed when he licked his lips, then sobered. "May I please use your kitchen? Again?"

"Of course. Hi, guys." He grinned at Beth, high-fived Davy. "What needs carrying in?"

"I brought everything for the meal," she said, handing him a stack of bins. "I haven't got time to run back and forth. It's already eight and I have to serve at one thirty."

"Okay, you two, lead the way." He chuckled at Beth's delicate maneuvers with her bulging bag of salad fixings. Davy, on the other hand, wielded his two plastic tubs with such carefree abandon that Tanner caught his breath when they teetered dangerously, and held it until everything was safely stored on the kitchen countertop.

"This is going to be tight." A hint of panic laced Sophie's voice. She who never panicked. With practiced ease she slid a pan that held perfectly sliced roast beef into the oven, covered it and set the temperature to warm the meat.

"It's going to be as perfect as everything else you make. And we're going to help you." He glanced at Davy and waited for his nod. Of course, Beth copied her brother. "What should we do first?"

"Can you peel potatoes?" she asked hesitantly, as if she thought he'd never used a knife on a tuber before.

Tanner gave her a look he meant to say, *You doubt my abilities?*

"Of course you can. You're Tanner Johns. You do everything well."

If she only knew. Tanner made no response except to return her smile.

"There's a bag in that yellow bin. Start peeling. Beth, you can whip the cream for my banana cream pie and Davy, you can chop carrots. Are you sure you don't mind?" she asked Tanner.

"I might have," he said, thinking of how desolate he'd felt only ten minutes ago and how her arrival had chased away his gloom. "But since I've just finished the most excellent cup of coffee from a wonderful machine someone gave me on my birthday, I'm in a very good mood."

He winked, relieved that for now the dark clouds had dissipated from his brain though he knew they'd return when Sophie and her family were gone and he was alone. Again.

Unable to constrain his need to touch her, he reached out to caress her cheek and whispered, "Calm down, Sophie. We're going to help you make this meal amazing. Trust us."

Tanner didn't miss the way her forehead furrowed and

her eyes narrowed at his choice of words. So she still found it hard to trust. Even him? Tanner was going to have to do something about that.

He'd thought about buying her a new stove. But then it occurred to him that Sophie would stop coming to Wranglers so often if she didn't need his kitchen. He wasn't about to end these sweet meetings. He enjoyed having her and the kids here too much.

"Make thinner peelings, please." Meeting his dour look, Sophie explained, "I know exactly how many potatoes I need. If you keep peeling half away I'll run out."

"Yes, ma'am." He saluted then returned to his work. But he couldn't stop watching as she moved around the kitchen, checking on Beth's progress, stirring the pie filling on the stove, encouraging Davy to keep going. "We have to do our best to help your mom make this a fantastic meal, kids."

"Why?" Davy frowned.

"Because this is a dinner for men and women who have worked to protect our country and keep it free," Tanner explained. "Some of them have even been injured, lost arms or legs or they have scars that will never get better."

"Why do they do it if they get hurt?" Beth turned off the mixer and waited for an answer while her mother checked the consistency of the cream.

"They do it so we can live here in peace. They do it so we don't have to fight people who don't like freedom." He watched them process that information.

"I don't know exactly what freedom means," Davy said with a frown. "You mean like we're not slaves or something?"

"Sort of. Freedom means we can live without someone trying to make us do things we don't want to do," he clarified.

"You mean like when Bertie wants me to kiss him and

I don't want to?" Beth's question stopped Sophie in her tracks. She stared at her daughter in shock. Tanner chuckled at Mama Sophie's dismay. She frowned at him so he cleared his throat and continued.

"Yep, sweetheart, sorta like that." He couldn't look at Sophie or he'd start laughing again. "There are some people in the world who don't want us to be able to go to church, or live without someone telling us what to do. Some people want to take what other people have and keep it for themselves."

"Like Josh," Davy said, nodding.

"Who's Josh?" Sophie's voice squeaked. Tanner felt a rush of sympathy. She was probably hearing about these particular issues for the first time and beating herself up that she hadn't known earlier and protected them.

"A kid at school who takes other kids' lunch treats and eats them," Davy replied nonchalantly. "That's why I always ask for two snacks." He grinned at his mother, obviously delighted with his solution.

"Good thinking, buddy," Tanner encouraged because Sophie seemed speechless. "Anyway, veterans are men and women who work so other countries can't take what we have."

"Like our treats you mean?" Beth frowned in confusion.

Tanner had to laugh out loud at that.

"I'll explain later. Okay, honey?" Sophie pressed a kiss against her daughter's hair. "This whipped cream is perfect. Can you chop up some dill for the salad now?"

"Sure." Beth bent over the task cheerfully, her concentration on the herb.

"I think Tanner is trying to say that we can thank these men and women," Sophie corrected with a wink at him, "by giving them a nice meal."

Tanner felt the impact of that wink straight in his midsection. A second later he was swamped by a rush of guilt.

She still thought the abandoning father he'd discussed with her was some unknown friend of his. He hadn't trusted her enough to tell her the truth.

Who was he to preach trust to anyone?

He worked steadily, doing whatever she asked while encouraging the kids in their jobs. Half an hour before the appointed time, Tanner sat in the driver's seat of the van with Sophie beside him.

"Are you sure this is the right way?" She checked a street sign, then her watch for the fifth time. "I'm going to be so late."

"No, you're not. There's the place over there. We came the back way. You need to trust me, Sophie," he teased, then inwardly grimaced. There was that word again.

"Yes, I do," she said. He couldn't move under her steady scrutiny. Finally she broke that stare. "Now if we can get it inside without spilling."

"Puhleeze, woman! Have some faith." Tanner shook his head in mock reproof. He climbed out of the van, took the heavy chafing dish with the beef from her hands and followed her inside the building. He made six more trips with the kids "helping."

In the kitchen, Sophie worked fast. Her two helpers had already arrived and had the beverages under control. Realizing he and the kids were now in her way, Tanner guided the children into the dining room where veterans were taking their places at the tables. He began taking orders for coffee, iced tea and water, including Davy and Beth as he chatted with each vet. Soon the two children were following Tanner's lead, ensuring each person had what he or she needed.

A minister Tanner didn't know said grace, then Sophie and her staff began serving. They worked quickly, Monica and Tiffany emptying the rolling cart as quickly as Sophie filled it. Tanner's admiration for her well-oiled operation grew as a murmur of approval flickered through the room, which now resonated with the delicious aroma of succulent roast beef. Someone invited him, Beth and Davy to sit at a table and moments later Sophie whisked full plates in front of them.

"Aren't you eating?" he asked, realizing a moment later that she wouldn't stop until her job was finished.

She moved through the room like the consummate hostess, refilling plates with a gentle brush to the shoulder, a soft, sweet smile and words he couldn't hear but knew would bring comfort. No one was left out of Sophie's generosity, he noticed, when men and women carried take-out containers. A man across the table said the meals would go to those veterans who couldn't participate in today's ceremony.

As quickly as a veteran's empty plate was removed by Tiffany, Monica replaced it with a towering slice of banana cream pie with whipped topping. Davy's eyes stretched wide when his mother set his pie in front of him though Beth only smiled and said, "Thank you, Mama," before she lifted her fork to sample hers.

When Sophie leaned over Tanner's shoulder, he couldn't help but inhale the fresh citrus scent of her hair as she handed him his pie. She turned her head to look at him and their gazes locked. Her lips were a hairbreadth from his. Tanner had to work hard not to lean slightly to the side and kiss her. As if she knew, she squeezed his shoulder and moved away quickly.

He ate his dessert in a trance, stunned by the depth of his yearning to be close to her, to be the one she turned to every day instead of only during emergencies. Sophie Armstrong was everything he'd ever imagined in a woman: warm, generous, kind, giving.

He was in love with her!

* * *

"You have the best ideas, Tanner." Sophie shifted a little on her comfy lawn chair under the shade of a mesquite tree and inhaled, letting go of the tension that had built up from the veterans' dinner and her stupid stove. "Thank you for helping me this morning and then inviting us to spend this afternoon at Wranglers."

"You're always invited to Wranglers Ranch, Sophie." The warm intimacy in his voice made her feel cherished. "You should take a break more often."

"What about you?" She shook her head. "I saw those three boys show up, heard them ask if they could ride your horses. You seemed to know them."

"Friends of Rod and Trent," he said in what Sophie considered a guarded tone.

"Oh." She pretended to study her pink toenails. "Have you heard any more from Tige?"

"No." He used Davy's squeal as he jumped in the creek to change the subject. "We've had another week of camp fill up. Two more and we'll have the summer filled."

"And you won't charge for any of them?" she asked curiously.

"No. Not unless we're asked to rent. Then I'll request a nominal fee." He smiled. "Don't worry, Sophie. Wranglers is well funded. Even if we weren't, donations have been coming in now that the word is getting out that we're here for all kids."

"Is that primarily Pastor Jeff's doing?" She smiled as Beth dipped one delicate toe in the water. A second later she plunged in, shrieking with delight. Because Tanner didn't answer she turned to glance at him, found him watching her. "Tanner?"

"Partly Jeff's. That street mission work he's doing gives him a lot of contacts with kids who need help. I'm glad he asked me to partner with him on that." He shrugged, then chewed on a stem of grass for a moment. "It's also due in part to Rod and Trent. I guess they talk up Wranglers Ranch quite a bit."

"No wonder. You've been great with them," she praised. "Does that mean you aren't worried about Tige anymore?"

"Not exactly. I don't want him to come here, if that's what you're asking." Why didn't he look at her?

"It isn't." Sophie frowned. "A few weeks ago you were seriously worried about him, though I'm still not clear exactly why. Did he threaten you or something?"

"Tige doesn't threaten."

"Well, something about him bothered you enough to hire that security outfit that now keeps watch on Wranglers." Confused and uncertain, Sophie waited for an explanation. "Yet today you seem almost nonchalant."

"I'm not nonchalant." Tanner's voice tightened. "The security guys haven't seen or heard anything and there haven't been any other incidents. Since kids are coming here, which is what I wanted, I'm trying to focus on what I'm here to do and leave Tige up to God."

"Yes, but—" Nervous about her burgeoning feelings for Tanner but hesitant to reveal them when he seemed to be distancing himself, Sophie finally asked the question that had been plaguing her. "Did you have a girlfriend when you lived on the streets?"

Tanner's head jerked toward her. His face tightened into a mask Sophie had seen only once before, for a few moments the morning after the fire.

"Why do you ask that?" he growled.

"Because you never talk about your past. I've told you all kinds of things about Marty and my past life," Sophie snapped, irritated that this sense of foreboding still troubled her. "But I know almost nothing about yours."

"There's nothing to know." Tanner smiled at her, but it wasn't his usual open smile. This one hid shadows in the back of his rich green eyes. The ball Davy and Beth had been throwing rolled toward him. As if relieved, he jumped to his feet to retrieve it. "I'm going to throw them a few," he said and walked away.

Sophie was about to nod but since he wasn't looking at her she clamped her lips shut, frustrated by the barrier that had seemed to come between them. Tanner laughed and joked with her children while she sat stewing about his attitude and lack of forthrightness. She yearned to be part of the fun the others were having but she couldn't settle. She wanted to trust Tanner was everything he seemed to be.

But what if she trusted him and he betrayed her?

Questions about Tanner and his past tormented Sophie until finally she rose and walked toward a gray-barked sycamore tree near their horses. She admired the beautifully arched white branches loaded with large star-shaped leaves before lifting down the knapsack she'd packed earlier. She took out a thermos of coffee and poured herself a cup.

And froze.

There on the ground, where Tanner had been sitting just a minute earlier, lay a picture. Sophie bent, picked it up and swallowed hard. It was a copy of an ultrasound picture of an unborn child.

Tanner's child?

Her knees buckled at the thought. Clutching her coffee, she sank onto a sun-warmed rock, unable to get past that thought. She sipped her black coffee, willing her hands to move, her brain to work, her thoughts to organize.

Sophie had no idea how much time had passed when she heard the kids' voices coming closer. Without even thinking she slipped the picture into the pocket of her capris not knowing why, only aware that she needed time to make sense of her suddenly tilting world.

"We're ready for a snack," Tanner said, his usual tone in place. Then he frowned at her. "Sophie?"

"Yes. A snack." She dredged up a smile while suppressing the urge to scream *traitor*. After all, she didn't know anything about this picture yet. "Good thing I packed some cookies."

"Are you all right?" His voice couldn't have been more caring nor could the hand he placed on her shoulder have been more tender. "Don't you feel well?"

"Actually I don't. I think I'll sit here and relax with my coffee while you guys have your snack." She returned to her former seat, away from his touch, his voice and those all-seeing eyes. "I'll be fine," she assured him when he kept watching her.

Of course she would be. She had to be.

Because if there was one lesson Sophie had learned it was self-reliance. But while she maintained her stoic face, her heart cried,

Whom do I trust now, God?

"There's something wrong so you might as well tell me what it is." Tanner sat on Sophie's lumpy sofa and waited for the ax to fall. "The kids are in bed, probably sleeping, and you don't have a job scheduled for tomorrow so you have no excuse to keep you from telling me what it is."

Sophie said nothing, simply reached into her pocket and slid something out. She set it on the coffee table in front of him. "You dropped this when we were at the creek."

Tanner knew she wouldn't ask him about the photo. She wanted to. He could see the questions filling her dark eyes. But she'd asked him about his past so often and he'd always rebuffed her. He knew she wouldn't ask again.

Explaining was the very last thing he wanted to do. But for ages he'd been telling her to trust. Now it was his turn to trust her—with the truth.

"The picture is of my son. He died before he was ever born."

Sophie caught her breath but gave no other visible sign that she was affected.

"I have to start at the beginning, okay?" When she nodded, he sighed. "Remember the friend I asked you about, the one who walked away from his pregnant girlfriend?" Her eyes flared and he nodded. "It was me. Her name was Amy and the day Burt invited me to live with him she'd just told me she was pregnant."

"But how— When…?" Sophie's lips pinched together. She sat back and waited.

"I know what I did was wrong. I know I should have taken care of her, at least made sure she was all right. I had a responsibility and I dodged it, ran away to a world I'd only ever dreamed about." Tanner could tell by her expression that Sophie was horrified. "I should have been there for Amy and I wasn't. I will always be ashamed of that."

"Why did you do it?" she whispered.

"I don't know if you can understand how unbelievable Burt's offer was to me." Even now Tanner was amazed that he of all people had been selected to live at Wranglers. "I'd been on the street for three months. I was scared, hungry, alone and going nowhere fast. I knew that if I stayed on the streets it wouldn't be long before Tige would convince me to start using. I knew I'd end up exactly like him if I did."

"Burt?"

"He said I'd have a home. I'd never had that, Sophie. Not a home of my own. He said I wouldn't be hungry, that he'd teach me how to work with horses. I was a mess with people," he joked but found no corresponding mirth on her face. "But I got along real good with his horses. Maybe because we both just want someone to love us." Admitting that was embarrassing.

"I see." Sophie frowned. "What did Burt say about Amy?"

"I didn't tell him." Tanner hung his head. "I didn't

think—no, I *knew* he wouldn't let me go with him if he knew about her and the baby. He'd been taking me out for lunch, to church, to the ranch—stuff I'd only ever dreamed of. He had a house, a place where he could be his own boss, and I knew from his church talk that he would never beat me."

"So you accepted." She said it as if she'd expected nothing more.

"No. I refused at first. But when I told Amy she told me to go. She was in love with another guy by then. She didn't want anything to do with me anymore. I figured it was the same old, same old. Nobody cared what Tanner Johns did." He studied her, praying, hoping she could understand his desperation.

But all Sophie said was "Go on," in that crisp, cool voice that was not the real Sophie, not the woman he'd come to care about.

"So I thought why not take what Burt was offering. Nobody would care. I could finish school and most of all, I could get away from Tige. So I gave Amy every cent I had, all two hundred dollars." He smiled, remembering how massive that sum had seemed. "And I walked away, all the way to Wranglers Ranch. And I'm still here."

"But—didn't it bother you?" Sophie wanted to know.

"Every day and every night," Tanner told her honestly. "I'd think about that baby, wonder when his birthday was, if he could walk or talk, what color his eyes were, if he was all right. I was desperate to know about my child. So one day I went back to find out." He stopped, the memory still powerful enough to catch his breath.

"And?"

"Tige told me Amy was gone. That's when I knew I'd lost any chance I ever had to have the family I'd always wanted." Tanner sat in silent shame.

He wasn't going to tell her that Tige had beaten him within an inch of his life because he wouldn't sell his drugs. He wasn't going to mention that he'd lain in pain under a sheet of cardboard for two days, until Burt had found him and taken him to the hospital. He sure wasn't going to tell her how hard it now was to keep going back to those awful streets, to keep some other kid from being as stupid as he'd been.

"I'm sorry, Tanner. No wonder you didn't want to talk about it," Sophie said in a very quiet voice.

"I'd talk about it nonstop if it meant he could have lived." He rose and picked up the picture, let his forefinger trail over the face he now loved. "It should have been me who died. I deserved it. Not him."

"I'm so sorry, Tanner." Her hand touched his shoulder in the briefest caress.

Tanner turned into her arms, desperate to find—what? Solace? Forgiveness? Love?

Sophie hesitated, patted his shoulder and then when he would have drawn her close, eased free and moved four feet away.

"I'm truly sorry, Tanner. But I'm glad you told me. You needed to tell someone, to let out the pain."

"I guess." He slid the picture into his pocket without taking his gaze from her. His heart sank. Sophie looked as if she was waiting. For him to leave?

As he studied her stiff figure he knew immediately that whatever she'd felt, or whatever he'd hoped she'd feel, was now gone. Sophie didn't trust easily. In her eyes, by leaving Amy, he'd betrayed in the worst possible way.

"I'd better go. See you soon?" He hoped.

"I'll be busy for the next few weeks," she said quickly. Too quickly. "But I'm catering your Independence Day celebration, remember? I think the kids are really looking forward to it."

"Yeah." So now they were employer and employee? "Sophie—"

"I'm really tired, Tanner. I'd like to get some rest. But thank you for today."

"Yeah. Sure." He walked to the door, took his hat off the hook and glanced around one last time. Something inside him died as he realized he wouldn't be coming back here again. Sophie didn't want a man she couldn't trust in her life.

Now she stood holding the door open, waiting to escort him out of her world.

Tanner walked forward. But he stopped on the threshold and, without pausing to think, did the only thing he could. He leaned forward and kissed Sophie Armstrong the way he'd always wanted to.

And to his utter amazement and joy, Sophie kissed him back the way he wanted to be kissed, as if he was precious, wanted. It was as if something stronger than either of them pushed them to break through the barriers they'd put up to protect their inner selves.

Against what? Against this powerful, heartrending certainty that no one could ever mean so much?

Tanner's arms tightened around the woman whose smile could make his day. Feeling Sophie's heart beat against his answered every question about what was important in his life. He'd never been happier than he was right now.

But Sophie wasn't his. By withholding the truth he'd lost her trust.

With regret dragging at him he loosed his arms and stepped back. He smoothed the tears from her cheeks, brushed her shiny brown hair from her eyes and traced her wonderful lips with one lingering caress.

"Goodbye, Sophie."

Then Tanner walked out the door to a future guaranteed to be the same as his past.

Alone.

Chapter Eleven

"Why doesn't Mr. Cowboy come here anymore, Mama?"

Sophie had been waiting for the question. Truthfully she hadn't expected Beth to wait more than a month before asking.

"Yeah," Davy chimed in. "How come we don't go to Wranglers Ranch anymore?"

"You still go, Davy," Sophie reminded him. "You work there two days a week."

"But that's work. School's been out for ages but I don't get to do fun things with Tanner anymore," her son protested.

"Tanner's busy. He has camps going for other kids. He doesn't have time to play with you." She pressed toothpicks with little flags on top into each cupcake. "Anyway, we are going to Wranglers today."

"Just to deliver food. Then you'll make up an excuse why we have to leave. Again." Davy's glowering face said he understood exactly what she was doing.

"I like Mr. Cowboy," Beth said quietly, favoring her mother with an intense stare.

"So do I." *Way too much for my own good.* "And for your information we're going to be at Wranglers Ranch until late tonight." Suppressing the bubble of joy inside her that matched her children's grins, Sophie said, "We're going to leave in twenty minutes. Please straighten your rooms and make your beds before we leave."

"Why? Who's going to see them?" Davy grumbled, pushing away from the breakfast table. "Nobody ever comes to this boring place."

"Boring," Beth added before she scooted off to her room.

Sophie couldn't argue with the truth. Without Tanner life *was* dull. But that was the way it had to be. She'd made that decision after he'd told her about his unborn child. Though it had been painfully clear that Tanner regretted his actions and though Sophie accepted that he'd been very young to make such a momentous decision, she'd realized that she didn't really know Tanner enough to trust him. Even now she couldn't get past her disappointment in his selfish actions. As she'd listened to his explanations with her heart aching for his loss, she'd accepted that he deeply mourned losing the son he clearly now longed for.

But accompanied by her empathy was the memory of her own suffering as a single mom, alone, desperate, terrified she'd fail her kids because Marty hadn't provided for them. His selfish decisions had cost her dearly. Still did. Even though Wranglers had boosted her income, even though Tanner had touted her skills so that she could now pick and choose jobs, Sophie still worried. What if, God forbid, something happened to her?

Sophie couldn't afford to love Tanner, though that didn't stop her heart from wanting his arms around her, or end her yearning for him to kiss her as he had. So she'd distanced herself by being brisk and businesslike and avoiding any chance of intimacy between them. Apparently Tanner felt the same because though he was always unfailingly polite and welcoming when she had a job at Wranglers or when he saw them at church, he no longer came to her house, teased her or made those affectionate gestures she'd come to cherish.

Sophie had contemplated walking away from her commitments to Wranglers and Tanner. But she couldn't do it, and not just because she'd spent the deposit he'd given her for Wranglers' Fourth of July party. Davy adored the skateboard she'd bought for his birthday, and the new stove in her kitchen was a necessity. But the real reason she hadn't canceled was because she couldn't bear to disappoint Tanner. Because he'd been disappointed too many times already. No matter how hard she tried to be cool and calculating, Sophie couldn't get rid of the strong love she felt for the rancher.

She was mad at God for that. How could He have let her fall for the wrong man again, and not just the wrong man but one her children adored? God had let their lives become intertwined with the ranch so much that this break with Tanner was causing her kids pain. That was the last thing she wanted and it only reinforced her feelings of distrust.

So Sophie slowly distanced herself from Wranglers, hoping Beth and Davy would find other things to fill their world. Clearly that wasn't working. Why oh why had God let this happen?

Stuffing down her yearning for things to go back the way they were, Sophie mocked herself. Pretending Tanner hadn't abandoned his girlfriend, and being with a man she couldn't trust was not the answer. Self-sufficiency was.

With a sigh for the trust that still eluded her, Sophie packed up the containers she'd filled with lunch goodies for the church-sponsored trail ride at Wranglers and tonight's barbecue, loaded the kids and drove to her job site. She would keep her word, provide food for today's party as she'd agreed. But once her Fourth of July commitment was complete, Sophie wasn't going back to Wranglers. Better to make a clean break. Davy and Beth would just have to deal with it.

"Hello, Mrs. Armstrong." The security guard nodded at the kids and waved her through onto Wranglers Ranch. That interaction combined with the sight of a new metal gate closing as she drove to the house gave Sophie a moment of anxiety, but she brushed it away. It had been weeks now and Tige hadn't made an appearance. Tanner was simply being cautious.

"Hey, Sophie. How are you?" The object of her thoughts opened her van door.

"I'm fine." Tanner looked gaunt, she thought. As if he wasn't sleeping well. Because of her? A trickle of guilt filtered through her but she ignored it and handed Beth and Davy items to carry inside.

"We'll have a hungry bunch of cowpokes today," Tanner said. He took the largest bin from her and indicated she should pile another on it.

"I have plenty of food," she told him, walking into the kitchen and hoping he wouldn't linger. Having him so near made her want things that could not be.

"And extra?" he asked quietly. "Tige's kids showed up with some friends."

"There will be enough for everyone." She glanced out the window. "The ranch looks very busy."

"It is." Tanner frowned. "We have so many coming every day. The day camps aren't enough. Originally I'd planned to build cabins so we could do overnighters but..." He leaned back on his heels without finishing his sentence.

"But?" she prodded. "That's not possible now?" she asked after nodding permission for Davy and Beth to go check on the rabbits.

"It's possible," he said quietly. "I'm just not sure how to go about it. I'm no builder."

"Can't you hire someone?" Sophie mixed the lemonade and added ice from his fridge.

"If I could find an architect with the right vision." He

met her gaze and shrugged. "I want a certain type of cabin that doesn't look out of place."

"I'm sorry," she murmured sympathetically while keeping her head averted, hoping, no, praying he would leave.

"Sophie, is everything okay?" There was a hesitancy to Tanner's question that told her he felt the chill she was sending his way.

"The food will be prepared and served as you requested." She couldn't help the stiffness in her voice. Hadn't she come through often enough for Tanner that he should know better than to question her? Why didn't he trust her?

As you trust him?

"Just checking." His slow, lazy smile reappeared for an instant, then dissolved when she didn't return it. "I'll leave you to it, then. Let me know if you need anything."

"Uh-huh." Sophie watched him go. If only... "Tanner?"

"Yes?" His green eyes lit up and his whole body language showed expectancy. Of what? Did he think she'd change her mind?

"Tige?" The light in his eyes died.

"Haven't heard from him." He clamped his Stetson on his head and walked to the door. "See you later."

Not if she could avoid it, Sophie thought, watching him stride across the yard with a longing she couldn't suppress. *Why did You let me love him, God?* her heart wept.

Trust in the Lord with all your heart and lean not unto your own understanding. In all your ways acknowledge Him and He will direct your paths.

Trust. It always came down to that. And, as usual, she couldn't do that. Couldn't trust Tanner. Couldn't trust God.

I'm scared to, she admitted silently. *Help me?*

"Sophie?" Monica studied her with a perplexed look. "I asked if you wanted Tiffany and me to start buttering buns."

"Yes, please," Sophie said in an effort to pretend everything was normal, which it so was not. Nothing had been normal since the day she'd met Tanner. And probably wouldn't be again unless she could get rid of this overpowering love for him. "I'm glad you're here early, girls. It's going to be a busy day. Happy Fourth of July."

Now get to work, Sophie, and forget Tanner Johns.

"Nice work with the decor, Moses." Tanner admired the array of banners and flags that decorated the ranch. "Wranglers is looking mighty festive."

"Thanks." The old man didn't look at him as he dug a stone out of Abishag's shoe. "We've got two lame horses but the others are good to go."

"We're going to need every one. The place is crawling with kids just waiting to get on a horse. Where's Lefty?" Tanner asked after he'd found nothing among their tack that needed repair.

"He and Bo took some beginners out for a short trial ride to test their skills. They'll be back in five." Moses's frown told Tanner he had something on his mind. "I been praying about those boys, Trent and the other one."

"Rod," Tanner supplied. "Why? Something wrong?"

"Don't rightly know," Moses admitted, scratching his head. "They seemed real worried when they were here yesterday. The bigger kid had a mess of bruises on his arm."

Tanner forced down a rush of anger. "It happens" was all he said.

"Yeah. Too often." Moses frowned. "They said they needed to tell you something but you were on that ride and they couldn't wait."

"I'll talk to them today, if they show up," Tanner promised.

"You talk to Sophie?" Moses lifted one bushy brow when Tanner frowned at him.

"About what?"

"Dunno," the old man said somberly. "Just seems to

me you two got some sorting out to do like maybe that girl you walked out on before you came here." Moses patted Abishag's side. "The one who was going to have your baby?"

Tanner gaped. "You knew?"

"'Course." Moses nodded. "Burt told me."

"Burt?" His face burned with shame. "I never told him about Amy or the baby."

"Didn't need to. Burt had a way of findin' things out." Moses smiled. "Smart old coot, that man. Kinda like me." He wheezed a laugh at Tanner's surprised face. "Burt an' me only look gullible, son."

"Yes, but—" Tanner couldn't get it to sink in. "Burt knew everything?"

"Pretty much. He found the girl, gave her some money and kept sending more every month after her new boyfriend dumped her." Moses stared off into the distance. "Even paid for a grave and a marker when your baby died so as you'd be able to mourn proper. Guess he forgot to tell you that part, but ol' Burt sure did love you, Tanner."

The private investigator he'd hired had said nothing about a grave. "I wish Burt had told me," he muttered.

"Reckon he was waiting for you to speak first." Moses slapped on his hat. "Wouldn't have made any difference anyway, would it?"

"Yes." Tanner unclenched his tense. "If I'd known where Amy was I might have apologized to her, tried to make it up to her or something." He met Moses's stare. "I should never have let her go like that knowing she was pregnant with my child."

"No," Moses agreed. "That wasn't right. I'm guessing your lady knows?" He lifted one of his bushy brows.

Tanner nodded and explained about the investigator he'd hired.

"Somehow he got hold a copy of the baby's ultrasound

from the hospital. I dropped it and Sophie found it. I had to tell her the truth when she asked," he muttered, embarrassed and yet relieved to tell Moses. "After hearing that, Sophie changed. She thinks she can't trust me, that I'd leave her and the kids vulnerable."

"Would you?" Moses studied Tanner with narrowed eyes.

"Never. I love Sophie. This past month has been agony. To see her yet feel that icy barrier between us—" Tanner squeezed his eyes closed against the pain. "She avoids me, makes excuses not to come here or sneaks away when I am."

"I know," Moses said. "Her boy told me she's not happy."

"Maybe that's why I can't make more headway with my plans for Wranglers. Maybe God can't use somebody who's messed up as much as I have." He stared at his dusty boots. "I always wanted a family, you know that. But that's not going to happen because I've made too many mistakes. I probably wouldn't make a good father anyway."

"Hogwash! Burt wouldn't have let it pass so neither will I," Moses chided. "God forgives. That's the very basis of our faith. We're human. We mess up. And God forgives."

"Yes." Tanner thought it through, then nodded. "But even so, I'm not doing what Burt wanted with this place. He had a heart for street kids and we haven't focused on only them. I can't make Wranglers into the kind of camp he envisioned."

"Burt was the best friend I ever had but he wasn't God. You gotta focus on figuring out what *God* wants you to do," Moses insisted. "Burt would have told you that God's your boss so you do what He's telling you to do."

"I'm not sure I know how," he admitted.

"You do, boy." Moses sounded just as stubborn as he had the day Tanner said he couldn't learn to ride. "The good Lord gave you talents to do what He needs done."

"We're back to that verse again, huh?" Tanner sighed. "The 'fan your gift into flame' one? But I don't have a gift, Moses. I'm just a plain ordinary cowboy."

"Ain't no such thing, son," Moses said in a dry mocking tone. "But you surely have been gifted."

"With what?" Tanner demanded. "And how do you and Sophie know when I don't?"

"Always thought she was a smart lady." Moses slapped him on the shoulder. "Don't you get it? You have the gift of leadership. Burt watched how the hands just naturally turned to you. They saw you as their leader when he wasn't there. After Burt died they knew they could count on you to keep the place rolling, to keep their jobs. You have a knack for getting folks to work together and that helps them give their best. Never knew anybody as good at getting folks to pitch in. Folks like that nice lady and her kids."

"Sophie won't be coming around to help much anymore," Tanner assured him gloomily.

"God told you that, did He?" Moses sniffed. "Don't matter what you think. God's got His reasons for bringing her here. He's got it all planned out."

"So what am I supposed to do?" Frustration made his voice sharp. "Hang around when I'm not wanted?"

"You be there in case she needs you." Moses glared at him. "You love this woman and her kids? Or are you scared of loving somebody like her, somebody who wants more from a man than just words? She doesn't need some guy who won't stick by her. She's got two kids to raise. You up for that?"

"Yes! I love her," Tanner almost yelled, irritated by Moses's pushing.

"Then prove it. Be there for her. Let God work out the rest." Moses grinned. "He brought you together. He can figure the rest out, too."

Tanner swallowed, humbled by the old man's faith. Moses trusted God. Tanner needed to do the same.

"Here comes Lefty. I gotta go help him." Moses leaned over to peer into Tanner's face. "Didn't upset you, did I, son?"

"I'll survive—"

"Mr. Cowboy!" Beth's voice echoed in the warm air.

"Since you think leadership is my gift, guess I better get on with directing this show." He couldn't quite believe that. Not yet anyway. "Thanks, Moses."

"You bet. Just keep your eyes on God and remember, Burt didn't choose no dummy." Cackling with laughter, Moses shuffled away.

Tanner forced the door of his brain to close on the thousands of questions that rippled through his head so he could deal with Beth's escaped rabbits.

I don't know if all Moses said was true, he prayed as he worked. *But I know I haven't trusted You enough. So I'm leaving Sophie and our relationship up to You. Please help her learn to trust me.*

Having turned over the woman he loved to the One who loved her even more than he did, and because he couldn't stay away, Tanner walked purposefully toward the kitchen with Beth to find out if the cook needed his help.

From now on Sophie Armstrong was going to find it hard to get rid of this cowboy.

Chapter Twelve

With the Independence Day party in full swing, Sophie hated to take a midafternoon break but she couldn't argue with the boss, especially when he was sitting on the bench right next to her.

"I meant to tell you." Desperate to distance herself, Sophie inched away from Tanner's big body. "Edna said to thank you for the flowers and for fixing her leaky faucet last week." She pinned him with her severest gaze. "Apparently you also helped Davy fix our coffee table and repaste the living room wallpaper."

"Edna and I were having coffee while she was watching your kids and Davy mentioned there were issues so…" He shrugged as if the chores were inconsequential. "No biggie."

"Well, thank you from her and from us." She hesitated to continue, to end things between them.

"Thanks but don't come around anymore?" Tanner chuckled at her expression. "I know you'd prefer that, Sophie. You've found me wanting in the responsibility department. And you should. I made a bad mistake ten years ago."

"Tanner—"

"But that was ten years ago," he reminded quietly. "I'm

not that dumb kid anymore. I've changed and I intend to prove it to you. You're not going to get rid of me." He leaned closer and covered her hand with his. "I love you, Sophie. I'm sorry if that isn't what you want to hear but it's the truth and I'll keep saying it until you start to trust me."

"I don't know if that's ever going to happen—"

"Sophie, we're out of lemonade." Tiffany waited for instruction.

Frustrated by her interruption at this most inopportune moment, Sophie rose, desperate to make Tanner understand that she wasn't going to change her mind and that he couldn't keep hanging around, waiting for that. It couldn't happen because having Tanner near made Sophie want things she couldn't have. She huffed a sigh of resignation and went to deal with the issue.

More kids arrived as afternoon turned to evening and each time Sophie needed something it seemed Tanner was there just in time to lend a hand, offer a suggestion or simply encourage her with generous praise. But by the time her barbecue supper was over Sophie began to lag. Somehow Tanner noticed that, too, and insisted she sit down with Davy and Beth, who'd been having a ball, Beth in the bouncy castle and Davy running errands for the hands who were kept busy with would-be riders.

"It's a really fun party, Tanner," Davy enthused. "I sure like making Moses's campfire pies."

Sophie made a face. All the food she'd prepared and her son preferred two slices of white bread with canned pie filling, cooked in a metal tin over the fire!

"I like these cookies your mother made." Tanner deliberately bumped his shoulder against hers, smiled when she drew away and crunched on his third cookie.

His smile warmed Sophie from the top of her head to the tips of her toes and finished in a warm fuzzy glow that made her want to snuggle against his side. Why did she care for him so much? She didn't want to, didn't want to risk what caring could mean—risking her security to trust in a guy who'd already proved untrustworthy seemed foolish in the extreme.

And so wonderfully alluring.

"What do you like best, Beth?" Tanner asked.

"I like people to be happy." Beth studied him. "Do you think this is what heaven is like, Mr. Cowboy?"

"Like Wranglers Ranch?" Seeing she was utterly serious, Tanner smothered his laughter. "Maybe."

"I like it when people are happy," she said with a frown. "I don't like arguing and fighting."

"Did you see someone fighting, Beth?" Sophie saw Tanner's immediate alertness. "Or arguing?" he added.

"Uh-huh." Her daughter's blue eyes darkened. Sophie was about to ask what troubled Beth when Tanner touched her arm and gave the slightest shake of his head. So she left it to him to probe further.

"Can you tell me about it?" His voice was so gentle.

"I didn't hear very much," Beth said. Sophie's concern escalated when her daughter glanced over one shoulder worriedly.

"It's okay, sweetheart," Tanner said in a very tender voice. "Just tell me what you did hear."

After studying him for a moment, Beth finally whispered, "It wasn't a nice voice."

"Was it a man speaking?" Tanner asked. Beth nodded. "What did he say?"

"Today's the day." She waited, her blue gaze riveted on Tanner.

"But sweetie, that's not fighting or arguing," Sophie chided.

"That was the other voice."

"What did it say?" Davy wanted to know.

Beth bit her lip. She looked to Sophie for reassurance. Sophie nodded and squeezed her hand.

"Tanner can't help unless you tell him, Bethy."

"He said, 'Tanner won't like it. You'll have to hurt him.'" Her voice cracked. "Are you gonna get hurt, Mr. Cowboy?" Tears spilled down her cheeks. "I don't want you to be hurt. I love you."

"I love you, too, Beth." Tanner lifted Beth onto his knee and hugged her in his strong, capable arms.

Sophie gulped, blinking away the rush of her own tears. Seeing the big tough rancher comfort her troubled, confused daughter brought a swell of love for him that she was helpless to stop. Again the questions rolled through her brain.

What if she trusted him with her love? Tanner had stuck with her, pitching in when he didn't have to. He'd taken care of her kids as well as any father could. Other than not telling her about his past he'd been totally up-front and a lot more than a good friend. What if she let herself accept everything he was offering her? What if she took a chance that Tanner Johns loved her enough to stick by her, no matter what?

What if she was wrong?

"You don't have to be afraid, Bethy," he said lovingly, brushing away her bangs to press a kiss against her forehead. "We have God caring for us, remember? Can you think of a verse that says that? How about, 'If God be for us, who can be against us?'"

"I have one, too." With the shadows chased away, Beth's blue eyes shone. "'Therefore I will not fear.'"

"That's a very good verse to remember, Beth." Tanner hugged her but his eyes narrowed as they met Sophie's. "Let's pray and ask God to keep everyone safe and happy today." He bowed his head and offered a short prayer that all visitors to the ranch today would learn more about God.

Then he gazed at her, his green eyes filled with tenderness. "And God, help us learn to trust."

Sophie's face burned with shame. Why couldn't she trust him? Everyone else seemed to. Thankfully Tanner didn't seem to notice her embarrassment since Lefty walked over and murmured something in his ear. Sophie heard the word *security* but little else. Then Lefty, grim-faced, stepped back.

"Okay, kids. When do you think we should cut that massive red, white and blue cake your mother ma—"

"Well, well. Isn't this a special family gathering? Hello, Tanner old buddy."

Tige. Sophie knew it immediately and cringed. Beside her, Beth snuggled against her and whispered, "Therefore I will not fear."

"Hey, Tige. Welcome here." Other than a slight narrowing of his eyes, Tanner showed no visible sign that he was annoyed by the man's arrival as he shook hands. "Glad you could come." His voice tightened a fraction when he said, "Hello, Amy."

Amy? As in Amy the mother of Tanner's son? Sophie's stomach dropped as fear took hold.

"Tanner." An apologetic look washed over Amy's thin, pale face. "I didn't want to come—"

"Why not? Everyone is invited to Wranglers Ranch's Fourth of July party, right, Tanner?" A cunning look filled Tige's golden eyes. "'Least that's what *my* sons told me."

The emphasis wasn't lost on Sophie and she'd doubted Tanner had missed it, either.

"Your sons are right." Tanner seemed nonchalant. "You're welcome here, Amy." He smiled warmly. "This is Sophie and her children, Beth and Davy."

"Nice to meet you," Sophie replied automatically in as friendly a tone as she could manage, taking her cue from Tanner.

"You, too," Amy said halfheartedly, barely glancing at her.

"Lulu sends her regrets. She's, uh, indisposed." Tige cackled, an evil sound that made Sophie shiver.

"I'm sorry to hear that. Would you like something to eat? Sophie's an excellent cook." Tanner didn't rise to the bait when Tige asked for whiskey. "Sorry. This is a ranch for kids. We don't keep alcohol here."

Lefty stood nearby watching so Tanner asked him to bring Tige and Amy coffee.

"The boys say this little lady makes some good pie. I could use a piece of that," Tige muttered after he'd taken a sip of black coffee.

"We don't have pie today but I made a big Independence Day cake," Sophie offered. "Want some of that?"

"Sure." Tige studied her. "So you're Tanner's new Amy."

"No, I'm the cook at Wranglers Ranch," Sophie said evenly. "Would you like to see the kitchen?" She aimed her question at Amy, who nodded eagerly.

"I've got some jobs for these guys." Lefty beckoned to Beth and Davy. He shot a look at Tanner, who gave a barely perceptible nod. "Come on, guys."

Clearly they'd worked this out beforehand. Sophie felt a rush of pure love for the big rancher's forethought in protecting her kids. She wanted them far away from Tige. She led Amy into the house.

"It's a wonderful kitchen to work in—" Sophie paused when Amy laid a hand on her arm.

"I'm sorry we butted in," she said quietly. "I only agreed to come because I owe Tanner an apology about the baby." She paused, frowned. "You know about that?"

Sophie nodded.

"I took off back then because I knew Tanner would have made me quit using and in those days all I wanted was my next fix," Amy admitted shamefacedly.

"I see."

"Tanner was always trying to help. He's the only guy I ever knew who stood up to Tige. I'm glad he got out." She waved a hand. "This place, this ranch, it suits him. My husband says Tanner's place is making a big difference to the city's youth."

"You're married?" Sophie said, surprised.

"To a cop. Can you believe it?" Amy laughed. "My husband suggested I agree to come with Tige. He said it was time I told Tanner the truth about the baby. But I think he already knows." She frowned. "Anyway after Tanner left with the old man, Tige said he came back to look for me." She frowned. "You knew that, too? Bet you didn't know Tige beat him so badly he almost killed him. Well, he did. You see, Tige was furious. He had lost control of Tanner and he didn't like that. Anyway I'd told Tanner I loved somebody else and that I was going away with him. And Tanner, being Tanner, gave me every dime he owned and wished me the best."

"But he should have helped you," Sophie protested. "He shouldn't have just walked away and left you to manage."

"It wasn't Tanner who left, Sophie. It was me. And with Tige's help I made sure he couldn't find me when that conscience of his took over." Amy shook her head. "To this day I don't know how God can love somebody as mixed up as I was. For a while I didn't believe He did. I guess I should explain."

"You don't have to," Sophie murmured.

"It would help, though, wouldn't it?" Amy nodded. "Because you're in love with him."

"I—"

"Tanner's one of those guys who deserves love. I wish I'd loved him back then but I couldn't even love myself."

"You weren't in love with Tanner?" Surprised, Sophie watched regret fill her face.

"I wish I had. But Tanner was only ever a safe place for me, a refuge from Tige's and Lulu's rages. That's why I latched on to him. I never once thought about what Tanner needed," she admitted. "Falling in love with my husband taught me that love isn't about yourself. It's all about the one you love, protecting them, trusting them. Even now I still struggle with trusting that Jack only wants what's best for me."

"How did you learn to trust?" Achingly aware that she craved this woman's confidence in Tanner's trustworthiness, Sophie paid attention.

"Ever seen that demonstration where a person closes his eyes and lets himself fall backward, trusting his loved ones to catch him?" Amy chuckled at Sophie's dark look. "Sounds horrifying, doesn't it? But that's kind of what you have to do. You can't have a relationship if you're always waiting for the other person to fail you. Because they will. Humans fail. If you put your trust in God, though, He never fails."

"Telling secrets, Amy?" Tige leaned in the doorway.

"Actually we were talking about her husband." Sophie stared at the bleary-eyed man, despising the smug look in his eyes. "Sounds like he's one of the good guys. Like Tanner." She wanted to escape Tige. "Since you're here at Wranglers Ranch maybe you'd like to go for a short trail ride, Amy? Or there's a walkabout trail."

"Trail ride sounds good. Would you show me where to go?"

Sophie was about to point until she realized the other woman had something else to say.

"I'll show you the way." She led Amy outside. When they were no longer visible from the house, Amy stopped her.

"This is far enough, thanks. That's my husband over there standing by the tree. The big guy with the green shirt," Amy said, love filling her voice. "He wouldn't let me come without him and now he's taking me home but I wanted to warn you first."

"Warn me?" A tickle of breeze made Sophie shiver though the evening was warm. "About what?"

"Lulu is here somewhere, and she and Tige are planning something." Amy's eyes darkened. "I don't know what but I know it isn't good. Tige has always resented that Tanner got off the streets, that he never got hooked, that Tige couldn't control him." Her lips tightened. "When Tige found out that his sons have been coming here, he was furious. He thinks Tanner is trying to take them away from him. Be very careful. Tige's dangerous and when he needs a fix he'll do anything to get it. He needs one now." She squeezed Sophie's hand. "Take care of Tanner, okay? You'll never meet a man you can trust more."

This from the woman whom Tanner had abandoned? Or had he?

Sophie was no longer so sure.

"I have to go."

A moment later Amy and her husband blended into the crowd, then disappeared, leaving Sophie bewildered and confused. She walked slowly, thinking about what Amy had said. After ensuring the kids were still safe with Lefty at the barn, Sophie was about to slip into the kitchen when she heard Tige's voice.

"So this place is all yours?"

"Burt, the owner, wanted the ranch turned into a kids' camp." Sophie could hear Tanner's hesitation and knew he didn't want to reveal too much.

"But you're in charge, right?" Tige pressed. "You're the boss here?"

"I guess." Sophie had a clear mental image of Tanner shrugging, as if being in charge meant little.

"Man, a place like this must be worth a fortune."

When Tanner didn't respond Sophie stepped around the corner to rescue him.

"Oh, you're still here, Tanner. Good. Can you help me in the kitchen, please?"

"Sure." He rose to his lanky height. "You hanging around for the fireworks, Tige?"

"Me, I love fireworks. Of course I'm staying," he said in a sly tone. The noise Tige made was not a laugh. "Hey, where's Amy?" he asked, suddenly sobering.

"Oh, she wanted to try her hand at our dart game," Sophie said breezily. "Maybe you would, too. There's a nice prize for the winner."

"Is there, now? A nice prize." Tige began to walk away but then paused to toss a "See you later, Tanner" over one shoulder. He grinned, his half-rotten teeth giving him a ghoulish look. "You can count on that, buddy. You owe me and I always collect on my debts."

As Tige walked away, laughing crazily, Sophie watched Tanner. She blinked when the handsome cowboy suddenly drew her into the shadows, into his arms and held her fast.

"Tanner, what are you—"

She couldn't say another word because Tanner Johns was kissing her as if she was the only thing that mattered in his world. And there under the whispering mesquite trees, Sophie kissed him back because she couldn't help herself.

She loved Tanner Johns.

Chapter Thirteen

"Oh, Sophie. I was so scared Tige would try something. I couldn't bear for you to be hurt because of me."

Tanner bent his head, unable to stop himself from embracing the woman who filled his world with joy, reveling in the way her lips responded to his, taking and giving. This woman, this special woman, was so dear. He couldn't help but reveal his deepest longing—to have her stay in his world as she'd stayed in his heart for so long.

"I love you, Sophie. I love you so much."

He bent his head to tell her without using more words how much she meant to him. To his delight her arms lifted and slid around his neck and she kissed him back with so much passion his heart sang with joy. When she finally drew away to catch her breath, he lovingly traced the delicate curve of her jaw, the graceful arch of her neck, only to home in once more on her lips.

"I love you, Sophie."

And then the dream ended.

Sophie pulled free of his embrace. "I'm sorry, but I can't love you, Tanner."

"Can't or won't?" he demanded. "After all this time, after everything we've shared, you're still afraid to trust me?"

Her nod killed every hope he'd clung to. He turned

away, unable to stand there and let her feel sorry for him. He wanted her love, not her pity.

"Where are you going?" she asked softly.

"I'm hosting a party, remember?" But Tanner paused because he knew his Sophie and right now she had something to say.

"Amy told me Tige is going to get even with you." She related the rest of Amy's warning about Tige and Lulu, then paused, waiting for his response.

"Don't worry. I'll handle it." Tanner took one step but her hand on his arm stopped him. Her glossy dark brown eyes met his.

"I misjudged you about Amy, didn't I?" she murmured. "She said you went back for her."

"You needed her to say that? You couldn't have trusted that I'm not a total jerk?" Looking at Sophie's beloved face, he felt utterly hopeless. If God had truly forgiven him for his mistakes, why couldn't He let Sophie love him?

"I'm sorry," she whispered, her voice brimming with regret. But what good was regret?

"It doesn't matter about then," he said, unable to cover the ragged tone of his voice. "It's the past. It has nothing to do with who I am now." He lifted his head, loving her beautiful face, hating that he'd caused her pain. "I'm sorry you won't trust me because I would die for you, Sophie. Because I love you more than life."

Reeling at the pain of never having Sophie's love, Tanner left. He walked to the shed where the fireworks were stored and sank onto an empty crate. There he silently poured out his heart to the only family he'd ever had—his heavenly Father.

"Where are your helpers?" Moses asked, surveying the spotless kitchen Sophie was still scrubbing.

"I sent them home." She glanced at him over one shoulder in concern. "I thought Davy and Beth would be with you."

"They were. Lefty's with them while I grab a coffee." He stepped in front of her. "You cryin', woman?"

"Don't be ridiculous. Why would I be crying?" Sophie sniffed and brushed away the tears from her cheeks. "I've just pulled off the biggest job of my career."

"That make you happy?" Moses asked.

"Ecstatic," she wailed.

"Huh. Funny way of showing it." He surveyed the kitchen, then said in a bland voice, "Hoped maybe you and Tanner finally got things sorted out." Moses poured a cup of coffee and creamed it. "Kid's crazy about you and yours."

"Kid?" she spluttered, ashamed of her tears but unable to stop shedding them.

"Compared to an old man like me Tanner is a kid." Moses grinned as he sat down at the table. "So you don't care about him. Too bad. Never find a better man than Tanner. He's got principles and integrity. Committed to make Burt's dream live. That takes guts."

"I know he's wonderful," she blubbered. Moses ignored her.

"Lots easier on him if he let the dream go. Sure, he'd lose the ranch but he'd still walk away with a big cash settlement and then he could chase his own dreams."

"I don't think Tanner would do that," Sophie said with a frown.

"Glad you at least figured that out about him." Moses shook his head. "'Cause he'd never do it. Not in a million years."

"You sound pretty sure." His certainty irritated her.

"Because I know Tanner." Moses's unblinking stare made her shift uncomfortably.

"You can't say it will never happen," she insisted. "You can't know that."

"'Course I can!" Moses glared at her. "I figured Tanner Johns out a long time ago. If you think he'd break his promise to the man he loved like a father, you're blind! Tanner's one in a million. Ain't nobody else I'd trust with my life more 'n him. Maybe it's a good thing you can't love him."

"Hey!" Sophie protested. "I never said—"

Moses ignored her.

"That boy's got a big job to do getting Burt's camp going." He shuffled to the door. "He sure don't need some 'fraidy-cat lady who won't trust him. You'll just hold him back from doin' the Lord's work."

Tossing her one last glare, Moses stomped out the door.

Indignation filled Sophie at the outspoken old man. But as she refilled the snack trays one phrase kept repeating in her head:

"Some 'fraidy-cat lady who *won't* trust him."

She prided herself on her strength, on her independence. But now she realized that her lack of ability to trust made her weak. Undependable?

Won't trust Moses had said.

Was trust merely a matter of will?

"This was a fantastic idea, Tanner." Pastor Jeff stopped him before he could move another box of sparklers into the truck bed. "That group of transient kids you found sleeping in the park the other night are having a ball with Moses. Got some ideas for a program we could start for them?"

"A few." Tanner chatted with the eager pastor for several more minutes, accepting his praise for Sophie's food while wondering if she'd ever come back to Wranglers. She didn't need his jobs anymore. Sophie's cooking had taken Tucson by storm and she was now in high demand.

When Jeff left, Tanner continued loading, praying for God to somehow intervene.

"You're the boss and you still hafta do this menial stuff?"

Tanner whirled around, hating the supercilious note in Tige's voice. He clamped his lips shut on an angry reply when he saw his nemesis had hold of a terrified Davy while Lulu gripped Beth by one arm.

"What are you doing, Tige?" he asked in a careful tone. "Let the kids go. You're scaring them."

"That's the idea, buddy." Evil blazed across his face. "A little insurance policy."

Lord, help!

Tanner suppressed his fear and smiled at the children he'd come to love.

"Hey, Beth. Davy. You okay?" They both nodded, obviously waiting for him to do something. "Why do you need insurance, Tige?" he asked, using his best conversational tone, though he already knew the answer because of all the questions Tige had lobbed at him earlier.

Where was security? Lefty? Moses? Sophie? His blood ran cold at the thought of her being trapped by Tige.

"You're a big shot now, Tanner. You're rolling in it with this place." There was a crazy gleam in the gold eyes that said Tige needed a fix and fast. In this state Tanner knew he'd go to extreme lengths to appease his cravings.

"How much do you need?" he asked, hoping he could talk Tige into being reasonable.

"Ten thousand." Triumph shone on Tige's desperate face. "Cash."

"The estate is entailed, buddy." Tanner laughed. "There's no way I could get my hands on that kind of cash," he scoffed. "You think a rich guy like Burt would leave his millions to a street punk like me?"

"He's lying," Lulu hissed.

"I'm not." Tanner tried to visually encourage Davy, who, oddly, seemed to be more nervous than Beth. Then he realized why.

Beth, eyes squeezed closed, was praying. But Tige held to Davy's throat a knife that Tanner recognized as one of Moses's artifacts.

"I got maybe fifty bucks on me," he said, slipping his hand into his pocket. "Nope. Forty," he said as he thumbed through some bills. "Take it." He held it out and almost heaved a sigh of relief when Tige made a forward movement.

"Tanner? Where are you?" Sophie's voice, breathless and oozing worry, preceded her through the bluff of trees that kept them hidden from the rest of the ranch. A moment later she appeared and Tanner's fears multiplied at the eager look on Tige's face.

"Oh, there you are. I can't find—" One look and she immediately assessed the situation. "Are you guys okay?" When she would have stepped forward Tanner grabbed her arm.

"The kids are fine, Sophie." He squeezed her fingers to reassure her. "Tige and I are just talking."

"Yeah." Tige's cackle gave Tanner chills. One slip of that knife against Davy's throat—*Lord, help us.* "We're talking about how much your kids are worth, Sophie. Tanner thinks forty bucks is gonna do it."

"Go back to the house, Sophie," Tanner told her quietly. Her terrified gaze met his. "The kids will be fine, I promise. Go to the house and pray."

"Pray?" Tige and Lulu hooted with derision.

Tanner ignored them. When Sophie didn't move he added, "Trust me. Please? Just this once trust me. I promise I'll protect them with my life."

Knowing he had no clue how to handle this, Tanner watched fear war with trust in Sophie's dark eyes. He ached for the worry he'd caused her. He should never have let her come to Wranglers today, not knowing what Tige was capable of. How many more mistakes did he have to make before he'd give up that silly dream of finally having a family?

"God is our help." Beth's clear voice pierced the tension of the moment.

A rush of joy filled Tanner. What a child!

"Beth trusts God," he said for Sophie's ears alone. "Can you?"

Finally Sophie nodded. "I will trust you both."

Tanner hugged her. *Please don't let me fail her trust.* "Go now," he urged, his lips grazing her ear. "And pray."

Sophie nodded, touched his cheek then turned to Tige. "If you hurt my children," she said through clenched teeth, "you will pay."

With one last look at Beth and Davy, she slipped out the way she'd come.

"Let's settle this," Tanner said with new resolve. "Before Sophie alerts security."

Fear and greed mingled on Tige's face. "I want more than forty dollars, Tanner."

"I've got two hundred tucked away. But I'm not getting it unless you let those children go." Tanner kept his face impassive and unyielding. He held up a closed hand. "I blow this whistle and security will be on you like fleas on a dog. You let the kids go, I'll drop it and we'll get your money." He inclined his head. "Deal?"

As he talked, Tanner kept edging closer to the pair, watching Tige, waiting for his moment. Sophie trusted him. He could not fail her.

"Take it, Tige," Lulu whined. "I'm hurtin'. I need somethin' real bad."

The moment he saw her fingers loosen on Beth, Tanner lunged forward and dragged the little girl free. Seeing what was happening, Davy jerked out of Tige's grip, grabbed Beth's hand and obeyed Tanner's yell to run. Tanner saw Beth and Davy race away and whispered a prayer of praise.

He realized his mistake the moment he felt the knife pierce between his ribs.

"Shouldn't have done that, buddy," Tige said as Tanner folded to the ground. "Now your lady and her kids are gonna pay a lot more than forty bucks." He and Lulu left.

Pain streaked through Tanner's body but he ignored it, knowing Tige would go to the house to hurt Sophie and find that money. Tanner couldn't allow that but in this state he would never be able to beat the couple back there.

"I need help, God." Suddenly he remembered the short-cut through the cacti. It was dark now and it wouldn't be easy to find the trail but it was much shorter. "Help me, Lord."

He pushed his way through, ignoring the thorns scraping his skin as blood seeped through his fingers and ran down his side. It didn't matter. Nothing mattered but proving that Sophie could trust him. Finally he made it to the back door and yanked it open.

"Tanner!" He felt Sophie's hand touch his. He laced his fingers with hers but he kept his focus on the doorway. A moment later Tige and Lulu appeared, dazed and confused.

"How'd he get here so fast?" Lulu asked.

"Here." Tanner held out his forty dollars. "You'll be a wanted man now, Tige. The cops will be here in seconds to arrest you. You'd better take this and go while you can."

Tige glared at him, hate and fear vying for supremacy. He grabbed the cash Tanner held out but before he could race away, Tanner said, "I forgive you, buddy. But don't come back here again unless you want to talk about God."

"Fat chance," Tige said and left with Lulu following.

Woozy now, Tanner grabbed the door frame. Sophie

slipped her arm around his waist, her tearful face inches from his.

"You shouldn't have risked your life, Tanner."

"I had to," he managed to say. "I love you, all of you. You're my world."

He had lots more to add but he couldn't make his mouth say it.

"Don't you dare die on me, Tanner Johns," Sophie said, her voice furious. "Not now. Not after saving my kids. Not before I—"

Tanner wanted so badly to hear this but he couldn't fight the waves of black descending on him.

Chapter Fourteen

Sophie lowered Tanner's unconscious body to the floor, resisting when Moses tried to pull her back.

"No!" She shoved his hands away and cradled Tanner's head on her lap, praying he wouldn't die before she could tell him how sorry she was that it had taken her so long to finally trust him. "Please God, help Tanner. Please?"

As if in a vacuum, Sophie noticed two security men rush in and heard Davy tell them what had happened. She watched Moses press a white tea towel against Tanner's side, saw it stain a dark crimson red in seconds. She felt Beth curl next to her, repeating verses she'd memorized. But all these things were background. Sophie's focus remained on the man whose lifeless body she held, the man who'd kept his promise.

The man she trusted.

"I can't lose him now, God." Not now that she'd finally realized that Tanner was a man to trust, to love.

Sophie didn't know how much time passed before Moses insisted she move away so the paramedics could attend to Tanner. She did but watched every move while she answered questions policemen lobbed at her. But when Tanner was loaded on a gurney, Sophie pulled free of Moses's restraining arm to grab Tanner's hand and walk beside him to the waiting ambulance, praying with every ounce of courage she possessed.

"Is the party over?" his beloved voice suddenly demanded.

"For you it is," Moses said in a gruff tone from just behind her. Of course Moses would be there. He loved Tanner, too.

Tanner said nothing for a moment. His eyelids fluttered, then lifted. He glanced around with a frown until he caught sight of Sophie.

"Hello, beloved," he murmured in the most tender voice she'd ever heard.

"Hi." The relief and joy flooding Sophie's heart kept her from saying more.

"Security caught your friends. They're not going to hurt anyone else," Moses said.

"That's good." He licked his lips and blinked again, trying to focus.

"You're going to the hospital now," Sophie explained.

He nodded, obviously groggy. But when he saw the ambulance door open he said, "Wait," in a loud, firm voice.

"Tanner, you need treatment," Sophie insisted. "Don't worry, you won't be alone. I'm going with—"

"No." He squeezed her hand. "Keep the party going. Make sure there are fireworks." He paused, grimaced and exhaled as if the effort to speak was becoming difficult. "I promised the street kids that we would have fireworks in the desert." He managed a crooked smile. "I have to keep my promise to them."

"And you do keep your promises, don't you?" How she loved the way his green eyes crinkled at the corners. "Because that's who you are. I know that now."

"Really?" He waved off the attendant's insistent urging to leave. "Just a minute. It's important."

"Because a stab wound isn't," the woman barked. But she moved back a step.

Sophie looked at Tanner and saw the man he truly was, a man who cherished and protected those he loved. Tanner Johns was the man for her. She knew that now.

"We can talk when I get to the hospital, okay?" Suddenly shy with so many interested onlookers, Sophie pressed her lips against his in a brief kiss. "I'll see you later, Tanner," she promised.

"Fireworks?" he asked.

"I give you my word that Wranglers Ranch will have the best fireworks for miles around."

"To go with the best eats," he teased in a husky tone.

Sophie couldn't help it. She leaned over and kissed him again.

"Gross." Davy made a gagging sound. "Mom, Tanner's got to get to the hospital. You can do that later." He pulled her arm so she had to back away.

"Thanks, kid." The grateful attendants loaded Tanner but before they could close the doors he called, "Keep praying, Beth."

"I will, Mr. Cowboy," she promised.

Then the doors slammed shut and Sophie lost sight of his smiling face.

Staying put while the ambulance with Tanner left was the hardest thing she'd ever done. And yet Sophie had no fear that Tanner wouldn't be okay. He was in God's hands now. She had no clue how to keep her promise to Tanner but she did know God was going to help her. And He would be with Tanner, too. All she had to do was trust.

"Come on, everyone," she said briskly. "I promised Tanner we'd keep this party going and we're going to do just that. Davy, you find Lefty and bring him here. He should be about finished with his rodeo display by now. Beth, you and I are going to make popcorn to pass around. Moses—"

"I know right well what my job is, missy." His indignation turned to laughter. "You sure grew some courage."

"Tanner taught me. 'If God be for us who can be against us?'" she quoted. "Right, Beth?"

"Yes, Mama." Content that her beloved Tanner was going to be okay, Beth walked inside the house ready to help her favorite cowboy's ranch.

The hands arrived in groups of twos and threes, their faces sober, fear waiting to grab hold. It was up to her to show her faith.

"Tanner's going to be okay," she assured them. "But he wouldn't leave until I promised we'd ensure the fireworks are every bit as great as he promised the kids. To do that, we'll need your help. Can we count on you? Can Tanner?"

"Yes!" they agreed in a cheer. "For Tanner!"

"Great." Teary-eyed at their respect for their boss, Sophie pressed on. She would trust God to help her keep her promise. "Moses says most of our guests don't know about Tanner's stabbing. Let's keep it that way with the celebrations continuing because that's what Tanner wants. Lefty, can you handle the fireworks?"

"I've helped out the city for years. In fact I taught Tanner. No problem." He selected three other men and told her they'd be ready in half an hour.

"Great." She heaved a sigh of relief. *Thank You, Lord, for Lefty.* "Moses, what else do we need?"

"Me and the boys will handle crowd control," the old man said and left immediately with his helpers.

"Davy, you, Beth and I are making popcorn," Sophie said before her son could follow the others.

"Aw, Mom! We didn't mean to get caught by that guy. We were just going to get some carrots for the horses."

"So you disobeyed Lefty and Moses when they told you to stay put."

Their shamed faces were answer enough.

After this evening's events Sophie needed to keep her children close. She'd have to deal with their disobedience later. But for now all she said was, "Do it for Tanner. Okay?" Davy nodded and got to work without complaint.

Somehow everything went off without a hitch. As she watched the spectacular display of lights, Sophie heard *oohs* and *ahhs*, gasps of wonder and squeals of delight with a heart full of thanksgiving. God had helped them fulfill Tanner's goal. As the final starbursts of red, white and blue filled the sky, the crowd burst into the national anthem. When it was over a hushed silence fell. Then Pastor Jeff spoke.

"Before we leave let's pray and thank the God of our land who has blessed us with this place, Wranglers Ranch." Pastor Jeff offered a short prayer, then wished the group a happy Fourth.

Her heart full, Sophie stood in the shadows with an arm around each child and listened to groups of chattering kids as they climbed aboard buses that would return them to the city. There were many positive comments but the best came from a teen who stopped to ask her if he could come back to Wranglers Ranch tomorrow to talk about God.

"Come back whenever you like," Sophie offered. She had no idea what Tanner could do for him but she knew he would do something because Wranglers Ranch was God's ranch and Tanner was committed to doing God's will. She trusted them both.

Now she needed to tell that to Tanner.

Groggy and in pain, Tanner wakened to semidarkness and Sophie by his bedside, holding his hand. She'd been dozing but must have sensed his return to lucidity for her eyes suddenly opened and she stared straight at him.

"Hello." He stopped, aghast to see tears rolling down her face.

"Thank you for protecting my kids," she sobbed. "But I wish it hadn't cost you so dearly."

Privately Tanner thought a little flesh wound was worth it if meant what he hoped it did. "Sophie—"

"I love you, Tanner," she blurted and dashed the tears from her eyes. "I'm just sorry that you had to get stabbed before I came to my senses and realized that. I also realize God is trustworthy. Even when I didn't feel Him, He was at work for you, for my kids and for me because He loves us with a love I can always count on." A tremulous smile tilted her lovely lips. "Why did it take me so long to trust the gift of love?"

"That's what I'd like to know," he said plaintively. He shifted in the bed so he could gaze at her. That's when he finally realized that in God's eyes his miserable past filled with terrible mistakes didn't matter anymore. God had blessed him with the opportunity to reach kids, and he'd sent Sophie to help.

"Tanner?" Worry tinged the edge of her voice. "Maybe I shouldn't have told you that. Maybe it's too soon—"

"Too soon?" He burst out laughing and then caught his breath as his side reminded him he wasn't totally fit. "I've been in love with you forever, woman."

"Really?" Her big brown eyes gazed at him with love. "Tell me again, please?" she whispered, squeezing his hand. So he did.

"I love you, Sophie. You make my days bright. I wake up wanting to share ideas with you and go to sleep thinking about all the things we can do together." He saw a tiny smile flutter across her face. "I love the way you challenge me to be better, to do more and to think outside the box. No one has ever cared enough to push me."

"Oh, Tanner." Her eyes clouded.

"Except God," he corrected. "But it took you to help me accept that if I wouldn't let go of the past and accept

God's forgiveness, I couldn't do what He needs me to do today." He made a face. "I couldn't 'fan into flame' my so-called 'gift.'"

"It *is* a gift, Tanner." Sophie's eyes pinned him. "Your ability to get people together is a God-given gift. That's what drew me to helping you spread the message of God's love through Wranglers Ra—"

"Sophie," he interrupted.

She looked startled. "Yes."

"My side hurts like crazy. I'm kinda befuddled," he said. "But will you please do something for me?"

"What?"

"Can you please get me a cup of coffee?"

She smiled but shook her head. "Nothing but water till morning. Sorry." She touched his cheek. "Something else I can do?"

"Oh, yeah." Tanner could hardly believe God had given him this woman to love. "Coffee isn't my top request."

"What is?"

"Will you please kiss me?"

"I was just waiting for you to ask." A pretty flush of color tinted her cheekbones.

"Don't wait anymore, darling Sophie," he pleaded.

She didn't kiss him immediately. Instead her fingers cupped his face, his eyes, traced a path over his nose to his lips and to his chin. Finally she spoke.

"I love you, Tanner. I trust you with my heart."

Then Sophie kissed him and when Tanner came back down to earth he decided that kiss and the ones that followed were well worth the wait.

"What are you thinking?" she whispered, her head resting lightly on his heart.

"That for as long as I can remember I've longed for someone of my own, a history, a heritage that I thought would make me worthy of God's love." He smiled. "Instead God sent me to Burt and to you and the kids to teach me that it's not my past that matters, it's what I do with my future."

"Mmm," she agreed.

"You are the love of my life, Sophie. You and the kids are so precious, Beth with her steadfast joy in life, and Davy with his generosity of spirit." Tanner hesitated, waiting until she lifted her head to look at him. "May I please be part of your family?"

Sophie began to cry. Tanner panicked until she explained.

"I'm crying because I'm so happy," she blubbered.

"I hope I never make you sad, then. I notice you didn't answer my question." He held his breath, exhaling only after she nodded.

"With one caveat."

"Which is?" How he loved her.

"It's *our* family."

"Deal. Seal it." He held out a hand but Sophie made a face.

"Really, Tanner?" She shook her head in reproof. "In this family we'll do things differently." This time she kissed him with a fervor that left Tanner breathless. "Deal?" she asked when she finally drew back.

"Absolutely." He leaned back against his pillow and promptly fell asleep. Deliriously happy, Tanner stirred from his drowsy state only when Sophie called his name. "Yes, love?"

"I forgot to tell you. The fireworks went off without a hitch and your ranch hands have Wranglers back to its pristine state, running smoothly and waiting for your return and the next event you plan."

"Sophie," he protested, cupping her chin in his hand and feathering his finger against her lips. "Do we really have to talk about the ranch right now?"

"Yes." She grinned. "Because Tige's sons asked Lefty if they could stay at Wranglers until they get their lives straightened out. Your retreat to help Tucson's needy kids is happening."

"With God leading, we'll do lots more, my darling Sophie." Tanner kissed the fingers he still held. "When are we getting married?"

The resolution to that issue was soon settled and sealed with a kiss.

Chapter Fifteen

Sophie married Tanner at a very private ceremony at Wranglers Ranch in September. At least they thought it would be private.

Tanner, having helped with one wedding, confidently assured Sophie he was capable of planning this wedding. He asked Mrs. Baggle to play for the event and insisted Beth choose a fancy dress in her favorite blue. He also bought a suit and Stetson to match his own for Davy and special-ordered cowboy boots for both children. Davy's were black and Beth's where white with blue stitching. Both children walked a little taller in them.

With everything ready, Mrs. Baggle hit a few notes signaling Tanner to walk to the front with his best man, Moses. He was astounded to see the patio filled.

"Who invited all these people?" he whispered to Pastor Jeff.

"Your guests come courtesy of Trent and Rod," Jeff said with a laugh. "You did tell them they were part of the family, remember? They're telling their new friends they intend on staying as long as they can since their parents are locked up. So they told everyone at church about your wedding with some help from Lefty and the other hands."

"Good. The more the merrier." Tanner smiled at Tige's grinning sons.

When Mrs. Baggle played the first chords of "Here Comes the Bride," Tanner inhaled, waiting impatiently to see the woman he so dearly loved. Sophie's neighbor Edna came down the aisle first, without a walker, resplendent in a gown of swirling fall colors, delighted to be part of the event. She took her place beside Moses, favoring him with a sweet smile that was returned so fulsomely that Tanner thought perhaps his friend also had found someone to care about.

Then Sophie appeared. She'd chosen a short ivory lace jacket and matching knee-length skirt that swirled around her pretty knees. Then he saw her boots—ivory, ladylike, lace-up Western boots. He smiled, his delight growing at seeing a jaunty ivory hat perched on the side of her head. She'd certainly embraced the ranch theme and he loved it, loved her.

Sophie walked slowly toward him, her gaze holding his until she paused just a moment to smile at her kids. Then she moved to stand in front of him.

"Wow!" Tanner barely heard the laughter as he gazed at his beautiful bride.

"Wow yourself," she murmured. "You clean up nice, Mr. Cowboy." Then sliding her hand into his, she turned with him to face Pastor Jeff.

"Friends, we've gathered today to witness the marriage of Tanner and Sophie." He continued to speak, explaining how God had drawn them together. "Sophie and Tanner will now say their vows to each other."

Tanner inhaled. He'd worked so hard to memorize the words that he felt in his heart. He wasn't going to let nervousness mess this up.

"Dearest Sophie. For most of my life I've dreamed of

being part of a family, but I never thought I was worthy. Burt offered me unconditional love, but when he died I figured I'd lost my chance to have a family. I sure had no clue how to make his dream come true. Then you came along, sweet Sophie, and hope bloomed. You taught me about love and showed me how to spread it around. From you I've learned to forget the past and focus on God's plan for the future. Because of you Burt's dream is happening. Because of us." He inhaled, then said the rest unrehearsed, from his heart.

"I promise I'll always be here for you, always love you, and always love Beth and Davy. I promise to work with you, with God leading us, to fan whatever gifts He gives us into flame. I love you, Sophie. And I promise to keep my promises to you. Forever."

He slid the solid gold circle of promise on her finger right next to the diamond solitaire he'd had specially designed just for his Sophie.

"Tanner." Sophie inhaled. A slow smile moved across her face. "I love you. I love the way you cherish me so I feel special. I love the way you encourage and support me. I love your joy in life, your love for my kids, your determination and grit to fulfill Burt's wishes. And I love that you've included me in the Wranglers Ranch ministry. But most of all, I love that I can trust you." She gave him a cheeky grin. "I know it took me a long time to get there but I know now that God knows what He's doing. It's going to be a great life and I can hardly wait to share it with you."

Sophie slid a plain gold band, exactly the style Tanner wanted, on his finger.

Then Tanner kissed the woman whom God had sent him, the one with whom he'd share a wonderful family on the ranch he loved, reaching kids who needed to know about God's love.

In the silence of that precious moment, Beth's voice penetrated.

"Know what, Davy? Mama should have known you can always trust a cowboy."

* * * * *

THE COWBOY
MEETS HIS MATCH

Leann Harris

For my grandbaby: you are the miracle child we prayed for, and your smile melts my heart.

Let the morning bring me word of Your unfailing love,
for I have put my trust in You.
—*Psalm* 143:8

Chapter One

Erin Joy Delong stood before the closed conference-room door. On the other side lay the truth she needed to face no matter how ugly. Grasping the doorknob, she took a deep breath and turned it.

All talking ceased. The air-conditioning clicked on, filling the dead silence.

Erin looked at each of the seven men seated around the table. No one would meet her gaze except for the stranger standing at the head of the table. A slide of his presentation on how to reorganize the bicounty rodeo lit the screen behind him.

Her knees nearly buckled. She hadn't gotten the job. No, the job of reorganizing the rodeo that her great-grandfather established had gone to a total stranger.

"Erin, we didn't expect you," Melvin Lowell, the rodeo board's president, said.

She didn't doubt it. "Sorry I'm late, but after I talked with dad's doctors at the hospital this morning, I ran into a big accident on the interstate just outside Albuquerque. Then, finding this unscheduled *Thursday* meeting proved tricky, since you'd moved it from the rodeo headquarters."

The men around the table shifted in their chairs as if

they were ashamed of themselves. They continued to avoid her gaze.

"How's your father?" Mel asked, as if nothing was off-kilter.

She stepped into the elegant meeting room at the new conference center. "He's improving from the stroke, but we won't know the extent of the damage for several days. I drove in as his representative on the board."

"Is that legal?" Norman Burke, one of the board members from Harding County, asked. "I mean, if he can't talk—"

"You can call my mother or the floor nurse at the hospital, Sylvia Carter, who witnessed Dad nodding for me to represent him until he came back."

"Oh."

Erin glanced at the man giving the presentation and caught the hint of a smile that crossed his face before it disappeared.

The muted brush of her boots on the carpet was the only sound in the room as she walked to the empty chair on the opposite side of the table and sat. In front of her was a slick folder that read "*Tucumcari Rodeo Proposal* by Sawyer Jensen." Her eyes jerked up and clashed with Melvin's. He didn't look away.

"I take it Mr. Jensen won the contract?"

"Yes, we voted for him at the last meeting," Mel replied, his head held high. "Didn't anyone tell you?" Too much satisfaction laced his voice. Most of the other board members kept their gazes fixed on the table.

"No, but you know with all the chaos that occurred the day of the vote and Dad having the stroke afterward, it was the last thing on Mom's mind."

Norman Burke glared at Mel. "Cut it out, Lowell. The lady has more on her plate than this rodeo."

"Of course."

If Mel's words were meant to be accommodating, they failed.

"You don't have to stay, Erin, since we've already hired Sawyer. I'm sure you're tired after spending that much time at the hospital. But we wanted Sawyer to meet with us and show us his plan again and answer any further questions we had," Mel said.

Panic spread through the room. Several of the board members looked as if they wanted to escape, but retreat was the last thing on Erin's mind. Her hometown needed this revitalization. A successful rodeo would bring in much-needed people and revenue to help their bottom line.

"Thank you for your concern, Mel. But, as I said before, I'll be Dad's representative until he's well enough to come back."

A couple of men shifted in their chairs; throats were cleared, but no one said anything.

"Sawyer, why don't you continue explaining your overall plan to us?" Melvin said, ending the tense moment. "I'm sure Erin would like to hear it."

"We're on page three, Ms. Delong." Sawyer nodded to his presentation folder.

Fingering the folder, Erin studied Sawyer Jensen. The handsome man stood over six feet with sandy-brown hair and compelling hazel eyes that did funny things to her stomach, which she ignored. He had a scar on his chin below the corner of his mouth. When his eyes met hers, there was no smugness in those green depths, but admiration, instead. She didn't understand his reaction, but it eased the blow. As she studied the man, she had the feeling that she'd met him before.

Sawyer started to explain his strategy to save the rodeo and put it back in the black.

Chalking up her body's reaction to stress and the long drive this morning, Erin opened the folder. She tried to follow Sawyer's presentation, but it seemed she'd gone deaf and blind. Looking up through her lashes, she saw Melvin studying her. She would *not* cry in front of him or any of the other board members. Nor would she cry in front of this stranger. That wasn't Erin Delong's way. When her ex-boyfriend had announced, at their high school graduation, that he was engaged to Traci Lowell, Mel's daughter, she hadn't cried, much to Traci's disappointment. Maybe Traci's father thought he could make her cry this time. Of course, the meeting wasn't finished yet.

By the time they adjourned, Erin couldn't tell what Sawyer had said. For all she knew he could've suggested they burn the old rodeo grounds down and sell tickets to bring in money.

Most of the board members hurried to where Sawyer stood, taking a wide berth around her to shake Sawyer's hand and comment on his presentation. Their guilty faces made her wonder if they thought she'd throw a fit or break down in tears if they got too close. She could assure them that neither would happen, but they clearly weren't going to take any chances.

Only Chris Saddler stopped by where she stood.

"I'm sorry you didn't win, Erin. I voted for you to get the job. With you being local, and knowing the history of the rodeo and what resources we have, I thought you'd be best, instead of an outsider."

Chris was one of her dad's friends. She stood. "Thanks, Chris, and thanks for the heads-up this morning. Being at the hospital, you lose sense of time."

He opened his mouth to say something more, then closed it. He nodded and walked away.

Mel was the last one to shake Sawyer's hand. "A good presentation. If you have any questions, just call me, Sawyer."

Snatching the slick folder off the table, Erin headed for

the door. Later, when she could think clearly, she'd read it over and evaluate his plan to see how it differed from hers.

"Ms. Delong?"

The deep voice calling her name sent shivers down her spine. It also stopped the other board members in their tracks at the door, no doubt expecting fireworks between her and Sawyer. Torn between wanting to plow through the bodies clogging the way out and facing the man with the wonderful rich voice, she straightened her shoulders, turned and faced him.

He stepped to her side. "Would you mind if we talked?"

Puzzled frowns crossed the board members' faces, and she heard a couple of them whisper.

"I'd love to, Mr. Jensen—"

"Sawyer is my first name."

"—Sawyer, but I last ate at seven this morning before visiting my dad in the hospital. After consulting with his doctors and my mother, I drove here. With the delay on the road, I never got the opportunity to eat. I'm probably not good company right now." Although it was only 1:40 p.m., food would help her thinking and dealing with this mess.

The man flashed a killer smile at her. "I haven't had anything, either, since breakfast in Amarillo, and I could use some sustenance, too. A full stomach helps me think and helps my attitude. Why don't we go and get a burger and talk?"

"So you think my attitude is bad?" she asked.

At the tone of her voice, groans erupted from the men at the door.

"No," Sawyer answered evenly. "I was talking about myself. And when I'm hungry, I don't listen well."

More groans.

She nodded. "Understandable."

His eyes twinkled.

Erin didn't know whether to grin at his cheekiness or ignore him. "What's there to talk about? You won."

"Well, with your late arrival, you didn't get to hear my complete proposal and I wanted the opportunity to discuss some of my ideas with you. Since you put in a bid, I'd like to get your reaction."

Was he teasing her? Did he want to rub her nose in her failure? She searched his face for any sign of duplicity, but found nothing. She needed some time to process all this, but she wouldn't let the board members see her disappointment. "I'm going next door to Lulu's Burgers. If you want to join me, I won't object."

The man didn't take offense at her tone. "Give me a second to unplug my computer and projector and pack them up."

So the equipment was his. She'd wondered where the board had found money to buy such nice equipment. "I'll be waiting next door."

She walked through the crowd of gawking faces clustered at the door, Mel's being the most outraged. Too bad.

Well, he'd been in more awkward places than this, Sawyer thought, but not many. There'd been that time, in Nevada, when the man who'd hired him to turn around the Western Days Rodeo had his wife and sister barge into the meeting and start screaming at each other. The women hadn't stopped screeching long enough for him to understand what the fight was about. Things quickly went physical, and the women threw anything they could get their hands on. Sawyer ducked a cowboy statue, but the owner wasn't as lucky and was coldcocked by a glass paperweight thrown by his wife. Of course, as a turnaround specialist, Sawyer had been in his fair share of tense situations and been able to bring the warring sides together.

Sawyer had seen the shock and sadness flash in Erin's

eyes before the protective shield came up to cover her emotions. His heart went out to her, or maybe it was just plain attraction that struck him like a fist to the chin. After his brother's recent marriage, Sawyer realized how alone he was now, and a restlessness settled inside him. The brothers hadn't really had a home since that little apartment behind the church in Plainview in the Texas Panhandle, but it hadn't mattered because they'd been a team. Together against the world. But now?

"You're not going to have lunch with that woman, are you?" Melvin walked back into the room.

Sawyer grabbed his laptop and the projector. "I am."

"Why?"

"Because I'm hungry."

Melvin sputtered. "But you won."

Sawyer nodded toward the outside glass door. Melvin opened it. When Sawyer had arrived this morning, he'd driven to the rodeo board's office, then followed Melvin to the new convention facility.

"Winning makes a poor lunch, Mel, and when Erin mentioned food, my hunger hit me like a kick from the old mule my dad worked with. And since the place is right here, why not eat?"

Melvin opened his mouth, but nothing came out.

"Besides, I'd think you'd want me to see if I could win the woman over, get her on my side. It will make things operate smoothly. I don't want any disruptions."

"Well, yes, but—"

"I'm glad you agree. It will make things better later on."

Sawyer stored his equipment in the long steel toolbox that ran the width of the bed of his truck. Turning, he faced Melvin and waited for the rest of his comment.

"Well?"

Mel glared. "Don't be surprised if she bites your ear off and spits it out."

"I'll consider myself warned."

Mel gave a curt nod and strolled to his car.

Sawyer's curiosity about Erin was piqued as he walked to the restaurant. His competition for this job was certainly much better looking than the one for the last job. Of course, from all the panicked looks thrown at Erin when she'd walked into the room, and from the dire warning just issued, he'd have to be on guard. The lady wasn't just a pretty face. But, as he thought about it, Sawyer couldn't shake the feeling that he'd met Erin somewhere before. Where, he couldn't say, but—

When he opened the door to Lulu's, the smell of burgers smacked him in the face, making his mouth water. Chrome-and-Formica tables à la 1950s vintage dotted the restaurant, with several booths by the windows. A jukebox sat close to the front door. Pictures from previous rodeos hung on the walls, along with ribbons from different 4-H projects. In the center of one wall was a large picture of Erin racing around a barrel, her long hair flying from beneath her cowgirl hat, her elbows out and her body low over the neck of the horse. A ribbon hung off the corner of the picture with a plaque below announcing State Champion. The picture impressed him. The lady knew her way around a rodeo, that was for sure, and he knew she'd have some ideas.

In a booth by the windows sat Erin. As he approached the table, she pointed to the opposite wall. "If you want to eat, you have to order at the counter behind you."

She wasn't going to make this easy, but, oddly enough, that didn't put a damper on his spirit.

He glanced over his shoulder. A large menu covered the wall behind the order counter. He turned back to her. "Recommend anything?"

"Try Lulu's chili burger."

He nodded and ordered the burger. When he joined her,

he noticed that she had opened his proposal. Sliding onto the bench across from her, he asked, "What do you think?"

"That you know how to put together a proposal."

"That's it?"

She placed her forearms on the tabletop and leaned forward. "I haven't read it all. Your slick marketing diverted my attention."

He didn't think she meant it as a compliment, but he couldn't help smiling. He'd impressed her. "Well, it's geared to do that."

"Let's see if the sleek outside matches what's inside." She looked down at the presentation.

If he didn't miss his guess, it would take a lot to win over this woman. He didn't mind competing with others for a job, but he would've liked to have known there was a hometown applicant in the running against him.

He studied her while she read his plan. The lady's long dark hair hung as a single thick braid down her back. If he didn't miss his guess, she had Native American blood flowing through her veins, but with a name like Delong, he wondered. She must be five foot seven or eight, since she stood just at the right height for him to kiss her with ease. The thought startled him and he must've made some sound.

"What?" she demanded.

He waved away the question. "Nothing."

She went back to reading.

Kissing her? That crazy thought had to be fallout from the wild morning he'd had, combined with his brother's recent marriage. Caleb's main focus now would be his wife, and the new baby they were expecting. But it left Sawyer feeling at loose ends. The brothers had depended on each other to survive their teen years. Well, they weren't teenagers anymore, but Sawyer felt a certain part of himself missing.

"I know you haven't had time to completely look over my proposal," he blurted out, "but did you have any follow-up questions to the presentation I made? Is there anything you might not have been comfortable asking in the presence of the others that I can answer now?"

The instant the last word fell out of his mouth, he knew he'd stepped in it. The fire in her eyes blazed. "I didn't mean—"

"Understand, Mr. Jensen, I don't suffer from shyness. I know my mind and will speak it. But I don't go off half-cocked, either. I'll know what I'm talking about when I open my mouth." She leaned in. "There's an old saying about keeping your powder dry until ready to fire. That's me."

He wanted to smile but resisted the urge. He knew better than to throw gas on a fire, but her strong spirit attracted him like metal filings to a magnet. "Good to know."

He had to admire her reaction. She didn't go ballistic, cry or stomp out of the meeting room like his last girlfriend would've or his mother. It looked as if she would give him a fair hearing. The thought surprised him. He sat back. Glancing over at the wall, he saw her picture again. "When did you win your ribbon?" he said, diverting his thoughts.

She glanced up. He nodded to her picture.

"Oh, that ribbon—high school."

Meaning she'd won a lot more. "Lulu helped sponsor me that year at the state fair. Since she helped, and raised money for me, I thought she should get the ribbon."

"I understand. My winnings helped put me through college. I competed in the summer and between semesters to earn enough money for school."

"Really?"

"I do know my way around a lasso."

With a thawing of her coolness, she leaned forward. He thought he caught a hint of respect. "I'm not just some college-educated busybody who thinks he knows how to solve the world's problems. My brother and I have been rodeoing since we were both teens." He rested his hand on the table. "I've lived it. The last time I worked and competed was last June in the little town of Peaster, Texas."

Her eyes widened in an 'aha' moment. "You were at the charity rodeo?"

"I was. I worked in tandem with my brother, riding pickup."

"I was there, too, competing in barrel racing. Talked with the organizer, Brenda Kaye, about how she put together the rodeo, hoping to pick up some ideas on how to save our rodeo."

"Brenda did a great job. When my brother confessed he wanted to marry her, I cheered."

"She's your sister-in-law?"

"She is, and getting her degree in counseling. She's an Iraqi war veteran and wants to help fellow vets."

Erin's expression softened, making him feel less like the monster who'd stomped her dreams.

The waitress showed up with a burger. "Here you go, Erin." The teenage girl placed the plate on the table. "Yours will be out in a minute, sir."

"If my burger is as good as this one smells, I can't wait." He grinned at her. "And my name's Sawyer. *Sir* makes me feel old."

She nodded. "I'm Rose. Mom cooks the best burgers in this part of New Mexico. Really, she's the best cook hands down." A ding of "order up" sounded and the girl disappeared.

Erin grabbed a French fry and popped it into her mouth as she continued to study his proposal.

The waitress appeared again with his burger. "Here you go, Sawyer. Enjoy."

"Are you still doing the work/study program in high school?" Erin asked Rose.

"Yup, and I have a ton of ideas I want Mom to try." She walked back to the kitchen with a little spring in her step.

Erin bowed her head, silently asking a blessing.

Sawyer liked that and joined her. When he looked up, she studied him.

He didn't say anything, but picked up the hamburger and took a bite. The flavors of chili and meat danced on his tongue. "You weren't kidding."

"Sawyer, I'm known for a lot of things, but being funny isn't one of them."

"So you don't laugh?" He took another bite of his burger. He felt some chili slide down his chin.

"How's the burger?" A rawboned woman stood at the end of the table. From her posture, the woman knew her way around the restaurant and wasn't afraid of hard work. She smiled when she saw the chili on his chin. "Ah, I see you're enjoying my special burger."

Wiping his chin, he nodded to Erin. "She wasn't fooling when she said this burger is the best."

The woman blushed. "Thank you. Our Erin is a treasure. Anyone who has a problem talks to her for ideas and advice."

"You're going to be seeing a lot of me in the next few weeks," he said after swallowing.

"Erin, did you acquire a new boyfriend that you didn't tell us about?"

Erin choked on her tea.

"No. He's not mine," she shot back. "Ask Mel about him."

Lulu frowned. "You're not making any sense."

Sawyer grabbed another napkin from the dispenser, wiped his hand and chin, then held out his hand to the woman. "I'm Sawyer Jensen. I've been hired to work on your rodeo."

"You didn't win the job?" Lulu glanced at Erin. "You okay with that?"

Erin sat quietly and studied Sawyer. "I'll let you know after I've read his proposal."

Eyes narrowed, Lulu focused on him. "You've got some mighty big shoes to fill, mister. Like I said, folks around here tend to depend on Erin."

Sawyer now knew that he wasn't the odds-on favorite of some of the people in town. He'd have to turn on the charm. "I'll try, ma'am. And I hope to consult with Erin here after she has finished reading my proposal."

"I'd like to hear her ideas, myself. Not that I don't trust you, but we know Erin."

"No offense taken."

"How is your father?" Lulu asked.

"The doctors think he'll recover, but how quickly they don't know. Right now they are still evaluating him. He's conscious, but not talking."

Lulu nodded. "I'm sorry about that. If you need anything, let me know."

Erin let down her guard long enough that he saw the worry in her eyes. "Thanks."

He took another bite of the burger, which confirmed what his taste buds had already told him. "Oh, this is good."

Several more locals entered the restaurant and clustered at the order desk.

Erin nodded at them.

Sawyer wanted to ask her about a good place to stay, but he wasn't sure she'd welcome giving him more advice.

Taking the last bite of her burger, she threw her napkin on her plate. "I'll finish your proposal tonight and get back to you after I've thought about your suggestions and plan of attack."

A reasonable response, but he'd keep up his guard. "Do you still ride barrels competitively?"

"I do and was in Denver competing when I got word about my dad's stroke." She fell silent. "Five days," she whispered to herself. She shook her head and picked up her thoughts. "I left the competition and dropped my horse at our family ranch before driving to see Dad. I didn't know the result of the vote on the contract until this morning when I saw you standing at the head of the table."

He tensed.

"Congratulations." She held out her hand.

He took it, and he felt an electric charge race up his arm, scrambling his brains. "Thank you. I welcome all input."

"Really?" Her arched brow and the twinkle in her eyes gave him pause. He knew a challenge when he saw one.

"Absolutely. Once you've read through my plan, I'd welcome your input."

"If you're pulling my leg or trying to smooth things over with the little lady, you've seriously misjudged the situation."

"No, I meant what I said."

"Good, because I'll have input."

"I look forward to it."

Her mouth slowly curved into a smile that could only be categorized as one of pure determination.

The door to the restaurant opened and a couple around Erin's age walked in. The woman had beautiful blond hair that fell beyond her shoulders. Under the ton of makeup she had slathered on, she might've been pretty, Sawyer thought, but she just looked hard. She scanned the restaurant, clapped eyes on them and marched to the table much like General Patton marching across France.

"Erin, what a wonderful heart you have." The woman's

voice dripped with sugar and venom. "I could've never eaten with the man who beat me out for a job I wanted, but here you are dining with our new turnaround specialist," she said. Her raised voice echoed through the restaurant. The smirk on her face told Sawyer this woman enjoyed Erin's humiliation.

Erin didn't look up as she calmly collected the proposal and put it into her tote. The man with the blonde looked panicked.

Sawyer held out his hand. "Sawyer Jensen. And you are?"

"Traci and Andy Hyatt," the man responded.

"My father is Melvin Lowell," Traci announced, as if that said it all.

Sawyer stole a look at Erin. She didn't look nervous or upset. She simply sat back.

Andy cleared his throat. "I'm sorry to hear about your dad, Erin. I always liked him."

Traci elbowed her husband.

"What?" Andy asked. "Detrick always treated me well. I'm sorry to hear about his stroke."

"Thanks, Andy," Erin replied. "Dad felt the same about you."

There was a wealth of meaning buried in those words. Andy glanced at his wife, who glared back.

"Watch your back with this one. You might find a knife there," Traci warned, pointing toward Erin.

Andy pulled his wife away from the table. "Let's order."

Erin didn't offer any explanation, but the tension the couple caused lingered.

In a small town there were lots of undercurrents that could take down an outsider in an instant, and Sawyer had just encountered one. You had to pay attention to body language and tone if you wanted to save yourself. He'd learned that lesson the hard way with his mom's constant stream of boyfriends.

"Can you recommend a place to stay while I'm here?" he asked, wanting to change the subject.

Erin's gaze settled back on him. "The board didn't arrange a place for you to stay?"

"No, it wasn't mentioned."

"Well, there are quite a few motels."

"What about that interesting-looking motel I saw a block over when I drove into town? The one that looks like a big sombrero?"

"Are you sure you want to stay there? It was built in 1937. We have more modern places."

"No, I kinda like its style. A blast from the past."

"Most of the rooms don't have TVs. And their phones are the big black rotary kind."

For some reason, the lady didn't want him to stay there. Why?

Before he could respond, a couple walked into the restaurant. They nodded to Erin and made their way to the order counter.

"I think I can handle that," he said.

Erin studied him, but before she could respond, they heard, "What?" The man at the counter said, "You're joshing me?" He looked over his shoulder at them.

"You sure, Lulu?" the woman questioned.

Instantly, the couple walked over to their table.

"You didn't win, Erin?" the man asked. "This is the stranger who won?" They looked from Erin to Sawyer.

Sawyer felt the gazes of the couple boring into his back.

"I can't believe the board voted for a stranger over one of our own, especially after what happened with your father," the woman added.

"It was a fair vote," Traci called out from across the room.

The man glared at her. "I think we all know how you feel."

Sawyer heard a strangled protest.

The man ignored it and focused on him and Erin. "Why go with a stranger? I know you and trust that your ideas would save the rodeo."

"I've just skimmed his plan, Bob, but I wouldn't jump to a conclusion before I've really studied it and thought about what he plans to do."

Bob considered Erin's suggestion. "Sounds good to me. I think the board needs to have a meeting tonight to let the rest of the town listen to this man's ideas. The longer we don't know what he wants to do, the longer we'll be in the dark, and I want to know what's happening from the beginning." He whipped out his cell phone and punched in a number.

Erin sat quietly as they listened to Bob.

"Mel, I just learned that you gave the contract for the rodeo to a stranger." He paused, obviously listening to Mel. "Okay, Sawyer Jensen."

Everyone in the restaurant listened, but Sawyer watched Erin's expression. Her defense of him to Bob surprised him. She wanted to give him a chance. He didn't know what to think or feel.

Bob nodded. "I think that's an excellent idea. I'll call around and we'll get enough people together tonight to listen to this man's ideas. At seven."

Another look passed between Erin and Sawyer.

"That's no excuse. If the board members from Harding want the same for their residents, they can do it tomorrow." Silence. "You may be head of the board, but that can be revoted."

Traci's gasp sounded through the room.

"Good. We'll gather tonight at the new conference center." Bob hung up and nailed Sawyer with a look. "We're going to listen to you tonight. You got a problem with that?"

"No, I'd welcome the opportunity to present my proposal to the residents."

"Good." Bob glanced at Erin. "I couldn't do less than check this guy out."

"Thanks, Bob."

"You always favored her, Bob," Traci shouted.

"And if you'd driven my son around while I was in the hospital and my wife was with me, then I might've favored you, too, Traci."

No comment came from the table behind them.

"Come on, honey. I'm hungry," his wife said.

With a final look, the couple walked back to the order window.

Sawyer knew it was time to leave. "I'd like to check into that motel."

"You sure?" Erin said.

"I am."

Shrugging, she stood and walked outside. "We could walk, but you probably have luggage and equipment that you need to put in your room, so we'll drive."

He nodded. "I'd like to ask one question."

Her shoulders tensed.

"Who's Bob?"

She visibly relaxed. "Robert Rivera owns the hardware/feed/tractor store. If you need something for your ranch or farm, chances are Bob has it or can order it or knows where to get it."

"And he's not on the rodeo board?"

"He used to be, but family stuff has kept him busy, so he resigned. He was on the board with my father and they usually voted against Mel. It made things lively."

"I'm sure it did."

"And be warned, things could get vocal tonight."

"I'll consider myself warned."

He swallowed his smile. She may have thought she could scare him away, but she didn't know who he was. His professional reputation as a man who could bring success out of defeat and turmoil was at stake. But more than that, there was something here in this town that called to him and he wasn't going to ignore that call. He'd turn the rodeo around and make it thrive. And the beautiful woman who would challenge him had nothing to do with it, he reassured himself.

It took less than three minutes for them to drive over to the next block and park in front of The Sombrero Motel, a prime example of art deco. The lobby was shaped like the high conical crown of a sombrero, surrounded by the curved brim of the hat sporting red, green and yellow stripes at its base. The hotel's color resembled a big swimming pool.

Erin still couldn't believe he wanted to stay here instead of one of the newer places. "Change your mind?"

"Nope. This place looks great." He carefully ran his gaze over the building.

"Carmen Vega, the owner, bought it ten years ago, when she came back from Denver after working for several different hotel chains. She grew up seeing The Sombrero and had always loved it, so she bought it and restored it."

"Good to know."

Pushing open the glass door, Erin called out, "Hey, Lencho, how's it going?"

The young college-aged man looked up from his reading. "Erin, what are you doing here?" He stood.

"I've brought you a paying customer."

"Good, things are kinda slow right now, but next week, we've got more people coming in. The historic-motel crowd of Southern California has booked the place."

Erin made the introductions, and Lencho handed Sawyer an old-fashioned registration card used circa 1937.

Sawyer stared down at it.

"Carmen believes in the full-blown experience," Erin explained.

Sawyer shrugged and went to work filling out the card.

Erin leaned over the counter. "What are you studying, Lencho?"

"Differential equations. I have to have it for the engineering degree."

Erin laughed. "I had a couple of courses that I could've done without in college. But fortunately I grabbed one of the bowling slots as my PE."

It took Sawyer less than two minutes to fill out the card.

Erin peeked at it. "No TV?"

"I want the full experience." If she thought she'd scared him, apparently she was wrong.

Lencho pulled the key out of a cubbyhole behind the registration desk. "You want me to show you to the room?"

Erin laughed. "If he can't find room two, the board's going to be in real trouble and needs to rethink giving him the rodeo job."

The youth stilled. "He got the job? I thought you applied for it."

She shrugged.

"But we're having an impromptu meeting tonight for the town folks to review my plan," Sawyer explained. "Please come."

"Bob organized it," Erin added.

The youth looked from Sawyer to her. "I'll be there. I don't want to miss any of that action." He rubbed his hands together. "We haven't had so much excitement since Denise Sander's burro got loose, ended up in Melvin's yard and ate the flowers, tomatoes and chilies growing in his garden."

Lencho gave Sawyer the key, an actual old-fashioned metal key.

"I haven't seen anything like this in a long time."

Erin's brow arched. "Full experience, remember?"

"True."

Motioning Sawyer outside, they walked the seventeen steps to room two. The motel consisted of twelve rooms with the sombrero-shaped lobby anchoring the east end of the structure. The twelve rooms surrounded a central patio covered by a pergola and scattered with various cacti. Massive Mexican clay pots dotted the patio area along with concrete benches decorated with Mexican tile. Room twelve anchored the far end of the three-sided structure. The lobby stood closest to the old Route 66.

"I'm impressed." He motioned to the patio.

"Carmen and her uncle landscaped the courtyard after they finished the rooms, using original plans the owners had drawn up when the motel was built."

They stopped at the door of room two, and he unlocked it. Stepping inside, he slowly surveyed the cool interior. The slick lines of the desk and chairs could've come from any of the *Thin Man* movies popular in the thirties. No TV, and a big black phone on the desk. Beside it was a Tiffany-style lamp with a cut-glass shade of brown, yellow and orange glass. A wonderful painting of the desert landscape at sundown hung on the wall over the bed. She loved this decor, but he didn't say anything.

"Does this meet with your approval?" She grinned at him, enjoying his reaction or nonreaction. She'd warned him.

He didn't bat an eye. "This is fine. Is there a Wi-Fi connection somewhere close?"

"In the lobby."

"Thanks for the heads-up."

"I hope you keep that positive attitude when we meet later tonight."

"I'm looking forward to it." No hesitation colored his response.

She wanted to grin. "I hope so."

Chapter Two

Erin had finally managed to find her footing. Her father's stroke had tilted her world off its axis, but when she had raced to the board headquarters today and found nobody there, she'd known another blow was around the corner. Talking to Mel's secretary about where they were, Erin knew. She thought she'd been prepared for the blow of losing out on the job she so wanted, but the instant she opened the door and saw Sawyer standing at the head of the table, she realized she wasn't. Why hadn't her dad called her with the news? How soon after the meeting had the stroke happened? Mother wasn't clear on the details.

She shook off the trivial thoughts. What was important was that her father had survived the stroke, not that she hadn't gotten the job. They'd spent countless hours on the phone, talking about what needed to be done in the update. He'd mentioned the other candidate that Melvin brought in, but Dad thought it wouldn't be a problem, at least the last time they talked, which was a few days before the vote.

She'd tap-danced her way through today's board meeting.

Pushing open the lobby door, she looked at Lencho. "How are you doing in your classes? Are you keeping up your grades?" Her dad had tutored the young man his freshman year in high school.

"I'm okay." He looked through the glass door and watched as Sawyer moved his truck from the far side of the office to park in front of his room. "How do you feel about that guy?"

She shrugged. "I'll be interested in hearing his plans tonight."

"I'm sorry that you didn't get the job."

Erin realized that the young man felt uncomfortable that she didn't win. "Don't worry. I'm not surrendering. I'll keep him on track. You remember, we didn't let you flunk out of algebra. Well, I'm not simply going to walk away from the rodeo and give up."

"No matter how much Traci lobbied for the other guy?"

The kid wasn't telling Erin anything she hadn't already figured out. "You got it."

"Good. Of course, I was surprised the guy didn't take the room with the TV."

"I guess we have a lot to learn about him."

"True."

"Does he know anything about rodeo?" Lencho asked.

Mel wasn't going to foist any greenhorn on the community, not even to please his daughter. "He does. He claims to have won several events at different rodeos."

The kid brightened. "Let's look him up on the internet." He opened his laptop and did a search on Sawyer's name. Erin walked around the counter and peered over his shoulder. Sawyer's name came up in the search engine along with a listing of his wins.

They silently read the list. He'd made a name for himself.

"Well, you're right. He's no greenhorn." Pointing to the computer screen, Lencho said, "He's got a brother, too, who did pickup."

"He told me."

They read about Sawyer's brother.

Taking a deep breath, Lencho shook his head. "He looks like the real deal."

He did, indeed, and from what they'd learned about Sawyer's and his brother's backgrounds, they were the real deal who participated in rodeo. Sawyer had the credentials to know what the cowboys needed, but Erin knew *this* rodeo and *these* people and knew the background that Sawyer didn't. "We'll find out tonight."

Erin tried to listen to the car radio on her drive home and ignore what had happened at the board meeting. She started to hum with Tim McGraw about heading down this road again.

But her wounded heart refused to let go of the hurt.

What had been the final tally of the board members? She knew Melvin hadn't voted for her. Of course, his daughter thought Erin was a cross between Godzilla and Cinderella's stepmother, but that stemmed from Traci's unreasonable fear that Erin would steal back Traci's husband, since he'd been Erin's high school sweetheart. Andy had wanted to marry Erin, but she hadn't wanted to settle down so soon. Going to college had been her goal but, no matter what she said to Andy, he never took her seriously. Traci often told Erin what a good catch Andy was and why not marry him? Traci thought Erin had lost her marbles not to take up Andy's offer. The instant he broke up with Erin, Traci swept in and captured her man. Erin had not been invited to the wedding even though it had been a Christmas affair. When Erin returned home the first time after she started college, Traci made it clear their friendship was over, much to Erin's surprise. Why Traci acted the way she did, Erin didn't understand. She got her man and Erin got to go to college.

How many other members of the board had followed Mel's lead in voting for Sawyer? Why had they voted for an outsider instead of a hometown girl? That's what hurt the most.

It's business, the logical part of her brain argued, but her heart said the vote was against her personally, not her proposal.

Pulling off the main road, she drove down the drive to the ranch house and parked her truck under the covered carport and breezeway that ran from the kitchen to the barn.

She didn't go into the house, and instead walked to the corral behind the barn to see her horse, Wind Dancer. The moment the horse saw Erin, she trotted over to the fence and head butted her.

Reaching out, Erin stroked the horse's neck. "Did you miss me, girl? I'm sure Santo took care of you." The horse arched her neck and then raced around the ring, coming to a stop in front of her.

Looking down at her long skirt and boots, she realized she needed to change. "Give me a minute, Dancer, and I'll be back."

It took less than five minutes for her to grab her bag from the truck, change into jeans and race back outside. Her brother, Tate, hadn't come home from school yet, and Erin didn't know where her aunt Betty was, but they'd show up.

Erin didn't bother with a saddle. She grabbed reins and a halter, opened the gate and slipped them on Dancer. Erin hopped on Dancer and rode out of the corral. Horse and rider started slowly, and then Erin leaned close to the horse's neck as Dancer picked up speed. They were in their element, racing across the high desert, dancing on the wind.

Erin could feel herself touch the face of heaven, giving

up her wound and the hurt of not winning the contract to reorganize the rodeo.

Finally, Dancer slowed to a walk and stopped. Leaning over, Erin rested her head on the horse's neck. "I was blind-sided when I walked into that meeting, girl. Felt as naked as the day I was born." She sat up. "So what am I going to do now?" She looked to heaven. "I need some direction here, Lord. I don't know what to do, but I know I'm not giving up." She thought for a moment and remembered the look of admiration in Sawyer's eyes when she'd initially faced off with Mel. There was something about the man that intrigued her and drew her. It didn't make sense, but then nothing in the past few days did. It was one of those times when you just held on to God and knew He'd guide you through the storm.

"Of course, Bob did set up the meeting tonight, so I need some wisdom there."

The instant the words were out of her mouth, she knew what she needed to do and that wasn't feeling sorry for herself.

Sawyer finished storing his things in the room and re-membered how Erin had watched him as he'd registered at the historic motel and surveyed his room. If he didn't miss his guess, she'd thought he'd call uncle and go to one of the newer chains. As he'd played along and taken the room, he'd discovered that he liked it. She intrigued him. He didn't know what he'd expected when she'd appeared in the conference room, but it wasn't the woman he en-countered. He didn't know quite what to make of her, but he had a feeling he'd find out. He'd walk cautiously around her until he knew what to expect. Would she be fair— or fight dirty like his mom and last girlfriend? He'd had enough of clingy and manipulative women.

Walking back to the lobby, Sawyer found Lencho hadn't moved from the desk and his homework.

"Is the room okay?"

Oddly enough, the room had the feeling of home—strong, sturdy, something that would be there for a long time. He hadn't had that experience growing up until his big brother had taken responsibility for the two of them. "It's great."

The kid studied him as if he didn't believe his ears.

"What I need are directions to the rodeo fairgrounds."

Lencho pointed to the brochure stand in the corner of the room. "You'll find maps there."

Sawyer retrieved a brochure and laid it out on the counter.

"So you beat out Erin for the rodeo job?"

Sawyer looked up and studied the youth. "I did."

"I'm surprised. I mean, everyone in town knows if you need something done, Erin's the one who can do it. And she always comes through."

"So I hear." He had his work cut out for him to win people over. "But maybe the board wanted someone who isn't familiar with anything here to look at the situation with new eyes. Suppose you're looking at one of your equations and can't see how to solve it. You've worked and worked on how to get the answer, then someone else looks at it and sees where you've gone wrong and points it out. The same is true with the rodeo. Maybe someone who's not familiar with it can see a problem, or even just do it a different way, and solve the situation."

Lencho thought about it. "That makes sense."

Sawyer studied the map to orient himself with the streets.

Pointing to where they were, Lencho said, "Go down to First Street, turn right, and when you get to US 66, turn west and on the outskirts of town you should find the fairgrounds."

"Thanks."

He followed Lencho's directions and, within ten minutes, found the grounds. On the north side sat the rodeo arena with chutes and corrals, and on the south side stood the football field. In between the two sat a midway with accompanying food stands and game booths.

After parking his truck, he walked through the grounds, inspecting the facility. It wasn't in bad shape but needed upgrades. He pulled out his cell phone and took pictures to document the conditions. As he stood on the bleachers, he could imagine Erin on her horse, flying around the barrels in the main arena. He would have liked to see that.

The thought caught him off guard. He was the last person on earth she'd want to run into, he imagined, unless it was an opportunity to offer her suggestions. Still, he would've loved to watch her race. Maybe he could in the future.

He sat and pulled a small notebook out of his shirt pocket and jotted some notes. Later, when he was back in his room, he'd update his PowerPoint, giving his initial thoughts, and incorporate the pictures he took this afternoon, pointing out how he'd redo the midway and food stands. He put the phone in his shirt pocket and headed back to his truck. He wanted to assess the roads leading into the rodeo grounds, which needed to be included in his overall plan, but as he drove away, he kept thinking of seeing Erin ride. When he worked on a rodeo, he never let his personal feelings interfere. There were a couple of times when the ladies he'd worked with wanted to take the relationship to another level, but he never did.

But this time—he stopped the thought cold.

What was wrong with him? Since his brother's wedding, Sawyer had been having all sorts of weird thoughts, and he chalked up his reaction to Erin as post-wedding blues. Did men get those? Surely that was the explanation.

Stepping into the house after her ride, Erin ran into Aunt Betty. Her salt-and-pepper hair hung in two braids, tied off with twine. Her colorful skirt and white blouse, belted at the waist, were her normal garb. Auntie preferred traditional Navajo dress. Besides, she teased, she couldn't fit into jeans the way Erin and her sister, Kai, could.

Mother had called her sister after Dad's stroke to come and watch over Erin's younger brother, Tate, a senior in high school. Mom thought Tate needed Betty's calming influence. Erin knew she should've come back with Auntie and Tate on Sunday, but wanted to stay to see how her father responded to the treatment the hospital provided.

"There you are. When I didn't find you, I knew you were out on Dancer."

"I can't fool you, can I?" Brushing a kiss across her aunt's cheek, Erin walked to the sink and got a large glass of water.

Betty studied her. "What's wrong, Daughter?"

In her mother's family, grown aunts and cousins called the younger members of the family *Daughter* or *Son*. It meant you were never alone and always had eyes on you, which was both a blessing and a pain. Erin thought about trying to divert her aunt's question, but no one got anything by Aunt Betty or Mother. They were nabbed every time they tried. Erin and her sister had learned not to try. Unfortunately, their brother, Tate, hadn't.

"I went to the board meeting in Dad's place. They hired the other person who applied for the job."

"What's the matter with those men?" Betty shook her head. "Someone should knock them in the head. They know you and how you've given to this town. If someone wants something done, you get a call, and that includes the children of board members. And they are not shy about asking for your help. You remember when Mel asked you to help Traci get through Algebra One? He wanted her to pass the class, but with you and your father tutoring her, she made a B minus. And then there was Chris Saddler's boy wanting help with his science project—"

"That's enough, Auntie. It's done." Erin didn't want to dwell on what was. She slipped her arms around her shorter, rounder aunt. "Thanks for believing in me," Erin whispered into her aunt's hair.

"You carry too much on those small shoulders. Not every problem is yours to solve, Daughter."

Erin stepped back, blinking her eyes. "True, but I have ideas on how to help the rodeo, and I cannot turn away. Besides, Dad wanted me to take his place on the board."

Shaking her finger, Betty said, "Rest and take care of yourself. We don't need another bird with a broken wing. With your father in the hospital, your mother needs you whole."

Erin couldn't deny that, but so far, her mom appeared to be bearing up under the load. "How is Tate doing?"

Betty didn't answer. She walked to the table and sat down. Erin joined her.

"What's wrong?" Her brother's freshman year in high school had been rough, and he'd given her parents no end of trouble, with skipping school and not wanting to go to church with them. But he wasn't given a choice whether or not to go to school and church. So he'd gone, and his sophomore and junior years had been better. He'd been doing well until their dad's stroke, then retreated into himself.

"Your brother acts as if nothing happened and life is fine. But I see behind the mask he's wearing. There's much trouble in his heart."

"I've worried about that. Kai mentioned he acted as if he didn't have a care in the world while at the hospital before

I got there. She said he'd even disappeared for a couple of hours and no one could find him." Erin shook her head. "We all know he's hurting, Auntie, but—"

"I thought he seemed off when I picked him up at the hospital Sunday night, but he said nothing to me on the ride home," Betty said, shaking her head.

"He's a man—a young one," Erin defended, "but a man. When was the last time your husband sat down and talked to you when he was troubled about something?"

Betty smiled. "You're right."

"The town's having an impromptu meeting tonight about the rodeo. I'd like to shower and change clothes before going back."

Betty narrowed her eyes, making Erin feel guilty. "What's the name of this person who won the rodeo contract over you?"

"Sawyer Jensen."

"I think I should go to this meeting, too, even though I don't live here. Your mother might want my observations."

"You sure you want to go?"

Betty's eyes twinkled. "There's more going on than rodeo discussion."

True, there were lots of undercurrents, but if Erin didn't attend it might look like she was hiding—and that wasn't happening. Besides, Sawyer might need her to referee. The thought made her grin. She discounted her reaction to the man.

"You're right, but I'm afraid the meeting will not be a peaceful one."

Betty shooed the concern away. "Have I ever been known to run from a challenge?"

"No, Auntie." And that's what made Erin nervous.

It appeared the entire town of Tucumcari had turned out for the impromptu meeting that night. Sawyer had his presentation cued up on his computer and plugged into the overhead projector. He'd added a couple of slides he'd taken this afternoon to bolster his points on the changes he thought needed to be made.

A wave of sound ran through the audience. Sawyer glanced up and saw Erin, an older woman and a teenage boy walk into the room. People pointed the group to the front row, where several seats were left empty. The trio made their way forward.

The older woman stopped at the edge of the stage and waved Sawyer forward. Erin stood behind the woman, but the youth walked over to the empty seat and threw himself down. He shot Sawyer a look that said he was bored. His body language echoed his disdain at having to be there.

Sawyer moved to the edge of the stage, then jumped down. "Ma'am. I'm Sawyer Jensen. And you are?"

"Betty Crow Creek."

He glanced over at Erin.

Betty cleared her throat. "I'm Erin's aunt. I'm here while Erin's mother is in Albuquerque with her husband."

Sawyer held out his hand. "It's nice to meet you."

Betty shook it. "You appear normal. Really, a handsome man."

Erin blinked.

To cover his surprise, Sawyer smiled. "Thank you."

Betty folded her arms over her chest. "I expected someone who had two heads and was maybe green."

Sawyer's eyes widened.

"Auntie!" Erin's strangled protest could be heard only by Betty and him.

His mouth twitched with humor. "Am I the ogre you were led to believe?"

"Erin only said you won. In *my* mind I expected a monster who'd turned my niece's world upside down." Betty glanced at Erin, and then turned back to him. "I'm the one who imagined you with green skin and living under a bridge."

So far, he was batting zero.

Melvin stood, stepped to the podium and started the meeting. Betty and Erin took their seats. Showtime.

Twenty minutes later, after Sawyer finished his program, he opened for questions.

Erin had listened carefully to the plan Sawyer laid out. She had to admit he'd thought of some aspects of the rodeo that she hadn't and his plans were good.

Bob stood. "Have you actually been to the fairgrounds yourself?"

"I went this afternoon and updated the slides in the presentation," Sawyer answered. "The board sent pictures so I could evaluate the situation, but after seeing it myself I changed and tailored some of my ideas for this facility."

"I can vouch for that," Melvin added.

Bob didn't look convinced.

A brisk discussion followed, with people asking questions and commenting on the presentation.

Bob stood again. "I'd like to hear Erin's plan, too, see how it compares with yours."

Erin stood, red faced, as she turned to her neighbors and friends. "The board evaluated both proposals and thought this was the better plan." That started another argument that lasted for the next ten minutes.

Erin looked around and knew this back-and-forth helped no one.

She motioned for everyone to be quiet, and it took a few seconds for everyone to quit talking. Traci glared at her from her second-row seat.

"I appreciate everyone's support and faith in me, but listening to my proposal won't settle anything. The board has already voted, and, after reviewing Sawyer's plan, I'd say he has a good one."

Several people started to protest, but she held up her hands. "I like his ideas on how to bring outside money to our rodeo and city. I hadn't thought about that.

"There were a couple of other ideas that surprised me, but I think they might work here. But I also have a few items that Mr. Jensen didn't think about, and I plan to suggest them to him and push to implement them." She grinned. "He won't remain unscathed."

Standing, Bob said, "You sure, Erin?"

"I am." She scanned the audience. "What we need to do is all come together and start working on the rodeo. A good idea is a good idea." She turned back to Sawyer. "No matter who came up with it."

She heard chuckles in the audience. "So, I think now that we've heard Sawyer's plan, we should get behind it and support it one hundred percent."

Melvin's mouth hung open, and his wife had to elbow him. From Traci's expression it looked as if she'd sucked a lemon, but Andy nodded to Erin.

Erin took her seat again.

Sawyer stood by the podium. "Any more questions or comments?"

The room remained quiet.

"Then I guess this meeting is over." Sawyer walked down the stage steps to the floor of the room, waiting in case anyone wanted to talk privately. No one came by. He didn't know if that was good or bad. But what he did know was Erin had stood up for him. That found a spot in his heart.

Erin's friends clustered around her, asking questions. This time, her brain had comprehended Sawyer's words, and she saw her neighbors' reactions. She'd been impressed. He'd put together a thorough plan to get their rodeo back on its feet. But she had modifications that could maximize his ideas.

As she talked with other residents, Erin saw out of the corner of her eye Sawyer packing up his laptop and projector. When he walked by Tate, her brother said something. Sawyer stopped. The two exchanged words, then Sawyer walked on.

Aunt Betty frowned and leaned close to Tate. "I may be old but…"

Erin couldn't hear the rest of what her aunt said. Tate shrugged and jogged up the other aisle out to their car.

What had that been about?

Now, several of the board members gathered in front of the stage around Sawyer. Bob joined them.

"I'm going to go through the facility tomorrow morning to do a more detailed inspection, making notes on what needs to be updated or replaced. I'd be happy to have anyone walk through with me," Sawyer announced to the room.

"I'll be there," Bob Rivera replied. "You going to notify the folks in Harding?"

"I will," Sawyer replied.

Bob nodded his approval.

Sawyer looked at Erin, silently asking if she would be there.

"You'll see me," Erin answered. She tried to keep her expression neutral, but felt a smile curve her lips.

He returned the smile, which made her heart light.

Later, when she and her aunt walked out to the car, Erin asked, "What was all that about with Tate and Sawyer earlier?"

"Your brother was just trying to give the new guy a hard time."

"What'd Tate say?"

Betty kissed Erin's cheek and opened the passenger-side door. Obviously, Auntie wasn't going to tell her.

Why?

Chapter Three

Sawyer parked his truck in front of his hotel room, grabbed his laptop and projector, and slipped out of the truck.

"Let me help you," Lencho called, walking to Sawyer's side and taking the projector.

Sawyer grabbed the key from his pocket and opened the door.

"I liked your presentation for the rodeo."

Sawyer nodded. "Good to hear."

"I did want to hear Erin's plan, and when she said it wasn't necessary, it surprised me, knowing how competitive she is." He shrugged. "But if she thought your plan was good, we can count on it." He grinned. "I know she'll give you her ideas, and she *ain't* shy about voicing her opinion."

"Really?"

Lencho opened his mouth to respond, but saw the teasing in Sawyer's face. Opening the door, Sawyer motioned Lencho inside. The young man put the projector on the desk.

"So, you're telling me that Erin will keep me honest."

Red ran up the teen's neck. "I didn't mean it like that, but if you give her your word, you better live up to what you've said."

"Good to know."

"And it's the same with her. If she gives you her word, you can count on it. And she has another thing. It's kinda related to her first thing. Don't lie. It ain't worth it."

"So you've been on the wrong side of her?"

"Uh, kinda. But it only happened once," he quickly added. "And you always know where you stand with Erin. I like it. She's not like other girls who want to play head games."

Obviously, the young man thought the world of Erin.

"Thanks for the advice."

"No problem." He left, closing the door behind him.

Sawyer locked the door and sat down in the flowered chair by the table in the room. The meeting tonight had been much easier than he'd expected, due to Erin's intervention.

Her actions puzzled him. He knew she wanted the job, so why'd she give up so quickly? He hadn't seen her proposal, but had it been inferior to his?

That thought didn't sit well with him. So what was it?

She had cut off Bob's insistence to prolong this process. But why? What motivated her? His experience with competitors was that they didn't act out of noble purposes. So, why'd she do it?

He stood and retrieved his laptop. Before he could boot up, his phone rang.

"Hi, Sawyer, how was your first day on the job?" Caleb, his older brother, asked. "Did it go well?"

"It's been an interesting day."

"Oh? What happened?" The tone of Caleb's voice changed from teasing to serious in a heartbeat.

"There was another competitor for the job, and some of the townspeople wanted to hear her ideas. She's local talent."

"She?"

Sawyer explained the situation with Erin and her qualified support tonight. "And the final twist is that she didn't know the results of the vote until she walked into the board meeting."

"So was there a big scene?"

"No."

Both men remained silent.

"Do you think she acted that way to stay in with the rodeo redo just to make your life miserable?"

After thinking a moment, Sawyer said, "No. She doesn't strike me as a woman with a sneaky side. So far she's been up-front and honest."

"You mean she's not trying to manipulate you like Mom?"

Sawyer thought about it. He didn't know Erin well enough, but his gut feeling told him no. "Tonight at a public meeting, she put an end to the argument about my winning."

Caleb didn't respond. Finally, he said, "Well, just watch yourself. We've been on the wrong side of people before."

"True, but enough about me, how's that wife of yours doing?" Sawyer wanted to get the topic off him and onto the new baby coming.

"She says she's okay, but she keeps puking. How could that be fine?"

Sawyer's concern spiked. "Is anything wrong?"

"Yeah. Morning sickness. She can't stand the smell of coffee anymore." The last words out of his mouth sounded strangled.

Sawyer laughed. "This is a new development."

"It is. The first time she threw up on me, I thought it a fluke. But time two and three, we knew.

"Herbal tea. She wants me to drink herbal tea. Have you ever tasted that stuff? Looks like dishwater and smells about as bad. I've seen stagnant creeks I'd drink out of before the stuff she's drinking."

"It's a small price to pay for me having a niece or a nephew." Sawyer wanted to laugh again, but took pity on his brother.

"Are you going to give up coffee to support me?" Caleb demanded.

"Nope. So what are you doing about it?"

"Running to the barn where Gramps brews a pot of coffee. Brenda knows what we're doing and stays away until ten. I'm wondering if I'll live through this."

Sawyer had to laugh. "You'll live."

Caleb mumbled something.

"You're going to have to gut it up, brother."

"That's what Gramps says, but I don't know if he knows what he's talking about. Do you know how many things could go wrong?"

"Trust him. He's seen his children and grandchildren born. He knows more than us. And Brenda being Brenda, if something's wrong, she'll see about it. Is she going to quit going to school?"

"No."

The quickness of his brother's answer told him that Caleb had made the mistake of asking his wife the same question. Sawyer grinned. "If she doesn't think she's in danger, then relax. I think your wife wants you to unwind and help her."

"If you say so, but I want you to be careful about the woman you told me about."

"Will do. Let me know how things are there." Sawyer hung up and sat staring at his computer.

Caleb thought Erin had another agenda. He'd have to be on his guard against her no matter how strangely his heart reacted to the woman. But there was still something about Erin Delong that he was missing. What?

* * *

The next morning, Erin arrived at the rodeo grounds before any other board member. She parked by Sawyer's truck, took the last swig of her coffee and got out.

"Ah, a lady who likes her coffee," Sawyer commented as he walked toward her.

"Guilty as charged. I haven't met a cowboy who doesn't run on it." She placed her travel mug in the center console between the front seats and closed the door.

"True." He shifted, then smiled at her. "I wanted to thank you for your words of support last night."

She nodded. "But, as I told Bob, I plan to have my say if I see things that need to be done." She had relived that meeting multiple times after she got home, checking whether she'd missed anything. The man seemed to rattle her thinking processes, leaving her to wonder if she'd lost her edge. Usually, she found it easy to cut through to the heart of the matter or see what drove a person. With Sawyer, she felt blind, groping in the dark. He made her feel nervous and off-balance. And what her senses told her, she didn't believe, which was a first for her.

"I'd expect nothing less." He nodded to her, but there was something else in his eyes that she couldn't nail down. Was that humor? Interest?

Before she could respond, Mel drove into the parking lot, followed by several other board members in their vehicles. Five minutes later, Harding County board members arrived. Bob Rivera also appeared. "Morning."

They walked through the empty rodeo grounds discussing Sawyer's plan and other concerns the board members had. Bob hung back and observed the tour.

"Who do you have a contract with to provide the rides?" Sawyer asked Mel as they stood in the empty area where the rides would be located.

Mel named the company they'd used previously to provide the carnival rides for the rodeo.

Sawyer frowned. "I wouldn't use them this year. I have the names of a couple of different vendors."

"Why?" Chris Saddler asked. "We've worked with that company for years."

Erin could always count on Chris to bring up questions she had. When Chris asked a question of Mel, he got answers. When she asked a question on the same subject, Mel gave her nothing but grief.

"The company you're using had a lawsuit filed against them last week, and their safety record is iffy," Sawyer answered.

The board members all looked at Mel.

"Did you know about their history?" Norman asked.

"This is the first I've heard of this."

Erin kept her mouth shut but met Mel's gaze. She and her dad had argued with him about the company, but he had pushed aside their concerns.

Mel ground his teeth and turned to face Sawyer. "I've heard rumors. We can look into your suggestions," he said reluctantly.

As they finished the tour of the grounds, Mel did a good imitation of a petulant child, with his stomping feet and bad attitude. The other board members grew uncomfortable with his actions.

"I think half these vendor booths should be offered to people in Harding," Norman stated.

"And if there are not enough people in Harding who want to pay for one of the booths, offer the rest of the booths to anyone in the state who wants to rent them," Erin added.

"Good idea," Bob Rivera said.

The others agreed.

"Okay, I can get those contracts reviewed and awarded," Sawyer added.

The group started toward their cars. Mel stepped closer to Sawyer. "You were hired for your talent and not anyone else's." Mel glared at Erin.

"So does that mean you don't want me to consider any of the suggestions from the other rodeo board members that vary from the original contract?" Sawyer spoke loudly enough for everyone to hear. "And does that warning include you?"

Everyone stopped.

Mel glanced around, then swallowed. "No, that's not what I meant."

"Good, because if any of the local residents or board members know of a way to cut costs to bring us in under budget, I want to know." Sawyer turned to the others. "I'll email updates weekly to the board members and have the changes posted at the rodeo office."

The members nodded and walked to their cars.

Mel shot Erin a last disgruntled look and trudged to his truck.

Bob waited behind with Erin and Sawyer. "Well, Mr. Jensen, you just got on Mel's bad side."

"Could be."

"Thankfully, you were already awarded the contract," Bob added.

"True, but once the project gets started, Mel will change his mind."

"Don't count on it." Bob nodded to Erin and Sawyer and walked away.

Erin stood there absorbing Sawyer's defense of her. It was the last thing she had expected from him, but there it was, warming her heart. It was something not a lot of people did for her. They always expected her to be the strong one, defending others. To be on the receiving end of it was like a gentle rain on her parched soul. "Thanks for your support." Erin didn't know how to handle this man. Too often, other professional men not from around here approached her ideas with skepticism. He didn't seem fazed by her suggestions but, instead, welcomed them.

He nodded. "I liked your idea to make sure all the booths were occupied."

Oddly, she wanted to preen over his compliment. "It's just common sense."

His rich laughter filled the air. "Sometimes common sense is the last thing that rules."

"True."

"I'm heading back to the rodeo office to go over the books for the last few years. I could use help from someone familiar with what's gone on before, and a board member would be perfect for the job."

The offer only added to her confused reaction to him. "I've got the morning free, so I can do that."

"Good."

They walked to their trucks.

"Growing up, I spent a lot of time on these grounds. I looked forward to September when the rodeo came," Erin said.

"I understand. Summers my brother and I followed the traveling rodeo wherever it went."

"What'd your parents think of that?"

His expression slammed shut, throwing her back on her heels. "My father died when I was young."

The tone of his voice didn't encourage any other questions. "I'm sorry." Erin didn't push. "I'll see you at the offices." She opened the door of her truck and slid into the driver's seat.

Pulling out of the parking lot, she glanced in her rearview mirror and saw Sawyer standing by his truck, studying her.

"I guess he thought I might get into his business. Too bad the man doesn't know me," she said out loud. A smile slowly curved her lips. "But he'll learn."

When Sawyer walked into the offices of the bicounty rodeo, Erin sat talking to the secretary.

"I appreciate your prayers, Lisa. Dad's improving a little each day."

The women stopped and looked at him.

"Did you get lost?" Erin asked, her voice light.

"No, but I drove through the rodeo grounds and confirmed that the back entrance to the grounds needs the road widened and marked."

"Excellent idea," Erin replied.

Lisa grinned.

"What?" Sawyer looked at both women.

"Erin proposed that last year, but Mel disagreed and wouldn't bring it up at the board meeting."

"Well, I agree with you."

"Good to know."

"Let's move into the other room and start working on this rodeo."

A small office stood behind the reception area. Down from the office was a meeting room where Sawyer and Erin could spread out. On one side of the room were bookshelves filled with binders of past rodeos. The notebooks went back to 1937.

"I see this rodeo has a long past." Sawyer nodded to the notebooks. "It's great it's been documented."

Erin pulled the first notebook off the shelf. Carefully, she put the binder on the table, opened it and slowly turned the pages.

Looking over her shoulder, Sawyer read the name of Clayton Delong. He stepped closer. "Clayton Delong? Is he related to you?"

She looked up. Suddenly, the air between them thickened with awareness. Her eyes drifted toward his mouth. Swallowing, she said, "He was my dad's grandfather. The rodeo has always been connected with my family, but as time has gone on, others in the community have bought in. When our rodeo combined with the Harding County rodeo, the Delong share diminished, but Dad still sits on the board."

Her interest in the rodeo suddenly took on a different dimension. This was family heritage. He could respect that and admire it, but he hoped he'd read her right and she'd work to make this redo a success and not want to make it about the Delong name. So far, she'd indicated she wanted the rodeo's success, but he'd been fooled before, so he knew not to let his heart lead the way. That didn't stop his heart from pounding at her nearness. He was here only to fix the rodeo, nothing more.

He swallowed the lump in his throat. "So this is in your blood."

"It is. But since the rodeo merged with the Harding County one, our family has not been as involved. Plus, I've been away at school and competing in barrel racing on weekends elsewhere, so I've not been here. Dad's called me and told me about the problems, but that's ancient history. Let's talk about your plan and how to implement it. And, if it needs to be tweaked, we can see about that."

Well, if he thought she'd back off, he realized he was mistaken. But he wasn't fazed in the least.

She opened the massive tote she had with her and pulled out his proposal, a notebook and several pens, setting them on the table. "I'm ready."

He knew a challenge when he saw one. "Let me get my papers."

She smiled in a way that indicated this wasn't going to

be easy. She would have her say. When he walked back into the room, he had his notebooks and her proposal.

She pointed to her proposal. "Why do you have that?"

"I found it in here when I was looking for the financial records for the losing years of the rodeo, and I wanted to read it."

"And?"

"I thought you had some good ideas, so let's discuss how we can incorporate them into my plan."

The corners of her mouth curled up. "Did you find the records for last year?"

"No, and I'd like to see those, to find out where the money was spent."

"My father, as a board member, has a copy of those records, but they're at home."

Erin stood and walked out to Lisa's desk in the reception area. "Do you know where the financial records are for the past several years?" Sawyer heard Erin ask.

"They are in Mel's office."

"Could we see them for the last year?"

"Sure, I'll get them."

Erin appeared back in the boardroom. Before they could get started, Lisa stood in the doorway. "Those records are not in Mel's office. I have last year's numbers on a flash drive in my desk. I'll bring it to you."

Several minutes later she reappeared. "I can't find the flash drive, either. It's not in my desk."

Sawyer met Erin's gaze.

"Lisa, that's okay," Erin reassured her. "If you find either the hard copy or your flash drive, let us know."

Once they were alone, Sawyer said, "That doesn't speak well of the record keeping around here."

Erin shook her head. "It's not Lisa's fault."

"Then where are the documents?"

"You'll need to talk to Mel. He's the one in charge."

So Mel was in charge of the documentation? The only reason Sawyer could think of everything disappearing was that Mel had something to hide.

For the balance of the morning, Erin and Sawyer went over his proposal page by page as they sat in the conference room. Erin wanted to understand his thinking and how he planned to execute his ideas. She'd prepared herself to argue her viewpoint, but much to her surprise, Sawyer didn't discount her opinion. He listened to her suggestions, considered modifying his plans, questioned her reasoning, then they came to a consensus. She welcomed his reasonable reaction, so different from Mel and some of the other men she'd dealt with in town.

"So, are you using some of the local residents in this rebuilding?" Erin asked.

"Is there a cement contractor in town?"

He knew there wasn't but wanted to make his point.

"No, we both know that, but there are local artisans who are excellent welders, and iron workers who know how to make the rodeo grounds more appealing for the visitors and horses. They could do some of the smaller projects. They'd welcome the work, and their hearts would be in the game."

Leaning back in his chair, he studied her. "I had planned on using larger companies out of Albuquerque for the main infrastructure components. But I'd like to encourage local craftsmen to bid on some of the smaller projects. I thought I'd add to the rodeo web page a list of the jobs that need to be done." Sawyer picked up his pen and tapped it against the table. "I have a budget I need to stick to, Erin. I don't think the board wants any overruns."

He had a valid point.

"But you might not reach all the local craftsmen. One of the local iron workers refuses to use the internet."

"So, if I wanted to advertise for local iron workers and other people to hire, where would I do that?"

She blinked. Her mind had geared up to argue for the local residents, and he'd short-circuited her brain. Again.

The glint in his eyes caught her attention. "Bob Rivera is the man who knows everyone in this county and the surrounding counties. We could walk down to his store and ask him. Or, better yet, we could list the jobs, post it in his store and ask for bids. It's not modern and high-tech, but some of the artisans prefer face-to-face business deals."

"I like that idea. Why don't we make that list, then go over to Bob's and post it? The sooner we fill the contracts, the sooner we get to work."

For the next few minutes they worked on Sawyer's laptop creating the job list. She'd been impressed he didn't ask the secretary or her to do it, but did it himself. Too often, she'd seen the guy in charge think the underlings should do the work.

"I should've had you type my econ paper." She laughed. "You're faster than I am. I flunked keyboarding in school and did the hunt and peck method my dad does. Why, even Tate is faster than me."

He chuckled, then saved the file and hit Print. Then he walked to Lisa's desk and waited for the printer to spit out the list, but nothing happened.

He quickly jotted down the jobs on a piece of paper.

"You did notice that I recommended the first thing they spend money on was a new computer and printer," Erin commented.

"I did. That will be one of the first purchases I make." He closed his laptop and notebooks and put them back in his office.

A glow of pride shot through her.

"Remember what I told the other board members? A

good idea is a good idea no matter who suggests it. I don't have a corner on the market."

As they walked down the street to Bob's hardware store, people came out of the buildings, seemingly curious. "Come see," Erin answered. The people followed behind. Erin heard murmured comments.

When they entered the hardware store, Bob and Tom Kirby, a local rancher, were at the checkout counter talking.

"Morin', Erin." He looked at Sawyer and nodded.

"Is there something I can help you with?" Bob asked.

Erin heard the other residents filing into the building.

"Sawyer and I have been discussing the rodeo redo and how to implement it. Sawyer needs the names of local vendors who want to bid on working for the rodeo."

"Oh?" Bob frowned at Sawyer. "I thought he'd want to use the big boys out of Albuquerque."

"I'm open to all bids. I do have a budget, but I want to include as many local vendors as possible. They know the history of the rodeo, and that could put a different spin on the work they do."

Bob considered Sawyer's words. He turned to Erin, silently asking if she believed this stranger.

"I think it's a good idea, Bob," she replied. "Locals would have a shot at working on the rodeo. It would give them a personal stake in the project and an opportunity to show off their work and maybe get other contracts."

"I think so, too," came a shouted reply from the back. "I'd be interested," a man called out.

Erin looked over her shoulder at the man who'd offered the comment and gave him a thumbs-up.

"Okay, give me the list of what you need, and I'll post it in the store. The folks behind you will read it and spread the word."

They didn't need the internet in this town. Word of

mouth was faster and the mode that had been used for over a hundred years, but Sawyer wanted to use the internet to bring younger people into the redo.

Sawyer pulled a slip of paper out of his shirt pocket and placed it on the counter. "Anyone who wants to bid can come by the rodeo board office." Sawyer turned to the group. "So read the list and, if you have any of the skills needed, come by and talk to me, then put in your bid."

Sawyer and Erin made their way through the crowd by the front door, leaving Bob and Tom with their mouths hanging open.

Erin laughed.

"What's so funny?" Sawyer asked.

"I don't think I've seen Bob that off-balance before."

"I do have that effect on people."

Boy, didn't she know it. No matter how much she wanted to dislike him for getting the job she'd thought was hers, he managed to throw something in her way that made it impossible.

"C'mon, Auntie, we're late," Erin said, trying to speed up her aunt and brother as they walked into the Hope Community Church.

"I'm not the one who caused the delay." Betty eyed her nephew. "What was Tate thinking about, wearing his torn cutoffs and old plaid slip-on tennis shoes with holes in each shoe to church?"

When Tate had appeared in the kitchen for breakfast, Auntie had sent him back to his room to change before he could touch any of the food. She'd ended her scolding with the threat that he had five minutes before she threw his breakfast in the garbage. Tate made it back in time to eat his egg-and-bacon flat-bread sandwich.

Entering the church, people clustered in different spots

in the main sanctuary talking. They turned and acknowl-
edged Erin and the family.

From the instant Bob had posted the jobs that needed to
be filled, a constant stream of residents had come by the
hardware store and rodeo board's headquarters. The board
members in Harding County got the word that they were
hiring for jobs to work on the rodeo. People had called and
stopped by the Delong home to check out the rumors about
jobs working on the rodeo. It'd been the talk of the town.
No, it had been the talk of the county, and late Saturday
night some jobs had appeared on the website.

As Betty, Tate and Erin made their way to the front
left side of the church, their regular place, several people
stopped and chatted about the rumblings in the county and
asked about Erin's dad. Finally, Tate threw up his hands
and just walked on and sat where he normally sat.

When the organist slipped behind her instrument and
started to play, people took their seats. The pastor welcomed everyone and announced the hymns for the morning. After they finished the first hymn, someone slid into
the pew beside her. When Erin looked over, Sawyer stood
there. He winked and started singing the second hymn.

The man had a marvelous baritone voice that flowed
around her, making her just want to sit down and listen to
him sing. Auntie looked around Erin and smiled at him.
Erin felt a dozen different people staring at them.

She didn't want to be the center of attention, but apparently she was.

The pastor announced upcoming church events and
welcomed Sawyer to the service. He also prayed for those
with needs, updating the congregation on Detrick's condition and asking God for a speedy recovery.

What the pastor preached on, she had no idea. All she
could think about was the man sitting beside her.

Before the final amen faded away, they were surrounded

by members of the congregation. Everyone wanted to meet the new guy in town. Pastor Antonio "Tony" Hooper walked over and introduced himself.

"I'm glad you decided to join us for church this morning. You are welcome."

The people around them agreed.

"Well, I wanted to find a church, since I'm going to be here a few months."

Respect filled Tony's gaze. "I'm glad to hear that. We are also grateful for the jobs coming into the county. And with you posting them at the hardware store, everyone knows about the opportunities."

"I'll credit Erin with that. It was her suggestion to make sure the local artisans and workers were given the opportunity to work for the rodeo."

"Well, that doesn't surprise me. Erin's always thinking about the people around here." Pastor patted Erin on the back.

"I'm hungry, Aunt Betty," Tate said loud enough to stop all conversation.

Uncomfortable chuckles floated through the room.

Betty looked at Tate, then Sawyer. "No doubt we're all hungry. Sawyer, come to the house and have lunch with us."

"I wouldn't want to put you out, Betty," Sawyer replied.

She waved away his comment. "I always fix too much since I'm used to cooking for eight people. Tate eats enough for two, and, although Erin has a healthy appetite, I'll have leftovers. And it will help your budget since, knowing Mel, I'm sure your meal allowance isn't that much."

"For sure," someone whispered.

Sawyer looked as if he fought a grin. "Betty, you've got me."

She nodded her head. "Follow us out to the ranch."

As Sawyer walked from the church, Traci appeared in

front of him. From the look on her face, she had heard what Betty said. "Surely, you're not going to eat with them."

Traci could be heard plainly throughout the parking lot.

"It would be ungracious for me to not show up since I've already accepted Betty's invitation."

Traci stepped closer and whispered something in his ear.

Taking a step backward, he smiled. "I look forward to it."

Traci glanced at Erin, gave her a cat-who-ate-the-canary smile and sauntered to her car. Sawyer walked to his own vehicle, parked not far from Erin's. Betty and Tate sat in the car. "What took you so long?"

He looked over his shoulder at Traci. "I tried to dodge a bullet but ran into a tree."

Erin knew exactly what he meant. She snorted. "I'll see you at the house."

As he followed her out of the parking lot, she laughed softly.

"That girl doesn't know when to quit," Betty mumbled.

"I know, Auntie, but you got to him first."

Betty nodded. "You can count on me."

"No truer words were ever spoken, Auntie."

Chapter Four

"He's still following you, Daughter."

Erin jerked her gaze away from the rearview mirror to her aunt. Erin simply shrugged and didn't defend herself.

"Are you upset that I invited him to lunch?" A satisfied smile curled Auntie's mouth.

Betty had never met a stranger without always feeling it her duty to feed them. "No, just surprised, since he won the contract over me, remember?"

"You're beyond that and already challenging him. Bob's wife told me about what happened yesterday. Little did he expect you to voice your opinions so quickly, but you have. Has he objected? Been unkind? Overbearing?"

Looking in the rearview mirror, Erin saw Tate roll his eyes.

"No, he hasn't. But—" She needed to quit while she was ahead.

Betty waited. "But what?"

"He read my proposal for updating the rodeo." All yesterday Erin thought about Sawyer, trying to sort out her conflicting emotions toward him. After another long ride on Wind Dancer, Erin knew her heart was involved.

Betty turned to her, her eyes wide and her mouth pursed into an O. "And?"

"He likes some of my ideas and wants to incorporate them, particularly my ideas for the midway."

Her aunt nodded. "A reasonable man. Good."

"But we've discovered a problem."

Betty frowned. "Oh?"

"The final figures for the last year are missing. We asked Lisa about them, but she couldn't find them. She had copies in several different places but couldn't find any of them."

The ranch house appeared, cutting off their conversation. The low-slung house and barn sat back off the road. When her great-grandfather had built the house and out structures, he'd used adobe, just as the natives of the area did. It had caused a stir among some of his friends but, during the hot summers, their home became the place where everyone met.

The driveway sat between the house and the barn with a covered breezeway connecting the kitchen door to the barn's side door. Beyond that, several corrals had been set up for Erin to practice her barrel racing. Her truck and horse trailer sat on the far side of the drive.

Erin parked next to the kitchen door.

Sawyer pulled in beside her and hurried out of his truck. He opened Betty's door and helped her out.

"Thank you." Betty glowed like a schoolgirl.

Tate clambered out of the backseat and slammed his door. He ignored everyone, walking inside. Sawyer's gaze roamed over the house, barn and corrals.

"Tate and Erin's great-grandfather built this place," Betty explained.

"Auntie, Sawyer's not interested in ancient history."

"No, I love to hear family histories," Sawyer replied.

Really? That was hard to believe. He'd be the first man she'd run into with that attitude. "Well, we better get inside. With the mood Tate is in, who knows what he's doing.

When I suggested driving to see Dad this morning, Tate didn't want to go." It only had been three days since she'd returned to Tucumcari, but she was willing to make another trip to Albuquerque if her brother wanted to visit the hospital.

"You're right." Betty hurried into the kitchen.

Sawyer stopped on the step up to the back door and scanned the yard. "Your family's got a nice setup here."

Erin picked up the tinge of sadness, or maybe it was longing in his voice. "Thanks. I miss this place when I'm away. There's a unique beauty in the starkness that calls to your soul." She shrugged. "I'll admit, it doesn't call to everyone, but for me, it—" She broke off and glanced up at him, expecting to see disdain, but instead she found understanding.

"I can see that." He opened his mouth to say more but shook his head and walked into the house, leaving her unsettled because she knew he understood her.

That had never happened before.

Betty spread a feast before him of a roast, beans, bread and local greens.

"You weren't kidding, Betty," Sawyer commented as they walked into the dining room. The room had French doors that opened out onto a patio, giving them a view of the horizon.

"My job is to feed others." Her simple statement reinforced her actions of putting out a big meal. "Didn't your mother do that, too?"

The innocent question from Betty felt like a right fist to his jaw, making him step back. Sawyer looked around to see if Betty or Erin had noticed his reaction. With all their preparations, they hadn't, but Tate had.

Sawyer searched for an appropriate response. He couldn't very well say when his mother wasn't drunk or feeling sorry for herself she couldn't manage to heat up a can of soup. They didn't need to know his past. "Mom wasn't the cook you are."

Betty stopped and her gaze caught him. He tried not to reveal anything, but her expression softened and she nodded at him.

After they prayed over the food, dishes were passed around. They discussed the morning sermon and how to live it.

Finally, Erin asked, "Did Uncle complain about you leaving?"

"No, he knows better. When his sister needed me to take care of her family, I went every time I was needed." She leaned over the table. "Uncle didn't protest then. There's food in the freezer, which he could live on for months, and if he didn't want that, there are neighbors around us who would make sure he's fed." Betty smiled. "The man won't go hungry."

"I remember the first time our parents took us to Aunt Betty's," Erin said, glancing at Sawyer. "Her kitchen is the biggest room in her house, and it's the busiest, with people coming and going.

"Tate wasn't interested in the crowd in the kitchen and found the big-screen TV in the sewing room."

Sawyer smiled, enjoying the light banter among the family. Good memories.

"That's where she made Uncle put the TV," Tate explained.

"If we had to have that fancy big-screen TV and not some normal one," Betty replied, "then I was going to make Uncle put it in my sewing room so I could watch it, too, while I sewed."

"Why Uncle let you put it there—" Tate shook his head. "He got his TV, didn't he?"

Tate shrugged and tried to suppress his smile.

"And the other boys in the neighborhood came and sat in that sewing room. They knew no shame."

"I'm surprised you let Peter and Sam Running Bear inside your house after they tried to push Tate and me down the mountain," Erin added.

Betty's eyes narrowed. "I told those boys if they ever tried that stunt again, they would never be allowed in my house to watch the big-screen TV or have fried bread."

Tate's features hardened. "You didn't need to fight my battles, Auntie. I can fight my own." He stood and stomped out of the kitchen, leaving the other three people staring at one another. Betty shook her head.

Sawyer could identify with the teen's moodiness. He stood and helped clear the table. "I wish I could've eaten more, but I didn't want to waddle to my truck."

"Don't worry." Erin put the bowl of fried bread on the counter. She pulled out freezer bags and began to put the excess food into them. "We'll either share it with others in the community or freeze it. Auntie has a reputation for feeding anyone who shows up at her door."

Sawyer stopped and studied Betty, wishing she could've been close when he and his brother needed someone like her. She returned his gaze with a penetrating one, then grabbed the bag of flat bread and shoved it at him. "For later."

At some level, he knew the older woman sensed the pain of his past. He'd known hunger. "You're doing good work."

Betty ducked her head. "There are too many people going without. My husband always had a job and we were blessed. I can do no less than share with others."

"And change lives," Sawyer murmured. "Thank you, ladies, for the meal. Now I need to go back and work." He paused. "Are your dad's notebooks here?"

"Yes, they're in the library."

"Think they might have the final numbers in them?"

"I don't know, but we should look."

He followed her to the library. She pulled down last year's notebook and handed it to him. They settled on the love seat and looked over the figures.

"These don't look like the final numbers," Sawyer commented.

Studying the final lines, Erin knew they weren't. "I agree. These look like working numbers." She glanced up into his face, realizing how close they were. She swallowed and his gaze didn't leave her face. "I'll look around to see if Dad has an addendum with the final figures." She closed the notebook and jumped up, feeling like a jack-in-the-box.

He slowly came to his feet, fighting a smile.

What was so funny, she wanted to ask, but she knew. Acting like a fifteen-year-old, which wasn't something she had done—until now.

"I'll have a listing of big contractors I need to call tomorrow. If you drop in, you can see who's shown interest in bidding."

"What time?"

"Let's try nine."

"I'll be there."

He nodded and left the room, leaving Erin clutching the notebook and feeling lost.

As Sawyer walked to his truck, he caught a glimpse of Tate disappearing into the barn.

"Tate, got a moment?" Sawyer called and waited for the teen. When Tate reappeared, the cautious expression on his face warned Sawyer to proceed carefully. "I hope I didn't barge in and ruin your Sunday lunch."

"Nah."

"I didn't mean for your sister to bring up those old stories."

"She's only a girl, and girls like to embarrass people."

Tread carefully, he warned himself. "You know what I think? Your sister remembers that time with laughter and joy. Both your aunt and sister are strong women."

Tate cocked his head. "They want to tell me what to do all the time. They think they're always right."

"True, but girls do that. It seems to me Betty was only defending her nephew. Maybe she went about it the wrong way, but sometimes we do wrong in trying to do right. I think they're acting out of love." He smiled. "I'd give them a break."

Tate shrugged. "If you say so."

"I guess when you've been raised by a mom who was afraid of making a decision, who needed someone to make up her mind for her, it's refreshing to meet a woman who can make a decision for herself."

Tate stared at him.

Sawyer wanted to snatch the words back. Tate didn't need his lecture. Sawyer nodded and slipped into his truck. As he drove away, Sawyer saw Tate standing in the driveway, staring at him.

Well, Tate wasn't the only one who was surprised. At lunch, sitting by Erin and across from Betty, Sawyer had found himself admiring them. From the conversation, he knew Betty felt a need to feed the hungry. He admired a heart so open that she'd feed anyone who walked through her door. Betty reminded him of the church people who'd housed and fed Caleb and him in Plainview.

Caleb and he had escaped an abusive home situation. After his father died, his mother turned into a helpless woman who went from boyfriend to boyfriend. The situation went from bad to worse until Caleb was finally declared an emancipated minor and moved out, taking Sawyer with him. The brothers moved to a little town in the Texas Panhandle, where the congregation adopted them.

Tate may have complained that the women in his life were suffocating him, but the teen didn't know how good he had it.

Monday morning Sawyer and Erin went over the bids that needed to be let.

The door to the boardroom opened and Mel stood there, looking like an angry bear.

"What's going on here?" He glared at Erin.

She opened her mouth to respond, but Sawyer replied, "We're working on plans for the rodeo. Would you like to join us in our session?"

Mel's jaw flexed. "No. That's why you were hired, but what is she doing here?"

"Didn't you read the email that Sawyer sent out last night?" Erin asked. "He invited any of the board members to the meeting this morning to get their input."

"Erin was the only one to show up this morning. I needed someone familiar with the area and people. She's helped with the logistics."

Mel didn't reply but turned to leave.

"Mel," Sawyer called out, "I wanted to see the final figures for the last year, to help improve the bidding, but I haven't found those records. Didn't Lisa contact you?"

Mel's back stiffened. "There are books here with the budgets in them."

"But the final ones are nowhere to be found," Sawyer replied. "The backup ones on the flash drives are missing, too, so I wondered if you have another copy somewhere."

"I do. At home, but Erin's father should have copies of them, too, for the last few years since he was on the board."

"We looked for those figures yesterday," Erin informed him, "but only found working numbers. After I went through the notebook a second time, I found a note

Dad scribbled inside that you'd provide the final numbers after the rodeo."

Mel's jaw flexed. "I'll bring the notebook by tomorrow before I drive to Las Vegas to meet with some of the board members out of Harding County. Is there anything else you need?"

"Las Vegas?" Sawyer asked, puzzled.

"Our Vegas, in San Miguel County," Erin supplied. "Our city is older than the Vegas in Nevada and dates back to 1835."

"Maybe the board should've gone with the person who knew this area," Mel grumbled. He eyed Erin.

Sawyer straightened his shoulders. Mel's words hit Sawyer wrong. Giving one's word meant the world to him. His mother's word changed with the wind or her feelings, and nothing that she promised or said could be counted on. "Feel free to revisit the decision to hire me, Mel. Let me know later today of your verdict. But realize you'll need a cause for the dismissal."

"I know the contract."

Mel stalked out.

Silence settled over the room.

"I'm sorry I didn't tell you about the note I found."

Sawyer studied the notebook in front of him, then looked up. "Not a problem."

Erin lifted her pen and tapped it against the table. "When you get on the wrong side of Mel, well, life's not pleasant. The board made a decision and while I would've loved to have gotten the contract, we need to stick with what we did. The county can't move with Mel's moods."

"Or his daughter's."

Erin bit her lip to keep from smiling. Sawyer grinned. She gave in and they laughed.

Sharing the humorous moment softened Erin's heart more.

"Don't worry. There's lots going on right now."

Before she could reply, her cell phone rang. She pulled it from her purse.

"Erin, this is Sheriff Trujillo."

Her heart nearly stopped. "Sheriff? Why are you calling?"

Sawyer's attention shifted to her.

"I have Tate here at the jail. I talked with your aunt and she said you were in town."

"What happened?"

"One of the deputies found him out at the rodeo grounds, racing around the parking lot. We nabbed him. You need to come by the jail and get him."

"I can be there in less than five minutes. I'm at the rodeo board office, working."

"Then I'll see you in a few minutes." He hung up.

Erin slowly put her phone on the table.

"What's wrong?" Sawyer asked.

Taking a deep breath, she looked at him. "My brother skipped school, and one of the deputies caught him at the rodeo grounds and brought him to the jail to cool his heels until a family member can come by and get him."

"Is he under arrest?"

"No, but I need to go see about it." She stood and threw everything in her purse.

"What are you going to do?"

"Other than strangle him?"

"That probably won't be helpful," Sawyer added.

"True, but what was he thinking of, skipping school?"

"He might be hurting and, being a teenage boy, he doesn't know how to reach out."

Sawyer's quiet explanation stopped her cold. He had a point. She knew her brother hurt, as demonstrated by his outburst on Sunday. She'd asked Tate later that day about the incident at lunch, but he'd refused to talk about the problem.

"So what do you suggest?"

"Well, since you won't be able to drive both yours and Tate's trucks, I could ride with Tate to the high school and we have a little boy talk. Afterward, I could drive back here with you."

"What if he doesn't want to talk?"

"Then we drive back in silence. It won't bother me, but your brother might feel more comfortable talking to another male."

The ring of truth in his suggestion convinced her. "Okay, let's go."

It took seven minutes to get to the jail. As they walked into the office, Sawyer whispered, "Keep cool. You might want to yell at your brother, but don't. You can yell at me later."

She hated to admit it, but Sawyer's perspective made sense. Clamping down on her emotions, she saw Tate sitting on the bench against the wall. His head jerked up when he saw her and Sawyer. Immediately, his slouchy posture disappeared and he sat up straight. He expected her to rain down on him, but Sawyer's words rang in her ears.

The sheriff appeared from around the corner where the cells were located. "Sorry to have to call you, Erin, with all that's happening in your family, but the deputy came across your brother doing wheelies in the rodeo parking lot and making such a racket with those pipes on his truck that I'm surprised the sheriff in the next county didn't catch him."

Tate's chin jutted out.

The sheriff stood in front of Tate. "So should I issue him a ticket for the illegal tailpipes on his truck, or you can make sure he gets back to school and I'll ignore those pipes for the moment?"

Tate wasn't the first teenager the sheriff had scared straight.

They looked at Tate.

"What do you want to do?" Erin asked. She had plenty of words and thoughts she wanted to share but battled her natural urges.

After a moment, Tate said, "I'll go back to school."

"And stay there," the sheriff added.

"Yeah, I'll stay in school."

"Okay," the sheriff said, "but those pipes will have to be fixed if you want to drive your truck anyplace other than the racetrack. Understood?" Turning to Erin, he added, "I think you should take away your brother's truck for a while."

Tate's expression turned to stone.

"I'd skip making him walk to school like my father did me," the sheriff added, his tone light, "but there should be consequences."

He returned Tate's keys and billfold, which had been taken when the teen was picked up, and the trio walked out of the jail. They crowded into Erin's truck.

Tate sat between Erin and Sawyer. "What are you doing here?" Tate snapped at Sawyer.

"That's enough," Erin replied, wanting to add that it was *his*, not Sawyer's, bad behavior that had caused the mess, but she felt Sawyer's gaze on her, helping her control her reaction.

"I'm here to help your sister with how we get you back to school," Sawyer calmly answered.

"I can drive myself."

"True, but can I trust you, Tate?" Erin replied, fighting for an even tone. "How good is your word that you'll drive back to school? As good as your promise to go to school this morning?"

Outrage and shame radiated in waves off the youth.

Sawyer caught Erin's gaze and shook his head, reminding her not to be too harsh on her brother.

Silence reigned in the truck as they drove the rest of the

way to the rodeo grounds. She stopped by the only truck in the parking lot. The boys slipped out.

"I'll follow you," Erin called out as Tate stood by the driver's door of his truck.

Her brother nodded and slipped inside.

Sawyer looked at Erin. "You did good back there with your brother." He reached out and squeezed her hand. Turning, he raced to Tate's truck. Moisture gathered in her eyes. He had seen both Tate's and her needs and met them. She didn't know whether to treasure the experience or be frightened of it. But she could get used to having him around.

Tate put the keys in the ignition.

Sawyer buckled his seat belt, then leaned back. "I'm ready."

Tate gunned the engine.

"I'd be careful. Why bring wrath down on your head if you don't have to?"

Tate glared at Sawyer but glanced in the rearview mirror. One look was all it took. He put the truck in gear and started driving at a normal speed.

After a moment of silence, Tate growled, "You going to lecture me about ditching?"

Sawyer recognized a youth spoiling for a fight.

"Nope."

Tate's body relaxed. "So, why are you here? Because I don't need a babysitter."

"True. I'm here because your sister needed some help making sure you get back to school. She might think she can tackle anything, but driving two trucks at the same time is something even she can't do."

Tate snorted and glanced at him. "There are some things Sis can't do. Besides, I could've driven myself and she could've followed."

"True, but what if you just took off on Route 66? Could she have stopped you?"

"I told her I'd go back and—" Tate swallowed hard.

Tate's reaction told Sawyer he'd made his point. "You have to admit Erin has a lot on her plate right now. Your dad, the rodeo and you. We all need help at some time."

"That's just a line," Tate snapped, his defensiveness rising.

"Not for me. I've been there. Needed help, and I got it."

"You're just saying that." Tate kept his eyes on the road.

"Nope. When I was fourteen and my brother sixteen, he took over the role of parent."

"Why?"

"My dad died of a heart attack, and my mom couldn't cope with the situation."

Tate didn't ask any follow-up questions. He wasn't at a place to trust a stranger, and Sawyer understood that.

After several moments, Sawyer asked, "I have a question for you. Is your sister as good as she claims to be? Is she reliable? We're working on the rodeo, and I want to know if I can rely on her to do what she says she'll do."

The youth's attitude changed. "Yeah. You can count on her. She's good. If you ask her to do something, you don't ever have to think about it again. She doesn't need a reminder. She gets kinda insulted if you do." He grinned. "When she focuses on a job, she won't quit until it's finished. She focuses so hard that she sometimes forgets the small stuff. I remember one time she walked through the kitchen without her shoes and probably would've left without them. Mom stopped her before she got out of the house. But, I'll admit, she's a little off on the small details. Mom calls it Erin's walking-in-the-clouds thinking mode. Erin sees the big picture."

"So you would depend on her?"

"In a heartbeat."

Sawyer nodded. "Good. I'll trust her, but you might try trusting her, too."

Tate's shoulders tightened, telling Sawyer his words had hit the mark.

To ease the tension between them, Sawyer asked, "Do you know anywhere around here where I could rent a horse and ride? Riding helps me to clear my head. I left my horse at my brother's ranch, so when I go home, I ride as much as I can."

"You can come out to our place and ride anytime you want. I like riding, too."

"You sure?"

"Yeah. Dad's horse is going to need to be ridden, so come and exercise Duke."

"Duke?"

Tate shrugged, trying to be cool, but the smile dancing around his mouth gave him away. "Dad loved John Wayne, so in honor of him, Dad named his horse Duke."

They pulled into the high school parking lot and Tate found a spot.

"Thanks for the invite to ride. I hope you'll think about what I said about your sister."

Tate studied him and nodded. They joined Erin at the front door of the high school and Sawyer watched Erin shift into her stern-older-sister mode. The awesome sight made him smile.

Erin tried to wait out Sawyer, hoping he'd talk about what he'd said to Tate on their drive back to town, but her anxiety won out. "So what did my brother say about why he skipped?"

"We didn't talk about it."

"What? Why not?"

"It's obvious you're not a boy."

She frowned. "What's that supposed to mean?"

He held up his hand. "What it means is you don't understand how a teenage boy's mind works. Pushing him would've just made him clam up. I'd be challenging his manhood. He needs some space, then when he feels safe enough or trusts enough, he'll open up."

As much as she didn't want to acknowledge it, his words made sense. "I'm worried that Tate is hurting and doesn't have any way to vent his feelings."

"Is there an adult male he could talk to? Maybe your pastor?"

"Tate's mad, and I think the last person he wants to talk to is our pastor."

"Anyone else?"

"Maybe Auntie's husband, Nelson, but he's not here and he doesn't want to leave his hometown in Bluewater to come and visit us. The last time Uncle left his hometown, it was to go to Vietnam."

"That would do it. Well, Tate invited me out to your ranch to ride, and I might—"

"He did what?" Her voice rose.

"I asked your brother if he knew where I could rent a horse to ride. He told me to come out to the ranch and ride your father's mount."

She felt her jaw drop.

"I told you I was a cowboy, and riding clears my head. Of course, I didn't bring my horse with me, so I'd have to rent a mount. He told me to come to the ranch and ride your dad's horse to exercise him."

Conflicting emotions raced through Erin. If Tate had invited Sawyer to the ranch, maybe her brother might feel free enough to talk to him. "No, no, I wasn't talking about your horse. I'm surprised my brother invited you to come and ride."

Shrugging, he said, "Hey, I'm a likable guy."

His comment didn't deserve an answer, but Sawyer

might have hit on a plan. "So, if you come out to the ranch, Tate might want to talk to you."

"Could be. If I come out and ride, and if Tate wants to talk, I'm willing to be a sounding board for him."

"Good. He definitely doesn't want to talk to me."

"That's because you're a girl and his sister. It's easier to talk to a stranger who is not emotionally involved."

He was right. She'd prayed that God would send help for her brother. "Thank you."

She'd just relaxed when Sawyer said, "I also asked your brother about you."

"Why?" She strangled on the word.

Sawyer looked out the passenger-side window, not in any hurry to answer. "I asked how reliable you are."

Curiosity raced through her. "What did Tate say?"

"He said I could count on you. If you were assigned a job, then I didn't need to worry. He laughed and said you had a walking-in-the-clouds mode and sometimes let the little details escape."

Erin's cheeks heated.

Leaning against the door, he studied her.

"I'll admit, when I get focused on something, I commit myself to the project and everything else falls away."

"He's proud of you. And he knows he can count on you."

Her eyes watered and her heart eased. "Thanks for talking with him. And for reminding me he needed my understanding, not my rebuke."

He nodded. "It wasn't brilliant insight, just experience."

Sawyer's words piqued her curiosity, but there was a look in his eyes that stopped her from asking about his personal life.

"Still, I appreciate it."

"No problem. I'm just passing along the encouragement my brother and I have received."

Again, he'd dropped another nugget from his past. "Care to explain?"

He smiled. "That belongs for another time."

She knew he'd slammed the door on his personal life, holding back, but for the first time she wanted to let her heart have free rein to get to know the man who made her smile and her heart sing.

Chapter Five

The rumble of Erin's stomach echoed through the cab of the truck.

Sawyer met her gaze and grinned.

Looking down at his watch, he said, "It's close to two and my stomach agrees with yours. Want to get something to eat?"

She hesitated.

"Skipping lunch isn't going to make anything better. Besides, you might have a different outlook on the situation if you're full," he added.

"Didn't you use that ploy before?"

"It works. And it's true."

She glanced at him and considered his words.

"So, do you want to stop, or do you need to be somewhere else?" he pressed.

"My life's here until Dad gets well, Tate's situation settles down and the rodeo gets on track."

"It sounds like you and I are free and hungry, so let's go eat."

"Do you always ooze charm, or are you just that hungry?"

"Hey, I'm a turnaround specialist, and my job is to bring

people together and get cooperation. When people are fed, they're much nicer."

"I know when I'm being handled, but I'm hungry."

When they arrived in town, Erin drove to Lulu's. The lunch crowd had already cleared, so there was no line. Once inside, Sawyer motioned for Erin to order first.

"Good to see you," Lulu said. "I attended the rodeo meeting last week and listened to Sawyer's plan. 'Course, things got a little rowdy toward the end. I liked how Erin settled things down."

"I did, too," Sawyer said.

Pleasure at his words washed through Erin. She felt as if she was fifteen and just discovering boys.

"And when word got out that local people could bid for a job working on the rodeo, that started everyone talking. It's been a long time since this much excitement has rolled through town. Why, my brother, Tom, is going to submit a bid to work on the redo of the iron works for the chutes out on the rodeo ground. I haven't seen him with that much bounce in his step in a long time. Thanks, Sawyer."

"I can't take credit for that. Erin suggested it. Well, I'd say she vigorously encouraged me to use local residents."

Lulu smiled. "That's our Erin."

"More than one person's told me that."

"It only made sense to use local talent so we can keep money here," Erin added.

"Well, we can use the work," Lulu answered. "So, what do you want for lunch?"

They ordered lunch and settled in a booth.

Erin sat across from him, and he studied her. She searched for something to say. He certainly held his cards close to his vest. He was a man who could be both charming and courageous, but kept his heart shielded. "Thanks for the help with Tate."

"Not a problem."

The tone of his voice didn't invite more conversation. Although she wanted to know more of what her brother had said, she respected that Sawyer wouldn't tell her what they'd talked about.

As he continued to observe her, she wanted to squirm under his scrutiny. Before she could say anything stupid, Rose delivered their burgers.

She vibrated with excitement. "Everyone's talking about the list you put up at Bob's place last week. Jobs. It sounds great. Where do Mom and I sign up for a concession booth? I know people in Harding County want to get in there, and I'm afraid there will be more people who want booths than we have."

"Ask the guy in charge." Erin pointed to Sawyer.

"Electricity, plumbing and sewage have to be addressed," he warned. "Can you and your mother do that?"

Rose gave him a "duh" look. "We do our own work here and do it better than most men."

Erin's eyes danced with amusement.

"I'm surprised, but I admire you."

"Hey, don't underestimate us country girls," Rose informed him.

"I'm quickly learning that lesson."

Sawyer had to remind himself these women in no way resembled his mom or ex-girlfriend. When he turned back to Erin, her eyes danced, and her lips turned up. It was good to see the lightness in her face.

"Okay, you're right."

"Glad you're getting the message."

He grunted and they dug into their hamburgers.

"I'm pleased that the people in this county are eager to help with the rodeo."

"It's a big part of our lives. And the folks who don't ranch have work keeping us ranchers supplied. Rodeo is our time to shine and brag. If you won bareback riding one year, you were the champ all year."

"And you won the barrel racing."

"I did." Pride shone in her eyes. "I had a couple of close calls when I was in high school, but I won. Those were the years I was the proudest." She nodded to the picture on the restaurant wall. "You asked about that picture before. That's one of those years."

He understood. It was a success that others in the community looked up to. Of course, once Caleb and Sawyer had settled in Plainview, his friends found other things besides his rodeo wins that they could admire him for, and they forgot about the two high school orphans living in the back room of the church. Glancing at Erin, he knew she understood.

"I'll contact Norman Burke this afternoon to put out the notice for local bids in his county. I wouldn't want them to say we neglected them."

Erin didn't respond. Looking into her face, he could see her preoccupation. Finally, she snapped out of her thoughts.

"Did you say something?"

"Harding County bids."

"Of course. I'm a little distracted right now. You were going to talk to Norm."

"You heard?"

The door opened and Mel walked in. Erin looked over her shoulder.

Mel's brows plunged into a deep V, making him look like a charging bull. He walked to the table and glared at Erin. She didn't squirm or shrink under his stare.

"Mel, what's wrong?" Sawyer leaned forward.

The man looked ready to explode. "The company that did work on the rodeo the last time called me this morning, and their president told me you wanted him to bid along with everyone else." Everyone in the café heard.

"That's true. What's the problem with that? All companies working on the rodeo reconstruction need to submit a bid. Those bids will be open for anyone to review."

Color flooded Mel's cheeks. He nodded to Erin. "She put you up to that?"

"No," Sawyer replied. "That's standard procedure taught in college. Since the counties are involved with this project, things have to be open to the public."

Mel raised his chin. "I wouldn't be taking advice from her." Mel pointed to Erin. "On our final vote to award the contract, her father voted for you over her, so that should tell you something about her skills." His gaze bored into Erin's. She withstood Mel's caustic words and didn't flinch. "We voted your plan, not hers."

Sawyer felt a flash of anger shoot through him and rose to his feet. Mel knew part of his plan was having everyone submit bids. It was the same in Erin's. Why suddenly was he complaining? What was going on? "I'm proceeding according to my plan, which the board voted on. Erin's answered my questions and filled me in on local resources. What I'm missing is last year's budget with the final figures that I asked for earlier. Did you leave it in the office for me to review?"

Mel rocked back and forth on his feet as if he readied himself to charge Sawyer.

Sawyer widened his stance and prepared for Mel's actions.

After studying Sawyer, Mel said, "I'll drop it by this afternoon." He turned and stomped out of the building.

Lulu raced out of the kitchen and hugged Erin. "Don't pay attention to that bitter old man. What's wrong with him? Pastor Tony, Father Jones, or Mel's pastor needs to get a hold of the man and do some talking."

Rose planted her hands on her hips. "Or someone needs

to talk to Mel's wife. Sharon wouldn't allow such behavior."

Sawyer watched as Erin talked with the other people in the dining room about Mel's cruel behavior.

"I don't know what's gotten into that man," Rose muttered. "I've never seen him so mean. I think I'd rather deal with a rattler than Mel right now."

The other patrons in the café agreed.

Erin grabbed her purse. She looked brittle, as if she were encased in ice. If another person talked to her, it seemed she might shatter. "You want a ride over to the office?" she asked him.

"No, I'll walk."

She nodded.

Sawyer opened the door and allowed her to exit before him. "If I have more questions, I can call you?"

"Of course."

Sawyer walked, mulling over the fact that Erin had taken several blows today and she still stood strong. He found himself admiring her. No, it was more than that. She didn't crumble at the least opposition, and she could be depended on.

And she was beautiful.

Smart.

And he'd be leaving when this job was done.

But a feeling inside him bloomed, no matter how hard his head argued against it.

Erin's mind went blank as she drove home. Everything seemed to have blown up at the same time—her father's stroke, losing the bid for the rodeo job and her brother ditching school. She could've dealt with all that, but the crushing blow that Mel delivered at Lulu's in front of her neighbors and friends—that her father voted for Sawyer over her—had brought her to her knees.

What's going on? Lord, I don't understand.

When had her father stopped believing in her? And she couldn't even ask him now since he hadn't remembered anything of the day of the stroke. Erin hadn't seen much of her mother since she'd decided to stay in Albuquerque to be close to her husband. Had Mother known about her father's vote? When Erin had seen her mother in the hospital, all that had concerned them was Dad's condition. He was alive, but no one knew what had been affected—memory, speech, motor function—but Erin hung on to the hope that her father would completely recover. Anything else, she didn't want to consider.

Mel had delighted in giving her the crushing news in front of a live audience at Lulu's. He could've lied, she told herself, but his claims were easily verified. What had she ever done to Mel to make him hold such contempt for her?

Traci. Erin knew in her bones her old friend feared Erin would try to steal away Andy if she got the job, which was ridiculous. Mel worried about it, too. By the time Erin got home, the entire town would know what had happened at Lulu's. Probably by tonight everyone in Harding and Quay counties would know, too.

Erin pulled into the driveway of the ranch. Tate wasn't back from school yet, so Erin could have a good pity party before she had to act as if everything was normal.

The instant Erin walked into the kitchen and looked at her aunt, Betty asked, "How did things go with Tate?"

"As well as could be expected. The sheriff told Tate he'd have to remove those noisy chrome exhaust pipes or only drive his truck at the dirt track. And he recommended taking away his truck for a while."

"Do you trust him to come home after all the trouble?"

Her heart jerked. "Yes. I think it's his cry to be heard. I pray I'm right." And if she wasn't…she didn't want to consider it.

Betty rose and walked to where Erin stood and enveloped her in a hug. Erin relaxed in Betty's arms. Erin didn't cry but let her aunt's love encircle her.

"Thank you," Erin whispered several minutes later.

Betty pulled back. "I called your mother and we talked. She wants to talk to you tonight. We'll have to drive him to and from school the rest of this week and probably next. He refused to answer why he ditched."

"Tate doesn't want to talk to his sister about what's in his heart."

Betty motioned for Erin to sit, then poured them coffee.

"That's normal. Men are hardheads, and a boy your brother's age doesn't know what to do with his heart."

"Could Uncle talk to him?" Erin asked, hoping.

"Of course, but we'd have to ship him to Bluewater, and Tate would know it was about his behavior, so would he talk?" Betty sighed and studied Erin. "Is there more that's bothering you?"

How her aunt sensed things, Erin would never know. "Sawyer helped me when the sheriff called that he'd picked up Tate. Sawyer rode with Tate back to school, so maybe he could help."

Betty studied her. "That's possible, but what are you holding back?"

Gritting her teeth, Erin didn't want to discuss what had been revealed.

Reaching out, Betty cupped Erin's cheek. "I've diapered you, cared for you as if you were the daughter of my body. Whatever you say will stay with me."

"Father voted for Sawyer to win the rodeo contract over me."

Betty's mouth puckered into an O. "Surely, you are mistaken."

She shook her head. "Mel happily told me while I was at Lulu's and announced it to everyone in the place. He's afraid that I'll influence Sawyer to do things my way. His argument was that if my father didn't believe in me, then Sawyer shouldn't, either."

Betty put her hands over Erin's and squeezed. "Something's not right here. You are the joy of your parents, and I've never heard your father say anything against you. You are his sunflower."

Erin tried to smile. "In his condition, I can't ask him why. I know it's small of me to question his decision, but—"

"It all seems so dark now, but believe, Daughter. Sometimes God takes us on a journey to let us see a different view. You will have to walk in faith."

The words washed over Erin like a gentle breeze. All she could remember was her father cheering her on when she rode barrels competitively, or his sitting in the front row, beaming with pride when she graduated from high school as the valedictorian.

Her entire life her father had supported her but, over the past few months, she'd noticed a change in him, a hesitancy that put her on alert.

"Thanks, Auntie."

They hugged, and Erin walked into her father's study, ready to search for the final addendum to last year's budget. But, as she surveyed his things, her heart ached with questions and doubt.

Sawyer walked into the rodeo office. The scene at the café had disturbed him. Why had Mel decided to humiliate Erin in front of everyone? The woman had held up under the man's ugly attack, but those small-town currents swirled around them.

When he entered the office, Lisa looked up. She nodded to the meeting room. "Mel brought the budget for the last year."

He nodded.

"Is everything okay?" Lisa asked.

"Mel seems on some sort of mission to hurt Erin."

"I heard."

The speed with which the news spread in a small town amazed Sawyer. None of the major cell phone carriers could've acted quicker.

"Could you explain the situation to me? I want to know when to duck." He moved toward her desk and collapsed in the chair beside her.

Lisa explained the complicated history of the two women and the one guy.

"But if Traci's happily married, why would Mel be so hard on Erin? She's been gone at school and riding the rodeo circuit."

Lisa leaned closer to Sawyer. "When the board decided to redo the facilities, Erin put in her bid. I think Traci's worried that if Erin's in town for that long maybe the feelings Andy had for Erin might flare back to life."

"That's ridiculous." Sawyer ran his fingers through his hair. "How long have Traci and Andy been married?"

"Almost nine years, but folks have noticed things are a little strained between the two."

A frown knit his brow. "You're telling me Mel's worried about the situation?"

"You asked what the problem was." Lisa shrugged. "It might not make sense, but there it is."

What a mess. "Thanks for the heads-up." Now at least he knew where the potholes were. Maybe he could survive this job. But he doubted he'd ever be the same.

Chapter Six

Late the next afternoon, Sawyer drove back from his successful meeting with the Harding County members of the rodeo board. They'd been excited about having their residents bid for contracts to do work for the rodeo. Norman had last year's budget and let Sawyer take the notebook to compare with the ones Mel brought to the office.

During the meeting, thoughts of Erin kept creeping into Sawyer's head while he talked to Norman. What had gotten into him?

When he passed the road leading to the Delong ranch, Sawyer went with his gut and decided to visit Erin. He'd go with the nagging feeling that he'd experienced all afternoon. Besides, he could use the excuse that he wanted to ride. He was a cowboy.

He parked his truck and saw Erin in the corral beyond, practicing her barrel racing. He sat for a moment and watched her ride the figure eights. Slipping out of his truck, he softly closed the door.

She didn't bounce in her saddle or yank on the reins. She leaned into the sharp turn, pushing down in the stirrups, keeping her weight off the horse's back. They worked in unison as a well-oiled machine. When she finished the last figure eight, she let her horse canter around the corral, cooling both her and the horse.

"You've got a good seat."

"Hours of practice."

Her face glowed, and her entire body appeared relaxed and at ease, the most relaxed he'd ever seen her. This was a joyful woman, who loved riding and competing. As she came toward him, he felt himself being drawn to that smile. Her bay-colored mare had a black mane and black points.

"Nice mount."

"Wind Dancer is a spoiled girl, but she loves to compete. The only thing she wants to do more than compete is to ride across our ranch."

Sawyer laid his palm on the horse's light reddish coat and stroked her.

Erin patted the horse's neck. "I needed to ride her again. We were competing in Denver when I got news of Dad's stroke. I drove home, left her here and then went on to Albuquerque. Both Dancer and I need the routine of doing the barrels. It's a comfort. She's a bit of a high-maintenance girl. You should understand."

"I do. Fortunately, my brother promised to keep my horse, Rescue, in shape.

"Thinking about it, I remembered more of you and your brother at the charity rodeo. You were quite a team doing pickup."

"Thanks. I was a little rusty at that affair, but Caleb wanted the backup. Pickup is Caleb's specialty, and when he practiced, I worked with him, so I've done it before."

"So why didn't you bring your horse with you here?"

"For a while, I traveled with Rescue, but he got tired of moving around, so I left him with my brother. When I was driving by your ranch, the urge hit me, and since Tate said I could ride anytime I wanted, I thought I'd go with the flow." He leaned against the fence post. "I'm sure Tate didn't think I'd take up his offer so quickly, but... Besides, Tate mentioned your dad's horse might need to be exercised, so on the drive back from Harding County, I thought about it. He'll probably be surprised to find me here."

"He's not home, yet. This is the first day we've driven him to school, and he wasn't too happy with me this morning. Betty took the evening shift." She dismounted, patted Dancer and looked at her watch. "Besides, having to endure his scowls and glares can only be tolerated once a day. He'll be glad for an excuse to get away from us. You're welcome to wait for him."

"I'll do that. Thanks."

After unsaddling Dancer, Erin walked the horse to the corral and let her loose.

Sawyer joined her at the fence. "Today, I drove to Harding County and talked to those board members about opening for bids," he said, leaning against the fence.

"Why not just call?"

"I did yesterday, but I wanted to see the county, meet face-to-face with people. They liked the suggestion of locals getting involved in the revitalization."

He caught her smile.

"It's good to see everyone get involved. The more the project is talked up and the word spread, the more support you'll have. Excitement will build and you'll get free publicity."

Erin didn't look at him, but kept her gaze on Dancer.

Sawyer wanted to say something to her about what had happened at Lulu's yesterday, or what he learned from Lisa, but if she didn't mention it, then he wouldn't. She seemed to be doing well today.

"I did get Norman's copy of the rodeo financials for the last year. Since he's the top board member in Harding it will be interesting to see how it compares with the book Mel dropped off after lunch yesterday and the one I've looked at here."

Erin turned to him. "Mel brought the notebook by yesterday?"

Sawyer carefully searched her eyes. "Yes, and I glanced at it last night, but I didn't see any final numbers." He shrugged. "I wanted to see if Norman and Mel even have the same estimates."

The sound of a car in the drive drew their attention. Moments later, the doors slammed and Tate appeared. He took in the situation. Betty was slow getting out of the truck.

Sawyer stepped away from the fence. "I had an urge to ride this afternoon." He knew that both Erin and her brother would understand. They were all horse people.

Tate rubbed his neck. "Ridin' sounds good to me, and since I'm being supervised, you can't object." Tate aimed his comment at his sister.

Sawyer inwardly cringed. Tate's heavy-handed approach invited trouble. "Since I don't know your ranch, a guide would be a good idea, if that's okay with you, Erin. If something happened to me while riding here—" he shrugged "—people might think it was your way of getting rid of the competition." He grinned, hoping his light tone would ease the tension between brother and sister.

She caught the teasing mood. "Well, you've got a point. I wouldn't want to be accused of letting our new rodeo wrangler get lost."

"No one would accuse you of ignoring your duty," Tate snapped.

Her brother's irritation at being driven to and from school was showing.

"Well, it's a good idea for you to accompany Sawyer."

Tate started toward the other horses.

"Just know, brother," Erin called, "we'll have a talk later about school today."

Tate froze. "Okay."

As they walked away, Sawyer gave her a nod of approval.

Erin smiled.

"When I drove up today, your sister was practicing her barrels," Sawyer told Tate as they rode past the practice corral. Sawyer wanted to get Tate's mind off school.

After several moments of silence, Tate replied, "She always practices. Both Sis and Dancer love it. Sis took Dancer with her to the university. I don't know how she practiced, but she did. I understood her wanting to ride, but others didn't." Tate's shoulders straightened with the pride that rang in his voice.

"I did the same and took my horse, Rescue, with me to school and rode on the weekends. You can relax and let problems melt away on the back of a horse. Life seems to come into focus." And no better place to pray than on the back of his horse. "It was only after I graduated and took jobs in different cities that I left Rescue at my brother's ranch. I do miss Rescue. When I call my brother, I ask about my horse before his wife."

"Really? You should use FaceTime to talk to your horse. It's what Sis uses every night to talk to Mom about Dad's condition."

"That's a good idea. I think I might try that the next time. Question is, will my brother take the tablet into the barn? But that won't replace riding my horse."

"True. Sometimes things aren't the way you want them." The comment trailed off.

There it was. Tate's cry for help.

"Yes, but things happen that we don't have a say in. When my dad had a heart attack, he didn't survive."

Tate remained quiet.

"So what'd you do?" he finally asked.

"There's nothing you can do but survive. I had my big brother and we got through it together. Got closer." Sawyer wouldn't tell Tate the other ugly part of his story. Tate needed to be encouraged, not depressed. "Your dad survived the stroke."

"But nothing's going to be the same. I should've been better and spent time with him."

Lord, help. "We can't go back and change the past, but going forward you can. You can be there for your dad in the future. And I know your sister is also struggling with your dad's stroke and with me winning the bid. I think you could help her."

"She's strong."

"True, but is there anyone there for her? We all need others to help us. I think she might like someone she could depend on to be there for her." Sawyer guided his mount down a wash.

Tate eyed him. "Really?"

"Yup. I knew this sheriff who had a reputation of being the best and, in his state, everyone depended on him, but when he went home, his wife made all the decisions in the house. The sheriff just needed a moment to be taken care of, but when he went to work, he was in charge.

"I couldn't change my dad dying. It took me a long time, and a lot of anger, to accept. But there was a pastor who showed an angry boy that he needed to let God into his heart and do the work." It still awed Sawyer how patiently and gently the pastor had guided two young wounded men.

Tate eyed him, then looked back at the landscape, his shoulders tense.

At least Sawyer had put the ideas into the teen's head. "I think we need to start back. We don't want to worry anyone."

Turning toward the ranch, an easy silence settled between them.

The first hurdle with Tate had been cleared.

* * *

They could see the ranch house on the horizon when they heard the ring of a meal triangle.

"We're being called to dinner," Tate said. "I'm hungry."

"You're a teenager and that's to be expected."

They traded grins.

"We need to hurry back, and I should get going back to town."

"Why don't you stay and eat with us?"

"I'm sure your aunt isn't expecting me."

"Didn't you listen last Sunday? My aunt loves feeding others. It's her thing. No one is ever turned away. In fact, she'll tackle you before you can come up with an excuse to leave."

Sawyer laughed. "Another determined woman."

Tate shook his head. "Us guys don't stand a chance between my mom, Auntie, and sister."

"Well, consider me on your side."

They rode up to the barn, unsaddled their mounts and put them in the corral.

Before Sawyer could walk out of the corral, Betty appeared on the porch and waved them inside. "I'm ready to put dinner on the table. Hustle."

"I told you," Tate whispered.

Sawyer didn't want to impose but thought he needed to excuse himself before he left to go back into town, eat and go over the information he collected in Mosquero, the county seat of Harding County.

Ten minutes later, Sawyer knew it was impossible to endure a tornado and remain standing.

As he sat next to Tate at the table, the teen couldn't help but smile.

Betty put the main dish on the table. "Erin, where are you?"

She raced into the room. "I'm sorry, Auntie. I was

looking through some of Dad's notebooks concerning the rodeo."

Erin settled across the table from Tate and Sawyer.

After saying grace, Betty started passing dishes. She handed Tate a bowl of greens to go with his roasted chicken. "How was your day, Tate?"

Everyone froze.

Tate refused to look at Betty. They hadn't talked about Tate's little stunt yesterday. Erin had told her brother they would wait a day to cool down and think about what happened. The only thing they'd determined was that Tate wouldn't be driving.

"I talked to your mother this morning. She asked about you," Betty said.

Sawyer leaned close and whispered, "I think she knows."

Tate's lips tightened.

"What were you thinking?" Betty asked.

"Auntie," Erin answered. "I think we've all been stressed with what's happened. It doesn't excuse it, but explains it." She met her brother's surprised look.

"True," Betty replied, "but remember what your mother and grandmother said—you do wrong, you pay the price. When all five of us kids were growing up, Grandma wasn't interested in excuses. Later, after we paid the price, paid the penalty, Grandma would sit with whatever child had done wrong, talk about what had happened and ask if we had learned a lesson. Or, she would have us think of a better way to have handled things."

"Tate and I were going to talk about it after dinner," Erin said.

Waving her hand, Betty said, "Now's a good time."

"I don't think Tate would want us to discuss the topic here over dinner."

"What Tate needs to know is that he's responsible for his actions," Betty replied.

"I know I'm stepping into an argument where I don't have a vote in the outcome, but I think Tate knows he's made a mistake." Sawyer glanced at Tate for permission to argue for him. The teen nodded.

Sawyer continued. "We talked on our ride. And I think he's willing to pay whatever price you think is appropriate."

Silence settled on the room.

Erin folded her hands on the table. "Mom and I talked. She thinks that what we've done so far, Tate not driving this next week but having either me or Auntie drive him, is a good start."

Tate opened his mouth to protest.

"How long?" Sawyer asked, jumping in.

"A week at least," Erin replied, "or until Tate builds our trust in him, again."

Sawyer turned to Tate. "I think that's reasonable, don't you?" To simply take away Tate's truck sounded like a reprieve to Sawyer, and he hoped the boy realized his mother had gone easy on him.

Tate didn't immediately answer. He slowly surveyed each person at the table. Heaving a sigh, Tate nodded. "Okay."

"Mom said that your truck needs to stay in the driveway. She'll take up the issue of the tailpipes with you when she comes home. It doesn't make a difference if you are a senior—ditching will not be accepted. There is a price to pay."

Tate's mouth tightened. "Does she want my keys?"

"No. She's going to trust you and give you the opportunity to show we can trust your word. What happens now is on your shoulders."

"I get it."

"Well, with all that taken care of, let's clear the dishes and Tate can finish his homework," Betty said.

Erin breathed a sigh of relief. The ride with Sawyer seemed to have helped her brother's attitude. She'd intended to talk privately to Tate and prayed Betty forcing the issue wouldn't backfire and, amazingly, it hadn't.

Erin owed Sawyer a debt.

"Thanks for helping with Tate."

"Not a problem."

"You mentioned you have Norman's books with you. Would you mind if I looked through that set, too, to compare with Dad's?"

Sawyer set the last dish on the counter. "No, I don't mind."

Betty waved them out of the kitchen. "Go, talk."

"I'll get them."

Sawyer disappeared out the back door and showed up in the library minutes later.

"I wonder if the figures in Norman's budgets are the final ones, because we haven't located a set yet."

"I hope so, too. I haven't been able to study Mel's numbers thoroughly yet, since we've been swamped with inquiries about jobs at the office, with people wanting to submit bids." He sat beside Erin on the small couch in the office so they could look at the figures together.

Opening Norman's budget to compare with her dad's, they had to dodge the front covers to avoid being smacked. With their dance, Erin and Sawyer bumped into each other, laughing and grinning like children. Suddenly, she felt Sawyer's warmth up and down her right side like the heat of a campfire. She froze. So did he.

Trying to ignore his presence, she compared the first pages of the budgets, but her stomach felt as if she had swallowed jumping beans. Turning her head, she came face-to-face with Sawyer. Inches separated them. She could see the green-and-brown color of his hazel eyes. A brown dot sat outside the pupil in the iris of his right eye.

They could hear the ticking of the grandfather clock in the study. She wondered if he could hear the pounding of her heart.

"These aren't final numbers, either. These are the same as the ones in the other notebooks."

His gaze held hers hostage, then he smiled, a soft, welcoming, toe-curling smile. "I'll compare all three notebooks when I get back."

Erin pulled the sticky note she found and showed it to Sawyer. "This is the note I told you about. Apparently, Mel told dad he'd get them the final numbers, but so far, we haven't seen them."

"And it seems no one has seen those numbers."

"So why are they missing?" Erin asked.

"That's the burning question we all want answered."

She closed the binder and held onto the edges. "It seems you keep coming to Tate's rescue."

"Well, I just wanted to help the kid along. I had my fair share of troubles as a teen."

"I wasn't criticizing, but thanking you."

He shrugged. "I know what it's like having your world turned upside down and not knowing how to act. I want to help."

She wanted more, wanted to know how his life had been turned upside down, but again he held back, not filling in the blanks. It seemed so unfair that their lives were open books but Sawyer volunteered nothing of himself.

Covering her hand with his, he lightly squeezed.

She didn't look up at him. "When you don't know what to say, it helps when someone else steps in. And there's been so much going on I wasn't as careful about Tate's needs." She stared at their intertwined hands and pulled away. "I don't think anyone was. With the rest of the people in the household women, Dad made sure Tate knew it was the boys against the girls. I guess Tate felt his only support was gone."

"Realize boys don't respond to 'Let's talk.' You could invite him to go riding or help him clean out the stalls, then you can try talking to him."

"That makes sense. Tate and Dad spent lots of time out on the range or in the barn. Sometimes, they liked to take their fishing poles and go to the creek and fish. That's a sport I don't understand, sitting there waiting on a fish."

"Spoken like a woman who doesn't understand the finer points of fishing."

She really should stand. Maybe then she wouldn't be so rattled, but her body refused to cooperate.

"Did any of the rodeo events appeal to your brother?"

She gathered her scattered thoughts. "He did 4-H projects. He won for raising the best heifer in the state when he was in the ninth grade. He earned a lot of money, but that didn't stop several of the boys at school from teasing him about just winning for raising a cow. They asked why he didn't compete in real rodeo stuff like bull ridin' or bareback ridin'. Dad told him—" Her voice trailed off. Suddenly, the light shone in her brain. Her gaze collided with his and she saw an understanding, and humor.

"Dad always did things with Tate and then talked with him. Ah, I see what you're saying. You have to *be* with them, doing their favorite activity before you can talk, unlike us women who can sit down and discuss things."

"I never doubted it."

Looking down at her hands, she shook her head. "Mom and Auntie tell me I should walk softly sometimes and see what's around me. See the path God has sent me down."

Leaning closer, he whispered, "I'd listen to them."

The door to the study opened, making Sawyer sit up straight. Betty leaned into the room.

"Your mother is on the phone."

Erin hadn't heard the ringing.

"She wants to talk to you. She's speaking to Tate now."

Erin and Sawyer stood.

"I need to get going." He grabbed the notebook he'd brought in and her father's. "I'll compare these with the ones Mel left, if that's all right with you."

She nodded and followed him out to his truck.

Betty and Erin followed. They stopped at the screen door and watched as his taillights disappeared around the curve of the road.

Betty wrapped her arm around Erin's shoulder and squeezed. "I think I know why that man got the contract."

"Why?" What was her aunt talking about?

Betty dropped her arm and turned to face Erin. "God sends us those people we need on our journey, and perhaps this family needed Sawyer to help us through this difficult time." Betty didn't wait for a response but continued. "Heaven knew your brother would have problems that neither of us could imagine, and He sent Sawyer. You must admit that Tate's experienced some bad spots that neither you nor I thought about. I know your mother wanted me here just as a touchstone and someone to feed you and Tate."

Erin couldn't believe her ears. "Really, Auntie? I was to lose so Sawyer could be here to help Tate?"

"I can see that. Remember, God knows the end of the story."

Erin frowned at Betty, confounded by her words.

"I can see you don't understand me. Open your heart and listen to God."

Auntie did have an uncanny way of knowing things, but

this time she'd completely missed the mark. Completely. Sawyer wasn't here to minister to her family.

So did she have a better explanation?

No, but it wasn't to help the Delong family, that much she knew.

But her heart called her out, saying she refused to face the truth.

Chapter Seven

Sawyer returned to the rodeo office. When he opened the front door, he stood for a moment, listening to the silence. He flipped on the lights and went to the meeting room. He could've waited until tomorrow to compare Norman's and Detrick's notebooks to the ones in the office, but he wanted to resolve the nagging question tonight.

He put the binders on the table beside the one Mel had left yesterday and compared the three. They all were the same, but none of them had final numbers.

Leaning back in his seat, he thought about the situation. The nagging feeling that something was wrong didn't go away. Instead, it got stronger. Why?

"What are you doing here at this hour?" Traci stood in the doorway of the boardroom.

"Working."

She slowly walked to the table, eyeing the notebooks. "It's after dinner and you should be in your hotel room, relaxing."

He swallowed his irritation. "I'm sure the rodeo board wouldn't object. I think they'd want the most for their money."

"Could be." She walked around the room.

Her sudden appearance made him suspicious. "What are you doing here?"

"I saw the light when I drove by and wanted to know who was here this late. I thought Dad might be here, and I wanted to talk to him." She studied the binders. "Why do you need last year's budget?" Her voice hardened. "And why three copies? I don't understand."

How could he get out of this mess? "I wanted to look at last year's budget to compare costs, and I couldn't find it. I asked the secretary where it was since it wasn't with the others. Oddly, her copies, hard and electronic, were missing, too. When your dad stopped by the office before he left town, I asked him where it was. Then, today, I got one from Norman when I was in Harding County. On the way home, I stopped by the Delong ranch to ride with Tate, and Erin gave me her father's copy."

Her eyes narrowed. "Aren't you showing a little too much partiality, stopping by Erin's?"

The tone of her voice made the hairs on the back of his neck stand up. He didn't like what she implied, but he needed to tread carefully in this situation. "Tate offered the opportunity to ride and, after driving all day, when I went by the Delong ranch, I knew I needed to unwind on the back of a horse. Ever have one of those days?"

Traci's frown eased.

"Yes, I have."

He picked up the notebooks. "It's been a long day, and I'm ready to call it quits." He motioned for her to exit the room before him, and he turned off the lights, then locked the office.

Traci tapped her lips with her index finger. "I have an idea. Why don't I document the rodeo redo with pictures? I could do a website and everyone in Harding and Quay counties will know the progress of things. And, if we need more people to bid on jobs that come up, we could put the notice there."

Traci had struck gold.

"I've already listed some of the job openings on the website, but I like your idea. You could do a new website and add a link to it or just rework the current site." The more Sawyer thought about it, the more he liked it.

"I can do it. I'm sure my dad would want me doing that."

A website would keep everyone informed and would keep Traci busy. He sensed that if she had a purpose, other problems might be avoided. "Go for it."

She smiled, leaned over and kissed his cheek. "Thanks. I'll work on it tonight."

Sawyer sat down on the bed, then pulled off his boots. What a couple of days. He should've been exhausted, but each time he closed his eyes, a different scene popped into his brain, from taking Tate home, to Mel gladly telling Erin her father had voted for him, to the trip to the next county with all those eager faces who wanted to bid on rodeo jobs.

He didn't know what Traci had planned to do when she'd shown up at the office, but it didn't matter, because her idea of documenting the redo on the website was a winner. He could see that as the best way to keep people updated and have all the contracts out there for everyone to see. He'd learned that secrets created gossip and gossip developed into grumbling, and he couldn't afford that in a small town.

Stretching out on the bed, he thought about the afternoon ride with Tate. Sawyer had read the situation correctly. The youth needed someone to talk to. Sawyer thought of Pastor Garvey, who had guided him. The man had shepherded both Sawyer and his brother, showing them what normal family life was. Garvey had stood in the gap, being there for them. Sawyer wanted to pass on that comfort he had received from the pastor.

He sat up and looked through the notebooks he'd brought back to the room with him. In the middle of reviewing the bid for last year's concrete work, his brain shifted to being stuffed beside Erin on that small sofa. His heart had sped up as if he'd been bull riding. He didn't like going with emotions, but this time had been different.

He had expected resistance from Erin over the rodeo— or some form of sabotage—since this had been his experience with other women in his life. Instead, she had contributed good, constructive ideas. Ideas that made his plan better, which awed him. How different was this experience from all the previous encounters he'd had with other females in his life?

The more he knew of Erin, the more she reminded him of his sister-in-law and not his mother or ex-girlfriend. So how did he deal with that? His mother needed both of her sons' input before she could make a decision. If not them, she sought the approval of her current boyfriend. Erin had her ideas, but she worked with others to accomplish her vision. What a difference. And he found he liked how Erin operated. A lot.

"C'mon, Sawyer, you like more than the way she operates." His words echoed in the room.

When Erin went to the rodeo office the next morning, she noticed Traci's truck sitting in the parking lot. Going into the conference room, Erin saw Traci sitting in front of her laptop. No one else was here. Traci looked up, wariness in her expression.

A dozen different thoughts raced through Erin's head, but what came out of her mouth was, "What are you doing here?" Not elegant, but not hostile.

Traci's jaw flexed. "I'm developing a new website for

the rodeo, listing all the jobs that need to be let. I also discussed with Sawyer last night a section of the site where the progress on the current work could be posted."

All of Erin's awkwardness dissolved. "I like that." The words tumbled out of her mouth, but she meant them. "You suggested that?"

Traci nodded and her shoulders relaxed. "I did. It only makes sense in this day and age. There is so much we could do with a website besides posting current job openings—we could show progress on work and collect ideas. The news would be at people's fingertips."

"May I see what you've done so far?" Erin asked.

"Sure."

Erin walked to where Traci sat and looked at the laptop.

"I thought this would let everyone know what the site was for and that it was the new one." A picture of the rodeo grounds was the banner across the top.

"I like that, and those graphics are good. There's a picture of Jessie Reynolds's winning ride on that bull several years ago that might look good with what you've got there. A collage effect, maybe."

"I hear ya. And there are other pictures we could add."

"True."

Erin sat and ideas started bouncing between them, and the awkwardness of the past few years melted away.

Forty-five minutes later, Sawyer walked into the office. The place hummed with activity.

"Morning, Lisa, what's going on?"

The secretary laughed. "I don't know what you did to Traci, but she's in the boardroom with Erin working."

His heart beating fast, Sawyer raced to the boardroom door, worried about what he'd find. Someone knocked out. Books scattered around. Broken furniture. "Everything okay in here?" He hung on to the door frame.

Erin and Traci looked up.

"Are you always this late?" Traci asked.

"I ate and had coffee," he mumbled, feeling as if he'd run into the door.

"We've been working on the website for the rodeo overhaul for some time," Traci replied.

"If you have suggestions on how we've set it up, or linked the new site to the old, now's the time to put in your two cents' worth," Erin added. "If we officially want to use the new website, then the board will have to approve it, but adding it shouldn't be a problem."

Still dazed, he walked to the table, sat and reviewed what they had done.

"We're almost done, and we're to the point where we need your input on the jobs you want to list and other general information you want given out to the public. Later, I'll take pictures," Traci added.

"Okay." He felt disoriented, as if he'd been plunged into a new reality.

Traci smiled. "Once I got home, all sorts of other ideas popped into my head. We can document the changes, have a blog, open it to suggestions, and everyone can follow the progress and feel involved."

Sawyer shook his head, still unable to believe the change between the women. Was he dreaming?

"I agree," Erin said. "This is a good way to give information out. The more people know, the easier I think it will be. Of course, Sawyer could be the arbiter of the suggestions."

He felt rooted to the floor.

Lisa peeked in and grinned at Sawyer, giving him a thumbs-up, and went back to her desk. Still dazed, he wandered out to the reception area.

"What just happened in there?" he asked, collapsing in the chair by Lisa's desk. "I was prepared to throw my body between the combating opponents. Instead, they've started working together as if they've known each other for ages."

"They have." Lisa's eyes watered up.

"What?" Sawyer panicked.

"It's nice to see those two working together again. Once the initial excitement wears off, there might be some stiffness between them, but at least they're talking." She smiled at him. "Thank you."

Erin appeared at the door to the boardroom. "Sawyer, you need to write up the jobs—and the sooner the better. Traci will have the links to apply for the jobs. Or, if you need me to do that, I will." She disappeared back into the boardroom.

"Did a tornado just run through the building?" he mumbled.

Lisa grinned. "It did, and you're fortunate you're still standing."

The morning turned into a whirlwind of activity with Erin and Traci working together on the website. Sawyer joined the group, writing up the job descriptions. By one o'clock in the afternoon, they had the website up and running. Traci had promised to drive to the rodeo grounds and put the pictures of what needed to be done along with the job descriptions. They retreated to Lulu's for lunch.

Several of the patrons did a double take as if looking at a mirage, with Sawyer, Erin and Traci eating and laughing together.

Bob Rivera walked into the restaurant and froze when he saw the three of them at a table, talking. After a moment, he said, "Am I hallucinating?" He studied each person at the table.

Traci laughed.

"No," Erin answered. "You're awake."

He rubbed his neck. "Then what am I missing?"

"We've decided to set up a new website for the rodeo." Sawyer explained what they had accomplished so far. "It's linked to the old website."

Traci chuckled. Erin couldn't remember the last time she'd seen Traci smile. But this morning, it was like working with an old friend. They had meshed so easily. Erin knew exactly what Traci needed before she opened her mouth.

Bob hadn't moved and kept looking at them. "I'm still not sure this is reality."

Erin waved him in. "Bob, we decided walking down to your store and posting the jobs wasn't the most efficient way to do things. The people in Harding might miss out on opportunities, and this is the best way to get the news out."

"Aren't you worried that some people don't have access to the internet?"

Traci shook her head. "Everyone in either county has a child, grandchild or a neighbor that has access, and those teens are willing to tell their neighbors. Ever try to keep a secret from your teen? If you're worried, we can put the web address at your place."

The lightbulb went off in Bob's head and an 'aha' look crossed his face. "I hear you. I wasn't thinking."

Traci's prediction came true. By the end of the day, everyone in Quay and Harding counties knew about the website. Countless calls and emails had come into the office, which pleased Sawyer. He watched in awe as Erin worked with Traci. The secretary also didn't believe her eyes. She walked countless times into the boardroom and looked. The last time she walked in, Sawyer drew her to the side.

"What's wrong?"

"I keep thinking I'm dreaming and want to pinch myself."

"You're not."

She walked out, shaking her head.

As Traci, Erin and Sawyer left the office at five, Mel walked in. He speared Sawyer with a glare.

"What exactly is going on here?"

Mel's angry demand caught everyone off guard. Sawyer's protective edge roared to life by stepping in front of the women. "We've been working on an interactive website for the rodeo. Traci did the bulk of the work."

The smiles and laughter evaporated.

Sawyer's answer stopped Mel. His gaze shifted from his daughter to Sawyer and, lastly, back to Traci.

"What's wrong, Dad?"

Mel took a deep breath and stepped back. Obviously, he was trying to regroup. "I just drove back from Albuquerque, after talking with the company that does the concrete work for the rodeo. I wanted to see them face-to-face to make sure everything was all right with them. They noted how things had changed." Mel directed his comment to Sawyer.

Erin started to answer, but Sawyer cut her off. "Mel, we discussed this before. Doing it online will speed things up."

Mel's irritation didn't diminish. "I know, but the Johnson Brothers have been working with the rodeo for the last fifteen years and I wanted to explain to them face-to-face how we were doing the bidding now. Since they're the biggest concrete manufacturer in the state, it's assumed they'd get the job. It would've been nice to have a heads-up." He flushed, jutting out his chin.

"I'm sorry, Mel. I thought that's why the board hired me to bring this project in as close to budget as possible, but all jobs need to go through the same process. We want everything we do to be aboveboard, and we want to let everyone see our costs and be able to answer their questions."

Mel's mouth tightened. Sawyer's answer obviously

didn't sit well with him, but if he protested further, questions would arise.

He brought his chin down with a firm movement. "Next time, warn me. I just don't want to be hanging out there, looking like an amateur."

"The Johnson Brothers know better, Mel. There's a contract process they go through with government entities," Erin pointed out.

"I know that," he snarled.

Something wasn't right. Sawyer traded glances with Erin and Traci. From their expressions, they thought so, too. Why complain about something the Johnson brothers knew they had to do to get a job?

"Let's go, Traci. Your mom is waiting on us."

Mel and his daughter drove off in different cars. Erin and Sawyer stood there in the quiet night. In the distance, they could hear children playing and an occasional car or truck drive by.

Things were going so well.

"Where's your car?" Erin looked around the parking lot.

"I walked. I like the option of walking on this job." Sawyer stepped closer to Erin. "How's your brother?"

"I haven't gotten a call from the school or my aunt, so I assume everything is good."

"Since you didn't leave when school was over, I assume that Betty picked up Tate."

"Auntie and I agreed she would do afternoon duty if I'd take morning." She opened her truck door. "I don't know who is being punished the most—Tate, Auntie or me."

He walked around the car and stood face-to-face with Erin. "It will be worth the price in the end. You're showing him that he matters."

He wanted to say more than just "hang in there." She cocked her head as if she understood his old hurts. "I'll remember that in the morning when I have to dash to the school at eight fifteen." She opened her car door.

"You surprised me today," Sawyer said, stepping closer.

She stood in the V of the open door. "How's that?"

"When you learned about Traci working on the website, I expected you to object, but you didn't. You sat down and worked with her. Why?"

She hesitated. "Traci won several awards for her website designs. She's good and she has a talent for it, and for me to object didn't make sense."

Lots of people he knew wouldn't have taken that broad view. With every turn of the rodeo redo, this woman surprised him, kept him off guard. She acted with courage and grace, and his admiration for her was growing. No, it was more than admiration, but he wasn't ready to admit what emotion it was.

"Why don't you hop inside and I'll drive you to the hotel? I feel like there's a neon light shining on us for everyone to see." She unlocked his door from the panel on the driver's door.

"Are you going to ask more questions if you drive me to the hotel?" Sawyer asked.

"No, but I might answer some."

He raced around the truck and hopped in. Quiet ruled in the cab on the short drive. She parked in front of his room.

"I'm going to explain some things. Traci's ideas on the website were good, and I asked her about the different ideas she had for the setup. It made sense for her to do it."

"But you and she haven't been getting along," Sawyer commented. He had been talking to people in town. He didn't want to walk into a war zone.

"Traci does excellent work with her websites and graphics. She's set up websites for different people in town and around the county."

He stared at her, as if to make sure she wasn't teasing him. "Why this change?"

"Because, as Traci told me about her ideas, I suddenly realized how much I missed talking to her. How my life had diminished since our…dustup. Fight?"

"Fight? I heard it was more like a major battle."

"It ended our friendship. I really didn't realize the depth of her feelings for Andy. I knew I didn't love Andy enough to marry him. I wanted to go to college, compete on the rodeo circuit and do things I couldn't if I stayed here. I had big dreams, and getting married wasn't one of them." She shook her head. "Looking back on some of the comments Traci made, I can see she had feelings for Andy."

"I heard that blowout wasn't your fault."

"I could've handled things better, but I didn't try." She took a breath and rested her head on the headrest. "As a matter of fact, I think you should let Traci run the website. You could check out bids and then decide which ones are the best."

He considered her idea, but he wasn't that comfortable trusting Traci at this point. "I might ask you if the person doing the bidding is up to the job."

Erin nodded. "Sure, or ask the secretary. You could even check the person out with Lulu."

He noticed her list of who to check with. "Not Mel or Traci?"

"At this point, things are still too new and shaky." She shrugged. "Traci is too involved with her dad. And, lately, Mel's actions are off."

Lencho walked out of the office and he looked into the driver's seat.

Erin rolled down her window and smiled, feeling like a high school girl being caught by her parents out in the car.

"Is everything all right here?" Lencho asked.

"We're talking about the website." Sawyer leaned forward to see the teen's face. "You know that we took it live a few minutes ago."

"You're fooling me," Lencho said.

He gave the address of the domain. "Check it out," Sawyer instructed. "Tell us what you think and look over the jobs that need to be done."

"Lencho, we need you to spread the word about it. It's the future of rodeo, so we want to be cutting-edge," Erin explained.

Leaning down, he addressed Sawyer. "I like the idea. I'll go look." He turned and dashed into the lobby.

"Maybe we won't have to do any advertising."

"You're right."

Sawyer started to lean closer to brush a kiss across her lips. Then they heard a door slam. He jerked up straight and slipped out of the car and walked to his room.

What was happening? Next thing he knew, he'd want to court her. He needed to remember he had a job to do here and nothing else.

Chapter Eight

Erin sat in her dad's office. "Thank You, Lord. Dad's getting better and better." She took a deep, steadying breath. The doctors couldn't say the extent of the damage caused by the stroke. Time would tell. Since her sister was there in the city finishing her degree at the university, Kai would visit the hospital daily, bring her iPad and they'd FaceTime. Erin felt torn between driving to Albuquerque to be with her father and staying put, tending to the rodeo, which she knew he wanted. When she'd suggested coming to see him, both her parents had nixed the idea. They counted on her to oversee the redo.

Where had the week gone? The days melted one into another and there wasn't a moment when they weren't all busy. Lencho had his pulse on the pipeline of information. Within a day, everyone in the county knew about the job openings and every proposal had been bid on.

Sawyer asked about the people who bid on the different jobs and listened to Erin and Traci give him background on them.

Erin savored the process. The man listened to her. He argued his position. Sometimes his ideas were better than hers, and sometimes it went the other way. She loved it and had never felt so alive. She felt herself blooming, growing and being challenged in a way she hadn't before. The unique experience burrowed into her heart, especially after the near miss of a kiss in the library and again last night at his motel. The back door crashed against the wall and it sounded as if a herd of horses were running through the house. Erin stood, hurried to the library door and caught a glimpse of Tate's face, which resembled a thundercloud. He stomped past her and into his room, slamming the door behind him. Amazingly, the door stayed on its hinges. Erin looked back and saw Betty's sober expression. She shook her head.

Erin walked into the kitchen. "What's wrong?"

Betty sighed. "Some boy yelled out that Delong's ride was here. Another boy mentioned that his mama quit picking him up when he was in the first grade. It didn't go well after that." She poured herself a glass of water and sat at the table. "I wanted to get out of the car and straighten that young man out, but I knew it would make things worse for your brother."

Erin wanted to go and talk to him but stopped herself, knowing that Sawyer would recommend leaving her brother alone for a while.

"You're not going to talk to Tate?"

"No."

Betty studied her. "What happened?"

"Sawyer's made me realize that sometimes, with a young man, you don't have to have the answer immediately. You wait until they are ready."

"Ah, a wise man."

Erin shrugged. "I don't know if I'd call him a wise man, but he is helping me understand things from Tate's view."

"I think Sawyer's thinking is wise."

"I heard my name mentioned," Sawyer called out from the walk leading to the back door. Obviously their conversation had drifted outside. He walked inside. "Betty, did you say something about me being wise?" His eyes twinkled as he looked at her.

"And you have excellent hearing, too," Betty added.

He laughed.

"What are you doing out here?" Erin asked.

"It sounds as if you don't want me." He stood behind one of the kitchen chairs, looking from Betty to Erin with a wounded expression.

"What Daughter means is that your appearance is a surprise."

Sawyer studied her. Erin felt itchy under his gaze, remembering how close they had come to a real kiss.

"Why are you here?" she asked.

His eyes danced. "I realized the last time I rode how much I missed riding."

Tate's door opened, and he walked out of his room. "I thought I heard you."

"I'm here to ride."

The thundercloud lifted from her brother's face. "I'd like that. C'mon, let's go saddle the mounts." Tate headed outside.

Sawyer's gaze met Erin's. "That okay with you?"

Relief flooded her and she smiled. "That's an excellent idea."

He stepped closer and whispered, "I thought your brother might need some guy time after being hauled around all week by women."

"Thank you," she whispered and had to stop herself from brushing a kiss across his cheek.

"It would've been okay with me if you'd done it."

Her heart raced as if he'd heard her thoughts.

He turned and walked outside, leaving Erin with her mouth hanging open.

Betty laughed. "I've never seen a man able to confuse you like that."

Starting to protest, Erin saw Betty shake her head. Erin snapped her mouth shut.

"Good. Truth is good."

Sawyer and Tate rode north of the ranch house.

Stopping his horse, Sawyer took in the harsh landscape. Range grass grew in clumps. Tree-like cacti and shorter cluster groups of cactus dotted the horizon along with rocks and boulders.

Tate pulled on the reins when he noticed Sawyer had stopped. "What are you looking at?"

"There's a rare beauty to this land."

Tate turned his mount around and rode back to where Sawyer sat. "Are you sure the folks at the rodeo haven't hit you in the head?"

Chuckling to himself, Sawyer understood what Tate asked. "I guess you might think me crazy, but I like this place. I feel it in my bones."

"Now I know you're nuts."

Sawyer lightly kicked his horse into motion. "Why would you say that?"

"Because you see how harsh this land is. What's the beauty in that?"

"The simplicity. The starkness. The colors."

Tate looked at the landscape again and shrugged. "If you say so."

They continued riding. The land dipped, and they walked their mounts down into the gully below.

"How'd the week go?" Sawyer asked.

Tate's lips tightened.

"Has your sister told you what's going on with the rodeo? Have you seen the website?"

"I looked. I'm surprised Sis could do that."

"She didn't. Traci did. And she worked with your sister on it."

Stopping his horse, Tate blinked at Sawyer. "Are you trying to pull something on me?"

"No. It made me do a double take, too. But this week, they've worked together on the website, getting it up and running."

"That's unreal."

"Proves you shouldn't lose faith."

"All I know is that I'm a laughingstock at school. Baby Tate is what they're calling me."

Stopping his mount, Sawyer leaned on the saddle horn. "What it proves is that you're a man who takes his punishment without complaining. Ignore the other guys. They know you ditched and were caught. Let their stupidity roll off your back. You know you're paying for what you did. Be proud of yourself. I am."

"Really?"

"You got it. I've been on the wrong end of different situations. Some were my mistakes. Others weren't. I'll admit, I had a mouth as a teen." Sawyer remembered the beatings he'd gotten. "It took a while for me to smarten up. When my mouth almost got me and my brother beaten to a pulp, I decided it was time to change.

"You strike me as a smarter guy than I was. It might look dark now, but God's in control."

"What if my dad dies? I mean when Mom calls, she's always so cheerful, trying to hide Dad's condition, but I hear Auntie and Erin talking. They should be up-front with me. I mean Sis could pick me up after school and take me to see Dad."

The fear in Tate's voice punched Sawyer in the heart. "True, but a five-hour round trip is not something you could do during the week. Hey, the FaceTime exchanges are great. You get to see your parents."

Tate scowled.

"Sometimes moms try to shield their children." That

was an experience Sawyer had never had. "Be up-front and honest with your mom. Tell her you worry more not knowing. She'll respond. Has your sister talked about what they think is going to happen?"

"No. When I saw Dad after the stroke, he was pretty out of it. I know he wanted Sis to take over for him."

"True, but I don't think your father would want you to spin out of control. You want to be able to face him and lift your head up high and say, 'I stood strong.'"

Tate didn't look sure, but he nodded.

"I wanted to ask you if you like the rodeo. Have a specialty?"

"I love trick riding. Sometimes I work with Dad and the other wranglers, but I haven't competed."

"You've got to do what you love."

Tate stopped and stared at him. "You mean you're not going to lecture me about tradition? I need to compete since my great-grandfather started the rodeo?"

"No."

After a moment of thinking, Tate nodded and started riding. They didn't say anything on the ride back to the barn.

"Who's that riding back into the corral with Tate?" Mary Morning Star Delong asked as she entered the kitchen.

Her mother's voice startled Erin so badly that all sorts of bad outcomes raced through her mind. Had something happened to her father? Erin jumped up from the table and ran to her mother's side. "Is Dad okay? Why didn't you tell us you were coming home?"

"Your father's condition has improved enough that the nurses encouraged me to go home and sleep in my own bed."

"So Dad's doing better? Talking and moving his arms and legs?" Erin's heart danced at the news.

"He is, and he asked about you and the rodeo." Her mom's eyes glistened with moisture.

Both Erin and Betty smiled.

"But no one has answered my question about the man who rode in with your brother. I assume that truck parked in our driveway is his."

Erin nodded. "Sawyer Jensen. He's the man the rodeo board hired to do the rodeo overhaul." Erin had avoided telling her mother details of her initial meeting with Sawyer.

Mary studied her sister, then daughter. "And what's he doing here?"

"He's been out riding with Tate," Erin answered.

"Is that wise?"

Mary barely stood five feet tall, and had lost her slender frame years ago, but anyone who thought Mary wasn't a force to be reckoned with hadn't met her.

"Mom, Tate hadn't said anything about Dad, but all anyone needed to do was look at him to know he is hurting. Sawyer stepped in to help. It's been good for Tate."

"It's true, Sister."

Before anyone could respond, the screen door opened and the men walked in.

Tate froze and Sawyer bumped into him. He reached out and steadied the teen.

Her mom didn't wait for her son to say anything, but embraced him. She whispered softly in Tate's ear in Navajo. He nodded.

Mary stepped back and studied Sawyer. Although the height difference should've been comical, somehow Erin saw equally matched opponents.

"I'm Mary Morning Star Delong. And you are?"

Sawyer took Mary's hand and met her probing gaze head-on. "I'm Sawyer Jensen. It's nice to meet you, ma'am. I hope everything is all right with your husband."

"Detrick is doing better and encouraged me to come home for the weekend. I decided my children needed to see their mother."

"I'm glad to hear it. You have a wonderful family." He didn't retreat under her scrutiny.

Mary nodded her head regally.

Erin knew more would come. No one moved, waiting for Mary to continue. "So, you are the man who won the contract over my daughter."

Her mother didn't disappoint Erin. No bitterness or anger tinged Mary's words, just strength to learn the truth. Ground rules were laid out.

Sawyer didn't shrink away; instead, he stood up straighter. "I am, but Erin and I have been working together, and she's pointed out some places where I needed to improve my plan."

Tate snorted. Betty harrumphed.

Mary glanced at her son as to stop any further "comments."

"So, you and my daughter are working together?"

"We are. And Erin and Traci have been collaborating this week on the website for the rest of the county to see and use."

"I see." Her mother turned to Erin, and Erin saw the countless questions she would have to answer. "Many things have changed."

"Yes, the world's been turned upside down," Betty commented.

Erin fought ducking her head. Suddenly, she felt exposed in a way she hadn't since she was six and dyed her mother's prize lamb green for Saint Patrick's Day.

"Stay for dinner with us, Sawyer," Mary said. "I would like to learn more of your plan and the working relationship you've developed with my children."

Her mother had *that* tone, which no one refused. "Thank

you, ma'am. I appreciate the invitation, but I need to be back in town."

Shock ran through the kitchen from Erin and Tate to Betty and Mary. No one had ever refused Mary when she used that tone.

Mary quickly hid her reaction and studied him. Sawyer didn't squirm under her mother's penetrating gaze.

Slowly, acceptance filled Mary's eyes. "Then you must have Sunday dinner with us after church. I would like to learn more about you and what you are working on for the rodeo."

"I don't wish to be trouble, ma'am."

"Sometimes no matter how hard we try, we are. So stop fighting it and accept your role."

Sawyer blinked, then a smile curved his mouth. "I see the mother is as formidable as the daughter."

"Give in now," Tate said. "Your life will be simpler." He snatched a piece of bread out of the bowl on the table.

"I'd be delighted." He nodded and walked out.

Erin followed Sawyer to his truck. When he heard the screen door slam, he paused and turned.

"Is there something else?"

He stood there, open and ready to answer any of her questions.

She waited until she stood before him, not wanting her words to carry on the wind. "Thank you for reaching out to Tate."

Shrugging, he smiled down at her. "Like I told you before, I want to give to others the same help I got. Sometimes God puts you in a place, and you know you need to reach out."

"True." Oddly, Erin didn't want him to leave, yet. She wanted to talk to him about Tate or the way the rodeo was coming along, but she knew he needed to go. Stepping back, she said, "See you at church Sunday."

"I'll look forward to it and sitting in the pew next to you and listening to that lovely voice of yours."

She watched as Sawyer pulled away. No one had ever told her they liked her voice. She wanted to blush but knew she'd better keep those emotions under control unless she wanted to face her mother's questions. And, at this moment, she didn't want to talk about the feelings Sawyer inspired.

Sawyer looked through all the bids that had come in. He thought about the invitation he'd received from Erin's mother. He probably should've stayed, but he knew the family needed time to be alone and talk. Earlier, when he'd had dinner at Lulu's, the place had buzzed with excitement, and it just wasn't the usual Friday night joy for the weekend. Several people joined him at his table and talked about their bids and ideas on how to help with the rodeo redo. There were many good ideas, but he didn't know if he could rely on these people. Could they pull off what they proposed or were they simply ideas with no substance?

He wanted to talk to someone about it. He could call anyone on the board, but he finally admitted who he wanted to talk to. He dialed Erin's cell phone.

"Sawyer, is there anything wrong?" Erin asked before he could say anything.

"No. But when I had dinner at Lulu's, lots of people came up and talked with me. I had one business from Las Vegas that intends to bid on chute gates. I wanted to head over there tomorrow and look at their product. I thought we might go together to check them out, as well as some other vendors."

The line remained quiet. His thinly disguised excuse for a date flashed like a neon light. He held his breath.

"I'd like that."

His breath rushed out, and he could breathe again. "I'll be by there at nine."

"See you then." She hung up.

Had he heard a lightness in her voice?

"Stop it," he told himself. He was a thirty-year-old man acting like a boy with his first girlfriend.

But he couldn't help himself.

When Erin put her cell phone down, she looked up and saw her mother standing at the door to the study.

"Who was that?"

For some silly reason, Erin didn't want to acknowledge her caller. Somehow, she was afraid if she shared Sawyer's invitation, her delight might go away. "That was Sawyer. He wants to drive into Las Vegas tomorrow and see the work of some of the vendors who've applied to work on the rodeo. He wants my input."

Mary nodded. "That is good. So, are you going to go with him?"

"Yes."

Sitting on the couch, Mary patted the place beside her. Erin came to her mother's side. Mary touched her daughter's cheek and brushed back the strands of hair that had come loose from her braid. "He's a handsome man, Daughter. He seems strong enough to hold his own against you."

Erin felt as if someone had smacked her hard on the back, leaving her breathless and disoriented. "Mom, I'm not looking for a boyfriend."

"I didn't say you were."

"Then why mention it?"

"Because you need someone."

Erin didn't know what to think. "What are you talking about?"

"I'm talking about being afraid to give in to your heart.

This man seems to have a heart big enough to allow you to soar. I like what I've seen between him and Tate."

Erin stared at her mother, stunned. "What brought this on?"

Mary looked down at her hands. "My husband's sick. As I sat in that room with him and prayed for his recovery, I asked God how I would go on. I have been blessed with a wonderful man and realize how precious life is." Mary took her daughter's hands. "What I want for you is a man as good as your father. A man who's as strong as you, who can walk with your strength and know his own. And for your brother, I prayed for the maturity for him to deal with his father's illness. And when I saw Sawyer and Tate riding in, I knew that prayer had been answered."

Erin's mind floundered to understand what her mother was saying. "So you trust Sawyer?"

"I see that God has provided a way. I want to talk to the man, listen to his words. I want to know if he'll share his heart. But for now, he's helping your brother."

Erin squirmed. Surely this wasn't God's way. She'd lost her rodeo bid. "Did you know about the contract going to another person, Mom?"

Her mother shook her head. "Immediately after the board meeting, your father had the stroke. No one told me the results of the vote. I didn't know anything about what had happened until you called me and told me that Sawyer won."

Erin, her heart still hurting, whispered, "Why would Dad vote against me, Mom? He knew I wanted the job."

Mary gently squeezed Erin's hands. "I don't know, Daughter. I don't understand, either. Since your father has been in the hospital, the results of the vote never crossed my mind."

Erin blinked back tears. "I can't understand how Dad could vote against me. That's been the hardest part." Erin closed her eyes, fighting for control. "Mel delighted in rubbing it in."

Mary snorted. "Mel's heart is so closed I'm afraid there's not much left of it." Slipping her arm around her daughter's shoulders, Mary drew Erin close. "From what I've seen of the young man who won the contract, maybe God brought him into our lives to help. With your father's condition, the burden of doing the rodeo might have been too much. And it seems that your brother needed him, also. Help comes in strange ways. Accept it.

"He seems a good match for you. He's not afraid to stand up for himself."

Erin wanted to object, but realized how ridiculous that sounded. Town folks knew that any man who dated her had better speak up for himself, so when Andy had proposed and she'd refused, no one had been surprised.

"I can find my own man, Mother."

"I didn't say you couldn't, but understand that a smile or a soft word will not ruin your reputation of being a wise woman. People come to you for help in solving problems, wanting advice. Sometimes walking softly holds more power than brute strength. Obstacles can be conquered with honey. Soft words don't mean weakness, but a confidence, and sureness, in yourself, which will not retreat in the face of those who don't listen. A dependence on God to lead."

Erin blinked at her mother. Where was this coming from? "I will think on your words, Mother."

Mary stood. "That lesson took a long time for me to learn, but once I did, life fell into place." Mary brushed a kiss across Erin's cheek. "I look forward to talking with Sawyer on Sunday."

Sleep didn't come quickly for Erin, with her mother's words tumbling around her head, making her wonder at the truth.

Had she put up walls, hiding from others?

Was she running? And was she ready to stop? Could she give in to the desires of her heart concerning Sawyer? Her mother said she should follow those desires.

She mulled over the idea. What could it hurt except break her heart, but would it be worth it to have someone love her and share the burdens?

The next morning Sawyer pulled into the driveway of the Delong ranch. He walked to the back door and called out, "Mornin', is Erin ready?"

Betty motioned Sawyer inside. Mary and Tate sat at the table eating.

"Would you like some coffee?" Betty offered. "I also have my special coffee cake if you haven't eaten."

Before he could respond, Erin appeared in the kitchen. Dressed in jeans and a Western blouse, her hair flowed around her shoulders like a silken black cape. The belt buckle at her waist he recognized as the top barrel racer for one year. She also had on snakeskin boots. It matched his attire of western shirt, jeans and boots.

Erin looked at the people around the table. "Auntie, I'd like some of your coffee cake and a mug of coffee to go."

"Why don't you sit and eat with us, Daughter?" Mary asked.

From her reaction, Sawyer knew Erin didn't want to stay.

"Mom, we've got a lot to do today for the rodeo. We need to get going."

Mary didn't respond except for a knowing smile.

Erin grabbed two travel mugs and poured coffee. "Do you drink it black?" she asked Sawyer.

"Yup, straight up."

She put the top on his mug and handed it to him. Grabbing the creamer, she fixed her coffee. Betty handed her two pieces of coffee cake. "You're the best." Erin brushed a kiss on her auntie's cheek.

Pausing at the door, Erin walked to her mother's side and hugged her.

"Remember my words," Mary whispered.

Erin nodded.

"I agree with Sister," Betty added.

Tate frowned and looked from his mother to his aunt to Erin. "What's going on?"

Betty smiled. "Too bad life is wasted on the young."

"Huh?"

Sawyer opened the screen door and heard Betty say, "Love is in the air."

"Where?" Tate asked.

Both the older women laughed.

Erin marched to Sawyer's truck, trying to ignore the conversation going on in the kitchen, but Sawyer cocked his head and grinned.

Great, how was she going to explain what had just happened?

Chapter Nine

Sawyer finished the last of the coffee cake, licking the crumbs off his fingers. He laughed. "Oh, I'm going to want another piece of that when I get back." He took a swig of his coffee.

"Both Betty and my mom are great cooks. Unfortunately, I did not inherit their talent."

Sawyer took his eyes off the road and looked at her. "It strikes me that maybe you didn't want their talent."

Erin chuckled. "Wow, you nailed that. How'd you guess?"

"Both my brother and I did rodeo growing up. I think Caleb could've given me a run for my money, but he wanted a steady paycheck to support us, so he developed the talent of being the best pickup rider in the business. He's as good as me in saddle bronc riding and bull riding."

He could see her mulling over the crumbs he gave her. She nodded. "True. You're one of the few people who's ever guessed that I wasn't interested in cooking."

"We each have our talents, and your talent lies elsewhere." He threw her a grin. "You could evaluate failing companies and write up plans to save them. My professors would've loved working with you."

"That's an idea. I just finished my MBA from University of New Mexico in Albuquerque. I could add to my credentials."

"Ah, you're one of those number crunchers."

Her laughter filled the cab of the truck, delighting him. That first day, when she marched into the conference room, he never would've expected to hear her tease him. "Dad understood my talent, but Mom wanted me to be more like her. I can cook, but if you don't give a snort, then most of what you cook is average. You can't be something you're not."

"I hear you." He pointed to the floorboard between them.

"There, by your feet, is an accordion file with the bids we've received so far. I wanted to go over them with you."

She found the file between the front seats and opened it. They spent the drive to Las Vegas scrutinizing each bid and talking about the person or business who had submitted it.

They finished reviewing the submissions just as they entered the outskirts of the city.

"Would you mind if we went to my mother's jewelry shop before we attend to the rodeo business?" Erin asked.

"Your mother owns a jewelry shop? Why'd no one say anything?"

"Well, with the rest of our lives falling apart, it slipped my mind." She directed him through the streets of Las Vegas.

"Mother's other talents include jewelry making, weaving and gardening." Erin looked down at her lap.

From the slump of her shoulders, Sawyer guessed that Erin felt her lack of artistic talent made her feel inadequate. "Remember, we all have different paths to walk."

Her head jerked up, and her gaze collided with his. "You're sounding more and more like Auntie."

"She's showing me new ways."

"My mother has an abundance of artistic talent, but she can't add a line of numbers and cares nothing about keeping her books straight or dealing with payroll. And don't get me going about paying taxes or dealing with dissatisfied customers or paying suppliers in a timely manner. But, somehow, some way, Mom charms them, and they forgive her. I'm trying to get her to hire a full-time manager again so all she has to worry about are her creations."

"From what I heard from folks in town, you're the person that straightens out problems and fixes mistakes."

She didn't reply, but he saw her consider his words.

"You've done that for your mom, haven't you?"

The answer shone clearly in her eyes.

"It doesn't matter."

Erin directed him to the part of Old Town that housed her mother's jewelry store. The long adobe structure had been built in the early 1900s, before statehood. The uneven wood walkway out front had borne countless feet that walked up and down the street.

They parked in front of the store. Before she could get out of the truck, he reached for her hand. "It does matter, Erin. Your mom's a smart woman, and if she wanted to, she could hire a manager to take care of those problems."

"She had one." She got out of the truck before he could ask any more questions.

Shame on you, Mary Morning Star Delong, Sawyer thought. Why had Erin's mother kept her daughter tethered to her? The woman he met the other day knew how to run a business. This didn't feel right.

Opening the door, she called out, "Hey, Joe, I'm here to take care of that problem Mom had with Mrs. Gonzales's necklace."

Joe appeared in the doorway that led to the back room, situated behind the glass cases holding the different artisan's creations.

"Erin, what a wonderful treat to see you." He gathered her into a hug. He looked over her shoulder at Sawyer.

"Who do you have with you?"

Sawyer held out his hand and introduced himself.

"Joe Torres. How do you know Erin?"

"I'm working with her on the revitalization of the bi-county rodeo."

"I've heard about that. People are talking in town about it. Should be interesting to see."

Erin carefully explained about Sawyer's role in the rodeo. "Joe's been working with Mother for the last twenty years. He's the one who convinced Mom to start her own line of jewelry. When Joe's wife passed away, he sold his store and Mom bought it. He's been helping her on and off for the last couple of years. I've tried to get Joe to accept the job as manager, but all he wants is to spend time with his grandchildren."

Joe shook his head. "I'm glad to help straighten things out temporarily, but with those resorts in Taos wanting the pieces your mother contracted with them, and received a down payment for, things are tense. I understand your mother's heart, concentrating on your father first, but she needs to notify the customers and let them know what is going on. I don't doubt they will give her time."

"I know."

Erin and Joe sat behind the counter and discussed how to deal with things. Erin called the disgruntled customer and explained the situation.

"Give me a half hour to catch up on paperwork," she told Sawyer, then disappeared into the back.

Joe and Sawyer faced each other.

"How are things working out?"

Another defender. Sawyer's first impression of Erin had proved to be true. She was a strong woman, but she was not the kind he expected. "She's kept me on my toes and thrown me more surprises than I know what to do with. She has me dancing."

"And is this a problem?" Joe watched Sawyer carefully.

"No, it's not a problem, but if I think one thing, Erin comes up with another way to solve the problem. I'm learning to see her point."

Joe smiled. "The Delong women can have you doing things that you never expected. Of course, when my wife died, I wanted to lie down and die, too, but Mary wouldn't allow me to do that. She threw me a lifeline."

"Unusual women, both Mary and her daughter." Sawyer shrugged. "I could include Aunt Betty, too."

"True. She came into the shop one time, but I knew she held her own with her sister."

Sawyer told himself it was none of his business, but he opened his mouth and said, "Tell me, why does Mary hold her daughter for ransom with her finances?"

Joe sat back and studied Sawyer. "You are an observant man and the only person I know who sees that. Detrick refuses to acknowledge it, and none of Mary's family or friends find a problem with it. They just chalk it up to the artisan in Mary." He rubbed his neck.

"So, I'm not out of line with my conclusions?" Sawyer quietly said.

"No, you're on the mark. About a year ago, Mary called Erin to ask for help." He paused. "Erin earned her undergraduate degree in accounting then used her earnings from barrel racing to pay for her masters. She'd win enough for a year of school, take off and attend UNM in Albuquerque."

Sawyer smiled. "I know that story. I did that myself."

"With rodeo?" Joe asked.

"Yes." It amazed Sawyer that Erin and he had followed the same path to get their degrees. Maybe that's why he felt so connected to her.

"Ah, I see you understand. When Erin started writing

her master's thesis, I retired from the store. Mary refused to hire a new accountant, complaining about how much work it was to keep the books, create and care for the store. Erin volunteered to help until her mother found someone to take my place.

"That was some time ago, and I've seen the toll it's taken on Erin. I don't know if Mary even knows she's doing it. Maybe she's afraid to let go. Mary aids many. The daughter follows in her mother's footsteps. Perhaps Erin needs an advocate." Joe stared at Sawyer.

Sawyer's skin prickled, and the hair on the back of his neck stood up. If he took up this challenge, lives would be changed. "That's a big job."

"It will require a strong man who can tackle the situation."

Sawyer felt every word. "I'm here to finish redoing the rodeo. I'm not qualified to meddle in people's lives."

"Yes, you are. Of all the people surrounding Erin, only you've seen the truth. Mary Morning Star knows how to hire an accountant and the problem would be solved, but she ignores it."

"You've seen the truth, too."

Joe folded his arms over his chest. "True, and I have thought to battle this situation, but my heart is a friend to Mary. Your heart speaks to Erin. You can choose to help her or walk away, but think carefully before you decide."

Suddenly, the world shifted. He stood in a place he had never expected to be.

"Joe," Erin's voice called out.

"Think about it," Joe whispered, then walked through the doorway to the back.

They enjoyed a lunch in an outdoor café on the edge of Old Town. The food was a fusion of Navajo and Spanish styles.

"What did you and Joe talk about?" Erin took a sip of her iced tea.

"He told me how he encouraged your mom to create pieces of jewelry and explained how they worked together."

His answer came quickly, but she felt there must have been more to the conversation. "Did he explain why he wouldn't come back and work with Mom?"

"I think he wants the freedom to live his life."

"I can't blame him."

"So, why doesn't your mother hire someone to take care of her business?" He took a chip from the basket on the table and scooped up some hot sauce.

"I've told her she needs to do that. She says she's been too busy to interview a manager. And now with Dad sick—" She shrugged.

"How long has this been going on?"

Erin considered how long she'd been running interference for her mom. As she thought, she realized this pattern had been going on since she started writing her thesis. Comprehension slammed into her. When her gaze collided with Sawyer's, she knew he saw the truth.

"Too long." Feeling duped, she asked, "Why would Mom do that?"

"I'm the wrong person to try to answer that question. My mom wasn't a mom."

Erin heard that same pain again. "What do you mean?"

He sat back in his chair. "After my dad died of a sudden heart attack, mom couldn't handle the grief. Her world dissolved in an instant. Dad had worked for another rancher and we lived in a house on the property, but with Dad's death, we had to leave." He paused, lost in the old memories. "Mom went from a woman who fed us and kept the house to a woman who couldn't make a decision without either my brother's or my input. When that wasn't enough, she started seeking out boyfriends. The first couple of guys were nice, but my mom smothered them."

A knot in her stomach formed.

"The more men left her, the needier she became. The men she attracted had the attitude of 'it's my way or the highway,' and that didn't sit well with two teenage boys."

Erin covered Sawyer's hand, which rested on the table.

"I was the one with a mouth. If one of my mother's boyfriends hit her, I spoke up. I got my face punched several times."

He looked down at their hands as if noticing them for the first time. "It wasn't uncommon for Mom's boyfriends to beat her, and I'd tried to stop it, but I'd get beat up in the process." He shook his head. "You'd think I'd have smartened up, but I couldn't ignore it."

"That speaks well of you."

"No, I was the stupid one. Mom's boyfriends would tear into Mom when it was only me there. They knew not to start their garbage when Caleb was home. Of course, Caleb was older and bigger than me."

He looked into her eyes. "Do you know what Mom would tell me afterward? It was my fault. If I hadn't annoyed so-and-so, then it wouldn't have happened. Can you believe that?"

Her heart ached. "No, I can't. Your mom was mentally off-balance."

He looked down at their hands. The waiter appeared, and Sawyer paid the bill.

On the way to the truck, he pulled Erin under a tree, out of the view of people on the patio and gathered her into his arms. "I didn't mean to unload on you like that."

Tilting her head back, she looked up at him. He'd mentioned before his brother had been declared an emancipated minor. "What caused your brother to file to be on his own and take you?"

"You caught my references?"

"Yes, and I wondered what had happened."

He pulled her closer and rested his chin on the top of her head. She knew he needed another sympathetic heart to share his story with.

"Caleb was at work after school at the feed store. Mom and her boyfriend were drunk and arguing over the TV. I was at the kitchen table doing homework. Mom told her boyfriend she didn't want to watch his stupid show." He stopped. "The next thing I knew, I heard a choking sound and her boyfriend yelling things I won't repeat. I raced into the next room and found him strangling Mom. She clawed at his face and his hands, but she was turning red."

"I barreled into the man, knocking him off her. She scooted away and watched as the man started in on me. I put up a fight, but he got a couple of good punches to my face, bloodying me up good. When he drew back his hand to deliver the final blow—and I sometimes wonder if that blow would've been my last—it never came. My brother stood over me, like some kind of guardian. He told Mom's boyfriend if he wanted to beat someone up, try someone his own size."

"The man backed down and told us to get out. When we looked at Mom, she agreed with her boyfriend. We ran out the back door."

Her heart broke at Sawyer's mother's betrayal. When he looked down, Erin pulled back and saw wet spots on his shirt. She hadn't realized she cried.

She cupped his face. "I'm sorry."

He shrugged. "I told you about my mother so you could see that in the grand scheme of things your mother's actions are what I consider minor. I like Mary, but when we got to her jewelry store, something didn't feel right. Joe also knows that, for some reason, your mom is pulling you back to her."

She wanted to argue, but everything he said made sense. What's more, Erin already knew the truth he had told her; she just hadn't wanted to admit it to herself.

"So, you're not offended that I put my nose in your business?" He gently held both her arms above the elbows.

"No." Her mother's words rang in her ears. God had sent Sawyer to help their family. Her mother wasn't going to be pleased with his words. She rose up on her toes and tried to brush a kiss across his cheek, but he turned his head and their mouths met.

Shock raced through her. She should've pulled back, but she didn't. His arms slid around her waist. The warmth of his embrace and sweetness of his mouth soothed her heart. When he drew back, he looked down at her tenderly.

"I shouldn't have done that."

"True." Her eyes danced with joy.

He dropped his arms and stepped away. "Why don't we finish our business here in Vegas, then drive to Albuquerque and talk to the concrete manufacturer? I'd like to meet with him face-to-face, but I'll need to call him now and give him a heads-up."

Glancing down at her watch, she knew they had plenty of time. "I'm up for it."

"Then let me call him and arrange things."

It took only moments for Sawyer to set up the meeting. When he hung up, he grinned like a schoolboy, but he was a responsible adult. "It's set. C'mon, let's finish our business here then go to Albuquerque. We have a man to meet with."

"And while we're there, I'd like to stop by the hospital and see my dad."

"Absolutely."

As they drove to Albuquerque, Sawyer couldn't find his bearings from all that had transpired that morning.

He knew any questions about the bids could be answered honestly by Erin. The woman had a good sense of people and honestly appraised each bid. He found he could count on her.

That truth blindsided him. She was the first woman he'd ever trusted in that deep a way. When he saw what was going on at her mother's jewelry store and told her, she had listened to him. She hadn't called him names or accused him of wanting to ruin her mother's name, but realized the legitimacy of what he said.

He had told the truth and she'd listened. That was the first time he'd encountered that with a woman so close to him. He could honestly talk to her and she could deal with it, even if it wasn't an easy revelation. More than just admiration, he felt her pain and tried to relieve it.

Of course, he'd had no business kissing her, but he hadn't expected her to put her lips in front of his. That was an accident, but he wanted to repeat the happy accident.

As he glanced at her, his heart swelled. Erin was the first woman he had told about his mother. He remembered when he'd met his future sister-in-law and she'd confided that his brother had shared stories about their tough upbringing. That was when Sawyer knew something was up with Caleb and Brenda.

Was he in that same boat?

"What are you smiling at?"

Erin's voice jerked him to the here and now. "I was thinking about my brother and his wife. You met Brenda when you attended the rodeo there in Peaster last Memorial Day. She took over putting it on."

"I remember her. We talked a little about how she organized the rodeo. Of course, what our rodeo needed was an update."

"She's an amazing lady. She was a captain in the army

until she was injured when a bomb went off in the café she was at in Baghdad."

"I didn't know."

"She's more than tough enough to handle my brother. It's nice to see her boss him around." He grinned. "You would understand and appreciate her methods of doing things."

She turned to him, and her solemn look made him nervous. Finally her lips twitched, and a wide smile creased her mouth. "Are you calling me bossy?"

"If the shoe fits." His light tone matched hers.

Waving away his comment, she said, "We talked about the problems we've had with our rodeo. I got some good ideas from her, but didn't implement them. The board hired you."

"And do you regret it?" He really wanted to know.

Her mouth turned up at the corners. "Ask me when we finish the rodeo."

"It's a date." And as the words died in the truck cab, he knew it would be a *date*.

Chapter Ten

The meeting with the concrete contractor opened their eyes. Erin now stared down at the invoice for the last work the contractor had done for the rodeo. Twenty-five hundred dollars. The price listed on Mel's final expense statement, which he dropped off at the office, was for thirty-five hundred and eighty-four dollars.

"It's unbelievable," she murmured. Mel had always been hard to get along with, but to embezzle—she never would've thought he'd do that.

"It happens," Sawyer said, bringing her back to the here and now. They sat in Sawyer's truck in front of the concrete manufacturer.

"Mel's known to be difficult. Too big for his britches, as my mother always likes to say." She studied him. "Have you run into this sort of thing before?"

"Yes. As long as there are people, we'll have things like this crop up."

Erin looked at the numbers on the photocopy of the check. "Surely there's another explanation," she whispered.

"What would you like to do now?"

"I'd like to go see my dad in the hospital since we're here," she said, without looking at Sawyer.

He didn't respond.

"What's wrong?"

"Are you going to ask your dad about the discrepancy now? You don't want to upset him."

She turned toward him. "I won't do anything to harm my dad," she said forcefully, "but I wonder if he suspected something." Her last words trailed off.

"Maybe that was the reason he brought in an outsider," Sawyer offered. "If I tripped over the discrepancy, others would be more inclined to believe me than you. It could be chalked up to bad feelings between you and Mel. I know Traci would've gone with that explanation."

That was it. Her heart and soul latched on to the reason for her father's actions. "You're right. No one would've believed me, but—"

"With me discovering it, others would know I didn't make it up."

Her gaze fell to the copy of the check in her lap again, making sure she wasn't dreaming. "That's true." She hadn't understood her dad's actions, but with this explanation things made sense. "Let's go to the hospital and see."

Reaching over, he squeezed her hand. His unconditional support made her heart sing with joy in the middle of this mess. She felt heaven's direction in the midst of this madness—something to hold on to. No, *someone* to hold on to.

Mary Morning Star stood beside her husband's bed. When Erin and Sawyer walked into the room, she smiled at them.

"Mom, what are you doing here?" Erin asked. "You just came home."

"Tate needed to see his father. I thought you and Sawyer had gone to Las Vegas."

"We did, then did some rodeo business here."

Erin walked to her father's bed. Picking up his hand, she gently cradled it. "Hello, Dad."

"Erin," Detrick choked out.

"It's good to see you face-to-face instead of just on the iPad. You've had us so worried."

Detrick's eyes went from Erin to Sawyer. He saw the question in the older man's gaze as it traveled from Erin to Sawyer.

"I wanted…" Detrick started.

"Dad, don't worry about anything." Erin stroked his forehead, brushing away a tear. "I believe in you, and I know you had your reasons for your vote. I trust you."

Sawyer felt awkward watching the tender scene play out between father and daughter. Mary stepped to his side. "When Erin told me that my husband voted for you, I knew he hadn't betrayed her. Never in the years we've been married has he deceived his family." She looked up into Sawyer's face.

"I think you're right. Your husband had a reason to bring me in."

Her eyes narrowed. "Something has happened."

"We may have stumbled on to some information that could be explosive."

"I knew it."

Erin caught Sawyer's hand and pulled him forward. "Dad, this is Sawyer. I don't know if you've met him in person before."

The older man shook his head. "Read his plan." The uttering of the words exhausted him.

"Erin's been very helpful. A little bossy, but a valuable asset." Sawyer didn't want to upset the old man with the truth they'd uncovered, but Sawyer suspected he already knew.

"True," Detrick whispered.

Mary took her husband's other hand and gently smoothed his hair back from his face.

"You let Sawyer and Erin take care of the rodeo. What you need to do is get well."

"That's true." Erin ran the back of her fingers over her dad's cheek. "Sawyer's come out to the ranch and ridden your mount. He and Tate have gone riding a couple of times. Tate's not drowning in a sea of estrogen with Sawyer there."

Erin looked around. "Where are Tate and Betty?"

"They are with Kai, eating. We'll drive back after they finish their meal."

A smile spread across Detrick's face as he traded looks with Sawyer. He read a thank-you in the older man's eyes.

The door opened.

"Good evening, Mr. Delong," the nurse called out. "I've got your evening pills here."

Sawyer's blood turned cold. He never thought he'd hear that voice again.

Mary turned and greeted the nurse. "Good evening, Sylvia."

"I see you didn't follow my advice and stay at home this weekend," Sylvia replied.

"Tate needed to see his father, but I promise to go home tonight."

"You will not help him if you wear yourself out. He's going to need all the support he can get once home."

Mary accepted the gentle chiding.

Slowly, Sawyer turned and came face-to-face with his mother. When she saw him, she momentarily froze.

The rest of the world faded away, and his past came roaring back, nearly flattening him. He locked his knees to stay standing.

His mother recovered quickly and turned to Mary. "The doctor's here now and wants to talk to you. I'll get him."

"Do you think we can take Detrick home soon?"

"You'll need to talk that over with the doctor. I'll let him know you're here."

Sawyer didn't say anything as he stepped back to get out of everyone's way. The name tag on his mother's uniform said Carter. Where she'd gotten that name, he didn't know. The last he knew, her boyfriend's surname was Braddock. How many men had she gone through since him?

Sylvia glanced at him. "Who do you have with you, Mary?" Her voice cracked.

"This is Sawyer Jensen. He's working with our county rodeo board to revitalize our rodeo."

"He's a turnaround consultant," Erin added. She turned to him and smiled. But all Sawyer could see was his mother's face, and a flood of different, hard memories flowed in.

"It's nice to meet you, Sawyer." She gave him a tentative smile and nodded her head. Deep in her eyes he saw doubt and uncertainty.

He didn't trust himself to open his mouth. He simply nodded.

Both Mary and Erin glanced at him.

"Excuse me," he said, not trusting his reactions, and walked out of the room.

He didn't stop at the end of the hall. He walked to the exit and descended the stairs to the main floor. Emerging from the stairwell, he saw the door to the ground-level garden for the patients and families and pushed it open.

In one corner, he found a bench shaded by the building and sat, trying to regain his footing. He never thought he'd see his mother alive again. He'd often wondered what had happened to her. She hadn't bothered to contact her sons once she'd hit them up for money right after Caleb had been declared an emancipated minor. They'd moved away and settled in the small city of Plainview, south of

Lubbock. Sawyer doubted his mother had ever tried to discover what had happened to her sons.

They had grown into manhood despite their mother's actions, and both his brother and he imagined she was probably dead.

As he thought about it, his mother looked like a woman in charge of her faculties. She certainly had to be in order to be a nurse in the hospital.

He frowned. A nurse? When had that happened? Before his dad died, his mother had always taken care of her boys when they were sick, and she had a talent for making them feel better. She looked as if she had a peace about her, which brought him to the million-dollar question—what had happened in his mother's life?

"Thank you, Doctor," Mary replied to the doctor's final assessment.

"I'll look for a rehab center closer to home," Mary told him. "I think going home for his rehabilitation would help my husband."

"If you need anything else, be sure to have the nurses contact me." The doctor left the room.

Mary turned to her husband and smiled down into his face. "It's good news, husband. It will take work on your part to get you back to your old self, but I don't doubt you can do it." Mary cupped his cheek. "My heart nearly stopped, and your children have not known what to do, so you need to work hard to get better. And Tate needs you more than ever."

Detrick nodded.

"I'll look around, Mother, for a place closer to home," Erin said.

"All that is important is that your father gets well. Oh, I have one more question for the doctor." Mary hurried out into the hall.

Erin stepped to her father's side and grasped his hand. His eyes held a question.

"What is it?"

He glanced toward where Sawyer had stood.

"Are you wanting to talk about Sawyer?"

He nodded. Talking took effort, and he tired easily.

"I will say I didn't understand why you voted for someone else, but as the days go by, I see that vote in a different light." She squeezed her father's hand. "Sawyer and I have found some discrepancies in the last budget done for the rodeo update."

He squeezed her hand again.

"As we've talked about it, I realized if Sawyer found the discrepancy, others would believe him quicker than me."

Detrick's body relaxed.

"Is that it?"

He blinked and tried to speak, but the sounds coming out of his mouth weren't intelligible.

"It shook my faith, but I knew you had a reason."

A tear ran from the corner of her dad's right eye. She wiped it away.

There were other things she wanted to talk to her father about—how Sawyer had reached out to Tate and how she'd found herself enjoying her skirmishes with him—but now wasn't the time.

The door opened again, and Erin turned, expecting Sawyer. It was her mom.

"I'm going to find Sawyer and go home. Don't stay too late, Mom. We might tire out Dad."

"Ah, now it happens, the child is trying to become the parent," Mary replied.

"No, it's a daughter who is worried about her mother's safety." Leaning over, Erin kissed her mom's cheek and thought about asking her mother why she kept ignoring her accounts at the store, but now wasn't the time to confront her. Tomorrow they'd talk.

Walking out of the room, Erin looked for Sawyer. He wouldn't have left, but she did not see him. At the nurse's desk, she asked Sylvia, "Have you seen Sawyer?"

Sylvia's hand jerked on the computer keyboard. When she glanced up, she took a deep breath. "No, I haven't seen him on the floor. Would he have left?"

Erin rubbed her neck. "Not without me. We drove together from home."

Erin started to the elevator doors.

"Have you known him long?" Sylvia asked.

Erin turned. "No. He won the bid over me to take our failing rodeo and turn it around. I wasn't happy to have lost, but I will say he's much different than I expected."

"How so?"

Erin shrugged. "Well, first of all, the man's a cowboy who has won a championship belt buckle, so he knows his stuff. We don't have some egghead who thinks he knows what a cowboy and his horse need. Sawyer's lived it. But what's amazed me is that he's listened to my input to his plan." A laugh escaped her. "I might have lost the bid, but I wasn't going to walk away from our rodeo and let this stranger have free rein over it." She smiled.

"And he's been helpful with my seventeen-year-old brother." Suddenly Erin couldn't stop the words rushing out of her mouth. Here was the nurse who'd been with them from the beginning, who could give an unbiased opinion or at least a reasonably unbiased one. "Tate wouldn't talk to any of us women about Dad's stroke, but somehow Sawyer understood his turmoil.

"And for that I'm grateful." Erin shook her head. "With all the upheaval and craziness going on around the ranch, Sawyer recognized a lost teenage boy and reached out to him. When the sheriff called me about my brother ditching school, my first reaction was to rain all over him, but Sawyer talked me out of it. He's surprised me with his keen perception of the situation. Most men wouldn't follow through like he did, but he's gone riding with Tate and they've talked a couple of times."

"That's amazing for a stranger to do." Sylvia picked up a pen. "Sometimes what we think is the end is a turn in the road we didn't expect."

Erin had the strangest feeling that Sylvia wasn't talking about her situation now. The words came from experience.

A buzzer from one of the patient's rooms took Sylvia in a different direction. Erin walked to the elevator doors. Before she could push the button, the doors slid open and Sawyer emerged. He looked around. "Are you ready to leave?"

"Yes. When I didn't see you out here, Sylvia, the nurse, asked if you'd left without me. I told her no, that you'd driven me."

"I'm sorry. I went downstairs for a moment."

She waited for more of an explanation but didn't get it.

"Are you ready to leave?" The tone of his voice was flat.

The more he spoke, the more suspicious she became. "Yes."

With the exception of a Western music station out of Albuquerque playing on the radio, the ride home passed in silence.

Erin knew something had changed at the hospital, but she couldn't figure out what.

"I'm encouraged by how good Dad looks," she said, hoping to get a conversation going.

"Uh-huh."

"And I'll talk to Mother about her bookkeeping."

"That's good."

"And I think I'll ride my horse right into church tomorrow to liven things up."

"That's a good approach."

She turned and faced him head-on. It took him several minutes to realize she had stopped talking. When he looked her direction, he said, "What?"

"Where are you, Sawyer? Because you're not here with me in this truck."

"Things piled up on us today, and I'm just trying to sort them out." He looked back to the interstate.

His explanation could've been the truth, but she had this feeling in her gut it wasn't the entire reason he was so far removed from her. She didn't try again. The words of caution he'd offered before about Tate rang again in her head. *Don't push.*

It went against her nature. She wanted answers, to sort out the situation now, but something inside her warned her, and for the balance of the drive, nothing was said.

He pulled into the ranch driveway. Following her out of the truck, he caught up with her in a couple of steps and caught her hand.

"Are you okay?" He studied her face.

"Yes. Are you?"

He pulled her into his arms and held her close, resting his chin on the top of her head. His hand rubbed her back. She found comfort in his action, but wondered if he didn't need the comfort, too.

"It's been a long day and seeing your dad was hard, I know."

She noticed he didn't answer her question. Instead, he cupped her face and gently kissed her. It wasn't a kiss of passion but of comfort and solace. He brushed another kiss across her lips. "I'll see you tomorrow."

She stared after his retreating form, wondering what was going on with him, because she didn't have a clue.

Chapter Eleven

Sawyer stared at the ceiling trying to find his way through the maze of conflicting emotions. It'd been a roller coaster of a day, from this morning around the Delong table with coffee and inquisitive minds, to the joy of talking with Erin about the bids that had come in, to his discovery of her mother's use of her. Erin had honestly listened to him without any recriminations.

Her reaction rocked him back on his heels, but the coup de grâce was meeting his mother face-to-face in Detrick's room at the hospital. His knees had nearly buckled when he'd heard her voice. He thought he might be hallucinating, but when he turned, it was his mother—a better, healthier version of his mother, much like she'd been when his father was alive. But there was something more in her demeanor that puzzled him.

What was it? She didn't seem nervous or unsure. She moved with confidence. A woman at peace.

That thought blew him away.

The nurse in Detrick's room physically resembled his mom, but she'd changed from the inside out.

He should call his brother and tell him what had happened, but he wasn't ready to talk to Caleb.

Sawyer thought about calling Pastor Garvey in Plainview to talk to him, but what would he say? He saw a woman who was a dead ringer for his mom but acted nothing like the woman he'd known. Besides, his mother wasn't a nurse.

People can change, the thought came.

He rested his head in his hands and ran his fingers through his hair. He needed to know more before calling his brother.

Erin walked into the kitchen, where her mother stood making her special honey cake for breakfast before church.

"Did you and Sawyer finish the business you had in Las Vegas yesterday before you came to the hospital?" Mary asked. "You didn't mention anything about how things went."

"We worked while on the road to Vegas and dropped by your store."

"You two agreed on what needs to be done." Mary looked up from the bowl with a knowing smile.

"We have. Sawyer's an insightful man."

Mary smiled. "Did you ask him if he is part Navajo?"

Erin hoisted herself onto the counter and stole a few raisins from a bowl.

"No, I didn't ask him about that, but he asked me why I was doing your books at the store since you're such an insightful and capable woman, and why you didn't hire a bookkeeper or buy a software program that would track your sales and expenses instead of drafting your daughter into doing your books."

Mary paled. "What did you say?"

"I blinked at Sawyer, realizing, for the first time, that he was right about what was happening."

Mary pulled out a chair from the table and sat down. Erin jumped off the counter and squatted in front of her mother.

"What has frightened you, Mother?"

Mary cupped Erin's cheek, and her eyes glistened with moisture. "I realized that my firstborn was now a grown and very capable woman who had earned her undergraduate degree and is close to getting her masters." Mary took a breath. "I guess I feared you would feel you no longer need your mother and leave to make your own way. I didn't want to face that."

Rising up on her knees, Erin wrapped her arms around her mother. "I will never outgrow my need for you. But I know you want to see me spread my wings and fly. You and Father made that possible. Everything was possible. If I could think it, I could try it. I knew this because of you and Father. Never did you put any limits on my imagination. I've talked with other girls in college and heard how they were directed in the way their families wanted them to go, never paying attention to their daughter's strengths. I found this so foreign and wasteful of their talents. I appreciated my parents even more."

"So much has changed," Mary whispered.

"True, but you always said there is a merciful Lord who walks with us."

Mary laughed through her tears. "There is nothing more humbling than having to live by one's own words."

"Sometimes we forget and need to be reminded." Erin gently wiped the tears from her mother's cheeks.

Betty walked into the kitchen. She looked at them and asked, "What is going on?"

"The sharing of wisdom, Sister, and the reminder to live with one's words with grace."

Betty looked from her sister to her niece and frowned. "What?"

Erin stood and wrapped her arm around her aunt, drawing her close.

Mary took a deep breath. "My daughter called me out

on trying to keep her close. She assured me her love will continue, no matter where she is."

Understanding lit Betty's eyes. "It's hard, Sister, to let the first one go. Talk to me, I will help."

"Thank you, Auntie."

Sawyer slipped into the back of the church. He'd overslept and thrown on his clothes and dress shirt. He'd missed the song service. Instead of parading down the aisle, making a show of himself, he sat in the next to the last pew and listened to the sermon. The preacher spoke about forgiveness and said that if you forgave the person who wronged you, that forgiveness would free you. No longer would you have to carry around the crippling weight that ate your soul.

Sawyer's gaze drilled a hole into the pastor. Obviously, the man didn't know what he was talking about. He hadn't had to sleep out in the field behind his house when his mother entertained her drunk boyfriend who was spoiling for a fight.

"Let loose and let God heal your heart."

Sawyer folded his arms over his chest, throwing up a barrier. His heart and head weren't interested.

The pastor said the final prayer, and the organist played the closing hymn.

As people filed out, Sawyer didn't move from his place on the pew, still struggling with the message.

Tate sat beside him. "You plan to sit here all day? Church's over. I thought you were eating with us."

When Sawyer looked around, he saw Erin, her aunt and mother standing at the end of the pew. They'd witnessed his struggle.

Fighting his awkwardness, he stood and pasted on a smile. "I'm ready."

Mary cocked her head, studying him, as if she could read his confused heart. She nodded.

"I'll follow you to the ranch," Sawyer told them. "I'd be more than willing to have Tate ride with me."

Within minutes, they were on the road.

"Sis was worried that you might not show up today."

Sawyer shot a glance at Tate. "She say why?"

"No. But she kept looking down the aisle while we were singing."

"I overslept."

"I hear you. One time I slept through my alarm for school and managed to get ready in five minutes. Amazed my mom and sister. Dad knew I could pull it off." At the mention of his father, Tate seemed to deflate.

"Your dad looked good yesterday at the hospital."

"Yeah, he did when I saw him, but Sis acted kinda strange when she came in last night. I thought something had happened with Dad."

Hearing Tate alerted Sawyer that Erin had picked up on his agitation. "We did a lot yesterday. I think the relief your sister had after seeing your dad made her a little—uh—"

Tate grinned, waiting to hear Sawyer's explanation. "Yes?"

"Off," he said, finally committing to a word. "But I expect you to keep this conversation between us."

"You bet." The kid folded his arms over his chest and kept grinning.

"Anything I need to know before your mom questions me?" Sawyer asked on the drive.

Tate stroked his chin. "Just be straight-up honest with her."

"I hear ya."

"I know. Believe me, I've never gotten anything by my mom, and I've tried."

Sawyer laughed. He could see Tate trying to put something over on Mary. It was nothing like his experience with his own mom, who had managed not to be aware that her boys were even in the house.

"But Mom's fair."

Sawyer wondered how fair Mary would be since he won the contract over her daughter. So far she'd been reasonable, but he hadn't spent much time with her. He knew his mom would've been out for his hide if he'd won over the person she wanted to get the job. Her sons weren't necessarily the people she backed.

The ranch house came into view. Tate's prediction would soon be put to the test.

Erin threw her purse on the desk in the kitchen and walked to the sink to wash her hands.

"How are you, child?" Mary asked, stopping next to Erin. Her mom had been watching her all through church. Erin felt guilty, but for what?

"I'm fine." Her clipped response gave away the truth— she wasn't—but before her mother could pursue the topic, Tate and Sawyer walked in. Mary leaned close. "We'll talk later. We have much to discuss."

They'd already talked. What now? Erin turned and walked away. It took less than five minutes for them to get dinner on the table, and then Mary motioned for them to take their seats. Sawyer sat next to Tate and across from Erin.

After a prayer, Betty dished out a lamb stew and placed a piece of blue corn bread on the edge of the bowl.

It took a moment of Sawyer studying the bread to ask, "Is this supposed to be this color?"

"It's Auntie's favorite blue corn bread. Try it," Tate urged.

Sawyer had eaten worse. He took a bite and slowly

chewed the corn bread. The sweet taste of the cornmeal raced over his tongue. "That's good."

"Of course, so how was your trip to Las Vegas yesterday?" Betty asked.

Erin looked at her mother. "We got a lot of things ironed out at Mom's shop and with the different people working with the rodeo."

They discussed how Detrick looked and the plans for this next week. They'd noticed a weakness on her father's left side, which they talked to the doctor about.

"On the way home from church, Sawyer said he'd like to ride this afternoon." Tate turned to Erin. "Want to go with us, Sis?"

Erin liked the enthusiasm her brother displayed. More like the old Tate. Glancing at Sawyer, she saw him nod at her.

"You're more than welcome to join us, Erin."

Oddly enough, she wanted to go out with them. "A ride this afternoon sounds like a good idea."

"So, you are a championship rider, Sawyer?" Mary accepted her bowl of stew.

"Yes, ma'am. I won my buckles the summer of my freshman year in college. When I first got this job, Erin wanted to make sure I understood the needs of the men and women who compete in rodeo, so she questioned me."

Nodding, Mary said, "I'm sure she did."

Erin refused to look at anyone.

"My daughter has a heart for others and wanted to make sure those needs were addressed."

"Mom, Sawyer doesn't need to hear that."

"I've seen that strength myself," Sawyer answered.

Erin's head jerked up, and she saw him smile.

"And, I know her single-mindedness." He grinned, letting her know he was enjoying himself.

"Odd you should say so. Erin said the same thing about you."

"Mom," Erin protested.

Mary smiled calmly. "He complimented you, Daughter. He should know you hold him in the same regard."

Nothing like having your mother reveal your deepest secrets.

Sawyer's eyes twinkled when they met hers. "I guess that's why we get along so well."

Her heart fluttered. Sawyer was right. They understood each other on a deeper level. She had never felt this way about another man, and she didn't know exactly what to do with the feeling. Across the table, her mother and Aunt Betty grinned like satisfied cats.

Suddenly, Erin wanted to laugh, and, with her heart light, she couldn't wait to get out on the range, with the horse beneath her and Sawyer and Tate by her side.

The three of them rode west of the house. The high desert slowly descended to a small creek that ran through the property. The horses picked their way down the ridges left by previous flash floods.

The wind increased, and the clouds turned a greenish-gray color and looked as if someone had a giant hand mixer, churning them.

Her skin pricking at the sight, Erin said, "We should probably head back."

"Let's get to the river, then we can turn back," Tate replied. "It's not that far."

Sawyer and Erin traded looks. In this part of New Mexico, storms were notorious for rolling in at an amazing speed, and they should turn around and head to the ranch, but for the first time in a long time, Erin saw her brother smile and joke, so she pushed aside her misgivings. At the river, they allowed the horses to rest and drink.

Thunder rolled across the prairie, shaking the ground where they stood. Their horses started to dance with nervousness.

Sawyer stroked his horse's neck. "Your sister's right, and we should start back. Our mounts sense something coming in."

Tate didn't protest. Having ridden all his life, he knew to listen to his horse and the weather around. They mounted up and headed back. Starting up one of the sandy hills, a gust of wind hit Tate, and his mount lost his footing and stumbled backward, rolling over. Tate flew through the air and landed against a large rock. Erin and Sawyer dismounted and ran to him.

Sawyer got there first and gently rolled him over. Tate cried out. Looking at the odd position of his arm, Sawyer realized it was broken. The force of the wind pushed her into Sawyer. He caught her, steadying her. "You okay?"

Erin braced herself against his shoulders. "Yes."

Lightning flashed across the sky, with the roar of thunder immediately following. Tate moaned and opened his eyes.

"Tate, how are you?" she asked.

"My head hurts and my arm."

Sawyer looked around at the darkening horizon, taking in the swirling black clouds. "Normally, I'd say to wait for EMS, but with that storm barreling down on us, we can't."

"Can you get Tate up on his horse?" Erin asked.

"Yes." Sawyer scooped the teen up and put him in his saddle.

"Do you feel you can ride by yourself?" Sawyer asked.

"Yeah."

"You sure?"

The teen nodded, but his lips tightened, going white.

As Erin and Sawyer mounted their horses, another burst of wind hit them, peppering them with sand and debris.

Something slammed into her upper arm, making her shout in pain. When she looked at Sawyer, he'd slumped forward against the neck of his horse. Tate still sat in his saddle, but he didn't look steady.

"Sawyer," Erin called, but the roar of the wind swallowed her cry. Awkwardly dismounting, she went to Sawyer's side. He'd been knocked out cold, and a trickle of blood ran down the side of his face. Thankfully he'd kept his seat, slumping against the horse's neck. Her dad's horse, Duke, didn't rear, instead remaining steady and bearing Sawyer's weight.

She grabbed Duke's reins and wrapped her horse's reins around her jeans' belt loop. "Easy, Duke." She tried to reassure the horse, laying her hand on the horse's neck. "You're an amazing pro." Her right upper arm burned like fire, but she moved to Sawyer's side. A tree branch lay a little beyond where Duke stood. Had that hit Sawyer? The blood that had trickled down his face had stopped. She took off her belt and gathered Sawyer's hands around the horse's neck, anchoring Sawyer's wrists together.

"I'm depending upon you, Duke, to get him back." She took the reins of her brother's horse. "You think you can stay on the horse yourself or do you want me to ride behind you?"

"I don't know, Sis."

"Okay, we'll try me riding behind you."

She tied Duke's reins to the saddle of her brother's horse, then gathered Dancer's reins in the other hand and mounted behind Tate. The pain in her shoulder made the horizon go a little fuzzy, but she drew in a deep breath. "Is this going to work for you?" She saw the doubt and fear in his eyes, but he nodded. "You can grab my arm to steady yourself."

"Okay."

Lord, help, she prayed as she started the group home.

She carefully picked their way up the wash and gained the high ground. Once up on the prairie, the wind buffeted them. Sawyer remained hunched over his horse's neck, and Tate clutched her arm. Erin wanted to gallop, but keeping Sawyer and Tate on their horses was her main priority.

Suddenly the skies opened up and it started raining, drenching them to the skin. Sawyer moaned and started to move. She guided her horse to Duke. Laying her hand on Sawyer's back she called out, "Stay still."

He quit moving.

As the horses walked, she kept checking on Sawyer and Tate.

"I'm not going to make it, Sis."

"Yes, you are. You're part of *the people* and will not let a little rain storm stop you."

The horse stepped in a gully, jerking her and Tate. He yelled and went slack against her. A jolt of pain shot through her shoulder, making her see stars. When Tate started to slump, she wrapped her arm around his waist to steady him. She tried not to jostle his arm but hit it, causing him to moan.

She would make it, she told herself, fighting the pain and blackness crowding her vision. They all would.

It seemed like an eternity before the ranch house came into view. When she rode into the yard with two injured males, her mother and aunt raced out the back door.

"What happened?" her mother shouted.

"The wind managed to take out both Tate and Sawyer." Erin winced as she walked the horses into the barn. Her mother grabbed the reins.

"I think Tate's arm is broken."

Her mother and Betty reached up for him. Erin helped slide her brother off the horse as carefully as they could. She slowly dismounted with her shoulder protesting. Walking to Duke, she untied Sawyer's hands, and the three women tried to maneuver him gently to the ground, but with his weight and momentum, he crashed into Erin, knocking her backward, and then the lights went out.

Erin woke in the emergency room, looking up at the white-tiled ceiling.

"Good, you're awake." A man in a white lab coat and scrubs looked down at her.

"Where am I?"

"You're in the university hospital in Albuquerque. You suffered a dislocated shoulder, and after we popped it back into place, it appears something else happened to your shoulder. You have a nasty cut and deep bruise. Trying to support your brother's weight wasn't a good idea."

Memories of the afternoon came into focus. "I didn't have a choice. I couldn't leave my brother and Sawyer in that wash at the mercy of the storm."

"True, and I heard you're quite a hero."

She didn't feel like one. "Where are they?"

"The men who came in with you are both stable."

"I'd like to see them."

The doctor hesitated.

"The younger man is my brother."

"I know. He's in one of the other emergency bays."

She tried to get up but gasped at the pain. The doctor helped her lie back down. "Let the nurse tend to your arm before you go trotting off."

"Are my mom and aunt here?"

"No, they haven't made it. The helicopter was only able to bring in the three injured patients. Can you tell me what happened, so I know some background on the other two patients?"

She described what had happened on their ride.

He left the bay and Erin wanted to follow him but knew she had to wait for the nurse.

Twenty minutes later, Erin emerged from her cubicle, her arm braced in a sling. She found Tate at the other end of the emergency room bay. He was awake.

"What happened, Sis? All I remember is my horse rearing, then nothing?"

"Your horse rolled over and threw you off. Sawyer and I got you back on your horse, but then Sawyer got knocked out."

Her brother looked at her arm. She started to shrug, but the pain stopped her. "I don't know what hit me, but I got a whopper of a bruise."

"Are you okay?" he asked.

"Nothing's broken." She carefully studied her brother. "And you?"

"My forearm's broken, and I have a couple of cracked ribs. I don't have a concussion, but I do have a massive headache. I think I can go home today, but the doc thinks I should stay the night." Tate waved his arms. "He said something about us being out in the middle of nowhere and if I needed help it was better to be here for twenty-four hours."

"He's right. Besides, Mom would like you and Dad here so she can keep an eye on both of you."

Tate considered her words. "I guess you're right. Have you seen Sawyer?"

"Now that I know you're okay, I'm going to go find him."

Tate started to get up, but she gently touched his shoulder. "Wait for Mom."

Nodding, he lay back down.

At the nurses' station Erin found the doctor who had treated her. "Where's the other man who was brought in with us?"

"Are you his wife?" the doctor asked.

"No."

"Are you related to him in any way?"

"Work colleagues."

"Do you know if he has any family close that we can contact in this emergency?"

Erin's heart raced. What was wrong with Sawyer? "No. I know he has a brother, but I don't know his name or number. Wasn't his cell phone on him when they brought him in?"

The doctor turned to the nurse and asked her to find out if there was a cell phone in Sawyer's belongings.

Erin walked out of the ER and ran into Sylvia.

"What happened?" Sylvia asked, observing Erin's condition.

Erin rubbed her hand over her face. "There was a riding accident this afternoon with my brother, Sawyer and me. My brother's going to be okay, but Sawyer—"

Sylvia paled and stumbled toward the nurses' station inside the ER. "What's wrong with him?" she whispered.

"The doctor won't tell me what's wrong and needs to contact his family. I know he had his cell phone when we started the ride, but it wasn't in the helicopter when they brought him into the emergency room. We're looking for his brother."

The doctor saw Erin. "Did you find a relative?"

Sylvia spoke first. "I'm Sawyer's mother, and you can talk to me. I can give you any permission you need. I know his birth date and know what medications he's allergic to. What is his condition?"

Erin's mouth dropped open. "Surely—"

"It's a long story, Erin, but Sawyer's my son and I can give permission for treatment. I assume he isn't married."

Erin nodded.

After consulting with the doctor and signing the papers, Sylvia came back to Erin and sat down.

Erin studied the woman. "You're nothing like Sawyer described."

A sad smile curved Sylvia's mouth. "That woman's dead."

Chapter Twelve

Sylvia sat beside Erin in the chairs just inside the emergency room doors. "I'm ashamed of what kind of mother I was." She looked down at her hands. "That woman is dead."

Sylvia remained quiet for a long time.

"You don't have to tell me about it," Erin reassured her.

She shook her head. "Has Sawyer mentioned me?"

"Yes. I was complaining about my mother and he tried to reassure me—"

Sylvia's shook her head. "Surely, not your mother. She's been wonderful since your dad was brought in. She's been a rock for all of the other women who've had their husbands on the floor."

"What I've learned is that we all have feet of clay."

"That's hard to believe."

"It's true, as both Mom and I have discovered."

With her hands clasped tightly in her lap, Sylvia began. "The wheels came off our life after my husband died of a heart attack. I was lost. I depended on him for everything. Neither of us had parents. We knew each other from foster care. Two lonely souls were attracted to each other. We weren't in love, but married, just to have someone. Once Dennis died, there was no one except my two teenage sons.

Left alone with the responsibility for them, I panicked, and my boys suffered." She closed her eyes and took a deep breath. "What I would give if I could go back and change what I did. But I can't."

Sylvia explained what happened next with her series of boyfriends. "When you're in a program like AA, you learn to accept responsibility for your actions. It was my fault. I brought those men into our home. I don't blame Caleb or Sawyer. The best thing Caleb did was leave and take his brother with him."

Erin laid her hand over Sylvia's and squeezed. "He's an amazing man. I hate to admit it, but I'm glad he won the contract over me. He recognized things in my brother that never would've occurred to me, but once I knew there was a problem, I could do something about it."

"Where are they?" Mary Morning Star demanded.

"They are here, Sister," Betty said, holding Mary's arm.

"There you are, Daughter." Mary hurried across the room. Looking at Erin's sling, Mary stopped short.

"I've only got a bruised arm and my shoulder was dislocated. They put it back into place. It's sore, but I'll be okay." Erin stood.

Mary looked at Sylvia for a confirmation.

"That's true."

Tenderly, Mary wrapped her arms around her daughter and held her.

Betty stepped forward. "I thought your mom was going to pass out on me, too, when you went down." She explained how they'd waited for the helicopter, loaded in the three patients and then taken off.

"I don't believe your mother ever went the speed limit on our drive here," Betty added.

"How are your brother and Sawyer?" Mary asked.

"Tate's fine. They cast his arm and want to keep him

for the night for observation. But Sawyer hasn't regained consciousness. They want to run some other tests."

"Do we need to contact someone in his family to give permission?"

"No need," Sylvia spoke. "I gave it."

Mary and Betty stared at her. "I thought only relatives could give permission," Mary said.

"That's right. I'm Sawyer's mother."

Betty's jaw dropped and Mary gaped.

"How?" Mary asked.

"There's time for that later, Mom. Why don't you go and find Tate? I believe he wants to see you. Now, he would not admit it, being a boy his age, but he needs you, just like I need you."

Mary grabbed Erin's free hand and held it to her chest, then leaned down and kissed her. "Thank you for bringing your brother home. And how you managed to bring in two men and three horses, I'll never know, but I'm proud of you, Daughter."

After a moment, Mary and Betty headed off. At the door, Betty stopped and held up something in her hand. "Here's Sawyer's phone. We found it on the floor of the barn after the paramedics took the three of you off in the helicopter. I thought you might need it to contact Sawyer's relatives. Of course, you don't need it now, but why don't you keep it for him? You know how I am with this stuff." Betty gave the phone to Erin, then followed Mary.

Erin stared down at the fancy phone.

"He's come a long way since he was a teenager who was always begging for a fight," Sylvia whispered.

"Have you ever thought that he might've been trying to protect his mother?"

Sylvia's face lost all color.

The moment the words popped out of Erin's mouth, she knew she'd made a mistake. "I'm sorry, Sylvia."

"That's okay. You were only telling the truth." Unsteadily she rose to her feet. "I arrived early for my shift, but now I've got to get to work. See you later."

Erin felt as if she'd just crawled out from underneath a rock. She tried to access Sawyer's phone but didn't know the password. She thought and thought, wondering what he would use. What was his horse's name?

Suddenly the phone sprang to life. A name appeared on the screen: Caleb Jensen, Sawyer's brother.

"Hello."

The other end remained quiet.

"Caleb?"

"Yes and who are you?"

The man didn't sound welcoming. "I'm Erin Delong, and I'm glad you called."

"Why is that?" He didn't seem too pleased that she had answered Sawyer's phone.

"There's been an accident. I needed to get a hold of you so you could give the doctors permission to treat Sawyer for his injuries, but apparently, your mother works at this hospital and gave her permission."

"I don't know what joke you're trying to play, but it isn't funny." The tone of Caleb's voice let her know he didn't appreciate any foolishness.

"It's not a joke," Erin reassured him. "Sawyer, my brother and I were caught in a freak storm out on the range behind our ranch house, and we all ended up in Albuquerque at the University Hospital. You might want to come see him, and your mother."

"There's been a lot of miracles in the history of the world, but, lady, I don't appreciate you including my mother in that group. Why don't you give the doctors my number, and I'll talk to them."

"Then give me your number because I'll never get into this phone again."

Caleb told her his number and hung up. The man didn't sound happy, but knowing what she did about the boys' upbringing, Erin couldn't hold it against him. She found the doctor and gave him Caleb's number. The room swirled around her and she stumbled into the doctor.

"If you don't sit down, lady, you're going to end up in a bed next to your brother."

Erin knew he was right and walked to the waiting room at the end of the hall and sat. She laid her head back against the couch and prayed.

It was going to be a long, difficult night.

Finally, after several visits to her brother's and father's rooms, Erin ended up in Sawyer's room. Her mother stayed with her father, and Betty settled in with Tate.

Slowly, Erin walked to the bed. Sawyer still hadn't awakened. "This isn't exactly the way I thought we'd wind up. It was just supposed to be a ride, Sawyer, not some life-changing event." Picking up his hand, she held it to her cheek. "C'mon, Sawyer, wake up. I need to see your eyes. So much has happened that you'd love to know.

"You might've been unconscious, but you did a great job riding in, staying in the saddle. If there was any doubt about you being a cowboy, it's gone. And if you hadn't been there, I never would've gotten my brother onto his horse." She didn't mention the bruise she sported when round two of the wind struck. "You'll have to put that on your résumé—the man can stay on a horse even if he's unconscious."

"That's an impressive thing to put on one's résumé," said an unknown voice.

Erin looked over her shoulder and saw an older version of Sawyer. "You must be Caleb."

He nodded, stepping next to her. He pointedly looked at her clutching Sawyer's hand. "How's he doing?"

She didn't want to let go of Sawyer, but at the steely look from his brother, she released Sawyer's hand, gently placing it on the bed. "The doctors say he's doing fine, but for some reason, he hasn't woken up." Her voice got thick and she struggled.

Caleb studied his brother. "He was always the one to stir things up."

"I know. He told me he was always in trouble."

Caleb's eyes narrowed. "I'm surprised he said anything at all."

"He tried to encourage me when I got all wobbly about my mother."

"Oh?"

The word hung in the air.

"He saw something I didn't and inconveniently pointed it out."

Caleb smiled. "That sounds like my brother. He's got a talent."

"True, but the way he said it lessened the blow." She stared down into Sawyer's sleeping face. She wanted to run her fingers over his cheek but didn't think his brother would appreciate the action. "Was he always like that?" Looking up, she caught Caleb's look of surprise. He quickly masked it.

"He's had his moments."

What did that mean? "I've been impressed with Sawyer's ability to bring the town folks in. And, he's listened to suggestions."

"That's part of his job."

She found herself lovingly studying Sawyer. His beard showed, making it look as if he'd just ridden in from the range, and his brown hair could use a good cut. She pushed a lock back from his forehead, unable to hold back from touching him.

Tears welled in her eyes as she remembered how he'd

reached out to her and Tate without any hesitation. "No, what he's done for my family is more than just making the rodeo redo go smoothly." Looking up, she didn't hide what was in her heart.

Caleb swallowed. "You said something about my mother."

Erin stepped away from the bed. Of course, Caleb would want to know about his mother. "Sylvia's the night nurse on the floor above us where my father is. We met her when Dad was hospitalized for a stroke.

"When the helicopter brought us in earlier today, the doctors wanted a contact number for Sawyer. I told Sylvia, and that's when she revealed she was Sawyer's mom. He saw her yesterday when he came with me to see my dad."

The world clicked in place and she understood Sawyer's silence driving home last night. He'd come face-to-face with his mother. The mother who'd abandoned him, who'd sided with temporary boyfriends over her own sons. He'd been wrestling with the ugliness of his past.

"So, how'd you come by my brother's phone?"

Caleb's clipped tone snapped her out of the memory. "When my mother and aunt drove in from Tucumcari, they brought his phone with them since it had fallen out of his pocket when we pulled him off my dad's horse. That's why I had it when you called. Would you like for me to get your mother? I'm sure she could take a break."

Caleb shook his head. "There'll be enough time to talk to her later."

The tone of his voice said he was done talking about his mother and he didn't want to talk to her, either. But Caleb Jensen didn't know Erin wasn't one to back down. She wanted to stay with Sawyer a little bit longer.

"Do you plan to stay in Albuquerque for long? I think the hospital will allow you to bunk in here, but you probably need to check with the nurses to make sure it's okay."

He folded his arms across his chest and took on a steely look. "I don't plan on leaving my brother, so I guess I'll need to talk to his doctor."

"Check with the nurses' station just outside. They'll have the doctor's name and how to get in contact with him." Erin didn't move.

Caleb nodded and left.

She turned back to Sawyer, picking up his hand, again. "I hope you don't mind I ran your brother off, but he was trying to intimidate me. And he didn't want to talk to your mother, either." She stroked the back of her fingers across his cheek. "You need to wake up. I now know why you were so quiet last night and today before all of this happened, but you don't know this new woman your mom's become. She's nothing like the woman you told me about. Please open those beautiful hazel eyes."

She heard a commotion out in the hall. Rushing from the room, Erin saw Caleb facing Sylvia. From their body language, the confrontation wasn't going well.

"What right do you have to assume any medical decisions for Sawyer? You haven't been in our lives for the last fifteen years, so what makes you think you're allowed to make decisions now?"

Sylvia blanched as if her son hit her.

Erin moved to her side. "This isn't the time or the place for this discussion. Besides, Sylvia was the only one here when the doctors needed permission." She looked from mother to son. "Would you rather have had Sawyer not treated? What if there'd been a brain bleed? Would you have wanted them to waste time trying to contact you and not treat your brother?"

Caleb took a step back as if her words nearly flattened him. "I don't believe you. In emergency situations, doctors act all the time," he shot back.

"True," Sylvia answered, "but I was here. I told the doctors I was his mother, and maybe those extra few minutes made the difference. I don't know."

"Yeah, if that's true, why isn't he waking up?" Caleb snapped.

Sylvia's shoulders hunched, and her eyes filled with moisture. "I don't know," she whispered.

Erin glared daggers at Caleb, slipped her arm around Sylvia's shoulders and led her to the elevators. Nothing was said while they waited, but Erin felt the woman's pain.

Once they were inside the elevator car, Erin said, "He's speaking out of hurt and fear."

"I know, but what he's saying is true." Her stark words only reinforced the somberness of the situation.

When the doors slid open, Sylvia walked off. Erin looked down at her watch and realized that Sylvia still had time on her shift. Erin went to her father's room. Both of her parents were sleeping, and Erin slumped down into the single chair.

She tried to take in what had just happened. She didn't blame Caleb and Sawyer for their feelings about their mother and what had happened, but her sons needed to become acquainted with the woman their mother was now before they made any judgments.

"Oh, Lord, help us to deal with the situations we find ourselves in."

Voices drew Sawyer from his sleep. He recognized one voice, Caleb's, but not the other.

"I'm sorry, Son. There was no excuse. Forgive me."

"That's easy to say now," he said, "but it doesn't change the past."

"I know…"

The conversation slipped beneath the surface of sleep. When Sawyer next woke up, darkness surrounded him except for the night-light by the sink. He remained still for a moment, cataloging the sounds he heard. A cart with a wobbly wheel went by his room; he noted voices in the distance as people walked by. The smell of antiseptic filled his nostrils. He cast his mind back, trying to remember what had happened. Obviously, he was in the hospital, but how had he gotten here? What day was it?

The last thing he remembered was the sand- and windstorm. He'd just put Tate on his horse, mounted his own, then—nothing. When did it happen? Why was he in the hospital? He ran his fingers through his hair and felt the bump. He jerked his hand away from his head. He had quite a lump.

Obviously, they'd gotten Tate help, but there was a whole lot of memory missing.

The door to his room opened. Outlined in the light from the hall was a woman, and from her shape he knew it wasn't Erin. The woman stepped into the room and allowed the door to slowly close.

"You're awake."

His mother.

"How are you feeling?" She stepped closer so he could see her face in the light from the night-light in the room.

"Like I've been kicked by a bull."

"I'll tell the nurse you're awake." She disappeared. Several minutes later, she and the floor nurse walked in.

"Welcome back to the world, Mr. Jensen. I'll call and let the doctor know you're awake. You gave us quite a scare there." Before she left the room, she took Sawyer's vitals, wrote them down and patted his mother on the shoulder. "You must be excited your son's finally awake after two days."

"I am. It's an answer to prayer." Sylvia nodded. Once they were alone, she moved to the side of his bed but remained quiet for a long time.

Sawyer still didn't know what to think. He often wondered if his mom was still alive, but he never imagined her like this.

"I know you have a million questions, but I'd like to tell you what happened if you'd let me. If you don't, I'll walk out of this room and not bother you." She stood by the door waiting for his answer.

He didn't know what to think. Was this reality? Maybe he had had a psychotic break.

The floor nurse came in. "I called the doctor. The resident should be in within a few moments, and the doctor should be by tomorrow morning, first thing."

For the next twenty minutes he was poked and prodded.

When he looked around again, his mother had disappeared. That psychotic-break thing was looking better and better.

When he woke again, the room was still dark, but he saw a figure by the door.

She walked to his bed. Her hand shook as she crossed her arms across her chest and tucked her hands under her arms.

"I thought you'd skipped out on me again." He sounded like an eight-year-old boy.

"I'm still on duty on the floor above. This is my break."

The reason rang true.

"I wanted to try to explain some things to you."

As if that was possible, Sawyer thought, but he said nothing.

"After Caleb won his emancipation and took you away, my boyfriend left, blaming me that we couldn't get more money from you. I was alone. At thirty-five, I didn't know how to take care of myself." She paused, lost in some memory.

"I ran through a series of boyfriends who beat me and used me. My last boyfriend, before I got sober, beat me up badly and left me on the side of the road. I probably would've died if Neil Turner hadn't found me and taken me to the clinic that he runs here in Albuquerque. Neil is also a recovering drug user, and he recognized a woman at the end of her rope. It took me months to recover, but, fortunately, Neil's clinic had places for homeless and abused women like me. The people there encouraged me to go to AA. Neil took me to their meetings. He helped me find a job, an apartment and encouraged me to go back to school.

"Neil also took me back to church. I've been sober nine years, eight months and eleven days."

If he wasn't so angry, he might be impressed. "Did you ever try to find us, Mom?" Sawyer bit out. "Did you ever wonder about us? Ever give a rat's rear if Caleb and I were alive or dead?" He heard the harsh words coming out of his mouth but couldn't control them. They spilled out with a raging hurt he didn't realize was still inside him.

She flinched as if he struck her. "I wasn't sober most of those years, but the times I was, and remembered my sons, I wanted another drink or hit off a joint to drown my guilt."

She looked down at her hands. "I didn't want to remember the terrible things I'd done." Taking another deep breath, she continued. "I remember siding with my boyfriends against my sons. Allowing you to be beaten, and then blaming it on you.

"It's an ache in my heart that doesn't go away. Lately, I've wanted to hire a detective to find you and Caleb, but I hadn't worked up the courage. Forgive me, Sawyer."

In the shadows, he couldn't see her eyes, but he heard the pain in her voice. She waited.

"I don't know, Mom. Caleb and I lived too long supporting ourselves and only depending on each other. It's a lot to think about."

"I can't ask for anything more." She touched his arm. "Thank you. I have to go back to work." With those words she turned and left.

Light spilled into the room, then, as the door drifted closed, the light winked out.

Staring at the ceiling, Sawyer had never imagined how his life would change this day. It should've come with a neon sign warning Danger Ahead. Instead, it came with him oversleeping for church and riding out with an amazing woman.

He'd often wondered if his mother was still alive. Caleb never mentioned her, but Sawyer often thought of her. Even as a teen, something inside him thought that if his mom ever got her life together, she'd be an amazing person. Before their dad had died, they could depend upon her. She'd embraced her family, made a home, but once they buried Dad and were thrown off the ranch, she'd unraveled quickly. From the looks of things now, it seemed she had gotten her life back together.

She'd been going to AA. And caring for Erin's dad. Erin and Mary loved her. That he didn't understand.

Could he turn his back on his mom, ignore her? How could he forgive what she'd done? He remembered all the beatings he got, sticking up for her and then her siding with her boyfriends.

When he told Erin of that last beating he got, the memory seared his soul as if it happened yesterday. Sawyer remembered their mother yelling at Caleb to stop hitting her boyfriend. Caleb shook her off, pulled Sawyer to his feet, and the two boys ran out into the backyard. They'd slipped through the side gate and Caleb dragged Sawyer forward. When Caleb started to run, Sawyer fell. Caleb picked him up, slipped his arm around Sawyer's chest and half walked and carried him to the far side of the field behind their house.

When Sawyer's nose wouldn't stop bleeding, they walked to the clinic the next street over. They didn't dare go to a hospital emergency room because the authorities would want to know where their parents were. The clinic dealt with street kids and wasn't as strict. They treated first, then asked questions. Neither boy wanted to rat their mother out.

They'd taped up Sawyer's nose and made sure nothing else was broken. When it came time to pay, Caleb wrote an IOU and they'd slipped out the back door. Oddly enough, the boys had paid every cent of that clinic bill. It might've taken two years, but they'd paid in full.

After that incident, Caleb and Sawyer spent as little time as they could at the house. That incident had been the last straw for the boys. Caleb knew Sawyer couldn't take another beating like that. Often, they slept over with their friends. The father of one of Caleb's friends was a lawyer and helped Caleb file for his emancipation. Once granted, Sawyer lived with his brother.

Their mother visited them once when her boyfriend beat her up. She wanted money from them. They gave it to her, but the boys left the next week since school ended. That was the last time they'd seen their mother.

Sawyer closed his eyes. He knew his mother didn't remember half the things that had happened. Now that she was clean and sober, she wanted forgiveness. She had no idea of most of what she wanted forgiveness for. Could he do that?

He didn't know.

As he thought about the last few days, he still couldn't take in what Erin had done on Sunday. What had started as an afternoon ride where he'd hoped to talk to Tate had turned into a nightmare. From what he could recall, none of them should've survived that storm, and yet, obviously Erin had brought both him and Tate home.

Amazing.

She awed him. He lo—

His head hurt and he turned his head on the pillow, not wanting to think about it anymore.

Chapter Thirteen

Early the next morning, Caleb walked into Sawyer's room. He moved quietly.

"What are you doing here?" Sawyer asked.

Caleb jerked toward the sound of Sawyer's voice. He took several steps toward the head of the bed. "It's been three days since they brought you in. Folks were worried. Little did I know what a stinking attitude you'd have when you woke. It's a good thing I left my wife at home, because she could've given you a run for your money."

Three days? "Really?"

Caleb stopped. "Yeah."

Sawyer heard a wealth of meaning in that sound. But he noted something else in his voice. He grinned. "Is the morning sickness any better?" he asked.

"No."

"So, how did you know about what happened?" Sawyer asked.

"I called your phone, got Erin and she told me what happened to you. But then she continued on with an amazing story, which I found hard to believe."

Leaning back, Sawyer closed his eyes, as shocked by the story as Caleb. "Believe it. Mom's alive and working in this hospital. She's one of the floor nurses on the next floor up, where Erin's father is."

Caleb sat in the chair next to the bed. "If you'd told me you were attacked by little green men from Mars, I'd find that easier to believe."

"You're not the only one. I thought I was hallucinating when she walked into Detrick's hospital room as the nurse, but I wasn't. It creeped me out. There, standing before me, was a nurse who looked like our mom, sounded like her, but was a totally different creature from the one we ran away from.

"She wanted to apologize for her actions." The words had to sink in again. Sawyer still doubted what was going on. "How can you make right all the stuff that happened to us?"

Caleb studied his boot. "You think she means it?"

"I don't know. I'm living in this weird dream where I don't know anything for sure."

"So, how'd you end up here?" Caleb asked.

"Got clobbered in the head with something, probably a branch, during a windstorm on Sunday. Can't say, since the lights went out."

Caleb smiled. "I know. Apparently, your competition for this job brought you and her brother in through that rainstorm. She got hurt herself."

Sawyer considered his brother's words. "How do you know?"

Caleb sat in the chair. "I have a story to tell you and it's a whopper."

Erin walked into Sawyer's room a little after eight in the morning. She'd spent the night in one of the rooms on the top floor of the hospital reserved for family. Both Tate and she'd been released yesterday, but her father had had a complication. He'd suffered another smaller stroke, and the surgeons were debating if he should be taken into surgery. Sitting in the bed, Sawyer had his breakfast tray in front of him. Caleb sat beside the bed.

"You're awake." Relief washed through her. She'd prayed for Sawyer and her dad through the night. Every time the worst-case scenario popped into her head, she pushed it out. They would be okay. Crossing to the bed, she stopped herself from kissing Sawyer. "When you didn't wake—" She took a deep breath.

"He's been known to be contrary," Caleb offered.

He wasn't the only one, Erin thought. "I can believe that." She followed her words with a smile.

"In the middle of the night, my eyes popped open. It was a relief to see Caleb walking in here this morning. He said he'd talked to you on the phone."

"That's true. Mom and Aunt Betty brought your phone. Before I could figure how to unlock it to notify your brother, he called."

"Yes, Caleb told me." He looked at her sling. "I don't remember you getting hurt."

"There's a lot you don't know about Sunday. But, as I told your brother, you could put on your résumé—can ride while unconscious. I was impressed and grateful."

He nodded toward her arm. "So what happened to you?"

"The wind not only picked up the branch that knocked you out, it hit me in the back with something that made me see stars. A bad bruise to my clavicle, so I guess I can put on my résumé—isn't easily knocked off her horse." He didn't know the sheer terror that had coursed through her that day, and she wouldn't admit it.

The door opened. Mary, Betty and Tate walked in.

"Tate wanted to check on you before he left and went home," Mary explained.

"So how are you, Tate?" Sawyer asked.

"I'm okay. They checked me out and think hitting the

ground the way I did is the cause of why I passed out."
Tate shrugged.

"That's not uncommon. Both Erin and I worried that
your horse had rolled over on you. We couldn't tell."

"How long you going to be here?" Tate asked. "Are they
going to let you go today?"

"I haven't seen the doctor yet, but I feel fine. Ready to
go. And if I get sprung today, Caleb will drive me to your
ranch to pick up my truck."

With a round of final goodbyes, the group left. Mary
looked at Erin. "We'll give you a few seconds."

Erin nodded. She moved to the bed and stood by Sawyer's head.

"I'll be outside if you need anything, Sawyer." Caleb
left the room.

Once alone, she smiled at him. "I don't think your
brother was too thrilled with me. When I talked to him
on the phone, he wasn't impressed."

"He's protective of me."

"I know."

"And you've talked to your mother?"

His face froze and the curtain of his eyes closed. "Yes,
I've talked to her."

"I knew Sylvia as my father's nurse. She helped Mom,
talked to her when we were sick with worry, answered our
questions and arranged for Mom to stay in one of the guest
rooms on the top floor. When my sister, Kai, would drive
over from her apartment, she always had Sylvia update
her on Dad's condition. Kai thinks your mom is super. We
could ask her any question and she'd answer it."

She wrapped her hand around his and squeezed.

Erin continued. "I think what you and your brother
did to survive and do well is amazing, and I admire both
of you for doing it. But you've got a second chance with

your mom. Don't throw it away. The person she is now is amazing."

"You didn't live through our hell."

"True, but I know that you need to give your mom a chance."

"And have you forgiven your father?"

Ah, he took no hostages. "I did. We talked, and I think that God sent you here to do more than work on a rodeo. Maybe you were here to minister to each member of my family. And, maybe you're ready and your mom's ready to heal the wounds of the past."

He pulled his hand out of hers.

"I'm going back with Betty and Tate. Someone needs to be there to take care of the rodeo redo. If we're going to get things finished on time, we need to make some decisions."

"I think I can go home today."

She felt him withdraw from her. "Let's hope so, but I'll go back now, in any case." She wanted to kiss him, but Sawyer had put up a wall and didn't seem to invite the intimacy. "Goodbye."

With each step, she felt him growing more detached, leaving a chasm between them, and the bright light of hope dimmed.

The doctor released Sawyer from the hospital, but only after he made an appointment for a follow-up visit.

"Did you talk to Mom?" Sawyer asked Caleb.

"No."

"You didn't want to talk to her?" If Sawyer had a bad reaction, Caleb's stank.

"No."

"Then, I guess you'd better not tell your wife you ran into her."

Caleb's jaw flexed.

"Your wife might want your kid to have a grandmother."

"She'll have a grandfather."

"A girl? You're going to have a girl?"

Caleb's shoulders relaxed. "Yeah, they did a lot of tests on Brenda since she had so much internal damage from the bomb blast in Iraq. We didn't think we'd be able to have kids and had decided to adopt when we discovered our wonderful news."

That wasn't the only astounding news. Their mother had been thrust into their lives again.

"So, Erin was the one you were competing against."

"What?" Caleb's question brought Sawyer out of his thoughts.

"Erin Delong, the lady I've been dealing with." Caleb glanced at Sawyer and grinned. He turned his gaze back to the road.

"And why are you giving her such a hard time?"

"Whoa. Back it up. I call you and some strange woman answers, then tells me my mother gave permission for you to be treated. It kinda sets your world on fire."

Sawyer understood his brother's reasoning. A lot of things had happened over the past few days. He thought about the courage and grit Erin had shown with her back to the wall. Not many people could've pulled that off. "I'm still in awe of what she did. That was not an easy ride with me and her brother. She's got guts." His mind went to how she'd originally dealt with him and then worked with him on setting up things for the bids on the rodeo.

And she took advice.

"That's quite a smile. What are you thinking about?"

Sawyer turned toward his brother, since his neck was still a little stiff. "Erin and what happened on Sunday."

"What were you doing out in the middle of a storm?" Caleb frowned. "I thought you had more sense than that?"

"C'mon, Caleb, you ever get caught off guard?"

Caleb's cheek flexed.

"The afternoon started out perfect. No sign of a cloud or any forecast of one. I'd promised Tate a ride, and the poor kid needed some time with another guy."

"So how'd the girl get involved?"

"Erin's smart and listened as her brother and I talked. When Tate ditched school one afternoon, she listened to my advice before confronting him."

Caleb threw him a grin. "I'm impressed. She wasn't the troll you first thought she'd be."

Sawyer realized that he hadn't thought of Erin in those terms in a long time. "Well, I had just finished a couple of projects that had been real headaches. I was prepared for the worst."

Caleb didn't follow up with another question, and that wasn't like him.

"What's set you off?"

His brother didn't answer, but looked back out on I-40. They were halfway between Albuquerque and Tucumcari. They had another hour or hour and half left before they got to the Delong ranch.

Sighing, Caleb shook his head. "I didn't tell Brenda about Mom being with you. I didn't want to argue with her about the situation, but somehow or some way she'll find out. It's scary how she does that, but she'll discover it. I'm wondering when to tell her."

"The sooner the better," Sawyer added.

"Hey, buddy, you're in the same spot as me. I didn't see you embrace Mom and tell her all's well." The harshness of Caleb's voice took Sawyer aback.

"I'd just come back to my senses. You were awake the entire time." Sawyer stared at his brother. "Wait, how did you know Mom slipped into my room?"

"I got to the hospital long before you regained consciousness. I'd walked out of your room that night to get some coffee, when I saw Mom slip into your room. I stood outside the door and listened as she talked to you. When she came out and saw me, she opened her mouth, but I shook my head. I heard your response to her explanation."

A vague memory of Caleb arguing with someone floated through his brain. "So what if I snarled? You haven't done so hot yourself."

This was the first time Sawyer could remember them arguing. They'd been a team for as long as he could remember. That's how they survived. Now…

"We might call Pastor Garvey in Plainview and talk to him. And you could tell him about your becoming a father."

Caleb's hands opened out from the steering wheel and then regripped it. "We sound like we're fourteen and sixteen again."

"That's probably because we feel that way."

Sawyer shook his head. "Who would've thought?" But that's what they were going to do, talk to their pastor. Too bad he couldn't talk to his brother as easily as he talked to Erin when they'd gone to Las Vegas and Albuquerque. Of course, she'd turned his words back on him, so maybe he didn't need to talk to her. But if he couldn't get past this obstacle, would he lose Erin?

When Sawyer and Caleb pulled into the ranch driveway, the Delongs had just sat down for dinner. Tate jumped up and urged the men to join them. Sawyer had no more success refusing Mary's invitation than he had last week.

No one said anything about Sylvia, but she could've been at the table.

"So you're going back to school tomorrow, Tate?" Sawyer asked.

"I am and will have lots of makeup work to do."

"I don't doubt you will catch up," Sawyer reassured him.

"Sawyer tells me that you were a pickup rider in the rodeo," Tate said.

Caleb nodded. "I was, but I like staying in one place for more than a week."

"You don't miss the traveling?" Tate asked.

Erin tensed. What was going on with her brother? He kept saying he hated rodeo, but now suddenly he was asking questions about the professional circuit.

"No, I don't miss it. I'll say rodeo helped Sawyer and I support ourselves, but if we'd been given a choice, we probably wouldn't have gone that route."

Erin knew every word Caleb spoke was the truth, but you had to love your sport to put up with the traveling and never settling down.

After the meal, Erin moved to Caleb's side. "Thanks for answering Tate's questions. I put myself through graduate school like Sawyer with my barrel-racing winnings, but hearing it from a male's perspective made the statements valid."

"Not a problem. Rodeo saved both Sawyer and me."

"I know."

Caleb glanced at his brother, who was talking to Mary and Tate. "He told you?"

"He did. He wanted to show me that my mother's actions were mild and could be worked out, as compared to the problems you two had with your mom."

Caleb studied his brother.

"He was right, but he needs to follow his own advice."

Sawyer's words hit home, and Caleb snapped upright.

"I guess he's not the only one," she added.

Fire ignited in Caleb's eyes. "You don't know what you're talking about."

"Maybe, but I haven't read an exception in the Bible that Caleb and Sawyer Jensen get a waiver when it comes to forgiveness."

Caleb opened his mouth, then clamped it shut. "Sawyer, I'm leaving."

Immediately he joined his brother. "You're not going to drive home to Peaster tonight, are you? That's more than a seven-hour drive."

"I'd planned on it. I've done harder drives with no problems."

Sawyer stepped closer to his brother and whispered something. Caleb gave a single nod, then walked outside.

"Thanks for the meal, ladies." Sawyer followed his words with a smile. "I'll see you tomorrow."

Turning to Erin, he nodded to her and started outside.

"Sawyer," Erin called.

He stopped and turned. The closed expression on his face didn't encourage talk.

Her heart ached. "Remember what we talked about Saturday afternoon. You were right on target."

"If my mom would've been as good as your mom, it wouldn't be a problem."

"So your advice only works if the problem's someone else's?"

The muscles in his jaw flexed, and his gaze narrowed. She could see all sorts of emotions racing through his eyes. Finally, he turned and walked out of the house without giving her the courtesy of a response.

She wanted to rush after him and scream and stomp her foot. He willingly gave advice but, apparently, couldn't take it. She didn't know how their relationship would work if he could only give advice and not follow it.

But, inside, she knew that wasn't true. He'd listened before, but why not now?

Sawyer grabbed his cell phone and dialed Pastor Garvey's number, putting it in speaker mode. Caleb sat in the chair beside the table in his motel room and glared at him.

Pastor picked up on the first ring. Sawyer quickly identified himself. After a couple of minutes of polite talk, the pastor said, "It's good to hear from you, Sawyer, but I think there's another reason for your call."

"You were always good about reading me."

"I'm glad to hear from the Jensen brothers, but you don't often call to talk."

Sawyer looked into his brother's eyes. "We ran into our mother the other day."

The other end of the line remained quiet.

"I was hurt and taken to a hospital in Albuquerque," Sawyer explained. "Mom works there as a floor nurse. She's clean and sober and claims to be a Christian."

"That's good news. I know y'all never thought to see her again."

"She's in AA and church, Pastor."

"But she asked for our forgiveness," Caleb blurted out.

Sawyer, who sat on the corner of the bed, stared at his brother, surprised he'd revealed that.

"And you're not willing to do that?" Pastor Garvey replied.

"No." Caleb's hands fisted.

During the entire time Caleb had been Sawyer's guardian, he'd never mentioned their mother, which was why his brother's reaction now flabbergasted Sawyer.

"She's only asking for forgiveness, Caleb. Not absolution. There's a difference."

Caleb lurched to his feet and walked out of the room, slamming the door behind him.

"I guess my explanation didn't go over too well," Pastor Garvey said.

"His reaction has surprised me, but I'm having a hard time with it, too. How can we just forget how she wronged us?"

"Grace, Sawyer. Let God work in your heart and quit

worrying how you can forgive her. Just do it. It's a decision, not a feeling. Choose to do it."

"Thanks, Pastor." Sawyer looked down at his phone. Was it that easy?

No, doing what Pastor said wouldn't be easy. Of course, he'd advised Erin to do that very same thing with her parents. Had she done it? He didn't know, but their offenses didn't come anywhere close to his mother's.

But was there a measure of grace, a point where you stop forgiving? Jesus said to forgive seventy times seven.

Forgiveness?

He struggled with that question all night.

Chapter Fourteen

Sawyer and Caleb walked to Lulu's for breakfast. Sawyer had managed to convince his brother to spend the night by pointing out that Caleb now had a wife and child depending on him, and Caleb needed not to take risks, such as leaving Tucumcari at ten thirty at night. That did the trick.

"Lulu will feed you any meal you need," Sawyer told his brother.

Entering the restaurant, several people called out a welcome to Sawyer. He introduced his brother with pride to the residents, talked about his adventure in Albuquerque and the helicopter ride.

"I hear it was our Erin who hauled you all in," Bob Rivera said. He introduced the men with him, salesmen who made their monthly trip out to this part of New Mexico.

"It was her, indeed."

"That's not unusual for our Erin," Bob explained to the men at the table. "I remember one time when my daughter drove to Las Vegas. She blew two tires and ended up in a ditch. The cell reception in that area of the state is spotty, at best, and my daughter couldn't dial for help. Erin drove by, took her into Vegas, and then drove her back to her car to make sure the tow truck got it right. Erin picks up any challenge thrown at her."

It took several more minutes before they got up to the order counter. After ordering, they grabbed empty cups and walked to the coffee urn in the corner of the room. With Lulu's daughter away on a school trip, it was every man for himself, but Lulu's cooking made it worth it.

They settled at a table in the corner. Caleb looked around. "Looks like you found a home, with all the greetings called out to you."

Sawyer sat up straighter and thought about it. He'd felt at ease ever since he drove into this town. "Could be. Was it like that when you first went to the Kaye place?"

Caleb played with the handle of his coffee mug. "It was, and with each visit, I settled in more and more. I allowed myself to let down my guard. After the accident, the Kaye ranch became my refuge."

When one of the cowboys Caleb helped as a pickup rider in the ring got hurt, Caleb nearly folded with guilt and retreated to his friend's ranch. Sawyer had worried his brother wouldn't recover from the incident.

"The minute Brenda showed up, well, I knew she would have a major effect on my life."

Sawyer laughed. "Having met your wife, I knew she'd have an effect, too."

Caleb took a sip of his coffee. "So have you run across *your* Brenda?"

"Sawyer, your breakfast's up," Lulu called out.

They retrieved their meals and began to eat.

"Are you going to answer my question? I remember you pressing me hard about my wife."

Sawyer recalled the night they'd spent in the small living compartment of Caleb's horse trailer, talking. "Well, I've never met someone like Erin. I thought she would be a headache for me while I worked on this project, but she's helped.

"It was her idea to post the jobs for the locals, and in

the future, as I do other projects, I'll work it the same way as this one."

"The website is a great idea," Caleb said.

"Well, that came from another local, but without Erin pushing, it wouldn't have happened." He leaned in. "It's a weird experience to argue with her, because she argues back and meets my arguments with her own. She thinks and can be reasoned with, and I can change her mind." He shook his head.

Caleb grinned. "Did it throw you off your stride? Make you wonder what was happening?"

"It did. She's a strong woman, so unlike—" He clamped down on the word, not wanting to mention their mother. They purposely hadn't discussed their mother after they'd talked to Pastor Garvey, but they needed to. She was the elephant in the room.

Sawyer sat back and took a sip of coffee, determined to clear the air. "You know we're both going to have to deal with it."

Caleb stared down at the table. "I hear ya."

"And what? Did you talk to Mom?"

"No."

"Why not?" Sawyer pressed. He felt like a hypocrite, unable to do it himself, but things needed to be said.

"Why am I suddenly the bad guy here? How crazy is that?" Caleb demanded.

"Since you're going to be a daddy, you need to deal with some of the garbage we went through. Garbage left in our lives and stuff you don't want to pass on to that new baby."

"I'm not the only one. Have you forgiven Mom?" Caleb didn't pull any punches.

"No, but I need to."

Rubbing the back of his neck, Caleb sighed. "I need the time and space, Sawyer, to think it through."

"I hear you."

It wasn't until they stood outside by Caleb's truck that Sawyer brought up their mother, again. "I think if you talk to your wife about Mom, she might help."

"That's a frightening idea."

They patted each other on the back, then Caleb hopped in his truck and drove off.

It would be a struggle for the brothers to forgive, but Sawyer knew he had to. Was it as simple as Pastor Garvey said last night? Just do it? Surely not.

But when had Pastor Garvey ever steered him wrong?

Fifteen minutes later, Sawyer walked into the rodeo office. He arrived first, started coffee and sat in the boardroom with the contracts. Working his way through them, a hundred different thoughts bombarded him. He needed to get things going to meet his deadline.

The front door opened, and Lisa called out and joined him in the conference room. "I'm so glad to see you. When I heard about your accident, well, it shook me to my core. You, Tate and Erin. All three of you, and when the helicopter flew in—" She shook her head. "Folks met at church and prayed together. Then when you didn't wake up immediately, panic raced through this town. Bob kept us updated. The man hasn't ever seen so much business."

That sense of home embraced Sawyer again.

"Your prayers mean a lot to me. Thanks."

"That's what neighbors and friends do, hold up each other in prayer in times of crisis." She walked back to her desk.

Moments later, he heard the front door open again and Lisa squealed. "Oh, Erin." He heard talking and crying. Curious, he stood and investigated. Erin and Lisa stood by her desk hugging.

His eyes drank in the sight of Erin. What an amazing woman. He'd been a jerk at the hospital, he admitted to himself, cutting himself off from her, but after what had happened, he still didn't have his bearings and couldn't risk—what? His heart? His pride? And he'd just admitted he wanted to talk to her.

Finally, Erin noticed him and stepped back from Lisa. He noticed a tenseness in her body that he hadn't seen since she'd walked into the conference room that first day. She still had on her sling. "I'm a little late for work today, but it's not due to having to drive Tate to school. Mom's taking over that chore. He claims his broken arm won't interfere with his driving, but Mom wouldn't hear of it."

"I'm sure that was an interesting conversation." Amusement laced Sawyer's words.

She rolled her eyes. "You don't want to know."

"That's a teenager." For a moment, they shared memories of dealing with Tate. "Our detour to the hospital has created a backlog. So I welcome your help."

"Good, because I'm here to work."

"Then let's get to it."

Over the next two weeks, the contractors started work at the rodeo grounds. In that time, Sawyer saw Erin watching him, but she never brought up the accident, how she'd rescued him and Tate. She didn't trade on what she did, but when he thought about what had happened, Erin's actions overwhelmed him. She'd risked her life to save Tate and him.

And with his mother's reappearance in his life, Erin said nothing about his attitude toward Sylvia, but, like a thorn in his side, his reaction to his mother sat between them. He wanted to talk to her about his mother, then he didn't want to talk. He didn't know what was wrong with him, except there was a tugging at his heart.

Finally, one Friday afternoon, after they'd inspected the concrete work done on the rodeo grounds by the company from Albuquerque, they started back to Sawyer's truck. He'd planned to talk to Erin about his mother, because the more they danced around the issue, the more the distance grew between them.

Mel zipped into the parking lot and stopped his truck next to Sawyer's. "I need to talk to you two," he said, slamming the truck door.

Sawyer stiffened, waiting for the complaint to be thrown out. He noticed Erin also braced herself.

Mel rubbed his neck, sighed and took a deep breath. Finally, he pulled a check out of his shirt pocket and handed it to Sawyer. When he unfolded the check, it was for more than the amount of the discrepancy Sawyer had discovered on the books for the concrete bill.

Sawyer glanced at Erin, then Mel. "What's this for?"

"I know you've been comparing final costs for the rodeo and talked to the folks at the concrete company, so I don't doubt you've found the discrepancy." He took a steadying breath and continued. "I ran into problems that year. My wife had health issues, and I took the money."

"That's more than the difference, Mel," Erin said.

He shrugged. "Interest."

"Why are you doing this?" Sawyer asked.

"Because I couldn't live with it anymore. I wanted a clean slate. Besides, you two have made a difference in Traci's life. Putting her in charge of the website for the rodeo has changed her. I see the little girl I loved after she's been lost for a long time." Mel turned to Erin. "You could've made it difficult for her. I know she wasn't nice to you and caused all sorts of problems, but you gave her a fair shot and it's made the difference. And, I know Traci was worried about Andy, but her worries proved to be unfounded."

He grinned. "I figure I might as well straighten out my life, too." Mel smiled. "It sure feels good."

Sawyer heard all sorts of lessons in Mel's words.

"If you feel a need to report me to authorities, I'm prepared to own up to my mistakes."

Sawyer had been quietly talking to the members about what he'd found. They'd debated it privately, not wanting to get the authorities involved, worried it would take away from the rodeo relaunch.

"It's not my call, Mel. I've discussed this with the board, but I think the repayment of the money might satisfy them. I don't know if they'll want you to resign your position," Sawyer said.

Mel's face didn't cloud up. "I understand, Sawyer. I'll work with the board however they want to do it." He looked around at the new concrete work done that morning. "Looks like the company did a first-rate job. I'm thinking the day this place reopens will be something to be proud of." He turned and walked back to his car, whistling.

Erin and Sawyer stood there staring.

"I've never seen Mel like that. It's an amazing thing." She smiled at him. "It seems God has a lot of things in store for us all, and we'll need to keep our hearts open to receive those blessings."

Sawyer flinched at her words. He watched her walk to his truck. The woman didn't play fair.

After dinner that Friday night, the hospital called, telling Mary that her husband had been okayed for release. During the call, the doctor talked to her about the aftercare and the therapy that her husband needed. Since there wasn't a facility in Tucumcari that could handle Detrick's needs, he'd either have to hire a therapist who would come to the house several times a week or rent a room in Albuquerque where they could stay and finish the rehab.

When Mary hung up, she explained the situation to Erin and Betty. Tate had been allowed to spend the night at the high school, helping with the senior play. His teacher would bring him home.

Betty spoke. "Stay with me and Nelson in Bluewater until Detrick finishes his therapy. We're only forty minutes away."

"That's a possibility." After several minutes discussing different plans, Betty left and went to her room.

"What do you think, Daughter?" Mary placed her napkin on the table.

"It would be easier on you and Dad to stay in Albuquerque. If you stayed with Auntie in Bluewater, I think the drive would be too much. But if you choose to do that, Tate will need somebody here. I'm willing to stay with him, but I think you should involve him in the decision." At least she thought that would be the approach Sawyer would suggest.

Sawyer. Erin would love to discuss this with him, but he wasn't talking. He'd removed himself emotionally from her, leaving her heart bleeding. She'd finally fallen in love with what she thought was the perfect man, but he'd seemed to disappear in an instant. She understood the scars on his heart but prayed God would give him the strength to see those scars and not let them have power over him anymore. When Erin looked up, she met her mother's knowing gaze.

"What's wrong?"

Erin didn't know how to put it into words. "Nothing."

"Then why are you frowning?"

"Things are going well with the rodeo. And all the support we get is encouraging." Erin told her mother what had happened with Mel that day.

"I know, I noticed a heaviness in Mel."

Her mother saw with her heart as much as with her eyes. "Daughter, I hear your words, and I see your heart. What is wrong?"

Was she ready to open up? Who better? "Sawyer."

"That's the name of the trouble. What has he done?"

"You knew that Sylvia was Sawyer's mother."

"No, I had not heard that."

Erin explained what had occurred. "Both Sawyer and his brother want nothing to do with her. There is no forgiveness in either of them. Caleb seems more set against his mother than Sawyer, but I think Sawyer received most of the beatings. It's as if I'm dealing with another man when the subject of his mom comes up.

"I haven't said anything to him about it, but it's there sitting between us much like a huge rock—cold and solid. He was the one who encouraged me to talk to both you and Dad and straighten things out, but he seems unwilling to follow his own advice."

"He's not the first man to say one thing and do another."

Truer words were never spoken. "I fear if he doesn't settle this with his mother, it will poison his life. I don't want that to happen to him."

Mary leaned back in her chair and beamed. "So your heart has succumbed."

She did a double take. "What?"

"Your heart beats for Sawyer." Mother had *that* smile on her face that made Erin crazy. When her mom had that particular look, it said she knew the truth even if the other person didn't.

"Of course I have a heart for him. He's hurting."

"Not that way. Your heart beats with his."

Erin opened her mouth to protest.

"I'm sorry, Daughter, but too often I've seen you walk away from a man who wanted to court you, and you'd have none of it. I've seen you freeze out a man who would try to get to know you. Now that your heart is on the line, you will need to learn patience, and grace."

Erin shook her head, wanting to dislodge the cotton

in her ears. Surely she heard wrong. "What are you talking about?"

"Sawyer. He's touched your heart in a way no other man has."

Mary stood and placed a kiss on her daughter's forehead. "When the time is right, you'll understand. But don't fight it too long, or the opportunity will pass by."

"What are you talking about?" Erin still couldn't comprehend her mother's words. Or was it that she refused to understand?

"Trust your heart." With those final words, her mother left the room.

Erin stared at the doorway. She hated when her mom went all Native on her, giving her pieces of wisdom that she had to figure out. She wanted some concrete answers. And wanted them now.

Okay, Lord, I have no idea what Mom is talking about. Show me.

The next morning, after breakfast had been cleared, Mary called a family meeting. "I have decided to bring your father home. I will hire someone to come and give him therapy as often as he needs it. I know Betty misses her husband and needs to go home, today."

"But, Sister, I'm okay."

"Nelson misses you. It is time for you to go home. Besides, I don't want my son to be alone again, so his parents will be here." She turned to Tate. "I think if your father sees you, he'll know he has someone to work for. And he can be your support. I know he worries that you will drown in all this woman talk."

Erin hid her smile, not believing how her mother stated the problem. Mary wanted to get Tate involved with their father's recovery. "And he can see the progress on the rodeo grounds," Erin added.

"That would give him a goal," Betty said.

"What do you think, Son?" Mary asked.

Tate looked at Erin, then rubbed his hands over his jeans. "I think your plan, Mom, is a good one, but where are you going to find someone to come and help Dad with his therapy?"

"Before we leave the hospital today, I'll ask for a name."

"Sounds good," Tate replied.

"So, we're all agreed on the plan?" Mary asked. "Betty goes home and we go and get your father."

"Mom, why don't I stay here to get things ready? Besides, if you take Tate, he's stronger to help with Dad than me."

Tate's shoulders straightened, and he seemed to accept the responsibility. "I can do that."

"Then let's get going."

Erin went into town to see if Bob had any sort of shower chair for her father. He didn't but promised he'd order one.

Her next stop was at the rodeo office. The door stood locked. Where was Sawyer? She missed talking to him, discussing the rodeo; she missed being with him, missed his energy and the challenge he threw her way. There'd been a wall between them as they'd worked on the rodeo the past two weeks. He'd been polite, laughed with others, but she felt the barrier he'd thrown up, cutting himself off from her. She didn't know if others felt it, but seeing him every day and having him beyond her reach broke her heart.

Had his mother's reappearance thrown him that much off his stride that he couldn't recover? Was the hurt inflicted in his youth going to be the thing that defined his life? If that was the case, she needed to discover that now before more of her heart belonged to him.

Pausing by her truck door, she took a deep breath and finally admitted she loved him. Her knees buckled.

She didn't welcome the truth. If Sawyer couldn't find it in his heart to forgive his mother, how would he react to her if she made a mistake? Or a child of his own who made mistakes?

He had reasons for his feelings, the logical side of her brain argued, but her heart didn't buy it.

After a quick stop by Lulu's for a sandwich, she drove back home.

Not wanting to think about her confused feelings, she called Wind Dancer in from the field where all the horses were grazing. "Let's do barrels." That's all it took for her horse to come to her side. Erin quickly saddled Dancer, rode to the corral set up for barrel racing and started the workout. Maybe she could outrace any questions she had.

She lost track of time and used the workout to avoid facing the situation. She paused after the last run and realized Wind Dancer's sides heaved, but her horse would go again if asked. Erin knew it was time to stop. She patted the horse's neck. "Sorry, girl. I didn't mean to run you like that."

"It looked like you were running from something," Sawyer called out.

Her heart jumped at the sight of him. "I guess I'm not the only one."

He jerked as if she'd punched him in the chin. "I deserve that."

That wasn't the way to start a conversation with him.

Erin walked Wind Dancer around the corral, letting her cool down and catch her breath.

She didn't know what to say to him.

"Where is everyone?" He scanned the area.

"They went to Albuquerque to get Dad. The hospital

called last night, telling us that Dad can be released. Aunt Betty went home."

"Why didn't you go with them?"

"The house needed to be readied for Dad, so I drove into town to get a couple of things, which will have to be ordered." She opened the corral gate and led the horse forward.

"I thought your mom and dad might stay close to the hospital for medical reasons."

"The family decided last night to bring him home and have a therapist come to the house. We thought Dad might recover quicker here. Also, Tate wouldn't be without his father again."

"Good idea."

She waited for him to say more, but he just stood there looking at her. "Why are you here? Did I forget to do something?" She guided Wind Dancer into the barn, stopped and grabbed the cinch under the horse and unbuckled it. When she started to pull the saddle off, Sawyer stepped in front of her and lifted it from the back of the horse. He put the saddle on the saddle stand outside the stalls.

"You didn't—"

He leaned forward and stopped her words with a kiss.

Erin didn't object. She wanted to throw her arms around the man, but Wind Dancer was at the end of the reins.

When he drew back, he rested his forehead against hers. "I've missed you."

Wind Dancer shook her head, setting the reins moving. Sawyer raised his head.

"I need to tend to her."

He gave her room and allowed Erin to unbuckle the horse's reins and turn her out in the corral.

Her heart pounded as she faced him. Her gaze caressed his face. The lines etched in his forehead and around his eyes spoke of his restless nights. Welcome to the club. She hadn't had a good night's sleep in several days, wondering about him, praying for him.

"I went by the office today, but found it locked," she told him.

"I'd gone out to talk to the artist hired to create the mural on the wall between the restrooms," Sawyer answered.

The artist proposed creating a mural of a scene involving several horses thundering across the desert. The drawing he submitted could be framed and used as a piece of art. She walked to the corral fence and watched Dancer.

He stood beside her. "It's peaceful out here. I can see why your grandfather settled in this place."

She knew instantly what he meant. She felt a special connection to the land and the ruggedness of this place. He'd understood, too.

"I've missed you," he said as he moved behind her and wrapped his arms around her waist.

His warmth and strength surrounded her, letting her know she could rest on him. "I've missed you, too, but you put up a wall I knew I couldn't scale."

His arms fell away, and he stepped back. "I just needed some time to sort things out. With Mom suddenly appearing in my life, there's lots of old baggage I'm tripping over."

She couldn't fault him for that. "And have you come to any decision? Know what to do with those old bags?"

"No. I talked with the pastor who helped Caleb and me when we were teens. You remember me talking about Pastor Garvey?"

"I do, and what did he say?"

Sawyer ran his hands through his hair, then over his face. "He said just forgive her. I didn't have to feel warm and fuzzy or have a blazing revelation, rather that it was a choice on my part." He shook his head. "I thought he was teasing us. He wasn't."

"And you find that hard to do?"

"It makes no sense. Surely there's more to it. It can't be that simple."

"What your pastor said isn't simple. It's the hardest thing you do, but you choose to do it."

"So says the only logical female I've ever run across."

"So says my pastor and yours."

He stepped closer. "And have you done that? Have you practiced what you preached?"

She heard the challenge in his question and the tone of his voice. "Yes. I had this smart cowboy tell me that my mother was unconsciously using me. I talked to her and worked things out. You should try it. I also talked to my dad, too. I forgave him for voting for you instead of me, because I believe Dad had a plan.

"It wasn't easy, nor did I feel like forgiving, but I did it."

Whirling, she marched into the barn. There were stalls that needed to be mucked out, and she couldn't think of a better time than now to deal with that mess.

Chapter Fifteen

Sawyer stood there watching Erin march into the barn with a full head of steam. She'd certainly turned his wisdom back on him. Nothing like getting smacked with one's own words.

He could stand out here and think, or he could help Erin with her chores. She might kick him out.

No, she wouldn't do that. No matter how mad or put out you were with someone, if they wanted to help muck out the stalls, you'd let them.

He grabbed a pitchfork and a broom and headed down the rows of stalls.

She didn't look up when he stepped into Duke's stall, which was next to the one she worked in, but she didn't object. That was a positive indication. They worked quietly for the next hour, cleaning and putting out fresh hay.

As he worked, he thought and prayed. Pastor Garvey and Erin had told him the same thing, and he trusted both of them. Pastor Garvey had taught him a lot of things, and never had he led him astray. He'd backed up his words with scriptures. It was easy to forgive someone if they'd just lied or cheated you out of some money, but what his mother did fell in a different league. But, he'd never read any qualifiers in the Bible. In other words, there were no limits on forgiveness.

They had just finished putting clean hay in the stalls when they heard engines. Vehicles pulled into the driveway.

Erin walked outside. He followed.

Two cars pulled into the parking area. The family sedan parked next to Erin's truck. Inside were Tate, Mary and her father. A second sedan parked beside his truck. Inside sat Sawyer's mother.

The kick to his gut wasn't as dramatic as it had been the first time she'd entered Detrick's room. This time he felt a peace.

Erin walked to her family's car and opened her dad's door, squatting in front of him. "Welcome home, Dad."

He grasped his daughter's hand. Silently he mouthed, *Home.*

Tate appeared by Erin's side. "Let me help, Dad."

Erin stood and stepped back. Tate grasped his father under the arm. Sawyer moved closer and took Detrick's other arm. Together all three of them walked into the house.

As Sawyer looked over his shoulder, he saw his mother embracing Erin.

Could he do it?

Over the weeks that he had shut Erin out, he knew he'd fallen in love. Could he fix the problem with his mother, and would it open up the way for him to tell Erin what was in his heart?

Mary opened the trunk, and Erin saw different pieces of equipment inside.

Sylvia stopped by Erin, reaching into the truck. "Let me help with unloading the equipment you'll need."

Erin hugged Sylvia. "I'm glad you're here. Are you going to be the one doing physical therapy with Dad?"

"No, I'm not going to do it, but your mom wanted me to come out here on my day off and show her how to set things up until the therapist gets here on Monday."

Erin wondered at her mom's plan. For the next hour, things were carried into the house and arranged to help Detrick and Mary deal with her father's hopefully temporary limitations.

After completing the setup, Mary invited Sylvia to stay the night. "It's too late for you to drive back," Mary argued. "I would feel better if you stayed."

"I hadn't planned on it. I have nothing with me."

"If you need anything, you can borrow it from me," Mary countered.

"Please stay," Erin added, understanding her mother's motives.

Sawyer hadn't left. Erin looked at him. His expression remained neutral.

"Thank you, I will," Sylvia replied.

"Good." Mary turned to Sawyer. "I'd like for you to share dinner with us, too. Both you and Sylvia have become very important to the Delong family, and we want to celebrate with you."

Sawyer remained quiet for a long time. Finally, he said, "Thank you, Mary, but I need to get back into town. I have some business to take care of."

Sylvia's disappointment showed in her face. No one said anything when Sawyer walked out of the house.

Erin started after him, but her mother caught her arm.

"Let him prove himself, Daughter. If his heart kicks in, then you know you can depend on him. If it doesn't, then you'll know to let him go."

Her mother's request made sense, but letting Sawyer walk away was the hardest thing Erin had ever done in her life.

* * *

Sawyer lay on his bed in his motel room and stared at the ceiling, wrestling with his decision to forgive. Was it worth it?

His entire future rested on *this* decision, because he knew if he chose to hold on to his resentment, he'd lose Erin.

Before he came to this city, there had been a calmness inside him, but now there was no peace. He knew both peace and love were within his grasp.

"Okay, Lord, You win. I forgive Mom."

He expected a huge weight would be lifted off his shoulders, but nothing happened. No lightning. No earthquake. He sat there a moment in the quiet. He'd done what he needed to do, so where was that marvelous moment of peace? It hadn't shown up. Now what?

He needed to tell his mom his decision. Glancing at the clock, he saw it was only ten fifteen. They would still be up, and he wanted to see his mother tonight.

With the radio off, the drive to the Delong ranch passed in silence, but the silence wrapped him in harmony.

He pulled by his mother's car and turned off the engine. Before he got to the back screen door, Erin appeared.

"Hi."

That soft welcome sound settled in his heart. He smiled at her, and she opened the door. Everyone at the table looked at him. "Excuse me for interrupting, but could I talk to Sylvia for a moment in private?"

Sylvia's eyes glistened.

"Why don't you go in the library?" Mary said. "Do you know where it is, Sawyer?"

He nodded and escorted his mother to the room. He looked straight into his mother's eyes and saw hope, fear and longing. "You asked me the other night if I could forgive you." He cleared his throat. "I've wrestled with the decision. How could I do it, let go of all the stuff in our past? But the pastor who taught both Caleb and me said it was a conscious action and not feeling.

"I forgive you, Mom, and want to put the past behind us and start over."

Tears ran down Sylvia's cheeks. "That's all I'm asking."

"You may not like me or who I've turned out to be, but I think we should get to know each other," Sawyer added. She started sobbing, and Sawyer didn't know what to do. He looked around and saw Mary and Erin standing at the door.

Mary motioned for him to hug his mother. He stepped forward and awkwardly wrapped his arms around Sylvia. She fell into his arms. He felt the sobs that racked her body and panicked. "Mom, did I do something wrong?"

She looked up and shook her head. "No. You did everything right."

That didn't make any sense. Why cry?

Erin slipped into the room and a placed a hand on his back. "You're doing good. Your mom is just overwhelmed with gratitude."

Sylvia stepped back and smiled at him. "You've given me a precious gift, Sawyer. Thank you."

Mary placed her arm around Sylvia's shoulders and walked her into the kitchen.

Erin stayed in the room with him. "That was a wonderful thing you just did for your mom."

He rubbed the back of his neck. "I've thought about what you said. Prayed. And I knew I had to toss that anger before I could tell you how I feel." He gently framed her face in his large hands. "Meeting you changed me. I saw a strong woman who could make a decision, argue her point of view and not give in to resentment or feel offended.

"You knocked me off my feet. No, you plowed me over,

and I'm glad you did. I love you, Erin, and I want us to spend the rest of our lives together. Will you marry me?"

Tears ran down Erin's face, and this time he knew what to do. He kissed her and drew her to his chest.

When he pulled back, he wiped the tears from her cheeks.

"You're an amazing man. I never thought I'd ever meet someone like you. I'd be an idiot if I didn't say yes, and I'm no idiot."

"True," he whispered before kissing her again.

He heard laughter in the hall.

Epilogue

The opening day of the bicounty rodeo fell on a clear eighty-degree autumn day.

Sawyer walked up behind Erin and wrapped his arms around her waist. They'd been married two months. Their wedding was supposed to be a small affair at Lulu's, but everyone in the county came, so they'd moved it over to the convention center.

Erin looked around their still-unfinished house. They would operate their new business out of this place. The barns were the first thing done, and both Sawyer's and Erin's horses enjoyed their new home and each other.

The only thing that hadn't been resolved was that Caleb still hadn't come to grips with his mother. Sawyer assured her that his brother would.

When they arrived at the rodeo grounds, the first thing they saw was Caleb hugging his mother. His wife gave him a big kiss over the infant she held.

"It looks like your brother's come to terms with things," Erin whispered.

"I think it was that new baby girl that brought him around."

"So, you wouldn't mind having one of your own?"

He momentarily stared at her, and she got nervous. They

hadn't planned to have kids so soon. Then understanding set in.

He hugged her and yelled, "Mom, you're going to be a grandma again in—" He turned to Erin.

"Seven and a half months, give or take."

"Around Valentine's Day." He let out a shout and laughed.

How amazing was what God had in store for her? She hadn't lost the bid for the redo of the rodeo; instead, she'd won. And won big.

* * * * *

The sun was low in the western sky by the time Micah Fisher
hitched a ride to the edge of town. The driver let him out at a dirt
road that led to several Amish farms. He'd never been to visit
his grandparents in Indiana before. They always came to Maine.
But he had no trouble finding their place.

As he drew close to the lane that led to the farmhouse, he
noticed a young woman standing by the mailbox. A little girl was
holding her hand and another was hopping up and down. They
were all staring at him.

"Howdy," he said.

The woman only nodded, but the two girls whispered, "Hello."

"Can we help you?" the woman asked. "Are you...lost?"

"*Nein.* At least I don't think I am."

"You must be if you're here. This is the end of the road."

Micah pointed to the farm next door. "Abigail and John Fisher
live there?"

"They do."

"Then I'm not lost." He snatched off his baseball cap, rubbed
the top of his head and then yanked the cap back on.

Micah stepped forward and held out his hand. "I'm Micah—
Micah Fisher. Pleased to meet you."

"You're not *Englisch*?"

"Of course I'm not."

"So you're Amish?" She stared pointedly at his clothing—tennis shoes, blue jeans, T-shirt and baseball cap. Pretty much what he wore every day.

"I'm as Plain and simple as they come."

"I somehow doubt that."

"Since we're going to be neighbors, I suppose I should know your name."

"Neighbors?"

"*Ja.* I've come to live with my *daddi* and *mammi*—at least for a few months. My parents think it will straighten me out." He peered down the lane. "I thought the bishop lived next door."

"He does."

"Oh. You're the bishop's *doschder*?"

"We all are," the little girl with freckles cried. "I'm Sharon and that's Shiloh and that is Susannah."

"Nice to meet you, Sharon and Shiloh and Susannah."

Sharon lost interest and squatted to pick up some of the rocks. Shiloh hid behind her *schweschder*'s skirt, and Susannah scowled at him.

"I knew the bishop lived next door, but no one told me he had such pretty *doschdern*."

Susannah's eyes widened even more, but it was Shiloh who said, "He just called you pretty."

"Actually I called you all pretty."

Shiloh ducked back behind Susannah.

Susannah narrowed her eyes as if she was squinting into the sun, only she wasn't. "Do you talk to every girl you meet that way?"

"Not all of them—no."

Don't miss
An Unlikely Amish Match *by Vannetta Chapman,*
available February 2020 wherever
Love Inspired® *books and ebooks are sold.*

LoveInspired.com

ACKNOWLEDGMENTS

The quotation on page 69 is from the article "Adaptation," by Richard C. Lewontin, in the September, 1978 issue of *Scientific American.*

The idea for the "annihilator" propulsion system described in this story came from a proposal of Peter G.O. Freund and Christopher T. Hill in their letter, "A possible practical application of heavy quark physics," in *Nature,* 16 November 1978.

What a tyrannosaur does with its hands was suggested by Charles J. Liptak in a letter to the editors of *Science News,* October 14, 1978.

I would like to thank Jerry Rasmussen, Michael Rosenthal, Alan Snyder, and Karen Preuss for reading the manuscript and making good suggestions.

RE-ENTRY

Countdown: Earth, 204 N.E.

Physician, heal thyself.
—Luke IV, 23

The snake eats itself, the dog chases its tail.
—G. Spencer Brown, *Laws of Form*

"Can you go home?" Susan had asked him, and in his profound hangover he'd profoundly misunderstood her. What she'd wanted to know was whether he was awake, and strong enough, and steady enough, to walk out of her life. Preferably forever. It was not a friendly question.

But he'd taken it metaphysically, and for a moment his foggy brain had wrestled with possibilities. *Could* he go home again? What would he do differently, if suddenly he were given the chance to do it all over?

"Take these," she'd said, thrusting a triad of pills at his face. His half open eyes had recognized a battery of lipotropin derivatives: energy, good will, a sense of well-being, waiting under his nose. The clouds of depression would lift, the sun would come out, the bluebird of happiness would sing.

He'd shifted his gaze to the gray-brown San Francisco fog outside Susan's soleri window. Lying on his back on her couch, looking straight up, he couldn't see anything else. Cold poisonous tentacles of despair, coiling over the glass half dome. And inside his skin, it was worse: he could smell the dried sweat and the vomit, taste the congealed mucus on his tongue. Oh, he'd been a very naughty boy this time. . . .

"Come on, Phil, take it and get out of here. Chemical sympathy is all you get. I've got work to do."

He'd taken the pills, dreading the memories they would restore. Then Susan had hauled him off the couch and pushed him through the door.

Those were his first wobbly steps on the way home.

Stage One: from Earth to Darwin, 206 N.E.—and before

1

Humboldt drove upward into star-spangled space, balanced on a column of fire from her annihilator engines. All her crystal promenades and portals were ablaze. On this "night" (by the ship's clock) the regal liner was more than three months from Earth, and only hours from Earth Station, the binary black hole system that gave forth on all the known accessible worlds of the Starry Archipelago.

Barring some unimaginable last minute emergency, *Humboldt* would proceed unchecked, diving with headlong grace into the space-time vortex around the orbiting holes, to emerge in no time in the vicinity of Darwin's Star a few dozen light-years away. The passage of the holes was scheduled for three o'clock in the morning, ship's time; before then there would not be the slightest interruption in the smooth .8-gee acceleration *Humboldt* maintained for the comfort of her passengers.

Those passengers gathered now by twos and threes and fours, to recline in leather-cushioned luxury beneath the sunset desert sky and battlemented mud walls of ancient Timbuktu. Palm fronds rattled in the cool breeze from the air conditioners. Boredom alone would have brought them to tonight's lecture in the Sun Grove lounge; that it was to be delivered by Philip Holder insured a full turnout.

Now if only Phil himself would turn out, fretted Evan Bruneau, *Humboldt's* sensie-handsome young Third Officer. He smiled warmly at Vivee Chillingsworth, and her diamonds, and her escort Robby Fain. Fain winked at Bruneau as he steered the widow Chillingsworth under the grape arbor and into the lounge, but Bruneau knew that Robby was only teasing.

Bruneau was beginning to fear the worst; the good doctor Holder was very distinguished indeed, but more often these

7

past couple of years for his epic binges than for his contributions to the annals of medicine.

Not that Bruneau was a moralist. His major task was to keep *Humboldt's* passengers entertained on the ship's long, long voyages among the major ports of the Archipelago, and Holder, a frequent passenger, was an invaluable resource: he had an intimate knowledge of the cultures of the inhabited worlds, gained through years of research, and he was an incurable raconteur. In return for Holder's services as a lecturer, Bruneau was happy to cancel his bar tabs.

It was after 21:00 already. If Holder didn't show up in a couple of minutes, Bruneau would have to send a steward around to the bars (*Humboldt* had eight). And if Holder wasn't in one of them, Bruneau would be forced to admit defeat. He'd show the travelogue sensie instead, and his name would be mud.

Of course he'd know damn well where Holder was. That was another part of their unspoken arrangement: Holder took his pounds of flesh (all female, mostly young), and somehow Bruneau managed never to think of the introductions he arranged as pimping. Perhaps that was unfortunate—in the present case it left him no excuse to go rousting one guest out of another's bed. (Excuse me, Loa darling, but Phil *promised* . . .)

But here came Loa Westcliffe now, fully dressed in diaphanous jumper, and all alone.

Bruneau grinned with relief. "So nice to see you here, Loa darling."

"Where the hell else would I be, dear?" Westcliffe asked, tossing metallic green locks. "Phil show up yet?"

"I couldn't say, really, I just . . ."

"In other words, no. If I were you I'd run quick as a bunny down to the Mirror Room and fish him out of his martini, or you're not going to have a show tonight." Her pale gray eyes were not smiling; she did not take the prospective loss of an hour's amusement lightly.

Bruneau went white, and without wasting a word he bounded toward the lift with improbably long and accurate strides.

Meanwhile Phil Holder sat all alone, sipping thoughtfully on what would have been his second Scotch after dinner—if he hadn't skipped dinner. A perfectly sane man would not have taken the risk of intoxicating himself even a little in the last hours before an act so audacious as the one Holder now contemplated; Holder, though, was neither completely sane nor completely foolish. He knew his capacity for alcohol with intimate precision. He wanted people to believe he was drunk as usual; moreover, the drinks would take the rasping edge off his nerves, as much a danger to his plans as alcohol's dullness. And even granted that all the excuses he could think of amounted to no better than a pile of shifting rationale, still his drinking would serve as an excellent test of his sincerity: did he dare remain sober?

He checked his wrist unit: 21:10. Where the hell's Bruneau? Doesn't he care?

Holder took another sip of the foul-tasting Scotch—reputedly an excellent unblended variety from Lothian, which he drank only for the sake of its unmistakable odor. He hated Scotch. He grimaced and put down the bulb. Glass clicked against glass. Glass everywhere.

He rubbed his hand over his face, feeling rubbery skin, trying to avoid his yellowing eyes in the bar's ubiquitous mirrors. He'd just as soon never see this particular version of his face again, anyway: a fortyish face, handsome in a soft-edged, dissolute sort of way, tanned almost black and engagingly wrinkled by the suns of a dozen worlds—yet somehow looking preserved.

The mirrored walls of the lounge, intended to make a modest space seem larger, closed in on him instead, mocking him with his own image repeated endlessly around him, a dozen decadent versions of himself converging at infinity reflected in the walls of this alcohol-filled killing bottle.

He was saved by the sudden appearance—a dozen desperate appearances at once—of Evan Bruneau. "... slap my wrist if I'm pushing, but this *was* the night you ..." Holder watched Bruneau try to get control of his face, which reflected relief and contempt before settling into determined obsequiousness. Holder almost laughed, but he was truly grateful for Bruneau's timely arrival.

"Oh Jeezus Ev, I've let you down again, have I? Probably too late now, huh? Lemme buy you drink, anyway. . . ."

"That's awfully good of you, Phil, but you could do me a much, much greater favor." Bruneau grinned sweatily. "The fact is, it's just a tad past 21:00. . . ."

Holder peered owlishly at his watch. "Say, you're right

rain, Ev. There's still time!" Holder pushed himself vigorously away from the bar, stumbling against Bruneau. " 'Scuse. Guess me arse is numb."

Bruneau steadied the shorter man with one hand and pressed his thumb against the countertop charge plate—for all his fumbling, Holder had never been in danger of paying his own bill. Bruneau steered Holder firmly toward the door.

The lift flashed upward, past a dozen opulent decks visible through the clear extruded crystal of the pneumatic tube. Holder leaned cozily on Bruneau's shoulder and closed his eyes. "Ev, 'd I ever tell you about the time at Epseridan U. when I was so sozzled and I was supposed to give this speech so I . . ."

"Sent your friend on instead, pretending to be you?"

"I *did* tell you!" Holder exclaimed with delight. "And he was so damn convincing! Ran through all the charts and graphs, knew 'em better than me. Had to call a stop to it, though," said Holder sternly. "He made too much sense to be a real ep'demiologist . . . mislead the public . . ."

"Don't get any ideas, Phil. It wouldn't work." Bruneau sighed.

"Oh hell, *I* know that." Holder was indignant. "These people already know *you*."

"But if you really don't feel up to it . . ."

"Relax, kid. I'll be fine," said Holder, miffed. He stood up straight as the lift doors whispered open.

The projected stars of the desert night twinkled more brightly as the sky light dimmed in the Sun Grove. Holder stood remarkably steady on the edge of the low dais, holding the room controls in his left hand. He'd warmed up his audience with professional aplomb, starting with a few jokes about drunken professors. Imperceptibly, not letting on that he was turning serious, he began including scraps of real ideas in his banter.

In the shadows at the back of the room Evan Bruneau allowed his gold-braided shoulders to relax—it looked as if Phil were going to pull it off after all.

" . . . the truth now—it's the lure of the primitive that brings you all to Darwin, isn't it? Even I still feel it, and I was born and raised here. Even though I know better than you that it's a tailor-made brand of primitivism." Holder laughed.

He fiddled with the room controls as he talked. Slowly an image began to fade in all around him, filling one whole end of the darkened room: tree ferns and fat cycads growing out of dark rich humus, and farther away, the mist-shrouded shapes of giant redwoods. The plants were merely life-sized, but nevertheless so big they seemed out of scale. Nothing moved in the dim ruddy light, not even the tendrils of mist; Holder had not yet activated the scene.

He kept talking all the while. "Once upon a time, in the good old days—you know what I mean; I call it the Garden of Eden syndrome—one way or another we all keep trying to go back. Now, a few years ago I spent some time with the yogis on Ichtiaque. I learned some things from them, I learned some things about them, I was lucky enough to solve a problem that had eluded other investigators. . . ." A few members of the audience murmured politely to indicate they were aware of the research that had won Holder the Freund Prize. ". . . whereupon a collection of armchair experimentalists decided to give me a prize for it," Holder said blandly, cutting the sycophants dead.

Bruneau was surprised at the acid sharpness of Holder's tone; Holder was a man who usually lapped up praise. But Bruneau thought that, all in all, Holder was doing remarkably well.

Bruneau looked at the holofilm with interest. The scene was new to him; Holder's talks usually began with panoramic views of Upper Cretacia from Mount Owen, one of Darwin's more inspiring vistas. Holder had brought the forest scene to full illumination, and had tapped the button that allowed partial animation. Fog drifted through the trees; water dripped in fat splashes from the spiny fronds of the cycads; insects flitted through the shadows. The motion cycled on an imperceptible dissolve, every few seconds—whatever happened later in the scene, Holder was saving it.

It wasn't a professional sensie with smelly-feely tracks, yet it filled the visual field, and even standing at the back of the room Bruneau felt he was inside the tableau.

"The yogis, attempting to get back to a presumed state of harmony with Nature that never could possibly have existed, are the strictest imaginable vegetarians," Holder was saying. "No animal products of any kind: no milk, no eggs, they won't even kill ticks. Yet they were afflicted by a very specific disease that, so far as we knew, could only be transmitted by eating the meat of infected loquemels, funny little goat-like creatures indigenous to the planet. As it turned out, the thing that was making the yogis sick was probably also keeping them alive."

Holder fingered the controls and the scene stopped cycling. He looked incongruously at home, standing amid the fronds of the prehistoric forest in his dark conservative suit and cape, but of course the primeval jungle was illusory. His head was cocked back and his eyes were fixed on a spot a few dozen meters back among the dark tree trunks. Unconsciously, every eye in the audience followed his gaze.

"Seems the disease was carried by a parasite that infested wild loquemel. In the larval stage, this tiny bug lives in besan pods. Besan provides the yogis with a staple part of their diet, and they were unknowingly eating an awful lot of the little grubs with their carelessly cleaned besan—thereby catching the disease. But those same grubs were providing them with their only complete proteins! Without that animal protein they would have been just as bad off, or worse." Holder chuckled. "We couldn't tell them that, of course. We persuaded them to switch to a different source of besan that just happened to be crawling with healthy bugs."

At this moment there arose repeated loud crashes in the brush, coming from the place in the trees Holder was watching. Over the sounds of vegetation being shredded and crushed came a different, more ominous sound, a guttural, slavering gurgle, mingled with violent expulsions of breath.

Holder seemed oblivious to his audience's mounting tension. After all, they were all sophisticates; they'd all seen a thousand skillfully produced sensies, replete with the most ingenious special effects.

Almost casually he attempted to undercut the excitement. By the way, I was thirteen when I took this piece of film, on an expedition organized by my father. Good old Dad. For those of you who go in for this sort of thing, it was shot with Leitz, with the reference beam reflectors set back there on the trunks of those sequoias, about four meters up."

Bruneau was among those lulled into looking for the equipment Holder mentioned. As his eyes searched the background, the branches of the redwoods whipped aside and Bruneau found himself staring down the throat of a roaring *Tyrannosaurus rex*.

Even though he was a dozen meters from the toothy apparition, Bruneau jumped. A collective gasp went up from the audience.

Holder giggled. "Oh come on, this is just a kid's home movie. In a couple of weeks you'll be on Darwin, where you can see the real thing."

The animal stepped forward. "There! Did you see it?" Holder shouted.

He flicked the controls and froze the tyrannosaur in place, cycling on a snorting breath. The bulk of the great beast's sixteen-meter length was back in the brush. Its huge head was carried relatively low and thrust forward, with rows of sharp teeth curved like Arabian daggers. Its nearly 9,000-kilogram weight was balanced on colossal three-clawed drumsticks in a running stance: head, body, and ridiculous stick-like forelegs ahead, massive tail out of sight behind.

Holder answered his own question. "No, none of you were paying attention." He reversed the film, and the forest swallowed the creature's head. "Down there, to the right! Look!" he shouted, as he instantly switched the film to forward. Smooth naked skin glimmered in the shadows of the underbrush.

Holder froze the image: it was a very young man only partly visible through the foliage. He wore a necklace of long curved teeth, a coil of rope over one shoulder, and apparently nothing else. His color was a rich, translucent bronze, his long golden hair flew out in braids behind his shoulders, and he sported a full blond beard and mustaches.

"The very picture of the perfect barbarian, eh?" Holder said cheerfully. "He could be a Viking, a Celt, even a Cromagnon—right down to the skin color. How many centuries have gone by since people were that pale?" Holder walked through the immaterial forest undergrowth until he was standing beside the frozen figure. "How did this outlandish creature come to be here, playing anachronistic cave man?"

Holder stood still a moment, then walked back toward the front of the dais, leaving the ghostly shape behind him. His voice was suddenly mournful. "In a way, I've spent my life trying to find the answer to that question. I've even written treatises on the so-called feral tribes of Darwin. But I still don't know." In the darkness Holder's expression was unreadable. "Unhappily, I was never able to discuss it with our 'primitive' friend, here."

Evan Bruneau's ears pricked up. Holder's voice sounded

dejected, but peculiarly insincere. What mischief was he about?

Holder started the film. The running man disappeared instantly into the undergrowth. The tyrannosaur bellowed and exploded from the trees, taking three frighteningly rapid strides forward. Muffled curses and squeals of fright came from the audience in the *Humboldt's* lounge.

The odd daintiness of the animal's bird-like gait was more than offset by the visible, audible effects each time a clawed foot hit the ground: the entire scene shook dizzily with each thudding step, betraying the unseen laser recorder's vibrations on its tripod. The nightmare animal stopped in the middle of the mossy clearing, the red expressionless eyes atop its skull staring fixedly from under bony orbital ridges. Its mouth hung open, and its breath came in liquid grunts.

Bruneau shivered. He was awfully glad now that Holder's film was mere sound and picture. Even in his imagination, the stench of the carnivorous dinosaur's hot, wet breath was almost overpowering. Then a horrible thought occurred to Bruneau—just as the great reptile's head twisted and darted forward into the brush.

There was a horrible scream, indisputably human.

"Oh, really, Phil, you mustn't!" Bruneau protested loudly, taking a step forward.

"For those of you who are still with me," said Holder, "have a look at this...."

Then Bruneau realized he'd been completely fooled; Holder had not been sober for an instant! The whole episode was a boozy practical joke. Nauseated groans and shouts failed to deter the intoxicated doctor, who continued to expound. Bruneau lunged toward the stage to interfere, but found his way blocked by members of the audience who were in a hurry to leave.

Inside Holder's "home movie" too, there were running figures. Bruneau had time to make out a boy in his early teens—Holder himself?—running toward the thrashing in the bushes, and a middle-aged man who suddenly caught up to the boy and cuffed him out of the way.

Bruneau was almost to the dais now. The fern leaves lowered over his head. And then the tyrannosaur stood erect. It, too, towered over Bruneau, so high and awesome that Bruneau almost stumbled in fright. The red gobbets that dripped from its jaws resembled nothing like a man.

". . . incidentally demonstrates the answer to a question that puzzled paleontologists for ever-so-long, before the re-creation of rex," Holder was remarking, nonchalantly. "Scientists could conceive of no possible adaptive purpose for the creature's tiny forelegs. . . ."

"Phil, for God's sake!" Bruneau shouted.

"But they are quite useful, as it turns out," said Holder.

The carnosaur ducked its head and lifted a pair of short, curving little foreclaws to its mouth. Then it began . . .

"Picking its teeth," Bruneau murmured. "Oh, God." He jumped onto the dais and walked toward Holder. "Phil, please. . . ."

Holder looked at him. "My g'ness, Ev." A bewildered expression came over his face; he blinked. "Have I gone too far?"

"Yes, Phil. Much too far indeed," said Bruneau, trying to hold his temper.

Holder peered at Bruneau, apparently puzzled by the anger in his friend's voice. Confidence drained out of him.

"Come on, Phil," Bruneau sighed, feeling the barest twinge of remorse. "I'll get you safely to bed."

"Oh. Sure. Sure, Ev, I'll come with you." Holder absently tossed the room controls into the make-believe bushes.

"Oh, *Phil!*" For a moment the exasperated Bruneau considered searching for the controls, but decided it was more important to get Phil Holder safely put away. He took him by the arm; Holder stumbled against him.

Bruneau escorted the confused doctor out of the room, guiding him gently past a number of angry guests who jostled him and hissed their spite. But as Bruneau made his way slowly up the aisle he noted that a good many passengers seemed not the least upset by the graphic sensie display. Bruneau saw Loa Westcliffe and Robby Fain and Vivee Chillingsworth among the audience who continued to watch in slack-jawed masturbatory rapture as, behind Bruneau and his bewildered charge, in the depths of the starship's elegant lounge, the apparition of *Tyrannosaurus* continued to munch, and pick delicately at the stringy remains of its dinner.

2

"Clarissa Sirich was in at the beginning; indeed, as became apparent only much later, her presence defined the beginning as such, though she was not herself the initiator of those historic events in Cole's laboratory. Born on April 25th, 1979 O.E., her name was originally Margaret Tanner, and she was the daughter of the renowned research biochemist . . ."

(from *Darwin: A Millennium of Conservation*)

Stefan Lazarev was twenty-two years old, an experienced operator of heavy equipment, but more used to the suburbs of Moscow than the permafrost regions of the sub-Arctic. He had lately been recruited by the Komsomol and assigned along with a half dozen other *bulldozeristy* to a railroad construction camp north of Tommot, where he was helping to build a major new spur connecting the Baikal-Amur Mainline at Nagornyy to the city of Yakutsk on the Lena.

On this particular afternoon Stefan was working alone, following a line of stakes set out the day before by a surveying crew, cutting an access road through the birch trees and stunted firs with the blade of his big American Cat.

Spring comes late to the taiga, but brings with it a profusion of sweet wildflowers and lush green grass and long warm afternoons that stretch into soft, perfumed twilights. In such a climate love blooms as quickly as the flowers. The tousle-haired youth was thinking about a girl named Valentina from the track gang, not about safety, as he brought the noisy diesel to a halt near the banks of a little brook.

Stefan climbed down from the Cat and stood still a moment, feeling the sun on his face, hearing the whisper of wind in the leaves. Then he carried his lunch tin to the dappled shade of a ring of birches. His only concession to caution was to bring along a beat-up old hunting rifle against the sudden, if unlikely, appearance of a bear.

He was little prepared, then, when having chewed his way through half a chunk of black bread he heard a sudden agonizing groan behind him. He leaped to his feet, spewed out his mouthful, and snatched up the rifle. Spinning around, he was just in time to watch with horror as his Cat's enormous steel blade slid beneath the surface of the earth, followed by a rattling splash of gravel. The little meadow brook was pouring into a crater where lately his wonderful new machine had been parked.

To lose a bulldozer! He refused to believe such a tragedy had befallen him. He raced to the edge of the hole and peered down in anguish.

Stefan had been warned about ice caves, and at the time he had thought he was paying attention to the lectures. But perhaps only bitter experience can convince one that the ground over much of Siberia is no ground at all, but only a thin layer of top soil over ice many meters deep, many millennia old. With each annual thaw the ground cover becomes rotten and treacherous.

Stefan sat on the soggy ground beside the hole and fought back tears. After a long while he came to his senses, realizing that the Cat could be salvaged easily enough by the work camp's big crane, and that the immediate need was to retrieve his loose tools and personal gear. The bulldozer was tilted up at a sharp angle, its blade facing him about a meter and a half below. He stood and leaped down onto the wide curved blade.

It was spooky, clambering around in the cold dripping halflight, swearing, and hoping that the massive machinery would not sink further into the ice in the next moment. Eventually Stefan had gathered all the gear he could get his hands on and began to climb back out of the chill pit.

While he was studying the frozen face of the sinkhole, looking for a sturdy handhold to help him to the top, Stefan saw the vague dark shape of the ice-locked mammoth.

Sheer accident brought Hank Cole and Yurii Amosov together for the 1999 annual meeting of the International Society of Cryobiology in Sri Lanka. Cole was in the Colombo Hyatt's veranda bar waiting for his wife and son to return from a shopping trip, and Amosov wandered in to wait for the restaurant to open. Both events being delayed, the two men got to talking.

Cole wasn't even attending the meetings—he and his family were vacationing and he'd dropped in to say hello to a colleague from the States. As a molecular geneticist, Cole had a passing acquaintance with some of the techniques of cryobiology, but it wasn't really his line.

It wasn't Amosov's line either, but he was at the meetings on purpose. A vertebrate paleontologist, a successor of the energetic Vereshchagin at the Zoological Institute in Leningrad, he was seeking to learn more about the effects of different conditions of freezing and thawing on mammalian cells, hoping to apply this knowledge to the study of Pleistocene animal tissues recovered in various states of preservation from the frozen tundra.

Amosov and Cole hit it off immediately, and after a couple of drinks the two men—both possessed of impish senses of humor—had concocted the most outrageous scheme. . . .

A few months after Stefan Lazarev's bulldozer fell into an ice cave Hank Cole's lab at Stanford received a shipment by air from Leningrad. Cole's graduate student Margaret Tanner helped open the well-insulated case of steel-jacketed bottles bearing the multilingual label, "Warning: Liquid Nitrogen. Do Not Open Manually," with a long list of detailed instructions. Inside the bottles were tissue samples taken from many parts of the body of "Natasha," history's first completely preserved adult woolly mammoth. None of these samples were in the best imaginable condition. Most, frozen too slowly, had been damaged by salt concentration as the cells dehydrated and shriveled, and a few, frozen too fast, had suffered disruption from needle-like ice crystals. A tiny fraction of the cells, however, exhibited nuclei in excellent states of preservation.

DNA is an extraordinarily stable molecule (if it were not, inheritance would be a very chancy business indeed), and from the nuclei of Natasha's cells Cole proposed to obtain enough intact DNA to model a typical set of somatic cell chromosomes. The ultimate aim of the study was to compare the mammoth and the modern elephant by locating those genes that specified slightly different sequences of amino acids in proteins otherwise common to both creatures.

It was important to know that any differences were indeed due to evolution and not to several centuries in the deep freeze. Applying sophisticated statistical analysis to many different partial models—some visual, derived from electron micrographs or soft X-ray replicas, others mathematical and chemical, based on advanced electrophoretic, chromotographic, and enzymatic techniques—an idealized mammoth genetic sequence was at last obtained.

Cole and Amosov wrote up a spate of papers, signed them jointly, and sent them off to the journals. But they did not sit back and wait for notoriety to strike.

Selecting several slices from Natasha's intestine, Cole carefully brought the frozen tissue to the normal internal temperature of an elephant's body, using a buffering solution Amosov had derived, which included "antifreeze" glycoproteins from the blood of Arctic fish. Cole's choice of intestinal cells was not random. Evolutionary theory suggested that the association of digestive and reproductive functions was not God's dirty joke—cells near the gut were the best nourished, and had the best chance to survive.

Cole microsurgically removed apparently perfect nuclei from choice thawed cells and slid them gently into fresh denucleated cells from living African elephants. If the mammoth's genes could function without error inside the elephant's cells, it would be good evidence that the Cole-Amosov model was correct. Several months passed. Cultures descended from some of the transplants continued to thrive.

Then Cole proceeded to thaw another set of mammoth cells. This time the recipients of the mammoth's DNA were an elephant's egg cells. An application of hormones started the hybrid gametes dividing and multiplying *in vitro*.

While Cole, dressed in an immaculate white coat, performed these delicate sterile operations in the gleaming stainless-steel environment of his laboratory in the handsome biochemistry building, Margaret Tanner and two other grad students wrestled with the realities of biomedical research on an earthier level. Several hundred yards from the School of Medicine a rude wooden compound had been set up under the shade of huge eucalyptus trees on the dusty plains of Leland Stanford's famous horse farm. The farming that went on inside the compound had nothing to do with horses.

A half dozen female specimens of *Loxodonta africana* had been borrowed from the San Francisco Zoo along with an amused keeper. Every day an adult African elephant typically consumes thirty-five kilograms of hay, alfalfa, oats, or vegetables. Cole's students spent their days with pitchforks and shovels in their hands, not microscopes.

After consultation with expert breeders Cole had decided to impregnate the elephants with frozen sperm from the nearest captive bull, who lived in Portland's Washington Park (most zoos would as soon do without a male's nasty temper). The complex changes in the uterus brought about by the onset of pregnancy can be mimicked by applying estradiol and progesterone, but Cole wanted to take as few chances as possible. The impregnation itself was done manually by Cole's unfortunate pupils.

The eggs fertilized by the testy Portland bull did not long survive. In a series of messy, intricate operations, Cole aborted the six cows and at the same time replaced their nascent embryos with glass-grown blastocysts from his laboratory.

Now there was nothing to do but wait. One after another, all but one of the pregnant elephants aborted again, this time spontaneously. Examination showed fatal developmental flaws of the fetuses. Cole and his long-suffering students all but gave up hope.

Two years passed, and all that time a 40-year-old cow name Mabel held on. She was a taciturn beast, and nothing seemed to upset her. Already she'd been the mother of two natural young. Nevertheless, Cole had long since resigned himself to the inevitable.

Miraculously the impossible arrived before the "inevitable." Hasty phone calls between Palo Alto and Leningrad brought Yurii Amosov on a special Aeroflot jet just in time to be on hand the day Mabel, the African elephant, gave birth to a perfectly healthy young woolly mammoth.

They named her Stefania, after Stefan Lazarev, the workman who had been her unwitting godfather and who, all unknowing, had brought her back from the dead. Her foster mother would nurse her for six years, like any ordinary elephant calf. In twelve years she would be mature, standing almost four meters high at the shoulder, covered with a fine wool undercoat with long black wiry hair growing through it, and sporting spectacular in-curving tusks three meters long. Stefania would always be an affectionate beast, willing to scratch her keeper's scalp with her curiously double-"fingered" trunk in return for a handful of carrots.

But on her birthday no one yet knew what to expect. They

could only hope that a living creature had been brought back from ten thousand years' extinction, once more to walk the earth in majesty.

And from the sidelines Margaret Tanner watched, and pondered, and laid vague plans for the future.

3

Pinpoints of reflected light glistened wetly on the surface of Holder's half-open eye. He stared straight down. He had not stirred for hours.

A few centimeters beneath his nose, myriad filaments of glittering optical fiber snaked around shadowy struts and beams. He looked through the floor of his first class room-with-a-view, past its structural bones, its arteries of plumbing, its light-fiber nerves, down through the ship's outer crystalline skin. The whole sparkling skyscraper dropped away beneath the feet of Holder's bunk, where he lay face down, his head and one arm dangling over the side.

The cliff-like face of the ship was a multi-faceted array of glowing crystals—emerald, ruby, amethyst, yellow diamond—revealing themselves on close inspection as instrument ports, observation galleries, promenades, and individual suites whose walls had not yet been opaqued for privacy this night. Far below, a pearly corona of light escaped beyond the edges of the energy shield surrounding the veiled stern engines, the only visible sign of the annihilators' unbearably bright flame.

Despite the immense structure's velocity of some 60,000 kilometers per second, twenty percent of light speed, nothing betrayed *Humboldt's* motion through space. Nothing moved at all, except here and there a shadow cast on a yellow pane of quartz.

Before Holder stirred, all those shadows would stop moving.

After the fiasco in the Sun Grove, Evan Bruneau had steered Holder to his suite, just managing to get his evening cloak off him before Holder batted him away, groaning. Bruneau had straightened him out on the bunk, pulled off his boots, spread a thin blanket over him, and then retreated, blanking the lights as he went. Holder was already snoring loudly.

A few minutes later Holder had started thrashing about—ending up half off the bunk with the blanket bunched under him, presumably more comfortable. In the course of these seemingly unconscious struggles he'd hit the bedside opaquing controls. turning the walls and floor to "clear." He hadn't moved since.

Amid the jeweled wonders below him, one dark area held his attention: a cluster of large, wedge-shaped objects blackly silhouetted against the luminous hull like bats clinging to the roof of a crystal cave. These were *Humboldt's* planetary landers, winged launches she routinely used to communicate with more remote ports of call, planets that could not conveniently provide their own high-orbital shuttles.

Darwin was by no means remote, being a prime attraction for wealthy tourists. The planet had a well-appointed orbiting entry station with comfortable service to the surface. Therefore, with superspace insertion due in less than fifteen minutes and Darwin still some weeks away, Holder doubted anyone but himself was giving the landers any thought.

The soft, soothing precisely polite voice of *Humboldt's* computer sounded from the room's speakers, at a level of volume just sufficient to be clearly audible to any passengers who might still be awake. "Ladies and gentlemen, in exactly ten minutes the *Humboldt* will cease acceleration in order to prepare for superspace insertion. This will result in a temporary condition of weightlessness. After our ship emerges from superspace we will perform a simple maneuver in order to align our main engines for deceleration. Immediately thereafter weight will be restored. The total period of weightlessness will be approximately five minutes. During this period, for your comfort and safety, restraining netting will enclose your beds. To insure that everyone is safely restrained, your rooms will be placed under automatic surveillance in exactly three minutes from now. . . ."

Holder did not move. He knew, as most seasoned travelers did, that the surveillance cameras were never really turned off. Holder listened as the computer explained that anyone who did not wish to stay in bed during the weightless period would be "assisted" by a crew member.

". . . therefore we now suggest that all passengers not in bed return to their beds, lie down, and make themselves *comfortable*. Thank you! Ladies and gentlemen, in exactly nine minutes the *Humboldt* will cease acceleration in order to prepare for superspace insertion. This will result in a temporary condition of weightlessness . . ."

Superspace insertion required extraordinary precision, but there were no tricks to it. Provided a ship entered the spacetime hyperfold at Earth Station at just the right point, she would emerge from superspace at Darwin Station. It was that simple. If the ship entered the fold at some other point, she would emerge near, say, Tau Ceti, or Brindle, or any of a few dozen other selected planetary systems—or for that matter, at any point within a spherical radius of a couple of hundred light-years that happened to be blessed with a double black hole system. A ship's point of exit depended wholly and simply on its point of entry. *Humboldt* had been riding a reference beam from Earth Station's robot navigational monitor since acquiring the beam two weeks out from Earth.

Penalties for straying from the beam were severe. A misguided exit from superspace through a single black hole was inescapably final: the ship and its contents would emerge as a shower of radiation, never escaping the far event horizon, serving only to enlarge the mass of the hole. Not only were double-hole Stations essential to avoid singularities, by providing a fold in spacetime rather than a tunnel through it, but also to provide null-gravity paths that could keep a ship from being ripped apart by tides.

Thus a ship could leap a hundred light-years with ease to reach Ichtiaque or New Albion, while other star systems only a few light-years from Earth remained effectively off limits forever, accessible only through vast stretches of ordinary spacetime.

The properties of hyperfold Stations had been thoroughly understood for centuries, in an empirical way, and interstellar travel was commonplace—even safer than air travel near a planet's surface. Besides the well-known properties of double black holes, however, there were certain other properties, little spoken of, speculative in the extreme, known only to a few—and never tested. Until tonight.

". . . will now enclose your beds. Please lie still. Do not be alarmed. The restraining nets will leave an ample space for ordinary movement. They will be withdrawn shortly, immediately after weight is restored. Should you require assistance, do not hesitate to use the call button at the head of your bed. . . ."

The tough, fine restraining net unfurled slowly from under the left side of Holder's bunk. Carried smoothly up and over him on half-elliptical tracks mounted on the head and foot boards, the leading edge of the net would fasten to the right side of the bed by means of evenly spaced electromagnets.

Holder moved his dangling right hand slightly at the last possible moment. A magnet in the descending net came to rest on his hand, failing to make contact. He now had a space between contact points, less than a meter long. The netting material should give just enough to allow him to slip through.

Patiently he waited, as he had for hours, drawing on the mental disciplines he'd learned during a year spent on Ichtiaque. With ironic detachment he reflected that had he learned all the yogis desired to teach him he would not be embarking on this bizarre journey. But he was "nailed to the Wheel of Life," as the yogis would have had it—he made use of their teachings only to control his body, not his awful moral hunger.

". . . do not be alarmed. Weightlessness will begin now. Do not be alarmed. . . ."

Finally he felt it: acceleration stopped. The faint quantum glow at *Humboldt*'s stern vanished. Holder pushed gently against the floor with his fingertips. His whole body floated off the bed.

He waited yet another half minute. He knew the safety officers used that time to make a quick video inspection of the passenger quarters, to satisfy themselves that all civilians were safely under lock and key.

Now. Holder rolled upside down in the space between the top of the bunk and the free-floating net. He grasped the edge of the net firmly, and pulled himself into the gap. For a second he wriggled and kicked, and then he was clear.

Three minutes to zero.

He reached under the bed and snatched the canvas satchel he had placed there. In the luminous dark glittering with pinpoints of fire, he swam like a dark diver among schools of flashlight fish. A strong kick of his stockinged feet against the wall sent him darting to the door. He yanked it open, knowing as he did so that an alarm sounded simultaneously on the control decks above.

Outside in the corridor a red panel blinked frantically over his head, but he paid no attention to it. Kicking with all his strength against the door jamb, he flew flat and fast down the dimly lit corridor toward the center of the ship.

Two minutes and forty seconds to zero.

He felt heady. Hours of enforced immobility followed by sudden strenuous activity were exacting their inevitable toll. But he had known what to expect.

He reached the ship's central galleries. Without pausing in his flight, he hooked his free hand over the molded acrylic banister of one of the ship's three grand staircases. He neatly executed a ninety-degree turn straight "down," boosting his flight with a double kick against the rail. He held his eyes open long enough to judge his trajectory. Then he closed them against the onrushing vertigo that tried to persuade him he was falling to his death.

The annihilator and the superhydrogen tanks that fed it took up the whole of *Humboldt*'s core; the ship's human activities were concentrated in a thin husk wrapped around this stem. The helical staircases, along with the transparent elevator tubes, descended the full height of the ship, winding around unobstructed shafts of open air down which passengers could peer to savor the space liner's majestic length.

When he opened his eyes he had hurtled past twenty decks. He had two minutes and twenty-five seconds to zero.

Still no interference from the crew! He knew they were coming; they knew where he was. But so far he was ahead of them. A fierce flush of excitement welled up in him. His plan was working without a hitch!

He swung his satchel overhead, veering a few degrees in his headlong flight, rolling over in midair. The roll caused him to misjudge his aim—he collided painfully with the banister, taking the blow on his upper arm. He gasped. Grimacing, he fumbled for the next floor's railing. He managed to hold on for an instant, just long enough to flip him end for end. At the next story he hit the rail with his shins. Then he managed to hook both his hands over it, sliding a couple of meters, burning his palms, with his satchel bumping the uprights. Finally he came to a stop on the stairs.

He checked his wrist unit. Two minutes.

Almost dispassionately, Holder noted that his breath came in sobs, that he had cracked his shins and wrenched his shoulders and blistered his hands. He was not a young man. He'd had no illusions about that, though. All in all, things were going remarkably well.

He sailed up the stairs to regain the floors he'd missed. Now he could see *them* coming, two elevators descending in their transparent tubes, away around the curve of the ship on either side of him, coming at him fast but still ten floors away.

A glance at the corridor marker assured him he was where he needed to be: D Deck, four floors above propulsion maintenance; Corridor 27, 270 degrees from dorsal zero. Lander D-27 was reached through this corridor. Again he launched himself into the air.

The corridor doglegged at the end, debouching in the small loading room alongside D-27's main hatch. For safety, there were airlocks leading into the corridor and, opposite, into the lander. They were always closed. They would cost him a precious few seconds.

Holder bounced around the end of the corridor and came up against the clear quartz wall that held the lock into the padded loading room. His heart leaped into his mouth.

There were guards in the room!

Holder's head spun. How had they gotten here ahead of him? There was a third entrance to the room, a small non-airlocked hatch from a maintenance tube that paralleled the corridor—and sure enough, that hatch stood open. So much for physical access. But how had they *known*?

It must have been Bruneau. Evan must have put two and two together and directed the security detail to this loading room, this particular lander. Holder had talked way too much back in the beginning, a couple of trips and a couple of years ago; he'd asked Evan too many detailed questions about the capabilities of the captain's launch, D-27, and about the procedures followed during superspace insertion. Back then all this had been a flight of fancy, a joke, really—not the life and death commitment it had since become.

Precious seconds passed while Holder thought. The guards inside the room floated impassively, making no move toward him. Their dark face-plates hid their expressions; they might as well have been a pair of robots. They knew Holder was trapped between them and the larger force who even now must have reached the end of the corridor.

Holder stabbed his finger at the guards, and then toward the maintenance hatch through which they'd come. Then he pointed toward himself, and toward the outer airlock. At first they did not move, but when Holder reached for the emergency trigger, accessible from both sides of the wall, they reacted in startled horror.

He deliberately opened the safety cover. From the corner of his eye he could see the panicked guards diving for the maintenance hatch as he tripped the delay.

A moment later a thousand kilograms of steel disintegrated under the impact of the explosive charge, half bursting into the corridor on a flat trajectory, the other half into the room. In the absence of gravity the debris scattered elastically.

That explained the dogleg in the corridor, of course. Holder had barely gotten around the corner and gotten his mouth open and his fingers in his ears before the lock blew up.

The smoke and crash of the explosion brought the pursuing security squad, halfway down the corridor, to a momentary halt.

Holder darted quickly into the loading room, flew across it, grabbed and spun the wheel of the second lock with his feet braced against the wall—he had no time to wait for the motors. Chunks of shattered steel still bounded around through the thick gray smoke, along with ripped-out shreds of padding. A jagged piece of metal tore the cloth on Holder's thigh.

He noted with relief that the maintenance hatch was closed.

He swung back the inner door of this, the primary lock. It was smaller but far more massive than the first lock had been, a vital orifice penetrating *Humboldt's* skin. No explosive charges here—they could only do more harm than good.

Holder guessed he had about thirty seconds remaining—less than he'd hoped, but still barely enough. He'd planned to close this hatch behind him, but he abandoned that idea; it would take too long. The ship's emergency systems would handle the decompression by filling the airlock with polyfoam.

He unlatched the outer door, which was in fact the hatch of the lander. The lander door sucked open, hydraulically cushioned against the crushing weight of air inside *Humboldt;* Holder braced himself in the wind. The lander was fastened to *Humboldt* by the skin of its belly. Holder reached up to pull himself into the craft's fuselage, grasping the edge of the floor.

He heard a clang behind him. Probably the security guard. "Phil! For God's sake, man, what are you doing? You'll kill yourself!"

Evan Bruneau was climbing out of the maintenance hatch. The guards were nowhere in sight. Bruneau's face was twisted in pain.

"Get out of here!" Holder screamed at him. "I don't have time to fool with you! I'm blowing a hole in this ship!"

As Holder turned to plunge into the lander he realized Bruneau was still coming. Then he saw the blood trickling from Bruneau's ears.

The man was deaf. The shock wave from the exploding hatch must have caught him inside the maintenance tube. The guards, too.

"Oh, sweet Jesus." Holder turned back away from the lander. He grabbed the heavy door, hooking one hand around the grip provided for this purpose, and slowly began pulling it to.

Bruneau was floating toward him, his mouth agape, his fingers outstretched. But Holder was faster, sealing the heavy hatch between them, cutting Bruneau off from his sight. He took the precious seconds needed to dog it shut.

Bruneau wanted to save his life. Holder could not sacrifice him in cold blood. True, he was late now. That might cost him his life after all. So be it.

Ten seconds left.

He pulled himself into the lander and sealed its hatch. He pulled himself rapidly, hand over hand, past the half-dozen lounge chairs toward the cockpit door. He yanked it open, and thanked God it wasn't locked. With no time to force it, it could have condemned him absolutely.

He settled himself into the pilot's couch, yanked the acceleration harness down over his shoulders, reached into the breast pocket of his tunic, and pulled out a programmed code sliver. He jammed it into the slot in the lander's autopilot and slammed the "start" sequence switches.

Holder hardly had time to take half a breath before D-27 snapped its shackles and hurled itself in a backward dive away from *Humboldt.* Through the quartz plates over his head Holder could see the great length of the starship wheeling in the sky at what seemed an agonizingly slow pace. D-27's rockets fired in exact sequence, following the program meticulously. Now it flew parallel to the parent ship, upside down, with nose pointed astern.

Out here, away from the glow of the ship's myriad windows, Holder could see the stars again. They shone cold and needle sharp, unblinking. Therefore, either he was still in time or they had already passed through the hyperfold and it was all over. . . .

He dared look at his wrist unit. He could hardly believe his eyes. He had two whole seconds to spare! He looked up, allowing himself a smile.

As he did so, the universe all around him went dark, as the stars sucked into a point behind his back, in the same instant blurring and disappearing in red smears.

The rest was an image constructed from nerve impulses that reached him an eternity after the event they recorded had ceased to exist: over his head, a hundred meters up, the *Humboldt* stayed the same; they were inside the hyperfold, both *Humboldt* and the little lander that had budded off her at the last instant, and already the lander's rockets were exploding with maximum power, and Holder was dragged deep into his couch, his cheeks sagging under violent acceleration, and *Humboldt* was gone.

Before his eyes all was double vision. He didn't know if it was because he was losing consciousness or only because of the familiar momentary sense of time reversal inside the fold. Perhaps both. Lose consciousness he did, as his stolen craft accelerated away from *Humboldt* with all the power it could muster.

Philip Holder slid into oblivion. If he had calculated incorrectly, even by a fraction of a percent, he would never wake up.

4

Angelica Claymore's private bird climbed swiftly to 15,000 meters and locked into the westbound security traffic lane

At 2,000 kilometers per hour she would have a couple of hours to brush up before her plane reached the west coast.

Word of the bizarre incident aboard *Humboldt* had reached Washington the day before, after traveling more than a week at the speed of light. *Humboldt* had radioed through the relays at Darwin Station and Earth Station immediately upon emerging into Darwin's Star space, but Earth Station relay was a long way from Earth, and moving forty kilometers farther away every second.

Claymore satisfied herself that the rocket plane was functioning as it should, then swung her couch away from the control panel. The acceleration restraints retracted as she did so. She rose from the couch, crossing the cabin to the plane's bar unit and punching a sequence on its keyboard. Most people addressed bars vocally; Claymore avoided talking out loud to robots.

The *espresso* would take a few moments. Anything done right takes time. While she waited she gazed out of one of the plane's forward windows at the banks of cloud far below, folded like whipping cream against the sinuous ridges of the Appalachians.

The cloud deck shrouded the squalor of the surface. Looking down, Claymore felt a shiver of triumph. She had made it to the top, almost to the very top. The plane that carried her far above the stink and jostle of the tubes was in itself a symbol of her status and value to her government, to Speaker Macklin himself. An optimistic symbol: though held aloft on slender wings in a rarefied atmosphere, the plane was perhaps more secure in its place than she.

Mentally she changed the subject. *Humboldt* must even now be nearing Darwin under heavy deceleration. Unlike Earth, Darwin was near its stargate. There were dark rumors that someday Earth, isloated as it was, would become just too expensive to carry on the scheduled runs. Even now, only the wealthiest, or those on official business, could afford to travel. Earth Station's extremely eccentric orbit meant that inevitably the center of civilization would move to other worlds— Epsilon Eridani was making a bold bid—leaving Earth to slide into cultural decline, a teeming ant heap of poverty in a Galactic backwater.

All the more reason to stay on top of the heap.

The bar unit pinged and Claymore reached for the tiny porcelain cup, easing it out of its friction cradle under the coffee spigot. She took it to the hand-carved teak table in the back of the cabin, sat down in her leather-upholstered lounge chair, and slipped off her shoes. For a luxurious second she allowed her toes to wriggle in the silken pile of the ancient Turkish prayer rug. She leaned back in her chair, reached into her case and withdrew a fileslab, and flipped on the book projector. Crisp printed words flowed brightly through darkened space in front of her eyes. She took a sip of her coffee.

> *Holder, Philip A.—Infofile Class 3 (fact), Security Access Only. Date of birth: 164 N.E., 6.103 × 10⁶ secs Gs (25th Deca, local). Place of birth: General Hospital of Cuvier, Cuvier, Galapagos, Republic of Darwin (Darwin, Darwin's Star).*
> *Current citizenship: Republic of Darwin.*

Duration code showed the file to be a long one. Evidently the agents had made an extra effort because Holder was an offworlder by citizenship and birth, a Darwinian at that. His father had held middle and upper management positions with the Rangers, as the Darwinians called their civil service, and Holder had been privileged to enjoy a comfortable childhood in a variety of spacious, interesting surroundings.

Just in these simple facts Claymore found cause to dislike her quarry. That helped: it made her senses sharper, the quest more urgent. It was also essential if she were going to self-induce an override to her anti-assassination conditioning. Her ability to do so was one of the things that made her so valuable to Security. But though possible, it was not easy, even for her.

Her own childhood had been somewhat different from Holder's. Her parents had been artists, struggling to earn a living in the legitimate theater, her mother as an Assistant Creator, her father as a gladiator. Claymore remembered the long tube rides from the slums of Westchester to Shea Coloseum to watch the Sunday afternoon productions. When she'd been very small her father had always been among the first rank. Often he'd won, but how she'd cried when he'd been killed or dismembered! On those occasions her mother had kissed away her tears, assuring her that, after all, it was only a Circus. Later on she could rarely distinguish him in the pageants; he was usually assigned to play a galley slave or a

Christian, or one of a horde of mudmen or Amerinds or Titanian jellywings, all of whom always died in anonymous heaps in the background.

Shortly after Claymore had earned her manual labor permit at the age of seventeen her father had applied for brainburning. She never saw him again. Brainburning was as good as death as far as relatives were concerned—better, really, since no decisions had to be made as to the disposal of the remains.

Claymore was sure she was personally responsible. She thought it must have been the cost of her vocational education that had so exhausted her father before he reached the age of forty. . . .

> . . . Sex at birth: male; Current sex: (unchanged); Race: sapiens sapiens (see illustration this locus. Access class 2 infofile this locus for genetic sequence abstract and profile, and psychological assessment.)
> Education (formal): University of Darwin (n.d.), University of Epsilon Eridani, B.S. '86; U EpsEr, Ph.D. '88, M.D. '90; Internship, Trebler Medical Center (EpsEr) '90; Residency, TMC '94; Research Fellow, University of Papua New Guinea (PNG, Earth, Sol) Center for the Advanced Study of Cultural Patterns of Health '94-'96; Certification: Pan-Eridanian Board of Medical Examiners, '96; Academic and scholarly awards, honors . . .

At eighteen Claymore apprenticed herself to the local Courtesans' Guild, knowing she was lucky to be accepted— the competition in New York was world class. Her small salary, minus an essential clothing allowance, went to her mother. Coming home one morning to the room they shared in alternating shifts, she found a note taped to the communicator screen. In her mother's hand, it said only, "You must live your own life."

She received the routine official notification later that day. Her mother had applied and been accepted for brainburning. She knew better than to try to learn anything more through government channels.

Claymore was skilled at her new craft and was quickly promoted; too much training is inefficient if youth is wasted. She cultivated a theatrical clientele, hoping to learn something of Circus politics. She heard that her mother's recent writings had been rejected, viewed as skirting on sedition, though no formal complaints had been lodged. As an Assistant Creator, Claymore's mother rarely had the opportunity to do more than simply develop the tech sheets needed to flesh out the Ringmaster's stale notions of spectacle. Sedition? Perhaps she had directed a thousand flower girls to arrange themselves to spell out, "Speaker Macklin Sucks."

The truth, as Claymore found after she dug a little deeper, was as clichéd as the Ringmaster's "creations": the Ringmaster had insisted, Claymore's mother had resisted, to the penultimate degree.

Revenge was out of the question. The best Claymore could do was resolve never to find herself in the same position. She managed to convince herself that she despised men (excepting only the memory of her sainted father). Thus she was able to remain unaffected by male demands. She was smart enough to hide her indifference.

> ... *Residence: Parnassus, San Francisco, Alta California (USNA, Earth, Sol)* //*Update: research mission to Darwin commenced 7 March 206 (Earth local) aboard Licensed Space Liner Humboldt, in progress*// //*Update: voyage of Humboldt interrupted by . . .*//

Claymore jabbed a finger at the book projector before it stuttered into realtime and started feeding her satfax.

> ... *Employment: Research Professor of Epidemiology, University of Alta California Medical Center, San Francisco (access class I infofile this locus for security assessment)* ...

No one stayed at the forefront of the oldest profession for more than a few seasons. Claymore had to find a way out or become a candidate for brainburning, or at least drug maintenance, herself. Fate intervened, in the form of a handsomish, youngish aide to the Director of Security Services. Looking for kinky action, he found instead an excellent imitation of the girl next door, and instantly infatuated himself—partly because he saw through her cheerful accommodating smile to the contempt beneath. That anyone should presume to be contemptuous of *his* looks, charm, breeding, and position so captivated him that he determined to win her.

The usual gifts got him nowhere (he wasn't surprised) and neither did his proposal of marriage (he was only mildly surprised; after all, the *pro rata* community property share after a standard three-year trial was not that great compared to what an expert like her could earn as a freelance).

So he played his trump, offering her a job in his department. She feigned polite interest, allowed him to guess at cool indifference, but completely disguised her deep, desperate need. Finally he persuaded her to accept. Once the contracts were signed she never spoke to him again outside of business.

Shrewd, adept, and ruthless, Claymore did not allow herself to be wasted as mere provocative bait in minor subversion capers. She sought and got advanced training—weapons, unarmed combat, air and space navigation, code, languages—and within five years she was an independent agent. Within ten she was practically a member of Speaker Macklin's family. She was at the top.

After a few minutes Claymore finished Holder's file. She'd memorized most of what she'd have to know immediately, though she'd go over the file several more times to absorb what she could of what subtleties might lurk between the telegraphic phrases. Restlessly she rose to her feet, bent over fluidly from the hips, and draped the backs of her hands against the soft carpet. She straightened and went to the window, her bare feet cold where they touched uncarpeted metal.

Below was a geometrically fractured brown smear, a dazzling expanse of blue, an even brighter expanse of white. Water-starved Salt Lake City, in ruins. Not much time before the plane reached San Francisco.

She sat down and pulled out a second fileslab. Its contents had been purloined from an internal computer hookup at UAC Med Center in San Francisco some years ago. Claymore had seen the file before; she was one of several agents who'd been unable to make anything of it. Now she was intuitively certain it had a bearing on the Holder case.

After the file contents had already been entered into the computer an attempt had been made to alter the address codes—a remarkably successful attempt by a mathematician of some skill. There was no longer any hope of ascertaining who had sent the memo to whom, although the fake ident codes were clearly fake, upon inspection.

Claymore chose transcription instead of voice. She studied the words that flowed in shadow before her eyes.

> . . . *instantaneous travel a shared illusion. One never emerges in the same spacetime one leaves, hence those tiny shifts in the phenomenal world we travelers have come to know so well. Are the freckles on your lover's nose slightly askew since last you said goodbye? There are a million billion yous, an infinity of yous, and you have a million billion lovers. What orgies of rediscovery all travelers might enjoy, if only they knew. . . .*

A warning tone sounded quietly in the cabin. The plane was about to land.

She rewound the fileslab and replaced it in her case. She went forward and sat in the control couch. Restraints enclosed her as she swung toward the console.

The plane banked and began to descend in a slow spiral. Below its long thin wings lay the San Francisco Bay Conurbation, scattered tall soleris poking up through the smog, rising from a thin crust of slums. Most of the bay itself was covered with floating suburbs connected to the shores by a spiderweb of bridges.

The tall, complexly articulated Parnassus soleri, the city's most populous and the seat of the Medical Center, reached up for the descending aircraft. Jets of flame shot down and forward from beneath the plane's wings.

An idea was forming in Claymore's mind. She thought she knew what Holder was up to.

The plane plummeted smoothly toward the Federal Offices landing pad that jutted from one side of the vast structure at the 120th level.

5

Holder's stolen craft spread its wings a bit wider, cupping cool dense night air. It dropped steeply, smoothly, through a cleft in sheer jungle-clad volcanic peaks. Holder watched through the cockpit windows as the moonlit vegetation slid by a few meters away, delicate as silver filligree. He marveled at the jungle's remembered beauty, and forgot to be afraid: the lander was more than competent to fly itself.

Soon the mountain valley opened onto a broad coastal plain, thick with shining palms. In the distance the low round moon spread a silver path upon the sea. The graceful, intelligent lander slowed to a hawk's lazy pace, wheeling in the night, dropping close to waving fronds.

A wide white beach opened beneath the lander's wings, coaxing it to extend those wings to their limit. The plane slid easily away in a curving dive that brought it within centimeters of the sand.

From the foaming surf great dark anthropomorphic shapes heaved up on hind legs, their webbed forefeet dangling, their shovel-nosed faces peering curiously at the passing shadow of the aircraft. Holder was delighted to recognize the silhouettes of anatosaurs momentarily distracted from their ceaseless grazing.

The lander gently pulled its nose up and allowed its forward motion to stop, settling easily to the sand on extended gear. Holder flicked off the instrument panel lights; the green glow faded and moonlight flooded the cabin. He settled back to wait for sunrise.

The placid herbivores in the surf were no threat to anyone, and though the jungle hid deadly carnosaurs, Holder had no fear of them either; their behavior was predictable. There were more dangerous bipeds in the night woods.

Best to stay put. The approach and landing had been silent; the lander had not fired its rockets once on the entire night side. Holder was confident that the particular route he'd worked out with the aid of the lander's computer had neatly evaded Darwin's anti-poaching defenses. He had memorized the location of every sensor installation on the planet.

Two weeks on short rations had served him well. Most of that time had been spent under plus-one deceleration, and even within the tight confines of D-27's small passenger cabin he'd been able to get a considerable amount of exercise, entertaining himself by measuring his progress in push-ups and sit-ups. He was a good deal harder and leaner than when he'd jumped from *Humboldt*.

And perhaps a bit saner as well. That stunt he'd pulled in the lounge the night he'd jumped—he'd justified it to himself as a diversionary tactic: poor old Phil Holder drunk, crazy, over the hill, passed out for the night or maybe the week. He could have achieved the same end without displaying his raw wounds, without leaving a testament of anguish. Perhaps he preferred to be remembered with disgust; perhaps he'd wanted others to agree with his assessment of himself.

What he'd almost done to Bruneau had shaken him. There he could not hide behind the excuse that his life was his own to risk if he wished.

For two weeks he'd been locked up with himself, with no means of escape except suicide. There was no alcohol in his bag or anywhere aboard, there were no hallucinogens or painkillers or tranquilizers. He was clean.

There was only The Plan, the best drug of all. "Lord, give us this day our daily delusion." Between sane and sick, and insane and healthy, he'd take robust madness any day.

He went to sleep.

By the time the hot yellow globe of Darwin's Star rose over the eastern sea, Holder had already walked a half a kilometer away from the little black lander, trailing a single set of footsteps in the unblemished sand. He heard a fluttering whistle behind him and turned to look back at the trim, powerful craft that had served him so well for the past two weeks.

As he watched, the metal bird came to life. Sand exploded from beneath it. It rose straight up into the air on a searing jet of thermonuclear flame. At an altitude of twenty meters the lander dipped a wing and turned east. It flew low over the ocean, straight at the rising sun, gathering its wings as it accelerated. A few kilometers from the beach the plane soared into a chandelle, screaming upward on a vertical trajectory that it could have maintained easily all the way into free space. But it rose only half a kilometer before pulling over into a tight half loop. In seconds it was flying straight down again, still accelerating.

Lander D-27 was a very smart machine, but with no one aboard it lacked the instinct of self-preservation. It followed Holder's programmed instructions without hesitation, ending its life in a mighty eruption of sea water.

Away to the south a herd of grazing anatosaurs, doubtless the same ones Holder had glimpsed the night before, gazed impassively at the distant geyser. When the sea ceased bubbling they went back to their feeding, poking broad ducks' bills under the water to crop seaweed growing close to shore. Holder turned his back on the dinosaurs and trudged northward up the pristine beach that stretched endlessly before him.

He carried his canvas satchel and wore the clothes it had contained: khaki trousers and jacket with flaps and straps and pockets sewn all over, a broad-brimmed canvas hat, and stout walking boots. He was the very picture of the well-turned-out jungle tourist.

He was headed for the mouth of the great Marsh River, a broad stream that drained most of eastern Cretacia; although its delta lay almost fifty kilometers to the north Holder had good hopes of reaching it before nightfall. Darwin's day was long (the terraformers had seen to that), and the coarse beach sand provided good footing, not like the powdery coral stuff found on the stormier shores of tropical Earth. Except for a few streams flowing into the sea which Holder would have to wade, there were no major obstacles between his present position and the estuary.

There he would pick up bushbuggy traces that eventually wove themselves together into a rutted, single lane road, paralleling the river and leading thirty kilometers inland to Copeville, the major port on the Marsh.

He would have to spend a night alone in the swamps. After that it was only one more short day's walk before he began to change the shape of history.